linked. The visitor who wishes to explore its

, of which in spite of clearing and

Though of old a palace, the labyrinth

full circuit still needs the guidance that of old was

partial reconstruction we have only today

us in many directions and in places artificially

a fragment of a fragment, is discontinuo

provided by Ariadne's clew'

Sir Arthur Evans, The Palace of Minos (1902)

VP

Valley Press

The Unauthorized B

iography of Ezra

Maas   The Unautho

rized Biography of

Ezra Maas

By Daniel James

The Unauthorized Bi

ography of Ezra

Maas   The Unauthe

rized Biography of

Ezra Maas

The following biography was completed without the authorisation of the Maas Foundation. Enquiries about Ezra Maas should be directed to: www.ezramaas.com.

To Elliott, Evie, and Etta

Foreword

And on the threshold of being no more, I succeed in being another[1]

This book is dangerous. You need to know that before you begin. Once you have turned the page, you will understand why. You could walk away now and leave the story unread, but having come this far, I suspect you will not. Only those willing to risk everything can hope to discover the truth.

The manuscript you hold in your hands is the only biography[2] of the artist Ezra Maas. It was written by my friend Daniel James, and it is a true story.

This is the last surviving copy of a book that was originally more than 800 pages long. I have done my best to put these pages in order, but I fear I have failed both you and Daniel. I am not the writer he was. Nor do I share his unique perspective on the world. These are my friend's words and no one else's. Where there were gaps in the narrative I have included Daniel's journal entries in their place, as this is what he intended himself, and where his own notes were incomplete, I have done my best to finish what he started, without interpretation. As such, I must assume some ownership of this final version of the text. *This thing of darkness, I acknowledge mine[3]*.

I'm sorry that I am not able to tell you my name, or how I came to be in possession of this manuscript. I know this may lead to speculation, but I have no intention of meeting my friend's fate. There are people watching me as I write this, and I am not as reckless as Daniel was. He knew the risks when he began this book, and though it cost him everything, the pages I deliver into your hands are proof of his final victory. The next chapter belongs to you.

There is nothing left to say. I have run out of time, and words betray me.

---

1. Samuel Beckett, *The Unnamable*, Grove Press, (2009), p.171

2. Note to reader: I have followed Daniel's notes as closely as possible while reassembling this manuscript in the five years since his disappearance. The surviving pages, with their disruptions and fissures, contain at least three overlapping narrative threads. First, there is Daniel's investigation into the life of Ezra Maas in his own words, supported by relevant news clippings, correspondence, partial footnotes, references, images, transcripts, and additional notes. Second, I have included the surviving chapters from Daniel's biography of Ezra Maas, featuring rare and unseen interviews, letters, and archival material. Last, there are my own editorial intrusions, both within footnotes such as these and elsewhere in the text. I have taken every effort to keep these to a minimum. As publisher, you will have your own notes and you are free to alter the text however you see fit. Similarly, if you choose to publish the manuscript, every reader who purchases the book will have his or her own interpretations, along with other narrative layers that I can never hope to identify and catalogue. In this way, the voices will continue to multiply, and the manuscript will be endlessly reborn – Anonymous.

3. William Shakespeare, *The Tempest*.

All that remains is regret. I hope you will forgive me, but that may be too much to ask. If nothing else, please understand that I had no choice.

Some stories are more dangerous than others, and true stories are the most dangerous of all.

This is not a biography. It is a true story.

Anonymous

Man behind the Maas?

Controversial journalist Daniel James denies growing speculation that he is set to reveal the truth about enigmatic artist Ezra Maas. **Sarah Chandler** investigates.

Daniel James last night admitted he is working on a new book, but denied any connection to Ezra Maas who disappeared seven years ago in one of art's biggest mysteries.

The writer and journalist, who famously turned his back on the newspaper industry after a much-publicised split with former employers News International, was questioned about the book as he left the Joseph Glass Memorial Awards in London.

James has attracted considerable criticism during his controversial career as a journalist. His writing, modelled on the New Journalism of Thomas Wolfe, Joan Didion, Hunter S. Thompson, Norman Mailer, and others, sees the line between fact and fiction blurred in an unorthodox hybrid, where the colourful events of his own life often overshadow his subject. Despite accusations of disregarding the truth and established journalistic practices, James's boundary-breaking work has been championed by a number of literary figures, including Phillip Roth, Umberto Eco, and Paul Benjamin.

"His writing is the only journalism I read," Benjamin states. "Where others see only the author's narcissism intruding into the text, I find James's deviations on the form to be a radical dismantling of how identity and fiction are constructed, and a unique commentary on the collapsing distinctions between life and art.

"If the sense of unreality running through his work is disconcerting, it is because his writing portrays life, not as we may want it to be, not how it used to be, but as it is now. In his search for literary truth, James is giving us a new kind of biographical fiction for the 21st century."

Others have been less favourable, including former Culture Minister Patrick Vasey, who famously branded James an "egomaniac" and claimed the writer had "never seen a mirror he didn't like." In 2008, Tate Modern boss Alan Leibniz accused James of plagiarism, while News International executive director John Atkins, unhappy with James's vicious attack on the news industry, described him as "a minor talent with a major gift for self-promotion". Literary agent Alex Renner, who parted company with James in 2009 after a protracted legal battle, said the former journalist was "obsessive and unstable", adding: "It's only a matter of time before he self-destructs".

As divisive as the writer has become in recent years, if the speculation is accurate and James has landed the job of writing the biography of Ezra Maas, it would easily be his most intriguing project to date. Reclusive artist Maas has

> 'Maas was a reclusive genius who disappeared from public view...many thought his story would never be told.'

not been heard from since 2002 when he announced via his website that he was withdrawing from public life to begin his "final and most important work". In the years that followed, the artist's estate, managed by the Maas Foundation, categorically refused to elaborate on the status of the artist other than to say he was "in seclusion" and that he would re-emerge when his work was complete.

However, in November 2005, after police were called to a reported disturbance at the Maas estate, Helena Maas, the artist's estranged wife and official spokesperson for the Maas Foundation, was forced to admit that the artist had been missing for three years. The hugely influential and radical artist, who first became famous in the 1960s before going on to win, and receive nominations for, a host of prestigious awards – including the Nobel Prize for Literature, and the Turner Prize – is notoriously reclusive. Little is known about his private life and very few photos of him exist. His refusal to give interviews or make public appearances since he first emerged on the art scene has only increased interest in his personal life and methods. There has even been speculation that the name Ezra Maas is a pseudonym for another famous artist or collective.

Unsurprisingly, a number of biographers have attempted to tell his story in the past, without success. BBC Head of Arts George Wallas puts this down to a combination of legal threats, confidentiality clauses, and the intense loyalty of the artist's family, friends, and supporters.

"Ezra Maas was a reclusive genius, an outlier and iconoclast even amongst the avant-garde. Today, his name has all but disappeared from the public consciousness, but in the art world, and especially to his followers, he is regarded as one of the most important artists of the 20th century," Wallas said.

"From his early fame in the late 1960s, Maas immediately distinguished himself from his contemporaries by rejecting celebrity. He took the New York art scene by storm, exhibiting a series of radical conceptual and guerrilla artworks at live happenings in the East Village, while choosing to remain anonymous and unseen. Maas was known to be intensely private in person and relentlessly controlled his own narrative by refusing to give interviews or have photographs taken. Naturally, this only added to the intrigue surrounding him and helped further capture the imagination of a disenfranchised generation. He was hailed as a prodigy by a number of respected critics and developed a cult-like following."

Wallas added: "At the time, Maas was compared to reclusive writers and artists like Thomas Pynchon and JD Salinger, with a touch of Howard Hughes's eccentricity. For contemporary audiences he is probably best described as the 'original' Banksy, as famous for the speculation around his identity as he was for his artworks.

"To this day, very few photographs of Maas exist, and the rare insights given into his life and art are either impenetrable or contradictory. Combine this with wildly different stories about his background, nationality, age, and physical appearance, and it's not hard to see why so many believed that his story would never be told."

All this changed recently, however, as rumours grew that the Maas Foundation were set to officially announce the artist's death following news of a scheduled inquest. James's interest in the artist is the latest twist in the tale. His publisher, William Wilson and Company, last night issued a brief statement confirming that James had been working on a new book for the last three months, provisionally for release later this year, but denied any connection to Maas. A spokesperson for The Bleed magazine, where James was former editor, said it had no knowledge of the book. The Maas Foundation declined to comment.

---

4. *The Guardian's* article as it originally appeared in the print edition of the newspaper during its Berliner era. On the following pages, I have also included the online version in a larger typeface. You will notice that it has some minor editorial differences from the original - Anonymous

3

Controversial biographer to reveal the truth about Ezra Maas?

Daniel James denies growing speculation that he is working on a book about the reclusive artist who disappeared seven years ago in one of the art world's biggest mysteries.

Sarah Chandler
guardian.co.uk Thursday 25 March 2011 10:08 BST

Biographer Daniel James last night admitted he was working on a new book, but denied it had any connection to missing artist Ezra Maas.

The writer and journalist, who famously turned his back on the newspaper industry after a much-publicised split with former employers News International, was questioned about the book as he left the Joseph Glass Memorial Awards in London.

James has attracted considerable criticism during his controversial career as a journalist. His writing, modeled on the New Journalism of Thomas Wolfe, Joan Didion, Hunter S. Thompson, Norman Mailer, and others, sees the line between fact and fiction blurred in an unorthodox hybrid, where the colourful events of his own life often overshadow his subject. Despite accusations of disregarding the truth and established journalistic practices, James's boundary-breaking work has been championed by a number of literary figures, including Phillip Roth, Umberto Eco, and Paul Benjamin.

"His writing is the only journalism I read," Benjamin states. "Where others see only the author's narcissism intruding into the text, I see James's unique combination of biography, auto-fiction, and the historical novel as questioning the representation of lived experience through language. I find his deviations on the form a radical dismantling of how identity and fiction are constructed, and a unique commentary on the disintegration of subject and object, as well as the collapsing distinctions between life and art.

"If the sense of unreality running through his work is disconcerting, it is because his writing portrays life, not as we may want it to be, not how it used to be, but as it is now. His work is giving us a new kind of biographical fiction for the 21st century. James has surpassed both the biography and the historical novel in his search for literary truth."

Others have been less favourable, including former Culture Minister Patrick Vasey,

4

who famously branded James an "egomaniac" and claimed the writer had "never seen a mirror he didn't like." In 2008, Tate Modern boss Alan Leibniz accused James of plagiarism, while News International executive director John Atkins, unhappy with James's vicious attack on the news industry, described him as "a minor talent with a major gift for self-promotion". Literary agent Alex Renner, who parted company with James in 2009 after a protracted legal battle, said the former journalist was "obsessive and unstable", adding: "It's only a matter of time before he self-destructs".

As divisive as the writer has become in recent years, if the speculation is accurate and James has landed the job of writing the biography of Ezra Maas, it would easily be his most intriguing project to date. Reclusive artist Maas has not been heard from since 2002 when he announced via his website that he was withdrawing from public life to begin his "final and most important work". In the years that followed, the artist's estate, managed by the Maas Foundation, categorically refused to elaborate on the status of the artist other than to say he was "in seclusion" and that he would re-emerge when his work was complete.

However, in November 2005, after police were called to a reported disturbance at the Maas estate, Helena Maas, the artist's estranged wife and official spokesperson for the Maas Foundation, was forced to admit that the artist had been missing for three years. The hugely influential and radical artist, who first became famous in the 1960s before going on to win, and receive nominations for, a host of prestigious awards – including the Nobel Prize for Literature, and the Turner Prize – is notoriously reclusive. Little is known about his private life and very few photos of him exist. His refusal to give interviews or make public appearances since he first emerged on the art scene has only increased interest in his personal life and methods. There has even been speculation that the name Ezra Maas is a pseudonym for another famous artist or collective. Unsurprisingly, a number of biographers have attempted to tell his story in the past, without success. BBC Head of Arts George Wallas puts this down to a combination of legal threats, confidentiality clauses, and the intense loyalty of the artist's family, friends, and supporters.

"Ezra Maas was a reclusive genius, an outlier and iconoclast even amongst the avant-garde. Today, his name has all but disappeared from the public consciousness, but in the art world, and especially to his followers, he is regarded as one of the most important artists of the 20th century," Wallas said.

"From his early fame in the late 1960s, Maas immediately distinguished himself from his contemporaries by rejecting celebrity. He took the New York art scene by storm, exhibiting a series of radical conceptual and guerrilla artworks at live happenings in the East Village, while choosing to remain anonymous and unseen. Maas was known to be intensely private in person and relentlessly controlled his own narrative by refusing to give interviews or have photographs taken. Naturally, this only added to the intrigue surrounding him and helped further capture the imagination of a disenfranchised generation. He was hailed as a prodigy by a number of respected critics and developed a cult-like following."

Wallas added: "At the time, Maas was compared to reclusive writers and artists like Thomas Pynchon and JD Salinger, with a touch of Howard Hughes's eccentricity. For contemporary audiences he is probably best described as the 'original' Banksy, as famous for the speculation around his identity as he was for his artworks.

"To this day, very few photographs of Maas exist, and the rare insights given into his life and art are either impenetrable or contradictory. Combine this with wildly different stories about his background, nationality, age, and physical appearance, and it's not hard to see why so many believed that his story would never be told."

All this changed recently, however, as rumours grew that the Maas Foundation were set to officially announce the artist's death following news of a scheduled inquest. James's interest in the artist is the latest twist in the tale. His publisher, William Wilson and Company, last night issued a brief statement confirming that James had been working on a new book for the last three months, provisionally for release later this year, but denied any connection to Maas. A spokesperson for The Bleed magazine,[5] where James was former editor, said it had no knowledge of the book. The Maas Foundation declined to comment.

---

5. *The Bleed* was an independent, multidisciplinary arts magazine founded by Daniel James in Newcastle upon Tyne in the mid-2000s.

Daniel James[6]
Chapter One

Nothing is more real than nothing[7]

It began with a phone call in the dead of night. A client with no name, offering me a deal that seemed too good to be true. Everything I had ever wanted. All I had to do was write a book. The true, untold story of the artist Ezra Maas. There was never any doubt in my mind that I would say yes. It wasn't the money. It was the chance to make history. I had been a writer for hire, a ghost for so many years, but through Ezra Maas I would live again. I would be the one to uncover the truth about him, no one else, and it would make my name. It was the moment I had been waiting for my entire life.

Within hours of the call, I knew something was different. I felt the change in the air. The world was new again; alive with possibilities. I retraced Maas's footsteps and relived his past, from the day he was born through nearly seven decades of secret history. Every step towards the truth took me deeper into the darkness. Every discovery brought me closer to the end, sat at a typewriter in a burning room, with the pages of the manuscript strewn around me like fallen leaves. A burning room, where the air shimmers, the walls blister and bubble, and the ceiling writhes like a living thing, a sea of black smoke. The walls are full of cracks. Eyes and ears move from gap to gap, ceiling to floor, watching me, willing me to write the final words.

Outside my window, the city is on fire. Buildings fold in on themselves and the only landmarks are those of the dead. Across the street, they are nailing someone to a cross. They knock another man's head off his shoulders and kick it along the road. In the trees, ugly spirits[8] whisper,[9]

---

6. Note to reader: The chapters marked 'Daniel James' feature the story of the author's investigation into the life of Ezra Maas. It is impossible to discount the possibility that some of what you are about to read may contain fiction. As a biographer, Daniel's style was uniquely creative, from handwritten notes and illustrations, to photographs and other documents, appearing throughout this manuscript, both within Daniel's story and the biography itself – Anonymous.

7. Samuel Beckett.

8. This is the first of multiple references to 'ugly spirits' throughout the manuscript. I will explore the origins of this phrase, and its connection to the writer William Burroughs, later in my commentary – Anonymous.

9. "Doom! Doom! Doom! Something seems to whisper it in the very dark trees." – DH

waiting for me to make my move.

Sleep is dangerous. That's how you lose time, and I have so little left. I need to stay awake in these final hours, counting down the clock until the end. All through the night the clock ticks and the typewriter clacks. Click clack, click clack, click, click, click, ding, all through the night. I slide pages under the door each morning, but at the end of every day they reappear in the book, sometimes just as they were, other times marked with savage red hieroglyphics that I don't understand.

There was a woman here earlier, more than one in fact, but they've all gone now. All the pretty birds have flown. I can't remember their names. It's no longer important. All of the women were the same woman in the end.[10] I remember each of them, but I try not to feel anything, anymore.

I can't let a little thing like pain distract me now. Not so close to the end. Not when the pages of the book are almost full. Even now, I wonder whether there will be a last page, or will the book keep writing itself after I am gone? It's always changing. Sometimes I forget how it began.

It started as a biography.

Just as we can never know what someone else is thinking, biography can never be true. Its limitations and thresholds mirror the boundaries of our own minds. We can never know another person's thoughts the way we know our own. Each mind is a locked room.[11] We can put our

---

Lawrence in 1923, writing about America.

10. The women Daniel was seeing during the years he spent working on the book appear throughout the manuscript. However, while they are each described differently, these relationships have a tendency to overlap and blur together in a variety of ways, often to the point where it is difficult to tell one from another. This has led me to suspect that this was a conscious decision on Daniel's part and these 'characters' all represent one woman, with the details of her life, her name, and her description, intentionally scrambled to obscure and protect her identity. It could also reflect Daniel's increasing inability to distinguish between the world of the book and its characters, and his life outside the manuscript. My reading has always been that the positioning of Daniel's relationships in the text acknowledges his awareness of a core aspect of his own personality, a need and a hunger for escapism that is at the very heart of his psyche. Whether it is through alcohol, books, noir fantasies, film, music, or women, he is compelled, time and time again, to escape from reality. You can read more on this subject in the psychological profile provided by Dr Cassie May, featured later in the manuscript – Anonymous.

11. As Sigmund Freud wrote: "… consciousness makes each of us aware only of his own states of mind; that other people, too, possess a consciousness is an inference which we draw by analogy from their observable utterances and actions, in order to make this behaviour of theirs intelligible to us." In *To the Lighthouse*, Virginia Woolf also described it beautifully when she wrote: "What art was there, known to love or cunning, by which one pressed through into those secret chambers? How, then, she had asked herself, did one know one thing or another thing about people, sealed as they were?"

ear to the wall and our eye to the keyhole, we can speculate about what could be inside, and the secrets it might contain, but we can never open the door. Not your mother or your father. Not your children or your closest friends. Not your lovers or your enemies. No one. Their inner lives will always be a secret to you. Biography will always fall short of reality.

I had made a career out of turning people's lives into newspaper and magazine articles, but it was just an illusion. If biography was a simulation, then my work was no more than a convincing facsimile. At worst it was a lie. And that was not the legacy I wanted. I dreamt of creating works of art, not fiction masquerading as reality. I became obsessed with creating the perfect replica, more real than real, and in doing so became afflicted by what Umberto Eco[12] termed 'reconstructive neurosis'. I wanted to walk through the door into someone else's life, enter the locked room, and return with the truth.[13]

Ezra Maas was the one. I knew it instinctively. No one had told his story. His art was filled with strange, autobiographical fragments and symbols that said everything and nothing, so dense with meaning that it overflowed, haemorrhaging in possibilities. Maas didn't have to hide his secrets, he casually scattered them on the ground for all to see and watched the trees grow up around him. For in a forest of signs[14] nothing could be seen clearly at all.

I believed I could navigate my way through and return home. I was different from the others who had come before me, from everyone. I was special.[15] And maybe I was right. It led me here after all, to this burning room and the pages you hold in your hands right now.

It was only much later that I realised the price of my ambition. To

---

12. Umberto Eco (1932 – 2016) was an Italian novelist and philosopher.

13. Arguably, Daniel's quest was fundamentally flawed from the outset. He was searching for an absolute truth that did not exist, and he was seeking to express it using a language that could not truthfully reflect reality. In this sense, he was doomed to failure from the beginning. "Words are a lie. They do not speak of the true nature of things." – Anonymous.

14. "Forest of signs" was a line from the Baudelaire poem '*Correspondences*' and was also the name of an exhibition at the Los Angeles Museum of Contemporary Art, featuring the work of Ezra Maas in 1989.

15. Daniel's notes reference an essay on non-religious transcendent experiences. One of those cited in the essay is the writer Philip Pullman, who reportedly underwent an experience of this nature in 1969. He describes how it left him feeling that "everything was connected by similarities and correspondences and echoes." However, Pullman also cautioned against those who sought out or who tried to engineer such experiences, warning that any attempt to do so was in his eye "an act of monumental and self-deceiving egotism."

throw open the door and enter another mind, to inhabit someone else's life so completely, to wear their skin and speak with their voice, to feel their thoughts and know their secrets as well as you know your own, to cross this boundary... *Pour voir Dieu, c'est de mourir.* [16]

In my arrogance I walked through the door, but when I turned back the entrance had disappeared. Inside there was a mirror, but I didn't recognise the face looking back.[17] I spoke, but I couldn't hear my voice. I looked into my eyes, and for the first time I didn't know what I was thinking. Where once there had been a constant sea of voices, all flowing together like instruments in a symphony, now there was only silence. I looked into the mirror, and for the first time I didn't trust my own face. I had trapped myself in a locked room full of mirrors and endless reflections. She was right after all. I was a million broken pieces, reflecting nothing. I picked up a shard of myself and began to cut...

It began as a biography, but it became so much more.[18] All that matters now is how it ends. Every word is true, but each page undoes the one before it. The book is a living void,[19] recovered from the edge of absence, visible more in its influence on the things around it than in itself. Only I can end it.

The final chapter is in my head, but before I can write another word I must

---

16. Translates from French as: 'To see God is to die.'

17. From Daniel's handwritten notes: "Our faces are a representation of the real. A second-hand truth. We can only experience the sight of our own faces through others, through reflections artificial and organic. We see the world through our own eyes, looking out from inside our head, a locked room we can never open, an insoluble mystery. The room and everything inside it is all that matters, the conscious mind is the true self."

18. Although my opinion counts for little, I think there is a strong case to say the manuscript incorporates elements of both poioumenon and historiographic metafiction. Poioumenon (from the ancient Greek meaning 'product') is a term coined by Alastair Fowler to refer to a specific type of metafiction in which the story is about the process of creation. According to Fowler: "The poioumenon is calculated to offer opportunities to explore the boundaries of fiction and reality – the limits of narrative truth." Works of historiographic metafiction, as defined by literary theorist Linda Hutcheon in '*A Poetics of Postmodernism*', are described as "those well-known and popular novels which are both intensely self-reflexive and yet, paradoxically, also lay claim to historical events and personages." Historiographic metafiction is an almost exclusively postmodern form, involving textual play, parody and historical re-conceptualization.

19. The book, particularly in its indirect influence, can be seen as an example of what Reza Negarestani, in his *Cyclonopedia: Complicity with Anonymous Materials*, describes as 'Inorganic demons'. He writes: "Autonomous, sentient and independent of human will, their existence is characterised by their forsaken status... Inorganic demons are parasitic by nature, ... they... generate their effects out of the human host". See my other related footnotes on the subject of forbidden texts, later in the manuscript – Anonymous.

go back to the beginning, and this time you will come with me. Every reader changes the story, bringing it to life and making it real, every reader plays their part, just as I have played mine. I must remember my lines, one last time, and recite them once more without feeling.

The light flickered, the projector whirred, and Ezra Maas flooded the room. His art, from floor to ceiling, colouring everything, the whole room, the four walls that had become my world. I had the sound turned off, but it didn't matter. If the film was what I believed it to be, it would be my first glimpse of the man whose life I had spent the last two years trying to unravel. I hoped if I saw his face and studied his movements, if I looked into his eyes, it would give me insights into the man that my research and field work had failed to do. All the people I had interviewed, all the books and articles I had read, all the journals and academic papers I had trawled through, all the news clippings and recordings, every location I had visited. I felt no closer to the truth. No closer to him. Only one or two photographs of Maas existed and each one looked different. Maas as a boy bore little resemblance to how he looked in his twenties , and looked even less like the man he became in later years. His voice on audio recordings posed the same problem. I might as well have been listening to different people. One voice was light and melodious, another like sandpaper and glue, but it was never the same twice.

The film was the key. It would unlock the entrance to the labyrinth. But it didn't come without risks. I looked down at four words scrawled on the back of a hospital admission form. *Don't watch the film.* Jane had written her warning with such force that she had nearly torn through the page. I pushed the note away from me, letting it fall to the floor. The time for warnings was over. My finger hovered over the button for a split second as I considered her words one last time before pressing play.

I listened to the purr of the projector as I sat back and watched, a heavy glass tumbler of Rittenhouse[20] in my hand. The footage played through from start to finish three dozen times before I saw it. Even then I was convinced I was imagining things. Exhaustion must have finally got the better of me. I left the hotel and walked out into the city, came back

---

20. Daniel drank the special Bottled-In-Bond 100° expression of this iconic American rye whisky produced in the tradition of the classic Pennsylvania or 'Monongahela' rye whiskies – Anonymous.

and slept. I showered, dressed, and made myself a fresh pot of coffee, but when I sat back at the projector and watched the film again it was still there, bathed in a shimmer of yellow light, staring back at me.

I found it hard to believe it had been there all along and no one had seen it. A series of messages embedded within the footage, concealed by a complex sequence of numbers and colours, repeating at irregular intervals. I had been hoping for a glimpse of Maas's face, but I had discovered something more than that, a greater truth hidden beneath the surface. This wasn't the first time I had come across numbers and colours in the life of Ezra Maas. My mind searched for everything I had uncovered ██.[21]

I tore the room apart until I found it. A code book given to me by the daughter of a psychologist who had treated Maas as a child.[22] It was the only copy that existed and the key[23] to unlocking Maas's mind.[24] The signs and symbols, the colours and numbers. I had to discover their meaning.

I spent hours examining the spools of 35mm film, holding it up to the

---

21. This is the first of several sections of the manuscript which have been blacked out, or redacted, presumably by Daniel himself as if he realised late in the writing process that some information was too dangerous to include in the final version of the text. By the end, he was working on a single hard copy of the manuscript so any changes he made would have been permanent. Rather than attempt to restore these sections, I have chosen to leave Daniel's omissions and ellipses as they are – Anonymous.

22. For more on this, see Ezra Maas Chapter Two and the interview transcript with Child M on Pg. xx – Anonymous.

23. In this case, the Bion code book was a literal decryption key.

24. Daniel does not go into detail about the method he used to unlock Maas's code, perhaps to prevent others from following in his footsteps. This would be highly unlikely without the Bion code book, which Daniel destroyed. However, I have done my best to reconstruct the method he used based on the notes I could recover. The code appears to be a polyalphabetic/polynumeric cipher – essentially the substitution of letters and numbers for other symbols – combined with an asymmetric cryptographic algorithm such as the RSA algorithm, which was devised using Number Theory in the late 1970s. Simply put, each letter of the message is replaced with a large prime number and multiplied together. The number is shared, for instance by embedding it into a film, but in order to decode the message you must divide the total prime number back into its specific constituent primes. This would be impossible without a decryption key. In Maas's case, I believe he further expanded on the use of a polyalphabetic cipher to include elements of cryptography and stenography by creating decryption keys using colours as well as numbers. However, it is my suspicion, based on Daniel's notes regarding Maas's films, that he inverted his colour associations to further conceal his intended message. Maas is known to have used a process known as 'solarisation' to reverse the colours in some of his experimental films in a manner reminiscent of a negative photo. It is possible to assign a numeric measurement to each wavelength of light, including fluorescent and solarised light. The use of colour in Maas's artwork and films has always been closely associated with his particular form of synaesthesia and I believe it was Daniel's intimate knowledge of this condition, based on the insight gained from Bion's files, which enabled him to see the patterns and unlock whatever messages Maas had left – Anonymous.

light, cross-referencing it against Bion's code, painstakingly writing down every possible outcome, every hypothesis, and then, as his message began to reveal itself to me piece by piece, recording every letter, every word, as I discovered their meaning.

~~tetragrammaton~~ /

~~a wavelength~~ /

~~mathematical algorithms and equations~~ /

~~the wave function of the universe~~ /

~~20,500 genes~~ /

~~a frequency~~ /

~~a unified field~~ /

~~geographical coordinates~~ /

~~the rest~~ /

The first message took me to London's oldest bank[25] and a safety deposit box, untouched for at least a decade , but reserved under my name. After I opened the box, everything would change once more, the walls of the labyrinth shifting around me. I didn't know it then, but the messages in the film, in all of his art, were a code only I could have cracked,[26] because Maas left them for me.[27]

The safety deposit box led to the discovery of the apartment in Soho

---

25. C. Hoare & Co, founded in 1672 by Sir Richard Hoare, is the oldest privately-owned banking house in England.

26. Only Daniel could have deciphered this code because only he had found the connection between Maas and Dr Alexander Bion, the psychologist who reportedly treated the artist as a child in the late 1950s. Bion's daughter provided Daniel with handwritten notes from the doctor's files including a code book, cataloguing the exact correspondence between numbers, colours, and letters in Maas's particular variation of ███████. Bion's handwritten notes were the encryption key that allowed Daniel to decipher the message Maas had embedded into the film footage. Maas's condition is explored in greater detail in 'Ezra Maas, Chapter Two' of Daniel's biography.

27. Steganography is the art and science of writing hidden messages in such a way that no one, apart from the sender and intended recipient, suspects the existence of the message. Generally, messages will appear to be something else: images, articles, shopping lists, or some other cover-text and, classically, the hidden message may be in invisible ink between the visible lines of a private letter. The advantage of steganography, over cryptography alone, is that messages do not attract attention to themselves. Media files are ideal for steganographic transmission because of their large size. As a simple example, a sender might start with an innocuous image file and adjust the colour of every 100th pixel to correspond to a letter in the alphabet, a change so subtle that someone not specifically looking for it is unlikely to notice it.

and the Maas Journals, to a greater understanding of the messages hidden in his work and the numbers counting down to his return, to the killers wearing animal masks, to the endgame. That was how I came to be here in this room; but where did it start? LA? New York? No, I had already seen so much by then. I need to go back further, before the months spent travelling across Europe, following stories of him from city to city, before Paris, Bruges, Berlin, Zurich and St. Petersburg, before Bilbao and Marrakech, before all of it. My search began in London, but that's not where it started. I need to go back to the very beginning.

Home.

Newcastle.

I remember now... There was a phone call. That's how it started. A phone call, a speeding car, and her. The headlights reached out before us, parting the darkness and guiding us through the night. It was 3am and I was in the back of a car with a woman. She had been my latest companion as I went another round with myself, living like there was no tomorrow, but without any of the pleasure that implied. I had the Schopenhauer[28] blues. The party was long over, but I was compelled to go through the motions, again and again, night after night, dancing to ghostly music in empty rooms, in the vain hope that greater and greater excess, however soulless, might recapture old highs and unlock past pleasures, that I might feel something, anything, again. My phone was vibrating impatiently inside my jacket, but for the moment I had better things to do with my hands. I pulled her close.

'Your phone is ringing', she said, between kisses. 'How far to your place?'

'We're not going to mine,' I replied.

She unbuttoned my shirt and slid her hands inside, the tips of her fingers cold against my chest, her teeth glittering in the dark as she smiled. It was about then that I remembered we weren't alone. I cast a glance at the front seat. Sam's gaze was politely averted.

'Eyes on the road, Sam,' I said, but he didn't turn to look.

He was focused on the night and the road stretching out before us. I turned back to her. We were two damaged people looking to each other for an escape, two bodies in the night pretending the past and future didn't exist. It would have been so easy to keep going, but I had played this game too many times. She looked up at me with sad eyes as I began to button my shirt up again. I took her in my arms and held her gently, her head

---

28. *"A man can do what he wants, but not want what he wants."* – Arthur Schopenhauer (1788 – 1860) was a German philosopher. His works included *The Will as World and Representation* (1818).

resting on my chest. Light flooded the back of the car, fading in and out like the tide, so that we were illuminated one moment, invisible the next. More than invisible, we had disappeared inside the light.[29] When the car finally stopped, she was almost asleep. I eased myself free from her and stepped out into the night air.

'You'll kick yourself in the morning,' she said.

'It's already morning,' I replied. 'The night just doesn't know it yet.'

I walked around to the driver side of the car as Sam rolled down the window.

'Make sure she gets back safely, will you?' I said.

'You do realise I'm not your fucking driver? You can walk home next time.'

'Ah, come on, Sam. You know I love you.'

'Fuck you,' he replied with a smile. 'I don't know why you brought her along, just to send her home.'

'She was with a guy earlier who was pushing her around, getting aggressive. I told her she could do better. She told him where to go.'

'Ha... yeah, you're a real white knight.'

I gave him a wink.

'Don't tell anyone.'

I watched the car's tail-lights recede into the darkness; a set of glowing red eyes that grew smaller until they disappeared altogether. Still, my phone continued to vibrate. I turned and walked into the night. The city had emptied itself of people, cars, light, everything. They had all slipped away like water around a drain. All that remained were the night people. Taxi drivers, bar staff, sex workers, stray dogs; a skeleton crew of the lonely and lost, drifting in and out, occupying the spaces in between, disappearing into the shadows at will. And still, the damn phone continued to ring. It was 3.53am and the caller display said 'private number'. I never answered my phone when I didn't know who was calling,[30] sometimes not even when

---

29. As a child, Einstein wondered what it would be like to travel inside a beam of light. In 1905 Einstein was working as a clerk at a patent office in Bern, Switzerland, a disappointment to his parents. He would return to his childhood questions about light, and his theories would change how we perceive the world. He later said: "You have to accept the idea that subjective time with its emphasis on now has no objective meaning... the distinction between past, present and future is only an illusion." – Anonymous.

30. This may seem like strange behaviour for a journalist, but not if you know Daniel and his circumstances. It was common knowledge among his friends that, like so many people who have an outwardly extravagant lifestyle, Daniel was living beyond his means and was in serious debt. It is my belief that the constant phone calls he received were from his many creditors and he was simply ignoring them. Only he can explain his full reasoning, but I suspect he

I did, but for reasons I can't explain that night I accepted the call, and everything changed.

'A few minutes ago, a contract was delivered to your agent,' a man's voice said on the other end of the line; cold and professional, devoid of any accent.

'What?'

The man continued as if I hadn't spoken.

'She wasn't very happy being woken so early in the morning, but she soon changed her mind. In fact, she's probably opening a bottle of champagne as we speak.'

'Who is this?' I asked.

'My name is not important. All you need to know is that I represent a client who wishes to engage your services.'

'Who's the client?'

'I'm afraid I cannot tell you that. My employer wishes to remain anonymous throughout this transaction. It is one of the reasons they are willing to reward you so generously.'

'Look, it's been a long night and I'm not in the mood for games.'

'This is not a joke, Mr James. We have already transferred an advance of ████████████ into your bank account. You will receive a further ████████████ when the job is done.'

'You're serious?'

'Always.'

I paused. If the money was real, it wouldn't be easy to turn down, and I was already intrigued enough to say yes.

'Okay... I'll play along.' The next question was obvious. 'What do you want me to do exactly?'

'We want you to write a book.'

And that was how it began.

---

simply hoped they would go away if he could avoid them for long enough. Psychologists refer to this as 'problem-avoidance behaviour', a common coping mechanism for those suffering from anxiety. His debts would also explain his willingness to accept less than reputable writing assignments to maintain his lifestyle – Anonymous.

PHONE TRANSCRIPT

Daniel James - Samuel Molloy
11.02.11[31]

DJ: I'm going to have to be more than a biographer on this one, Sam. More than a journalist. I need to be a kind of writer-detective.[32] I'm not just writing a book, I'm investigating a man's disappearance, the truth of his life and death, his final work of art. **11:38, 11 Feb**

SM: I remember watching my first Ezra Maas film at university, the one he filmed in the Ukraine. A twisted love story and treatise on adulthood. It changed the direction of my studies. He can't really be dead, can he? I always thought he'd live forever. **11:41, 11 Feb**

DJ: I don't know. He could be my anonymous client[33] for all I know. All I have are questions right now, but I'll find out everything by the end. I always do. **11:42, 11 Feb**

SM: I still can't believe they're paying you that much as an

---

31. As far as I have been able to establish, this conversation took place two weeks after Daniel received the phone call. I have partially edited the original, verbatim transcript, and others like it later in the text, in order to remove some of the stumbles, incomplete thoughts and ellipsis of actual spoken text, for the pure purpose of readability, and without actually changing anything that was said – Anonymous.

32. The similarities between the roles of writer, reader, and detective has been the subject of extensive critical debate. As Jeffrey T Nealon says: "The unravelling work of the detective within the story mirrors and assists the work of the reader, as both try to piece together the disparate signs that might eventually solve the mystery. The reader of the detective novel comes to metafictionally identify with the detective, as both the reader and detective are bound up in the metaphysical or epistemological work of interpretation, the work of reading clues and writing a solution or end." Briggs, Robert, *Wrong Numbers: The Endless Fiction of... ...* Winter 2003, Vol.44 No. 2. However, as Nealon goes on to add in his own essay *Work of the Detective, Work of the Writer*, the work of writing is arguably more closely linked to the role of detective than reading: "The writer is the one who initially creates the disparate world of ruses and clues that is the mystery, but also the one who searches – perhaps more desperately than the reader – for its end." – Anonymous.

33. Much has been written about the identity of Daniel's anonymous client. There was some speculation that it may have been Giraud Bernault, the private billionaire chairman of multinational goods conglomerate YHWH and one of Europe's richest men. He is known to be a serious art collector and the private patron of a number of major galleries. Bernault is also reputed to own the largest collection of Ezra Maas's work, outside of the Maas Foundation. However, this theory was later discredited. For other theories, see the conversation between Daniel and the journalist Ariane Beauvais later in the book – Anonymous.

advance. It's obscene. **11:42, 11 Feb**

DJ: Well, it includes the cost of sending me around Europe and America. I'll not see that much of the money myself, once all is said and done. Anyway, it's a fraction of what they could make in return. Art is big business[34] and death is bigger still. Maas may have been a superstar in the art world in life, but there's a lot of money to be made from the dead. **11:42, 11 Feb**

SM: This has got to be about more than making money though. What else did they say when they hired you? **11:43, 11 Feb**

DJ: Not much. Just that they want a unique book for a unique man. That's why they chose me. They don't want a by-the-numbers biography and they don't want another analysis of his artwork. They want his inner life, the truth of who he really was. He might be gone, but you could write a whole book about the impact he's had on the lives of others. They all have stories to tell, they all hold a little piece of the truth. **11:43, 11 Feb**

SM: So it's *Frank Sinatra Has A Cold*[35] meets *Waiting for Godot*?[36] **11:43, 11 Feb**

DT: Maybe. Maas is another of those seminal figures. **11:43, 11 Feb**

---

34. In 2014, LVMH paid £111m for a new gallery, the Fondation Louis Vuitton in Paris, designed by superstar Canadian architect Frank Gehry – and yet this was a fraction of the value of the artworks displayed inside, which included several Maas originals, on loan from the Maas Foundation, and other masterpieces such as Cezanne's *The Bather*, Pollock's *Echo: Number 25*, Brancusi's *Bird in Space*, and Warhol's *Campbell's Soup Cans*. The art world is both a playground and investment opportunity for the world's billionaires – Anonymous.

35. Published in *Esquire* magazine in April 1966 and written by Gay Talese, *Frank Sinatra Has A Cold* is a legendary piece of long-form writing and a pioneering example of what would become known as New Journalism. Unable to interview an unwilling Sinatra, Talese instead observed him from a distance, interviewing his entourage, friends, family, associates, fans, and employs, combining fact with storytelling usually reserved for fiction. The result is a compelling and multifaceted profile of one of the 20th century's most guarded figures, as well as an exploration of the cult of celebrity at a turning point in American history.

36. Samuel Beckett's *Waiting for Godot* is a play about waiting: two men – Vladimir and Estragon – waiting for a third, Godot, who never appears. It is a play which resists interpretation and it has been said that "the first step towards engaging with the play is accepting that it won't supply solutions to its mysteries."

SM: Like God?[37] **11:43, 11 Feb**

DJ: Like Sinatra. Or maybe the book will be more like *Picasso*[38] by Gertrude Stein, crossed with Virginia Woolf's *Orlando*?[39] All I know for sure is that Maas's absence is the centre of the book. It's the catalyst, the inciting incident, and its effects reverberate through his past, present and his future.

SM: "An infinite sphere, whose centre is everywhere and whose circumference is nowhere."[40]

DJ: What's that? **11:43, 11 Feb**

SM: It's the classical definition of God. Maybe I wasn't so far off the mark after all? **11:43, 11 Feb**

DJ: Let's leave God out of this. This isn't a metaphysical quest, it's a detective story and Maas is the body in the library. **11:43, 11 Feb**

SM: Everything's a detective story to you. **11:43, 11 Feb**

DJ: Hey, there's a lot to be said for that structure. Nabokov and Robbe-Grillet both employed the structure of a murder

---

37. Sam appears to confuse Godot with God. A common misconception and an association denied by Beckett himself – Anonymous.

38. An intimate and experimental portrait of the famous artist, written by his friend, the highly influential American writer Gertrude Stein, who also wrote *The Autobiography of Alice B Toklas*, *Everybody's Autobiography*, *Tender Buttons*, and *Blood on the Dining Room Floor*, among other notable works. Stein, who was friends with Picasso, Hemingway and many others in early 20th century Paris, is credited with the phrase 'the lost generation' to describe these writers and artists. Picasso painted a portrait of Stein in 1906, currently on display in the Metropolitan Museum of Modern Art in New York. Allegedly when someone commented that Stein did not look her portrait, Picasso replied: "She will." Stein's response was to write a poem about Picasso, *If I Told Him: A Completed Portrait of Picasso,* first published in *Vanity Fair* in 1924, and later, the aforementioned memoir.

39. *Orlando: A Biography* by the modernist writer Virginia Woolf is a revolutionary novel, once described as a "hallucinogenic and interactive biography" by the actress who would later play the title character. It was written by the author in 1928 and fuses memoir, biography, and fiction. It has been claimed that the fantastical character of Lord Orlando – immortal and transgender – was based on Vita Sackville-West, and the novel can be read as the "longest love-letter of all time", from Woolf to her close friend and lover Sackville-West. The novel is also notable for its experimentation with biography and fiction, its satiric depiction of the history of English Literature, and its impact on gender and transgender studies.

40. This definition can be traced back to the *Liber XXIV philosophorum,* a Latin booklet by an anonymous author, potentially dating back to the 4th century – Anonymous.

mystery, or a search for a missing person in their narratives.[41] The first novel in Beckett's trilogy does the same and it recurs throughout Pynchon's work, too. **11:43, 11 Feb**

SM: Okay, okay, you've sold me… but there's one thing that's still bothering me about all this. Why come to you now? Maas has been missing for years. **11:44, 11 Feb**

DJ: There have been rumours The Maas Foundation is going to officially announce his death. I think that might have something to do with it. **11:44, 11 Feb**

SM: They'd need an inquest for that, and a ruling of death in absentia. **11:46, 11 Feb**

DJ: I know. I've been looking into it. I think the client, whoever it is, wants to have an unauthorised biography ready to print in anticipation of the Maas Foundation's next move. **11:47, 11 Feb**

SM: It's only a matter of time before the Foundation finds out you're working on a biography and shuts you down. You need to be ready for a call from their lawyers. The UK's libel laws might as well be designed to protect the rich and powerful. The deck is stacked against writers. I've heard horror stories of entire print runs of biographies being pulped before they even hit the shelves, just because of the threat of a lawsuit. **11:49, 11 Feb**

DJ: Libel ceases its protection on death. If Maas really is dead, the truth can finally come out. Maybe that's what this is all about. **11:49, 11 Feb**

SM: Maybe, but copyright is inherited. It'll pass to Helena Maas and the Maas Foundation and can last up to 70 years after an artist's death. You know as well as I do that copyright is abused every day to protect reputation.[42] They'll use every

---

41. As the renowned Marxist theorist Fredric Jameson wrote, in *Raymond Chandler: The Detections of Totality*: "Nabokov and Robbe-Grillet almost always organise their works around a murder: think of *Le Voyeur* and *La Maison de Rendezvous*, think of *Lolita* and *Pale Fire*… here the decorative event of the murder serves as a way of organising material into an illusion of movement, into the formally satisfying arabesques of a puzzle unfolding… "

42. Copyright law is often misused by estates to posthumously protect reputation, in place of libel law which ceases 18 years after death. An example of this is ▮▮▮▮▮▮▮, the widow of ▮▮▮▮▮▮, who used her inherited copyright law as his widow to do just that. ▮▮▮▮▮▮ also used copyright infringement to block a biography about him (his lawyers even had copies

trick in the book to stop you. **11:50, 11 Feb**

DJ: But they won't. **11:51, 11 Feb**

SM: What makes you so certain? **11:52, 11 Feb**

DJ: I'm the best. Besides, true stories have a way of getting out there. **11:52, 11 Feb**

SM: They've blocked other books before this one. You must have heard? **11:54, 11 Feb**

DJ: Of course, but they weren't written by me. Maybe it's my ego talking, but I know I can pull this off, Sam. This book... his life... it's mine to write. **11:59, 11 Feb**

SM: I don't doubt your ability or your tenacity, my friend. Far from it. I just can't see how you'll get the access. His family, his lovers, no one will speak to you. Hell, he's barely mentioned in the Cousteau biographies and he supposedly spent a year with him. Where do you start? **12:01, 11 Feb**

DJ: In the library. I've been reading as much about Maas as I can. Books, research papers, official records, financial and medical documents – everything I can get my hands on. There are some great online resources for investigative journalists[43] these days. You barely need to leave the house. **12:01, 11 Feb**

SM: Ideal for avoiding unnecessary attention. **12:01, 11 Feb**

DJ: Exactly. There'll be plenty of time for that later. **12:02, 11 Feb**

SM: So what's next? **12:02, 11 Feb**

DJ: Field work. I've already mapped out my travel itinerary, but I need to move quickly. The clock is ticking, and I'm going to have to write as I go. **12:02, 11 Feb**

---

taken off the shelves and online orders refunded) on the basis that the book infringed on his own planned autobiography. However, the belief was he just wanted to control the narrative and prevent further commentary on the accusations against him – Anonymous.

43. These include, but are not limited to, resources such as the International Consortium of Investigative Journalists' database, Companies House, Open Corporates, the European Data Portal, Open Interests, LittleSis, the Global Open Data Index, the Organised Crime and Corruption Reporting Project's investigative dashboard, and NICAR's Data Library.

SM: Just be careful. People aren't just scared of The Maas Foundation because they're so litigious. They're a weird crowd and they'll do anything to protect Maas's reputation, especially when there's so much money at stake. The global art market is worth billions. Law suits will just be the start. You need to be ready for a lot worse than that. **12:02, 11 Feb**

DJ: That's why I need to stay one step ahead of them.

SM: I'm sure his other would-be biographers felt the same way when they began, but they all gave up in the end.

DJ: They all missed what was right in front of them anyway. The man behind the myth is the real story, but they were blinded by his art. I think Maas knew exactly what he was doing. He beat all of his biographers to the punch by filling his work with autobiographical fragments that led people into a hall of mirrors, while he hid in plain sight. I don't believe a word of it. **12:07, 11 Feb**

SM: What do you mean? **12:07, 11 Feb**

DJ: There are serious gaps in the texts I've read about him. Things don't add up. I think it was all a game. And the ridiculous thing is, every newspaper or magazine that has written about Maas since he first became famous has re-used the 'facts' that Maas and his Foundation put out there. They've been controlling the narrative for so long that it has become the consensus of truth. **12:07, 11 Feb**

SM: You think he made it all up? Everything that's been printed about him over the years? Yeah, the guy is an enigma, but do you have any idea what doing something like that would take? You can't just fabricate your whole life. **12:10, 11 Feb**

DJ: Oh, you'd be surprised… You know that line 'the greatest trick the Devil ever pulled was convincing the world he didn't exist'? Well, I think Ezra Maas's greatest trick was convincing the world he did. **12:14, 11 Feb**

END

Ezra Maas[44]
Chapter One

A screaming comes across the sky.[45]

A blood-stained child held up to the light, skin mottled and blue, opens its mouth, fills its lungs with air for the first time, and screams. A baby like any other, emerging into a world of light and noise, its limbs flailing and eyes focusing as it searches for answers in the blurred faces of those around it. But this baby is like no other. At least, that is if you believe in fate. Those who do, believe this new-born was already special, already destined to change the world. Others claim that it was the world which changed him, that it was not fate but chance that made him into the man he would become, starting with events on a cold November day a few short years later, when he would cradle the broken body of his brother in his arms. His 'phantom twin',[46] covered not in the life-giving fluids of the womb, but the blood that should have been flowing through his veins. A child holding a child, desperate to save him, but unable to do so, and haunted for the rest of his life by his failure; irreparably changed by the first of many tragedies in his life. That day was still eight years away from now. Today was January 1st, 1950.

Before his years in New York and Paris, before international fame and critical acclaim, before exhibitions at the Museum of Modern Art, Art Institute of Chicago, Tate Modern, Documenta, the Venice Biennale, Prague's National Gallery, and the Musée D'Orsay, before the Kings Place Gallery, the Museu Nacional D'Art De Catalunya, and the retrospectives at the Rijksmuseum, Amsterdam, and the Gagosian, before the solo shows

---

44. Note to reader: The following chapters marked 'Ezra Maas' are all that remain of Daniel's original biography. They are based on handwritten journals recovered by Daniel during the course of his research. The Maas Journals contain a large amount of archival material, including letters, photographs and personal belongings. The Maas Journals, as Daniel came to refer to them, provided a highly detailed account of the artist's childhood and personal history, although their validity has been questioned by several sources. Daniel verified and expanded on the information from the journals, combining it with his own research and interviews, and unifying everything he had discovered into the biographical chapters presented in this manuscript. Sadly, the original copies of the journals, alongside much of the archival material recovered by Daniel, were later destroyed. The surviving chapters of Daniel's biography, collected for the first time in this book and beginning on this very page, are all that remain – Anonymous.

45. Pynchon, Thomas. *Gravity's Rainbow* (1973)

46. *The Maas Journals Vol.1 1950 – '60.*

in Salzburg, Munich, Bilbao, Montreal, Los Angeles, Hong Kong, Buenos Aires, and Seoul, before the White Cube in London, the East Side Gallery in Berlin, and the Kunstsammlung in Chemnitz, before the nominations for the Turner Prize , and the Nobel Prize for Literature, before the Golden Lion, before the Ordre des Arts et des Lettres, before £500m in art sales, before the cult following, before the controversy, before The Maas Foundation, before seclusion, before disappearance, before death, there was a child . A child smearing paint onto a blank canvas with the palm of his hand; a child opening his eyes, looking at the world and trying to understand and express himself through the act of creation . But this was even before that. This was God before the Big Bang.

At 00:03, in his first few seconds of life, he was just another blood-stained new-born, being held up to the light by a midwife in a hospital and handed to a man and woman, his parents Michael and Sarah Maas. Today was January 1ˢᵗ, 1950. The day Ezra Maas was born.

It should come as no surprise to learn that even a fixed date in time is subject to interpretation in the life of Ezra Maas. Like the majority of the seven decades to come, the exact date of his birth is disputed. The Maas Foundation, who write about his early years in almost exclusively hagiographic[47] terms, claim he was born in the first few minutes of New Year's Day 1950, a date that neatly corresponds with the suggestion that Maas was the 'zeitgeist of the post-war years and the spirit of the postmodern era'.[48] Other sources place his birth at November 1947, although it is difficult to determine the true date because his original birth certificate was destroyed in a fire at the Parish Church of St Michael at the North Gate, Oxford, in 1953.[49] This, along with confusion caused by the mistaken belief that he was a twin (his brother Daniel was born 10 months earlier, but they looked almost identical by all accounts), has contributed to the difficulties in determining his actual date of birth, difficulties of which the artist himself, and particularly The Maas Foundation, may have taken full advantage.

It may be best to start before his birth, and to discuss what we know of his parents and how their stories influenced the man and artist he would

---

47. Hagiography is the study of saints. The term 'hagiographic' has also been used as a reference to the works of biographers and historians perceived to be uncritical or reverential about their subject.

48. Atkins, T.J, *Critical Maas: A Life in Art*, Bloomsbury, London, (1987), p.24.

49. The birth and death records for the parish were being kept at the church as a temporary measure after water-damage to the registry in Oxford city centre caused by flooding during the winter of 1952.

become. His father, Michael, the grandson of Dutch immigrants, was a war hero turned travelling salesman, who suffered from depression after returning home from war. Ezra's mother, Sarah Wake, was an English-born dancer and actress who had worked as a performer in pre-war Paris. Although there is little evidence to support the claim, The Maas Foundation has since written that Sarah was involved with the French Resistance during the Second World War and that Michael's job as a salesman was, in reality, a cover for post-war espionage for the British Secret Service, which may also have involved his wife.[50] Whether the rumours of their post-war exploits were true or not, records indicate Michael Maas reached the rank of staff Sergeant and served in three campaigns, using his proficiency in French and German to help interrogate prisoners of war. He had the distinction of being one of the first soldiers to enter a liberated concentration camp, and fought at 'Bloody Mortain',[51] Normandy, in August 1944.

Following the war, he spent a six-month period on 'denazification' duty in Germany, living in the Weissenburg area, before returning to England where he was treated for 'combat stress reaction'. Michael and Sarah are understood to have first met in France in 1942 and kept in touch throughout the war. The couple were married in 1947 at the Parish Church of St Michael at the North Gate, Oxford.[52] The period between this and the birth of their first child two years later is relatively undocumented, although The Maas Foundation speculates that Sarah continued to work for Whitehall, while Michael, ostensibly at least, worked as a salesman for the Oxford-based branch of American engineering firm, Yoyodene,[53] which specialised in aeronautical parts. This work regularly took him to London and elsewhere around the UK and Europe. Ezra's brother Daniel was born in 1949 and almost died after complications with the delivery,

---

50. See the limited Maas biography available at www.ezramaas.com

51. Otherwise known as the Mortain counter-offensive, in which 2 – 3,000 Allied soldiers died in six days, attempting to repel a counter attack by German forces following the Battle of Normandy in August 1944.

52. The tower of the Parish Church of St Michael at the North Gate, Oxford, dates back to 1050, making it the city's oldest building. An interesting fact in addition to this is that the font was removed from the former St Martin's Church at Carfax and was likely the same one that William Shakespeare stood at during a baptism at St Martin's, where he acted as godfather to a friend's child.

53. This should not be confused with Yoyodyne, the fictional defence contractor featured in Thomas Pynchon's novels *V.* and *The Crying of Lot 49*. It is possible Pynchon was inspired by real-life Oxford based company Yoyodene.

believed to be intrapartum asphyxia.[54] He suffered a number of health problems in his young life, including viral meningitis and scarlet fever, but the most serious condition affecting him would go tragically undiagnosed.

Daniel and Ezra were incredibly close as children and due to the similarity in their appearance they were often mistaken for twins. Ezra, in particular, enjoyed this confusion and even at this young age seemed to embrace the opportunity to step into another person's skin. The pair were inseparable, and despite the events that were to come, Ezra is understood to have continued to refer to Daniel in the present tense for the rest of his life. The dedication, 'Daniel will always be with me',[55] in his debut novella, *XXXXXX*, is understood to refer to his brother. Due to his various illnesses, Daniel spent much of his time indoors and was a voracious reader. His collection of books, which would later become Ezra's, included HG Wells's *The Invisible Man* and *The Time Machine*, Jules Verne's *Ten Thousand Leagues under the Sea*, Franz Kafka's *The Metamorphosis*, *Ulysses* by James Joyce, *The Stranger* by Albert Camus, *Notes from Underground* by Fyodor Dostoyevsky, *At Swim-Two-Birds* by Flann O'Brien, and Herman Melville's *Moby Dick*. When not keeping his brother company, Ezra was almost always outdoors, exploring the nearby woods, building forts, and sword-fighting with tree branches. Although Ezra would later take on many of the bookish characteristics of his brother, almost absorbing Daniel's personality into his own, according to family members, it is clear he was initially more athletic and outgoing. Their uncle, H.W. Maas, described the brothers in a letter to a friend in Tangier, in 1956:

"Daniel and Ezra are incredible… like two halves of the same person, one reads constantly while the other is never still, mind and body, so different, but so close and so necessary to each other. I wish Michael and I had been the same…"[56]

Although Daniel was the more advanced reader, Ezra was light years ahead of his older brother in almost every other respect, speaking for the first time at eight months, learning to walk a few weeks later, and generally surpassing every area of child development well in advance. This included a remarkable, almost photographic, memory and an ability to process large and complex number patterns. However, it was the creative arts where his true passion lay. As a result, his early years have been compared to those of

---

54. Otherwise known as the impairment of oxygen to the brain during pregnancy and childbirth.

55. Maas, Ezra, *XXXXXX*, Sun Press, New York, 1967.

56. Kenner, Everett, (Editor), *H.W Maas: The Tangier Letters 1949 – 1965*, Routledge, 1980.

Wolfgang Amadeus Mozart and Pablo Picasso's and it is hard to disagree with the classification of him as a similarly gifted child prodigy.[57]

Where Mozart was composing music at five, and Picasso was sketching and painting realistic images at seven, Maas was already writing poems and complex stories, drawing friends and family, and devising performance and conceptual art pieces. Even by these standards, Maas was an exceptionally creative child. He would draw, paint, sculpt, write stories, and invent names for the characters in his creations, then take on their identities. This would sometimes last for days at a time, where he would only be addressed by his character's name, which was understandably frustrating for his parents. This fascination with self-reinvention can be seen throughout his career. He also excelled at school, although there were early signs of the rebellious, independent streak that would manifest itself repeatedly in later life. John Henry Simenon, now aged 93, taught Ezra at St Vincent's First School in Oxford, from 1956, and recalls[58]:

"You could tell he was special even then. Always writing in one of his notebooks, his little brow furrowed with concentration. Daniel – I mean, Ezra – I always did get those two mixed up… Ezra was a lovely boy… polite, respectful, and warm, as long as you didn't try to tell him what to do (*laughs*). He was always good-natured about it though… I know he had run-ins with other teachers who felt he was challenging them in some way, but not with me… I had no ego about it… I didn't waste my time worrying that he was more intelligent than I was, I knew it… It was clear to me almost straight away that he couldn't be taught in the same way as other children… It was for that reason that I recommended his parents took him to meet a colleague of mine who worked in child psychology at the university…

"His knowledge at such a young age was frightening. He would talk about Picasso, and Braque, and how Cubism had been the most revolutionary new art movement since the Florentine painter Giotto di Bondone,[59] five hundred years earlier… I actually had to look up Giotto as I hadn't heard of him; he was a young prodigy credited with introducing perspective to painting… Ezra seemed to gravitate towards young, radical artists whose breakthroughs introduced new ways of thinking and led to major paradigm shifts… I remember him talking excitedly about Dada,

---

57. We should always be cautious of accepting 'history' as fact, of course. History is just another story, after all. It is often based on personal accounts and, as we know, memory is unreliable, and people have agendas. Even the circumstances of Mozart and Picasso's lives, cited above in the text, are highly disputed – Anonymous.

58. During an interview with Daniel in 2011.

59. Giotto Di Bondone (1267 – 1337)

about Hugo Ball, and Tristan Tzara, and what it must have been like to be one of those young men at the Cabaret Voltaire in Zurich in 1915, planning to change the world... It came as no surprise to me when I heard many years later that Ezra had followed in their footsteps... "

By the age of six, Ezra's skill as an artist was becomingly increasingly evident. In a letter to her friend Joan Cartwright, his mother Sarah, who had dabbled in painting herself as a teenager and who acted as an early tutor to her son, wrote:

"He's already better than I ever was. It makes me want to stop painting altogether. I'm kidding, but I genuinely don't think there's anything else I can teach him. I'm so proud of him, of how good... no, that's not right... how great, he could become."[60]

Although art was his greatest passion, a school friend from 1956 to 1957, who wished to remain anonymous, claimed Ezra displayed gifts in a number of fields, and hints, albeit light-heartedly, at the resentment this may have caused:

"Ezra was just one of those children. He could have been a star of track and field, the captain of the football team, a budding artist, and a maths wizard, all at the same time... He seemed to master everything he tried his hand at. Naturally we all secretly hated him, and wanted to be him at the same time."[61]

Maas was also taught to play chess by his father, Michael, around this time and reportedly had a strong aptitude for the game, quickly surpassing his teacher and reaching an advanced level at an early age. Various accounts confirm that chess became a lifelong obsession of Maas's, who continued to play throughout his life.[62] According to notes from The Maas Journals, his interest in the game stemmed from its ability to help:

'... develop patience and discipline in choosing between alternatives, at a time when being impulsive seems very attractive...'[63]

The following year, in 1958, an eight-year-old Ezra visited The Ruskin School of Drawing and Fine Art, which was located relatively near the family home in Oxford. His mother, Sarah, knew the art historian Edgar Wind, who worked at the school and was eager to see her son's prodigious talent recognised. It was here that Ezra first met the American artist

---

60. This letter was discovered inside Vol 1 of *The Maas Journals* by Daniel.

61. This anonymous source was interviewed by Daniel in mid-2011.

62. *Knight Moves: Maas, art, and games of the mind, Look and Listen* Issue 2, Vol. 2, University of Maryland Press, (1989), p.33.

63. The 'Maas Journals' Vol.4.

R.B. Kitaj, who had recently moved to the UK. Kitaj, who would leave Oxford to study at the Royal College of Art in London shortly after this, was reportedly astounded by Ezra's talent.[64] The pair would later become friends, with Maas attending Kitaj's first solo show at the Marlborough Gallery in London in 1963, with his uncle, and briefly working with him in the mid-1970s.

It was two months after this visit that everything would change for the Maas family. The date was November 1958, and Michael's brother, Henry William Maas, had recently returned from Europe. Henry, or H.W. as he was more commonly known, was undoubtedly the 'black sheep' of the Maas family, although the true depths of his problems were not known at the time. If they had been, Ezra's parents, Michael and Sarah, would surely never have left their children in his care, although to blame him completely for what was to happen would be wrong. H.W. had also served in the Second World War, suffering a hip injury in the Provence-Alpes-Cote d'Azur region of France, which left him with a limp for the rest of his life. Following the war, he struggled to reintegrate back into society, turning to alcohol and drug abuse, and eventually left the UK in 1949 with dreams of becoming a poet. These dreams took him to New York, South America,[65] Mexico,[66] Tangier, and Paris. In New York, between 1950 and 1952, he would allegedly meet and befriend the beat poets and writers Allen Ginsberg, Jack Kerouac, and William S Burroughs, although he enjoyed little of their literary success. In Paris, he lived in the Latin Quarter,[67] and also in Montparnasse near the La Rive Gauche,[68] where artists had been living and working for decades, including the likes of James Joyce, Ernest Hemingway, and Pablo Picasso.[69]

If H.W. hoped the influence of these artists would transfer to him he was sadly mistaken, for his poems and other literary compositions remained largely ignored and unpublished by the journals he approached, during this period. It is not clear where or when, but at some point, during

---

64. The 'Maas Journals' Vol.1.

65. Allegedly on the trail of the legendary drug Yage, which promised the user telepathy.

66. Where he reportedly studied a form of Mexican picture writing known as codices.

67. The Latin Quarter is a Left Bank area in the 5th Arrondissement, Paris.

68. The Left Bank is the southern bank of the River Seine in Paris. This generally refers to the Paris of writers, artists, and philosophers, specifically the artistic community of Montparnasse, and figures such as Picasso, Rimbaud, Verlaine, Matisse, Sartre, Hemingway, and F. Scott Fitzgerald.

69. Interestingly, the Latin Quarter would also become home to Ezra in less than a decade.

his extensive travels, H.W. became addicted to heroin. Remarkably, he was able to keep this secret until shortly before his death. There were rumours of a morphine addiction before he left the UK, following his post-war treatment, but it seems that while abroad he turned to other forms of medication. H.W. returned to England in 1956, after legal problems caused him to leave Mexico,[70] and reunited with his brother Michael.

Full of stories of his 'success' as a writer in Europe and America, H.W. was able to negotiate his way back into the lives of the Maas family, convincing everyone of his sobriety and reliability, whilst masking his worsening drug addiction and depression. Initially at least, he had a very positive effect on the family, particularly Ezra and Daniel, while living in the spare room of their new rural home just outside Oxford. The boys' mother, Sarah, who had herself been a performer in pre-war Paris, enjoyed H.W.'s largely fictional stories of his bohemian life abroad, while the boys benefited from his extensive collection of books. Michael, who had always had a weakness for his brother according to reports, was pleased to have H.W. back. It also allowed Michael and Sarah to spend some time together away from the children, and this is exactly what they were doing in London, on the 19th of November 1958.[71]

H.W. had been left in charge of the boys and took to the idea enthusiastically. He planned on taking them into Oxford to visit the Ashmolean Museum of Art and Archaeology. However, the morning Michael and Sarah departed, H.W. received a letter from London publisher William Wilson and Co informing him his collection of poems had been rejected, and his mood reportedly changed. The trip to Oxford was cancelled and H.W. retreated to his room. Ezra and Daniel were happy enough to entertain themselves while their uncle slept. Daniel disappeared to his favourite spot in the attic, to read, while Ezra was playing in the garden outside. The day was much like any other, until shortly before 3pm. That was when it happened.

Daniel is understood to have been climbing onto a chair to reach a book, later revealed to be Conrad's *Heart of Darkness*, when he slipped and landed on an upturned nail, exposed in the floorboards below, suffering a

---

70. H.W. was allegedly facing undisclosed charges of obscenity, but decided to flee the country after his attorney disappeared, citing his own legal problems after an altercation with the son of a government official.

71. Michael and Sarah were planning to see the Oscar Rabin Jazz Band, at the Lyceum Ballroom in London's West End. They had booked a room at the Langham Hotel on Regent Street, and it was here that H.W. reached them by phone.

small but deep puncture to his neck.[72] By itself the wound may not have been fatal, but the bleeding would not stop because, unknown to his parents and certainly to the eight-year-old, he suffered from a severe variation of the genetic disorder haemophilia.[73] Unable to stop the bleeding, his face colourless and drawn, his strength already failing, Daniel struggled to push open the window of the attic and call his brother for help. Eventually picking up a hardback book in desperation, he threw it at the window and broke the glass at the third attempt. The book sailed through the air, landing on the grass near where Ezra was playing, its pages fluttering in the wind, followed by Daniel's weak voice on the air crying out for help through the jagged, broken glass. His white face was peering down at his younger brother, his small hand pressed over the wound, which bled relentlessly.

Ezra raced into the house and was up the stairs in seconds, climbing into the attic to find his brother passed out in a growing pool of blood. Sweeping him up in his arms, Ezra struggled down the stairs with his brother, screaming for help. H.W. did not respond, later claiming to have been sleeping, although the belief is that he was passed out either from alcohol, heroin, or a combination of the two. Ezra lay his unconscious brother on the sofa and tried to use the phone to call for an ambulance, but the line was dead.[74] Alone and frightened, the eight-year-old pressed a kitchen towel to his brother's neck, lifted the limp body into his arms, and began to walk.

Awakening at last, H.W. followed the trail of blood down the stairs and

---

72. It seems Daniel may have inadvertently penetrated the left common carotid artery in his neck, a potentially fatal injury even without haemophilia.

73. Haemophilia is a group of hereditary genetic disorders that impair the body's ability to control blood clotting or coagulation, which is used to stop bleeding when a blood vessel is broken. The disorder lowers blood plasma clotting factor levels of the coagulation factors needed for a normal clotting process. Thus, when a blood vessel is injured, a temporary scab does form, but the missing coagulation factors prevent fibrin formation, which is necessary to maintain the blood clot. A haemophiliac does not bleed more intensely than a person without it, but can bleed for a much longer time. In severe haemophiliacs even a minor injury can result in blood loss lasting days or weeks, or even never healing completely. In areas such as the brain or inside joints, this can be fatal or permanently debilitating. It seems strange that this condition was not known to the Maas family as severe haemophilia is often identified at birth, or during a child's early years during tooth extraction etc where excess bleeding may be observed. However, after investigating this, it appears that mild haemophilia, which can be missed, can worsen due to a number of genetic and/or environmental factors. It would appear this was the case in the tragic life of Daniel Maas – Anonymous.

74. It has been speculated that H.W. was responsible for disconnecting the phone line before he went to sleep in his room, or that in anger he had torn the phone line out after receiving the rejection from his publisher, but this is speculation.

out of the door. He ran along the lane looking for signs of the boys, but was unable to find them. At 3.21pm, Michael and Sarah received a confused phone call at their hotel from H.W., who had evidently reconnected the line, telling them about an accident at home. In a state of panic, they began the drive back to Oxford immediately.

The exact circumstances of their accident are not known,[75] but it seems that as they sped home, desperate to learn what had happened to their children, Michael's dark green Morris Oxford II[76] came off the road near Stokenchurch, overturned, and caught fire. Michael and Sarah reportedly died at the scene, trapped inside the wreckage of their car, never knowing what had happened to their children – how one lay dying, and the other had been changed forever.[77]

75. The Maas Foundation has suggested, largely based on Michael and Sarah's alleged counter intelligence activities during wartime, that there may have been suspicious circumstances relating to their fatal road accident. There seems to be little evidence of this, but it cannot be discounted.

76. Produced by Morris Motors Ltd, based in Cowley, Oxford, not far from the Maas family home.

77. It has been suggested by at least one interviewee that the deaths of Maas's parents and brother actually took place months apart, and were not as closely related as the above chapter would suggest, the implication being that either Maas or his Foundation intentionally reimagined history for dramatic effect and/or as justification for the artist's later behaviour. This has been aggressively denied by The Maas Foundation.

Westminster Coroner's Court

Westminster Coroner's Court
Horseferry Road
London
SW1P 2ED

RE: Death in Absentia

Dear Mr James,

Thank you for your enquiry. To clarify, death in absentia, or presumption of death, is a legal declaration that a person is deceased in the absence of remains attributable to that person. This declaration is typically made when a person has been missing for an extended period of time without any evidence that the person is still alive, or when the circumstances surrounding a person's disappearance overwhelmingly support the belief that the person has died.

In most common law and civil code jurisdictions, it is usually necessary to obtain a court order directing the registrar to issue a death certificate in the absence of a physician's certification that an identified individual has died. However, if there is circumstantial evidence that would lead a reasonable person to believe that the individual is deceased on the balance of probabilities, jurisdictions may agree to issue death certificates without any such order.

If there is not sufficient evidence that death has taken place, it may take somewhat longer, as absence does not necessarily prove death. In England and Wales, if it is believed that there should be an inquest, a local coroner, such as Westminster Coroner's Office for instance, will file a report. This may be done to help a family receive a death certificate that will bring some closure. It can also bring any suspicious circumstances into light. The coroner will then apply to the Secretary of State for Justice, under the Coroner's Act 1988 Section 15, for an inquest with no body. The seven years rule will only apply in the High Court of Justice on the settlement of an estate. Without a body an inquest relies mostly on evidence provided by the police and whether the senior officers believe the missing person is dead.

Although we cannot comment on individual cases, I will say ███████████████████████
███ 77
███

███████████████████

Senior Coroner

---

77. Note to reader: For legal reasons, including ████████ the remainder of this letter has been redacted – Anonymous.

Daniel James
Chapter Two

Art is a lie that makes us realise the truth[79]

Time passed differently when you were working on a book. How long had it been since the back of the car and the phone call that set everything in motion? I had stopped marking the weeks and months with units of time, I began to count in words instead. It took less than a thousand words for things to start falling apart. I kept moving, even though every instinct told me that something was wrong; the pieces of the puzzle I was trying to put together just didn't fit.

How many words did it take to get from St Pancras to the Gare du Nord? What was the word count when I reached Bruxelles-Midi, or the Gare de Genève-Aéroport?[80] I wrote 50,000 in the first three months, interviewing people in cafés and bars, galleries and museums, writing into the early hours; coffee in the mornings, wine and beer in the afternoon,

---

79. "We all know that Art is not truth. Art is a lie that makes us realize truth, at least the truth that is given us to understand. The artist must know the manner whereby to convince others of the truthfulness of his lies." Pablo Picasso, speaking in a 1923 interview.

80. Daniel's narrative begins in transit. The first chapter describing his work on the biography is presented as a literal search. He is seen as a man of action, permanently on the move, from city to city and country to country; following in Maas's footsteps and evading those who would prevent him from finding the truth. This is no accident of course and it is interesting Daniel chooses to begin his narrative this way. Perhaps even more revealing is what Daniel omits – and why – which can be discovered by consulting his private notes. Daniel's description of his time spent researching the life of Ezra Maas, in this and later chapters, would suggest he left London for Paris almost immediately after receiving the phone call that sets the story in motion. He depicts his search for the truth about Maas as a breathless race against time, from one atmospheric location to the next. This portrayal was, of course, a conscious choice on his part. In truth, Daniel spent more than three months conducting research and interviews in the UK before he ever set foot on the Eurostar to Paris. Part of this time was spent carefully planning his European and US itinerary, including exactly who he would interview, where and when, every location he would visit and why, with the rest of his time spent poring over letters and newspaper clippings, financial, medical, and property records, academic books and research papers, photographs, interviews, and more. He was far more organised, systematic, and professional than he chooses to show. In the novel, he skips over much of this research and instead chooses to portray this period of research as a kind of detective story, and his method as largely intuitive, almost like improvised jazz. He depicts himself throughout as a neo-noir literary detective, when in reality he was a post-DeLillo art journalist, who engaged with subjects intellectually as well as personally. He could explore the space between critical theory and personal reflection seamlessly, and was all too aware of his position as the 'detective' on more than one level, allowing his roles to merge and co-exist in parallel – Anonymous.

bourbon at night. I was staying at the Cité Internationale des Arts,[81] a complex of ateliers for artists in the 4th arrondissement neighbourhood of the Marais. My notebook never left my hands, regardless of the time of day. It was with me as I drank on the Left Bank in Montparnasse where Ezra had lived in the 1970s, it was in my hand a week later in the Groeninge Museum[82] as I stood looking up at *The Last Judgement* by Hieronymus Bosch with a painter who had known Maas, and it was with me in the office at the European Graduate School at Saas-Fee[83] with a lecturer who claimed to have had an affair with him. The notebook lay on the table, safely within reach, as I drank coffee at Teecafé Schwarzenbach on Münstergasse, and again during breakfast at a café opposite the De Pont Museum, Tilburg.[84] It was with me when I sat across from a music journalist, drinking cocktails in deck chairs on the Oststrand,[85] it accompanied me on my walk past the graffiti and murals leading toward the artists' collective along the Oranienburger Straße. It was with me as I danced at a 24-hour party at Berghain,[86] and as I entered the East Side Gallery.[87] It was there when I discussed *Absence*[88] with film students at the Gerasimov Institute of Cinematography,[89] and as I explored the State Hermitage[90] on the banks of St Petersburg's Neva River. It was with me as I interviewed the musical director at The Gran Teatre del Liceu,[91] and when I ate guisante lágrima with 'txipiron' juice and Zurrukutuna,[92] with

---

81. In Paris, France.

82. In Bruges, Belgium.

83. In Switzerland.

84. In the Netherlands.

85. On the banks of the river Spree, Berlin.

86. *The Guardian*: "Berlin's Berghain club is known for many things: its hardcore opening hours (no one arrives before 4am, and most stay until well past teatime), its DJs (who play some of the best techno in Europe), and its relaxed attitude towards sex in public."

87. A 1316m long section of the Berlin Wall located near the centre of Berlin on Mühlenstraße in Friedrichshain-Kreuzberg.

88. The short film allegedly directed by Ezra Maas.

89. Formerly the All-Union State Institute of Cinematography, Moscow.

90. The Hermitage museum occupies six buildings along the Neva River, including the Winter Palace, the former residence of the czars.

91. The opera house on La Rambla, Barcelona.

92. Sometimes described as Spain's 'green caviar', the guisante lágrima or 'tear pea' is a highly prized vegetable from the Basque country, grown by Spain's local farmers for its country's

a sculptor in Nerua Guggenheim Bilbao.[93] I almost lost it as I escaped through the crowds in Djemaa el Fna square, Marrakech, evading a group of men who were following me. I had to retrace my steps after I realised the notebook was missing, but I was able to retrieve it from the ground before escaping in a cab. It was my constant companion through all of this.

I wrote on the train, in the back of cabs, on the bus, everywhere. I would go to sleep with words swirling in my mind, wake up mid-sentence and reach over whoever lay next to me to continue writing. For months I lived and breathed the book, moving from city to city, country to country. I couldn't stop. There was always another person to interview, another lead to follow up, another location, where Maas had lived or worked, for me to experience and absorb into the book. I climbed into another car, another flight, another train carriage. I didn't know where it would take me. Everything was uncertain.

The rural landscape was bathed in a hazy, washed out light. As the train moved slowly through the country, the horizon was undefined, blurred at the edges. The skeletal trees and the red-tiled rooftops of farm houses emerged from the fog slowly, as if they were coming into existence just for us. Bruges itself was a different kind of dream to the Belgian countryside. A night-time place of tightly-packed cobbled streets that twisted and turned, ornate doorways and narrow townhouses, medieval footbridges and gloomy waterways that snaked through and around the old city. After arriving at the station, I headed through the Minnewaterpark, past weeping willow trees, and swans drifting along the water, and into the old city centre. After I dropped my bags at the apartment, I planned to have dinner at ███████████████████[94] where Maas allegedly ate during his years in the city.

It was a small, eclectic restaurant on Mallebergplaats, which had been run by the same husband and wife for almost 40 years. It was like having

leading chefs. Zurrukutuna is a rustic garlic soup, made with day-old pan Sopako bread and salt cod.

93. Nerua is a Michelin Star rated restaurant, within the Guggenheim Museum, Bilbao, offering visitors a taste of Basque country. Nerua takes its name from the Nervión River, the backbone of Bilbao.

94. The restaurant's name is a reference to a Roman Catholic order of chivalry founded in Bruges by Philip the Good, Duke of Burgundy, in 1430, to celebrate his marriage to the Portuguese Infanta Isabella. It continues to be one of the most prestigious Orders in Europe.

dinner in your eccentric aunt's living room, cluttered and overflowing with decades of ornaments and memorabilia, mismatched furniture, dolls, statuettes, vases, photographs, bottles, and candles. It appeared that the owners had thrown nothing away in the four decades they had owned the place. The restaurant had previously been an art café and gallery, and Maas had supposedly visited here while working with a group of Belgian artists in the 1970s. I ordered the Flemish beef stew with spiced apple, and two bottles of Papegaei.[95]

The restaurant owner was a tough-looking, sinewy woman with dark, heavily-dyed hair and garish jewellery, called Suzanne. Her husband, tall, gruff and moustachioed, was the chef. They were the only staff. After complimenting the quality of the food, and ordering another beer, I called her over.

'Back when this was a café, an artist named Ezra Maas was a regular here. At least that's what I've been told. Do you remember him at all?'

'Who?' Her dark eyes narrowed.

'Ezra Maas.'

Suzanne's body seemed to tense for a split second before she composed herself again. She began to adjust the table-setting next to mine, as if something more important than our conversation had come up.

'You knew him?' I added.

'A lot of artists passed through here back then,' she said, with a dismissive shrug of her shoulders. 'I can't remember every single one.'

'He was very famous at the time. You'd remember if Andy Warhol came in here, wouldn't you?'

I had meant it light-heartedly, but it sounded like a challenge to her memory, an insult at worst. She looked bemused for a moment and then smiled, almost despite herself.

'I never met Warhol,' she said simply. 'But Maas... yes, he did come here, a very long time ago. I heard he was dead.'

'So I've been told,' I said. 'Do you think it's true?'

'I wouldn't know,' she replied flatly. 'Why are you looking for him?'

'I'm not,' I replied. 'Not exactly. I'm researching a book about his life.'

'A biography?'

'Yes, that's right. What do you remember about him? I might be able to arrange for you to be paid, if anything you tell me makes it into the book.'

'I'm not sure I want to be in a book,' she said. 'Besides, I don't have

---

95. A strong Belgian pale ale, named after the word for 'Parrot,' with a distinctive pale blue label and parrot logo.

much to tell you.'

'But you do remember him?'

'Yes, he was part of a group – artists and their friends – who used to come in here back in the Seventies.'

'What did he look like?'

'Maas? He... I... Ha. You know, I can't really recall his face, now you've asked. Not exactly. I remember he had dark hair, and his eyes... there was something about his eyes... I'm usually good with faces, but his... it's a blur if I'm honest... I'm sorry. It's been 40 years since he was in here, and I'm not as young as I used to be.'

'None of us are,' I smiled. 'What else can you tell me?'

'He dressed well, and he was always very polite... didn't talk much. At least not to me. His friends were always in deep conversation. It all gravitated around him. I remember that much. He was the star.'

'Do you remember any of these friends?'

'I'm not sure... ' She paused and looked past me at the wall. 'But you might find them over there if you want to take a look?'

She gestured in the direction of a wall covered in photographs.

'You have a photograph of them?'

'It's possible,' she replied. 'I used to take photographs of all the regulars. You'll have to take a look.'

Her manner was so casual that I almost didn't register the significance of what she was telling me. Did she just say she might have a photograph of Ezra Maas and his entourage on her wall? She left me for a second to see to another customer. I stood up too fast, nearly knocking my cutlery onto the floor, and clumsily made my way between the tables to the wall of photographs.

There were dozens of faded pictures, some behind glass in a gaudy frame, others simply pinned to the wall. After a couple of minutes Suzanne re-appeared at my shoulder. She moved a bony finger over the wall as if she was divining for water, and finally pointed to a small black and white photograph.

'There,' she said. 'Those were his friends. They worked out of a little gallery on Korte Vuldersstraat.'

I studied the photo. It was a crowded shot of the restaurant from the mid-1970s. There was a group of people sat at a long table, with one or two others standing on the fringes. The composition of the shot had an eerie resemblance to Da Vinci's *The Last Supper*, albeit with 1970s fashions.

'Is Maas in this photo?' I asked.

'Let me take a look,' she said. 'No, I don't think he is... '

I couldn't hide the disappointment in my face. She saw this and pointed to a couple of men in the picture whose faces were obscured.

'One of those could be Maas,' she said. 'But it's difficult to tell without seeing their faces, and looking at this picture doesn't bring back any memories of him. I'm sorry.'

Suzanne took me through what she could remember about the other people in the photo. A young Belgian woman called Marianne who worked at a wine bar around the corner. An American student from Columbia University who wanted to be a writer. And, finally, a German painter who was part of the Fluxus[96] movement, but who died a few years later in a car accident. The others she didn't know. One of the men at the table might have been Maas, but she couldn't say for sure. Even so, she had been more helpful than she realised.

Although Maas had never been formally connected to Fluxus, the group had come up in my research before. I searched my memory for the other names she had mentioned, cross-referencing against people who had come up in my previous interviews. Her mention of a student from Columbia matched a story I'd been told in Paris about a young writer who had travelled to Paris to meet Beckett before setting off for the rest of Europe. If it was the same man, then I was due to speak to him when I arrived in New York in a few weeks. And it would be easy enough to check if Marianne was still working at the wine bar nearby. It felt like a couple of puzzle pieces were beginning to fit together.

'Can I borrow this?' I said, gesturing to the photograph. 'I'd love to include it in the book.'

'No... No. These are my personal photographs. They belong here in the restaurant.'

'I would only need it long enough to make a copy and then you can have it back, I promise.' I took 250 Euros out of my pocket. 'Call it a down payment. I'll pay you another 250 when I return the photo.'

She looked at the money and back at me.

'I need to think about it,' she replied. 'Take a seat and I'll be back in a few minutes.' Suzanne walked through into the kitchen. I looked back at the photo wall. It was hard to believe I could be looking at Ezra Maas, but it was somehow in keeping that I couldn't identify which of the men was him. His control over his own image extended even into the past.

---

96. Fluxus was an international and interdisciplinary group of artists, composers, designers, and poets that took shape in the 1960s and 1970s. George Maciunas is considered the primary founder and organiser of this loosely organised movement. Fluxus sought to change the history of the world, not just the history of art.

'Monsieur?' Suzanne called from behind me.

I turned around at the sound of her voice, and blinked as an old-fashioned flash went off. Suzanne stood a few feet away from me with a large Polaroid camera in her hands. She took the square photograph out and shook it until my image slowly appeared inside the white frame. My thick dark hair and blue eyes looked back at me. Suzanne unpinned the black and white photograph of Maas's last supper from the wall and handed it to me.

'What was that about?' I asked.

'Now we have a deal,' she said, as she pinned my photo to the wall. 'You have my photograph and I have your soul. You'll get it back when you return my picture – and the rest of my money.'

With the picture in my bag, I headed straight for the wine bar on Braambergstraat, which Suzanne had mentioned. It was set in a narrow red-brick building that dated back to 1637, with leaded windows and dark wooden beams. Inside, the bar was dimly lit and heavy on atmosphere. The owner, a small woman in her late '60s, treated me like her long-lost son and kissed me on both cheeks after I walked through the door. There was live jazz and blues upstairs that night on the mezzanine, and both floors were crowded. I took a seat at the bar and ordered a glass of Gewürztraminer[97] from the extensive wine menu, while the owner proceeded to greet every new arrival in her customary manner. A few glasses of wine later the musicians wrapped up their set with the Charlie Haden's *Quartet West* rendition of *Lonely Town*.[98] The bar began to empty out, the owner personally seeing each customer to the door. I took the photograph out of my pocket and placed it on the bar.

'Excuse me,' I said to her. 'Does a Marianne Dubois work here?'

'How do you know that name?'

I relayed the story I had been told by the restaurant owner and explained I was looking for a man who Marianne used to know.

'She did work here... but she moved away. What is this about?'

'Ezra Maas.'

Her eyes grew dark.

'I don't know anyone by that name,' she said, her voice cold.

'Are you sure? This photo... it looks an awful lot like you.' I smiled, trying to charm her, but she wouldn't even look at the photo, or me. Her eyes darted sideways. She was afraid.-

---

97. A flowery, heady-scented German white wine.

98. Written by Leonard Bernstein and recorded by Frank Sinatra in 1954 – Anonymous.

'I think you should leave,' she said. 'Marianne doesn't work here anymore, and I can't help you.'

'I didn't mean to upset you,' I said. 'I'm writing a book about Maas, that's all. I'm looking to speak to people who knew him.'

'Please go,' she repeated. A couple of her staff, a young waitress and a muscular kitchen hand, had started to take notice of our exchange and were now looking over, concerned. I decided not to cause a scene. Standing up, I put the photograph back into my bag and placed a business card on the bar.

'If you change your mind, my number is on the card.'

I waited in an alcove along the street, watching the wine bar, and the activity inside, through the leaded window. While her staff closed up, the owner made a phone call. She looked upset and agitated, and I couldn't help but wonder if it was connected to my visit. About ten minutes later she came out to meet a man who had arrived to collect her, and the pair walked off into the night. The entire city appeared to be empty as I followed them through the streets at a distance. There were no sounds, no voices, no cars, nothing at all. I walked across the square and over one of the small, arched footbridges. The surface of the water was so still and unmoving below that it became a perfect mirror of the flood-lit buildings and pitch-black sky above it; a city doubled. I felt like I had stepped back into a time when the city was under curfew. The streetlamps seemed only to illuminate themselves, the orange light keeping its distance from the shadows of the buildings. Even my footsteps seemed to generate the wrong kind of noise. It was as if the city's Gothic architecture separated sound and light from their sources, to create a maze in which your eyes and ears were perpetually deceived.

I hung back as they crossed the Burg Square, to prevent being spotted in the open, but I knew I was at risk of losing them in the side streets leading off Grote Markt. As I waited in the darkness I sensed something on my periphery. I turned quickly and saw a figure step back into the shadows. There was someone following me. I had to move. As soon as the owner of the wine bar and her companion were out of sight, I sprinted across the Burg and took the first left on Wollestraat, followed by another left across the river onto Braambergstraat in an effort to double back on myself. I had lost the owner of the wine bar, but in that moment I was more concerned about the man on my tail. I glanced back and saw that he was still in pursuit, walking quickly and purposefully in my direction.

The only signs of life came from flickering candlelight behind the steamed-up windows of a shop front on Jozef Suvéestraat. At first glance, it looked like a kitchen showroom, but there were people inside having drinks, like a private party. I took a chance and went in. On closer inspection, the showroom turned out to be an unusual, minimalist bar designed with a kitchen style worktop as a focal point, covered with hundreds of bottles of gin from around the world. There were only two or three tables and a solitary barman, who was dressed like he had just wandered downstairs in his pyjamas to serve drinks to friends. I kept my eyes on the door while pretending to look at the menu. After a minute, my pursuer walked past the window without glancing inside, his features obscured by the condensation covering the glass.

I ordered a gin and tonic, but the barman insisted I have it on the rocks, muttering something about tonic being sacrilege as he did so. I opted for a sophisticated-looking bottle with the emblem of a golden tiger.[99] After battling through a glass that tasted like pure alcohol, I found myself wishing I had discovered a late-night bourbon bar instead. Still, the place had served its purpose. I tipped the barman a 20 and asked if I could leave by the back door.

I wasn't far away from the apartment I had rented near Koningin Astridpark,[100] a former monastery garden turned into a public park, with a wooden bandstand and water fountain. It was a picturesque little neighbourhood, with a patisserie[101] on the corner and a boucherie[102] across the road; the kind of place I could happily have retired to in another life. The apartment had formerly been a fishmongers and had been converted into a tiny flat some years ago, spread over several levels with seemingly no attempt to adapt the layout. As such, the living space was a strange mismatch of oddly-shaped rooms, stacked one above the other, connected by a series of steep spiral staircases that I had noted would be deadly after a few drinks. The bedroom was in the attic, with a walk-in wet room and views above the city's uneven rooftops and spires, including the famous belfry in the Market Square. As I climbed the first flight of steps I heard the floorboards above me creak. There was someone upstairs. I continued up, step by step, my heart pounding, and found a familiar face waiting for me in the darkness.

---

99. Blind Tiger Liquid Gold.

100. The English translation is 'Queen Astrid Park'. This former Franciscan garden was named after Queen Astrid, who died in 1935.

101. Patisserie Schaeverbeke.

102. Butchery Maertens Brugge.

Child M

Date 15th Dec 1958

Name of patient ██████

Address

Admitted 11.12.58   Discharged

Diagnosis   NOT CONCLUSIVE

██████

SUMMARY OF CASE

HISTORY

██████ was admitted into this department complaining of general disorientation, he had been found wandering the streets in a state of some distress and agitation. He had caused something of a disturbance with other people and continued to do that on arrival at the unit.

PHYSICAL EXAMINATION

Fully conscious child aged 8 years
C.V.S, R.S, Abdomen, Nervous System - NAD.

INVESTIGATIONS

X-ray of chest shows no evidence of fracture.
X-ray of skull shows no bone injury.

PROGRESS AND TREATMENT

He was observed in hospital for 3 days during which time his condition improved a little.

RECOMENDATIONS

Further observation of ██████ is required. I recommend that he stays with the unit for a period of at least six weeks and that further tests are carried out during this time.

The following pages feature a partial interview transcript between an unnamed doctor, identified as D, and a seven-year-old child. At least one source has indicated this child, who is referred to as M in the document below, to be Ezra Maas. However, this has never been verified

REG. No.

392925

Child M

Date 15th Dec 1958

TRANSCRIPT: INTERVIEW WITH CHILD M

11:42am.

D: Can you tell me the first time you experienced this cross-wiring of your senses, as you described it to me earlier?

M: The colour of my mother's voice. Her words, floating above my head, seemed to change the air itself.

D: You're saying it didn't begin with the accident?

M: No.

D: But I understand you suffered a fall...a head injury...and later seizures. Are you saying you experienced this phenomenon even before that?

M: Yes, I've always been this way.

D: But you didn't tell anyone. Why?

M: I knew it made me different from the other children.

D: In what way?

M: The other kids talk to each other. They play with toys and pretend to be cowboys and Indians. I talk to numbers and words; they have colours, sounds, smells, textures. I can make them dance.

D: And why wouldn't you want to be different?

M: Would you?

REG. No.

392925

Child M

Date 15th Dec 1958

D: One of my colleagues described you as gifted,
potentially a savant. Do you know what that word means?

M: Why am I here?

D: I work in the field of cognitive science. Do you know
what that is? I'm studying the development of
intelligence, particularly the changing states of the
brain during childhood, to better understand the impact
of key genetic and environment factors. You were
recommended to me by a colleague who interviewed you
after the accident. He felt that we could help each
other.

M: Savant comes from the French word 'savoir', meaning
'to know'.

D: Yes, it does. My colleague said you scored
exceptionally in the IQ testing.

M: Did he use the Stanford-Binet or the Wechsler?

D: You're aware of formal IQ testing?

M: I read a lot.

D: The Wechsler.

M: I don't believe intelligence can be measured with a
test. In my opinion, both tests are extremely limited.

D: I agree.

M: Then why am I here?

D: If my colleague can be believed, you represent an
unprecedented opportunity for someone in my field. The
equivalent of being able to ask questions of a young
Mozart, Picasso, or Einstein. Moreover, I have a

OXFORD CENTRE FOR COGNITIVE STUDIES
CHILDREN'S DEPARTMENT

REG. No.

392925

Child M

Date 15th Dec 1958

particular interest in synaesthesia and the
extraordinary perceptual experiences it provides, which I
believe you can help me understand. As you can imagine,
this opportunity doesn't come along every day.

M: Einstein was a late bloomer, if you can believe the
stories; a disappointment to his parents as a young man,
still employed as a patent clerk in Bern in his twenties.
I believe some of this to be a myth, part of his legend.
It's interesting how myths are born, don't you think?

D: Perhaps Einstein wasn't the best example. Mozart then.

M: Why should I help you?

D: If your mind is as extraordinary as it appears to be,
then the whole world should know about it. You would be
famous.

M: I'm not interested in becoming a sideshow-attraction,
doctor. What if I don't want the whole world to know?

D: You're angry.

M: All I'm hearing is what you want; what you stand to
gain. You're going to have to do better than that if you
want me to help you.

D: Very well. Clearly you have an appetite for learning;
for knowledge. I could share my library with you and
become your instructor in the sciences.

M: Think bigger.

D: Bigger? The University? I see…Well, what if I could
arrange supervised access to the library as part of your
treatment? It would be highly irregular for a child, but
as long as we were careful and did not draw undue
attention to your visits, then it should be possible.

Child M

Date 15th Dec 1958

Would that be a sufficient incentive?

M: Unsupervised access, and I want to be able to withdraw books.

[PAUSE FOLLOWED BY INAUDIBLE SPEECH]

D: Can we begin? I'd like to test some hypotheses.

M: What kind of hypotheses?

D: Unlike my colleagues, I don't believe synaesthesia to be a neutral condition. It is my theory that synaesthetes have several cognitive and physiological advantages over non-synaesthetes, including superior memories, the ability to generate more vivid mental imagery, and increased creativity. You would appear to be living proof of my ideas. There are many different variations of synaesthesia - grapheme-colour synaesthesia being just one of them - but they are each consistent within the same individual, so while A may cause a red colour experience for one synaesthete and a blue colour for another, it will always be the same for each individual. Together, we could map your particular sensory associations.[102]

M: And what would you gain from such a map?

D: By studying you, I hope to better understand how your brain works, particularly how the visual pathways in your brain, which recognise letters and numbers, communicate with the area for colour processing, and importantly whether your gifts can be learned by others.

M: I hate to disappoint you, doctor, but I've read at least one paper exploring this idea already.

D: True, but that was a very small trial. And they certainly didn't have a test subject like you.

102. Bion appears to have done exactly that. His 'sensory map' for Child M was later recovered by Daniel who used it as a codex to unlock hidden messages concealed within Maas's artwork and films, adding further credibility to the theory that Child M and Ezra Maas were one and the same.

OXFORD CENTRE FOR COGNITIVE STUDIES
CHILDREN'S DEPARTMENT

REG. No.

392925

Child M

Date 15th Dec 1958

M: I told you. I'm not interested in being a guinea pig.

D: All I'm asking is that you talk to me. Explain to me, in your words, how you do what you do. Your creativity, your aptitude for language and mathematics, your ability to absorb and recall large, complex, amounts of information at will. I want to understand.

M: And you believe it is my synaesthesia that allows me to do these things?

D: In part, yes. But you also have an exceptionally high IQ and demonstrate a number of other intriguing behaviours on the autistic spectrum. As I said, you present a unique opportunity to study the developing brain of a genius-level intellect. I believe there is a great deal your brain - I mean, you - can teach us about how you interact with language, mathematics, and the arts, whether these gifts are genetic, or the result of your environment, your family, perhaps even the trauma of what happened to you. There are studies showing that neurochemicals in the brain, during moments of stress and anxiety, can stimulate...I'm getting ahead of myself...Well, let's just say, I know you think you've always been this way, but I would like to explore the possibility that it was the -

M: I won't talk about the accident, doctor. If you push me, this is over.

[SPEECH BRIEFLY INAUDIBLE]

D: Understood...Can we continue?

M: Yes.

D: Although you favour the creative arts - drawing and painting, sculpture, writing, performance - you have also demonstrated an extraordinary aptitude for numbers and

Child M

Date 15th Dec 1958

languages, solving complex arithmetic, reciting pi
numbers into the thousands from memory, and learning
French and German by the age of six.

M: That's right.

D: Your mother worked in France during the war. Is that
right? Did she teach you French?

M: Yes, but as I said I'd rather not talk about -

D: And your father...He lived in Germany for two years
after the war on denazification duty before returning
home. I understand he had a basic grasp of both French
and German, but you're fluent. I have a theory that
bi-lingual people see the world differently. By rapidly
and unconsciously switching between languages, between
tenses, nouns, cultural perspectives, they are
effectively re-wiring their brains, and increasing their
cognitive flexibility. We call it code-switching. I
believe your ability to learn language so quickly and so
effectively is linked to your gifts.

M: I find language beautiful, but I don't trust it. The
very fact that different languages reveal an alternative
yet equally valid perception of the world...of time and
space...exposes it to be false...a beautiful illusion.

D: That's interesting. I'd like to talk about that
further at some point. Can we move on to numbers for now?
How do you account for those abilities?

M: I see the meaning behind the numerals. They mean
something more to me than just symbols, they're bright or
dark, male or female, they have so many unique
characteristics which I know intimately, so that when I
think of large pi numbers or I'm asked to solve
arithmetic, I visualise the whole number as the shapes,
colours and textures that make it up, simultaneously, and

OXFORD CENTRE FOR COGNITIVE STUDIES
CHILDREN'S DEPARTMENT

REG. No.

392925

Child M

Date 15th Dec 1958

I instantly recognise the answer, in the same way that
if I asked you to think of a Tyrannosaurus Rex you can
imagine it straight away, you wouldn't have to work it
out by adding up the letters and syllables that make up
the word. The average person has a vocabulary of 45,000
words and yet we access it instantly, with no delay
between the brain constructing sentences and speaking
them. How is that possible? We can access numbers in just
the same way.

D: Remarkable...You explain your ideas very confidently...One
of the reasons I find you such a curiosity, in fact, is
that you do not display any of the characteristic traits
or behaviours of autism, or the high-functioning form
observed by my esteemed colleague Hans Asperger, such as
repetitive behaviours, difficulty in socialising,
isolation, and the loneliness that goes with it...

M: I never claimed to be autistic or anything else.

D: Not at all. What I see is an exceptionally intelligent
child who has learned to conceal any behaviours he does
not wish to show. What you are is frightening...Just
imagine if your gifts could be taught to other
children...you could change the world. But to replicate it
we need to understand it.

M: The left parietal lobe for numbers and the left
frontal lobe for language are both located in the left
hemisphere of the brain.

D: Correct.

M: I believe these regions of my brain are communicating
with each other more than normal, due to extreme neural
connectivity.

D: That's a fascinating theory. I'd love to run some
tests to try and monitor that hyperactivity. Of course,

OXFORD CENTRE FOR COGNITIVE STUDIES
CHILDREN'S DEPARTMENT

REG. No.
392925

Child M

Date 15th Dec 1958

if you're right and if it continued unabated...it could
lead to psychosis.

M: Perhaps...My point is, what I am cannot be taught. The
real question is why was I born this way? Is there a
purpose? These are questions I am considering and one day
I will have an answer.

D: You sound as if you would like to question God.

M: Why not?

D: The 'why' is something I'm also interested in finding
out...I've had some difficulty in acquiring your family's
medical history, but I understand there is evidence of
schizophrenia on your father's side and epilepsy in your
mother's. Can we talk about your brother?

M: I told you. I don't want to talk about my brother.

D: He was very different from you, wasn't he? Do you feel
you should have been able to save him?

[PAUSE]

M: Dionysus and Apollo were the sons of Zeus. Apollo was
the god of light, reason, and the representational arts,
a world of appearances, and fixed and individual
identities. Dionysus, on the other hand, was the god of
intoxication and rapture, intuition, formlessness, the
world under the surface, where individual identities
dissolve and merge with nature.

D: That's not what I asked.

M: You're not listening.

D: Okay...I'll play along. And you feel you were the
opposite of your brother, like Apollo and Dionysus?

REG. No.

392925

Child M

Date 15th Dec 1958

M: The sons of Zeus were complementary, not opposite.
Two sides of the same whole. Order and chaos, light and
darkness.

D: And which one are you?

M: Neither. I have no brother.

D: When your brother died, I understand you took on a lot
of his characteristics, leaving behind who you were, to
become someone new. I find this interesting.

M: Nietzsche wrote about the duality of Dionysus and
Apollo in The Birth of Tragedy.

D: That's right.

M: Nietzsche saw Dionysus as the first tragic hero and
that all those who followed him, from Prometheus to
Oedipus, were masks for him. His suffering is the
suffering of all men faced with the horror of an absurd
and meaningless existence. Did you know that, as a boy,
Dionysus was torn to pieces by the Titans? All that was
saved was his heart from which he was born again.[103]

D: Do you feel the tragedies of your life have driven you
to a world view, like Nietzsche, of nihilism?

M: You think I'm a nihilist?

D: I'm just trying to understand.

M: Nietzsche saw Dionysus, cut to pieces, as a promise
that life "will be eternally reborn and return again from
destruction".

D: Nietzsche was mad by the end of his life...I'd like to
talk about your parents again.

103. Nietzsche, Friedrich. *The Will to Power.*

Child M

Date 15th Dec 1958

M: No.

D: I insist. I believe their influence on you, in life
and death, alongside your relationship with your brother,
is key to understanding how your mind -

M: - was cut to pieces and reborn?

D: Exactly.

M: Doctor, I will not discuss my family with you again.

[PAUSE]

D: You will do as you are told while you are in my care.

M: You would exploit my family's deaths to make a name
for yourself in your field. That's all this is about.

D: I know it must be hard to think about -

M: The Romans had a god who had no antecedent in Greek
mythology.

D: Janus, the two-faced god. Do you identify with Janus?

M: From his single position in space, he sees both past
and future as the same. His duality allows him a true
vision of reality.

D: Yes, well...if you're not going to answer my questions
in a meaningful way I might have to rethink our
arrangement. While you reside in the university, under my
supervision, I have the power to grant privileges as we
have discussed, but I can also enforce restrictions. I
could recommend a stay at Cane Hill psychiatric hospital
for treatment if I feel it is necessary.

M: Are you threatening me, doctor?

Child M

Date 15th Dec 1958

D: I'd like to talk about November 11th. You were found wandering after the incident. Doctors described you as near-catatonic. You were reciting numbers, but otherwise non-responsive. Do you remember?

M: I remember everything.

D: You didn't talk for thirty-four days afterwards except to repeat these same numbers over and over: [Numbers blacked out]. What do the numbers mean?

M: I can't tell you that.

D: Why not?

M: It's a secret.

D: What kind of secret?

M: Don't worry Doctor. I know other numbers that might interest you...

D: What do you mean?

M: Numbers like...1 - 12 - 49...

D: What did you say?

M: You heard me. 1 - 12 - 49.

D: How do you know that date?

M: 1 - 12 - 49.

D: Stop it.

M: Why? Did something bad happen on 1 - 12 - 49? Something you'd like to stay hidden?

Child M

Date 15th Dec 1958

D: I don't know what you're talking about.

M: I think you do. I think you know all about 1 - 12 - 49.

D: I said stop it.

M: 1 - 12 - 49. 1 - 12 - 49.

D: Stop it!

M: 1 - 12 - 49. 1 - 12 - 49. 1 - 12 - 49. 1 - 12 - 49. 1 - 12 - 49. 1 - 12 - 49. 1 - 12 - 49. 1 - 12 - 49. 1 - 12 - 49.

[Interview terminated]

END

What do the numbers mean??

Daniel James
Chapter Three

When we look at a photograph, we are really looking at the return of the dead[104]

I switched on the light as I walked into the bedroom. Ariane stood with her hands on her hips and a look on her face that seemed to suggest I was the intruder. She wore a cream linen shirt with the sleeves rolled up to her elbows, and a pair of khaki trousers.

'You're late,' she smiled.

'And you're early,' I replied. 'I wasn't expecting you until tomorrow morning.'

'I thought I'd surprise you.'

'By waiting in the dark?'

'Did I scare you? You're white as a sheet.'

'Someone was following me,' I replied. 'I had to duck into a gin bar to lose them.'

'A likely story.'

'A happy coincidence,' I said, as I took off my jacket. 'But true all the same.'

Ariane was a freelance reporter who lived in Paris, and a friend since our days as trainees over a decade ago. I had called her to cash in a favour, and she had agreed to join me in Bruges.

'Were you really being followed?' she said.

'I haven't told you the best part yet.'

'What's that?'

'I finally sold my soul to the devil tonight.' I took the photograph out of my pocket and handed it to her. 'That was the price.'

She looked at it closely.

'A photograph of Maas?'

'Not quite... those were his friends in Bruges back in the '70s. He might be one of the men in the background, or at the dinner table with his face out of view, but the restaurant owner couldn't say for sure. I do have a couple of leads though, including an American writer whose name has come up a couple of times now.'

'And this is why you were followed?'

'Well, I also have a habit of pissing-off the wrong people.'

'This is true,' she replied.

---

104. Roland Barthes, *Camera Lucida* (1980).

The pig made the shape of a gun with his hands, pointed his arm at me and pulled an imaginary trigger, before disappearing along the alley. As soon as they were gone, I headed in the opposite direction as quickly as I could.

Once inside the Cabaret Voltaire, I found a quiet corner with my back to a wall covered with hand-drawn black and white artwork, where I could keep an eye on the exits. I had to tell Ariane what I had found, but there was no answer on her mobile or at her apartment in Paris. I thought about trying *Le Monde*, but I didn't want her newsdesk to know she was helping me. I decided to try her again later. She needed to know about Jane D's letter. If it was true, it could confirm a number of long-standing conspiracy theories about the Maas Foundation. It wouldn't be the first time they had been accused of being a cult, of course, but this was different. A woman was dead, and her last words had the unmistakable power and authenticity of the truth. Was that the real reason my hands were shaking? Not through fear, but excitement at having found a piece of the puzzle? Or was it still something else? Maybe what unsettled me most was my lack of reaction to a person's death, the absence of ordinary human emotions despite the brutal images that kept appearing in my mind. It was a curious thing, this emptiness inside me. I worried about myself sometimes. Why didn't I react like other people? I saw the world as a double exposure.[163] I was both the author and a character in my own story, simultaneously inside and outside. The distance caused by this division insulated me from the world, but every now and then, faced with an experience like this where I knew certain emotions were expected, it made me feel less than human.[164] I had been haunted by this strange simultaneity[165] for as long as I could remember.

---

163. In cinematography and photography, double exposure refers to the superimposition of two or more exposures to create a single image. In analogue photography, the technique involves opening the camera shutter more than once to expose the film multiple times, usually to different images. The resulting image contains the subsequent image/s superimposed over the original. It is often used as an artistic visual effect and can be used to create ghostly images or to add people and objects to a scene that were not originally there.

164. Fredric Jameson writes: "For Proust we can only be sure we have lived, we have perceived, after the fact of the experience itself; for him the deliberate wilful project to meet experience face to face in the present is always doomed to fail." *Detections of Totality*, Verso Press.

165. This phrase made me recall a line from Poe's Dupin stories and his detective's bi-part soul. From the earliest detective stories, the genre always placed an emphasis on cerebral activity, with the detective solving the crime through ratiocination, i.e. using reason and logic rather than physically tracking down the criminal. In the case of Poe's Dupin he also possessed a uniquely 'Bi-Part Soul' which allowed him to mirror the thinking of the criminal mind, becoming the double of his opponent, a characteristic which anticipates the postmodern detective fiction where the line between detective and criminal are frequently blurred – Anonymous.

I decided to check out of my hotel that night instead of waiting until morning, and took a night train across the border into northern Italy. In the days and weeks afterwards I continued on across Europe, never staying anywhere for more than a few days, sometimes doubling back on myself when I had to. I went where the story took me, and that meant abandoning the fastest route from A to B, or visiting places in a linear sequence, as any normal person would have done. Life wasn't linear, and if my book hoped to tell the truth it couldn't be either. Sometimes I would wake up and not know which city I was in, unsure whether it was day or night.

Where was I today? The train pulled into Moscow's marble-lined Belorusskaya station. I was staying at the Metropol, the historic Art Nouveau building where Bulgakov's *The Master and Margarita* was set, my days spent wandering the Red Square. I was back in Berlin, staying in an Altbau on a tree-lined twin avenue in Schöneberg. Where now? When now? I was in Paris, visiting the graves of Jean-Paul Sartre and Simone de Beauvoir, drinking coffee in Café Flore; I was exploring the bone-lined tunnels of the catacombs. You start to lose a sense of where and when. When your mind is in the book, your body could be anywhere. You open your eyes and you're in the back of a cab, you're in a train carriage, you're in a hotel room, you're standing on a platform, you're picking up your bags. You're on the conveyer at Tegel airport, the Aeroporto Leonardo da Vinci di Fiumicino, Luxembourg-Findel, Brno-Turany, Braganca Aerodrome, Zürich Flughafen, heading towards the departure lounge, you're leaving arrivals. You drift through an endless succession of non-places,[166] moving even when you're standing still, taking off as you're touching down, always moving, always writing.

Above the clouds everything was calm, but it was just an illusion. We were at 30,000ft and travelling at 510 miles per hour when the book reached 150,000 words. The narrative was breaking down. My life consisted of jump cuts[167] from one place to the next, my world was washed-out and colourless. I felt as if the book was an illness and I was dying, disconnected from everything, from everyone, but this was the way it had to be. The book was writing itself in my mind all the time and I had to listen carefully. The story was being transmitted and I was the receiver. It flowed through me and onto the page. The world of the book was more real than reality to

---

166. Airports, retail parks, and chain stores have been referred to as 'non-places' by Marc Augé, homogeneous spaces whose "ominous proliferation is the most visible sign of the implacable spread of capitalist globalisation", according to cultural critic and essayist Mark Fisher.

167. A jump cut is a technique used in film editing to draw attention to the constructed, artificial nature of the film.

me now; I was more there than here, living inside the pages and between the words, watching moments play out in my mind, a stream of images projected into my head, discontinuous flashes. I didn't know if other writers experienced this, but that was how it was for me. I was essentially transcribing and interpreting a succession of scenes as they unfolded in my mind, both real, imaginary, and somewhere in-between, drawn from people and places, research and books, from the stories I had been told and the things I had seen and felt. My conscious mind imposed structure and provided narration, bringing everything together, merging it all into one. It was a kind of possession. And the closer I got to the source of that possession, the greater my disconnection from my own life.

Ezra Maas: An Oral History
Part Two

Artists, writers, journalists, photographers, critics, friends, and others, who were around Maas during the years 1956 to 1996, give their impressions of the artist. Interviews by Daniel James.

☆

Suzy Sternwood, New York-based multidisciplinary artist, who collaborated with Maas from 1978 to the present.

SS: His was the art of survival, especially in his later years. For a man whose every move was watched, discussed and analysed, art provided Ezra with a unique means to express his individual experience in a private mode.

☆

Randall Mosley and Jacob Thompson, fellow students with a young Ezra Maas at the Ruskin School of Drawing and Fine Art from 1957-62.

RM: Ezra Maas? He always gave me the creeps. I never saw people's fascination with him. It was only because he was so young if you ask me. A savant? Hardly! I didn't think he was anything special.

JT: Ah, don't listen to Randall. He's just jealous.

RM: I'm not, you never–

JT: Randall could never get over the fact that they admitted Ezra to the school at such a young age, but the truth is he deserved his place. Professor [Edgar] Wind, the art historian, was giving guest lectures at the time and he was one of many senior staff who took Ezra under their wing. Wind was an expert in iconography and pagan mythology and Ezra was an apt pupil, always listening and asking questions, absorbing everything he could. Personally, I agreed with Wind and the others. Ezra was a prodigy in our midst and it didn't surprise me in the slightest when I began to see him appearing in the international press just a few years later.

☆

Perrine Sallis, curator of The Green Gallery in Paris, France.

PS: Encore aujourd'hui, bien des années après sa disparition, Maas continue de hanter la psychogéographie de la ville. C'est l'artiste des artistes, peut-être oublié par une grande partie du public mais toujours cité par ceux qui s'y connaissent vraiment dans les meilleures galeries d'art de Paris, influençant encore et toujours la nouvelle génération d'artistes d'avant garde.[168]

☆

Jean Highsmith, daughter of Dr [REDACTED] who allegedly assessed Ezra Maas in the 1950s following the death of his parents and brother.

JH: How did you find me?

DJ: A schoolteacher I interviewed in Oxford told me that Maas had been treated by a psychiatrist named Bowlby when he was a child. He remembered the name because Bowlby went on to become quite famous a few years later. Your grandfather's name is referenced briefly in Bowlby's authorised biography, alongside Dr Alexander Bion and the case of an unnamed child. It was the child's circumstances that caught my eye. Namely their similarity to stories I've uncovered about Ezra Maas's childhood.

JH: Here.

DJ: What's this?

JH: My grandfather's notes – the cases and medical histories he just couldn't let go – take them. He told me, before he died, that one day someone would come looking for his files. He didn't say which of them, but when I read the files for myself, it was obvious. I always wondered why he didn't ask me to destroy them... probably the same reason he kept the files himself all those years... Guilt... I suppose they were his punishment to bear, his mistakes... I want you to know that my grandfather was a kind and caring man, and a lovely grandfather to me, but there was always sadness in his eyes and I didn't understand why, until I read those files. They haunted him for almost half a century. I'm glad to be finally rid of them.

DJ: What are these codes for?

JH: The numbers? I didn't understand them either. Not at first. But once you read the file you'll see...

DJ: See what?

JH: What my grandfather couldn't forget.

---

168. Translates as: 'To this day, years after his disappearance, Maas haunts the psycho-geography of the city. He is the artist's artist, forgotten by sections of the public perhaps, but still referenced by the truly knowledgeable in Paris's finest galleries and studios, still influencing the next generation of avant-garde artists.' – Anonymous

Ezra Maas
Chapter Three

I is another.[169]

Andy Warhol was pronounced clinically dead on 3rd June 1968.[170] He had been shot. Of the three bullets fired at Warhol, it was the third and final shot that did the worst damage. The .32 calibre slug punched through his right side, piercing his lungs, oesophagus, spleen, liver and stomach, and exited out the left side of his back. He was dead for a minute and a half in the emergency room at Columbus Hospital, New York, until surgeons cut open his chest and massaged his heart back to life. Warhol was in surgery for five and half hours after that, as doctors worked to save him. They were successful, but his injuries were so severe that he had to wear a surgical corset for the rest of his life and never fully recovered.

Valerie Solanas,[171] a radical feminist, activist and author, was arrested for Warhol's attempted murder and later diagnosed with schizophrenia. She famously told police she had done it because Warhol had "too much control over my life". However, there were also claims that she had fallen under the sway of other charismatic figures on the '60s art scene who promised to support her work if she carried out the shooting,[172] However, this was never proven, and the claims have been highly disputed. Solanas was jailed[173] in the aftermath and the carefree, open door policy of The Factory was over. Some felt Pop Art died that day, too. The decade was

---

169. Arthur Rimbaud (1851 – 1891)

170. The year 1968 saw unprecedented outbreaks of violence and social unrest across the United States and around the world, including the student protests of that year, marches for Civil Rights, anti-Vietnam demonstrations, and the assassinations of Presidential candidate Robert Kennedy and Civil Rights leader Martin Luther King Jr.

171. Solanas was the author of the radical feminist SCUM manifesto, a scathing critique of patriarchal society which was published in 1967. She had moved to New York as a writer and met Warhol at the Factory, acting in one of his films.

172. Unnamed sources have linked Solanas with several extreme groups, including friends and followers of Ezra Maas. However, there is no evidence to suggest she ever met Maas himself or had any communication with him. In fact, Maas was not in New York at the time of the shooting. His whereabouts that summer are a source of speculation, with conflicting stories placing him in LA and back in the UK.

173. Solanas was initially judged unfit to stand trial after being diagnosed with chronic paranoid schizophrenia. She was eventually tried and sentenced to three years, but was released after one year. Solanas continued to stalk Warhol with threatening phone calls in later life, before disappearing and spending many years homeless, before dying at the age of fifty-two.

coming to a violent and nasty end. Many said it began two years earlier, not long after the arrival of a mysterious stranger in the city.

New York wears many faces. In time, Ezra Maas would come to know them all, while never revealing his own. This was the beginning of his second life, just six weeks after disappearing from his home in the UK following his uncle's fatal overdose. Based in Greenwich Village, he took his first steps towards becoming an artist in February 1966, selling paintings and sketches on a snowy corner of 12th Street and Broadway, outside The Strand[174] bookstore. In his previously unpublished paper, *Endangered Species: Exodus and Extinction in the work of Ezra Maas 1964 – '66*, Professor Paul Desmond writes:

"… the relocation to the US was also significant for another reason. It signified the death of the boy Ezra. Now only Maas remained, and this was how he referred to himself thereafter, yet another death in his life had preceded rebirth, geographical movement cleared a path for psychological reinvention…"[175]

While no definitive explanation has ever been given for how he arrived in America, it has been speculated that Maas was aided by twenty-one-year-old heiress Hilary Banford,[176] who was the daughter of US steel tycoon Robert Banford. The socialite was a familiar figure on the London art scene and was renowned for spending money almost as fast as her father could make it. According to Hilary's younger sister, Rosette, the pair first met at the National Gallery in London when Maas was just fifteen. The story goes that Hilary found Maas sitting cross-legged in front of Renoir's *The Umbrellas*[177] writing a poem inspired by the painting in his notebook. A contradictory (and less romantic) account of his departure from the UK describes Maas, with forged seaman's papers, bribing his way onto a merchant ship docked at Liverpool and making his way to New York himself. He lived in poverty for weeks and earned a living performing

---

174. A fiercely independent family business, The Strand Book Store opened in 1927 on Fourth Avenue, New York, which was known as 'Book Row', before moving to Greenwich Village; it reportedly stocked eighteen miles of books on its premises by the late 1960s. Maas's novella, *To Beg or Borrow*, had its unofficial launch at the store in March 1966.

175. Desmond, Paul. *Endangered Species: Exodus and Extinction in the work of Ezra Maas 1964 – '66*. pp.42-43. The original publication of this research paper was blocked by The Maas Foundation in 1989. A copy was posted to Daniel in 2012.

176. Banford (1944 – 1991) was often compared to Virginia Dwan, another heiress turned art collector and patron.

177. Pierre-Auguste Renoir began *The Umbrellas* in 1881 and finished it in 1885 – '86.

card tricks at Coney Island,[178] before a chance meeting with Hilary at Greenwich Village book store The Strand, where he managed to charm his way into her life. Either way, there is little doubt she provided Maas with much needed financial backing, even if their relationship, in a romantic sense at least, only lasted a few months.[179] Even at this young age, Maas's ability to seek out people who could help him was as finely tuned as his art.

Other stories of Maas's early days living in Greenwich Village describe how he often played chess 'for quarters' in Washington Square Park and various Manhattan chess clubs, while struggling to make a living as an artist. There were also rumours that to stay off the streets Maas had earned cash by volunteering for psychedelic drug-testing experiments, which were taking place in a number of college campuses in New York, and elsewhere across the United States, during the 1960s.[180] These stories were later linked

---

178. According to Daniel's notes on this period, Maas was taken under the wing of Coney Island magician, Fabulous Francis aka Bill Doyle and his wife Ada, who taught him sleight of hand tricks and other techniques. Daniel travelled to New York in 2011 with the hope of tracking down some of the carnival folk who Maas worked alongside, perhaps even Francis himself. However, the old magician was said to have died in the 1980s. For more on this see Daniel's chapter in New York – Anonymous.

179. It is understood that Ms Banford, later Adler, remained one of Maas's many financial benefactors for several decades.

180. From the late 1940s to the early 1970s, the CIA secretly conducted a large number of high-dose psychedelic drug experiments at universities, hospitals, and prisons across the US and Canada. This was Project MK-Ultra. It was officially approved by CIA Director Allan Dulles in 1953, ostensibly motivated by fears that Soviet, Chinese, and North Korean agents were using mind control, brainwashing, and experimental drugs to 'turn' US soldiers. The project's principle aim was to control human behaviour using drugs and other psychological techniques so as to give the US an edge in covert operations and during the interrogation of prisoners at the height of the Cold War. However, there have been suggestions that MK-Ultra's origins can be linked to Operation Paperclip, which saw high-ranking Nazi scientists recruited by the US after WW2, and also Operation Bluebird, which allegedly involved using amphetamines and barbiturates to hypnotise enemy agents into undertaking activity against their will. Between 1953 and 1964, MK-Ultra covertly funded more than 150 human experiments involving psychedelic drugs, paralytics, and electroshock therapy. Sometimes those volunteering were aware they were testing drugs, but on many other occasions dangerous hallucinogens and psychedelics were administered to individuals without their knowledge or consent. These illegal experiments have been linked with a number of deaths, as well as extreme, anti-social behaviour, acts of violence, and psychological problems later in life. Well-known MK-Ultra tests subjects allegedly include the author Ken Kesey, the gangster James 'Whitey' Bulger, and the 'Unabomber' Ted Kaczynski – a mathematics prodigy turned domestic terrorist who killed three people and injured twenty-three others in a nationwide bombing campaign. The project was officially terminated in 1973 and most of the documentation relating to the tests was destroyed.

to accusations[181] that Maas's sudden rise to fame over the next twelve to eighteen months was stage-managed by 'friends in high places', as well as controversial allegations which emerged over a decade later implicating the Maas Foundation as conspirators in the CIA-funded Project MK-Ultra.[182] This association was strenuously denied and never proven.

Maas was also a lover of independent cinema and reportedly spent his early days in New York educating himself in film, with regular visits to screenings at art houses such as the Thalia on 95th Street, and Dan Talbot's New Yorker on Broadway between 88th and 89th,[183] as well as retrospectives of Hollywood directors at the Museum of Modern Art.[184]

In order to build his early reputation, Banford encouraged Maas to give away some of his work for free on street corners in and around the East Village,[185] and arranged meetings for him with the power players on the New York art scene, including Leo Castelli, Sidney Janis and Julien Levy, which months later would lead to Maas's first solo exhibitions.

It was during this period, working out of a small studio space in the East Village owned by Banford, that Maas began to gather a following. People would crowd around the artist on 12th Street as he handed out artwork until the police told them to move along, causing fans and followers to congregate outside his studio.[186] Many were invited inside to watch Maas at work or engage in energetic conversations about art until the early hours. One onlooker said:

"Maas could walk into a room and every head would turn... it was like he was the sun itself... he was this radiant child, and everyone gravitated

---

181. It must be noted that many of these accusations came from Maas's rivals in the art world, who were understandably resentful of his rise to fame – Anonymous.

182. The public only became aware of Project MK-Ultra in the late 1970s. This was due to the work of a number of individuals, including former CIA officer John Marks, who recovered a number of MK-Ultra files using a Freedom of Information Act request. His analysis of these files became the basis for his 1979 book, *In Search of the Manchurian Candidate*, which is partly responsible for bringing the project to the public's attention.

183. This was the Golden Age of postwar European and Japanese cinema. Maas reportedly admired the work of directors such as Fellini, Antonioni and Kurosawa, as well as the work of the French New Wave.

184. Programmed in the early '60s by a young Peter Bogdanovich, who would go on to direct *The Last Picture Show* among other films.

185. As documented by Art International Magazine Vol. 14, Issue 4. Spring 1970.

186. Allegedly sleeping in stairwells and in the alleyway outside for a chance to meet him, or see some of his work in progress.

towards him... it was incredible."[187]

Within weeks, these informal gatherings had moved to small venues, often spaces above cafes and coffee shops, and were formalised into live 'happenings'.[188] These events, organised by Maas's followers rather than the artist himself, usually featured the launch of a new artwork as the centrepiece, but also included performance art, mixed media, music, film, photography, dance, and public interventions. They were part exhibition, part social gathering. Loosely modelled after German 'Fluxus'[189] activities, these happenings began to attract greater and greater crowds, but Maas himself never attended. While early descriptions of Maas cast him as a charismatic street artist, he also had a reputation for being intensely private outside of his inner circle. A collection of his early artworks, brought together with his own text, was released in May 1966 as a unique, illustrated novella entitled *XXXXXX*.[190] This was the next step toward widespread fame and his work becoming synonymous with the counterculture and the social unrest across the US. *XXXXXX* was initially distributed guerrilla-style on A4 paper, typewritten and bound in yellow with an image of a Borromean Knot[191] stencilled on the front cover in red. Copies were passed around in cafés, bars, coffee houses,[192] schools, and colleges and it became the *de rigueur*[193] fashion accessory for the city's disaffected youth. Thanks

---

187. From one of Daniel's New York interviews 2011 – '12.

188. The term 'Happening' was first coined by Allan Kaprow. Maas can be seen as following in the footsteps of Kaprow, Claes Oldenberg, Red Grooms and others. Kaprow said: "Words, sounds, human beings in motion, painted constructions, electric lights, movies and slides – and perhaps in the future, smells – all in continuous space involving the spectator or audience; those are the ingredients. Several or all of them may be used in combination at any one time, which permits me a great range of possibilities."

189. The Latin word Fluxus means flowing, in English a flux is a flowing out. Fluxus founder Maciunas said that the purpose of Fluxus was to "promote a revolutionary flood and tide in art, promote living art, anti-art". This has strong echoes of Dada, the early 20th century art movement.

190. Allegedly written when Maas was fifteen, and taken to the US as one of his few belongings when he left England.

191. The Borromean Knot is a group of three rings linked in such a way that if any one of them is cut, all three become separated. French psychoanalyst Jacques Lacan used the Borromean knot as a way of illustrating the interdependence of the three orders of the real, the symbolic, and the imaginary. This corresponds to a rethinking of the relationship between language and the body in the subject.

192. Such as Caffè Reggio, the Commons, and Caffè Dante in Greenwich Village.

193. Roughly translates from French as 'out of strict etiquette' and is used to denote something that is done strictly because it is fashionable.

to Banford's connections, *XXXXXX* was picked up by Greenwich Village small press Sun & Co, who distributed the book on a wider scale. Within weeks, Maas's 'micro-cult' of followers had grown to include a number of hard-core devotees, who treated the book like an underground manifesto, filled with esoteric messages written just for them.[194] Critics were also enthralled, hailing *XXXXXX* as "a profound meditation of the postmodern condition",[195] although at least one reporter said they did not believe the book had been written by a teenager and accused Maas of plagiarising a number of other texts.

Despite this, *XXXXXX* became a defining publication for alienated and disaffected teens in late 1960s New York and continues to sell 50,000 copies-a-year[196] in the city to this day. The success of the book led to Maas publishing several short stories in *The New Yorker* and elsewhere, using a variety of thinly veiled pseudonyms. His artwork also brought him to the attention of other New York based artists, notably Andy Warhol, who was a regular in nightspots such as Max's Kansas City[197] which Maas and his followers were also known to frequent. Julia Deeley, a model and singer-songwriter, was a friend of Warhol and claims to have known Maas briefly:

"Maas was a regular visitor to The Factory[198] in the early days. Andy was infatuated with him. He referred to Maas as "that beautiful boy" and the brightest of all "superstars".[199] Maas wasn't interested in Andy in the same way and he certainly didn't want to be one of Andy's superstars, but there was respect there from artist to artist, and he always said he learned a lot from him… he attended Warhol's solo show at the Castelli Gallery later that year when Andy redecorated the space with *Cow Wallpaper*… Maas seemed particularly interested in what Andy was doing with film… I got the sense that he was absorbing everything he could from those early

---

194. XXXXXX was reportedly influenced by Max Ernst's collage novels, Une semaine de bonté (1933) and also experimented with techniques such as decalcomania to reveal hidden textures, messages and forms.

195. Greenwich Review, March 1966.

196. Note to reader: I'm not sure where Daniel got these figures. The book is currently out of print and has been for decades, it would appear. The rights are held by The Maas Foundation – Anonymous.

197. The famous nightclub and restaurant at 213 Park Avenue South, New York City, described by critics as both "viper pit and arcadia" and the site of many cultural and sexual unions.

198. At the time, The Factory was located on East 47th Street in Midtown Manhattan.

199. Warhol's Superstars were a clique of New York personalities – artists, drug addicts, socialites, sex workers and more – who came to be associated with the artist, including Edie Sedgwick, Ultra Violet, Nico, and International Velvet.

interactions with a view to pushing the medium further... Maas was clearly ambitious. He stopped coming by The Factory after a while and became one of those artists who were talked about a lot, but you rarely saw them... I heard a rumour he was agoraphobic, but I don't know if that's true... "[200]

It has been speculated that Maas, following Warhol's example, began recording his telephone conversations and keeping all of his personal correspondence to be used as potential 'art'. Maas was also rumoured to have been impressed with Warhol's use of assistants to increase his productivity[201] although he disagreed with turning art into a factory production line. Instead he saw the use of assistants as a way for him to distance himself from the press and fans alike, retreating from public view to concentrate on his art, while his followers dealt with the media and helped manage his business interests.

In many ways, this can be seen as the early origins of The Maas Foundation, although it would not formally take shape, and be named as such, until Maas's marriage to Helena Huston in 1980. Even at this relatively young age Maas was gaining followers, and supposedly had a wide circle of friends in the art world, but he was also determined to remain inaccessible to the media. He refused interviews and public engagements, something he would continue to do throughout his life, and told friends wildly differing stories about his life and background. The fashion photographer, John Jones-Parker, became friends with Maas in early 1967:

"Before I met him, they told me he was doing LSD, peyote, heroin, the whole lot..." Parker recalls. "But when I met him I didn't see signs of drug use whatsoever... in fact, while everyone else was high, it was pretty obvious he was clean... what did become apparent was the lies he would tell about himself at every opportunity, and he had others lying for him too... before long no one knew what was real and what was fiction... maybe not even him... the rumours of drug use and addiction... I wouldn't be surprised if he started those stories himself. It added to the image he was trying to cultivate... "[202]

Maas consolidated his growing success with a number of solo shows at the 10th Street co-op galleries, including Brata, Hansa, and Tanager.[203] He

---

200. This is taken from an interview Daniel carried out with Julie in New York in early 2012.

201. Warhol also did this to emphasize his view that art could not escape being treated as a commodity.

202. An excerpt from a full interview conducted with Parker by Daniel in 2012.

203. My own research has revealed that these three galleries had all closed by the mid-1960s. It

119

also exhibited at Virginia Dwan's New York Gallery on 57th Street, which had opened the previous year in 1965. Dwan,[204] a dark-haired, glamorous and wealthy art collector, patron, and philanthropist, was notable for her interest in male artists (who became known as Dwan's boys) and was an advocate of Minimalism, Conceptual, and Land art. Maas was becoming an established name, but he would never be part of the establishment. Even as his shows continued to grow in size he retained his radical nature and the respect of other avant-garde artists. As feminist performance artist Eva D recalls:

"There was no jealousy among us. We didn't say "Oh, now he's famous. He's sold out." It wasn't like that. We would talk about the implications of what Maas was doing, using the gallery space in a way that had never been done before; his work was fucking unreal. It pushed the boundaries. We all left thinking, "What does that mean?" and "What can I do to keep pace with this when I get back to my studio?" That's what was happening."[205]

It was also at this time that a number of spiritual and religious organisations reached out to Maas. Every week another group claimed he had converted to their belief system, but while Maas chose to remain publicly silent on the matter his friends stated he had no affiliation with any organisation, spiritual or otherwise, and that he was generally opposed to organised religion. However, due to Maas's continued reluctance to comment publicly about these stories, the rumours continued to grow. Joan Lauder, author of *A Decade of Counterculture*, was one of those who believed this was a very clever move by Maas:

"This was another example of Maas allowing rumours of his association with cults and pseudo-religions to flourish, for the very reason that if people were talking about all these bizarre theories then no one knew what he was actually doing... And whether he was behind it all or not, it was incredibly clever PR..."[206]

Although attempts were made to link him with everything from occultism[207] and ceremonial magic to Christian science, acupuncture,

---

is unlikely Daniel's research was incorrect as he was notoriously thorough, but it does raise the possibility that some of the people he interviewed about this period were either lying to him or giving him false information – Anonymous.

204. Dwan was heiress to the Minnesota Mining Company, which had annual sales of $30bn in the 1960s and 1970s.

205. From an interview with Daniel in 2012.

206. In *A Decade of Counterculture*, Oxford Press, 1985.

207. Maas's name was mentioned alongside the likes of Aleister 'The Great Beast' Crowley and

homeopathy, macrobiotics, and dianetics,[208] Maas was arguably most closely associated with Zen Buddhism and Hinduism during these months, with one group asserting he had been a follower of *The Gospel of Sri Ramakrishna* for several years, while others claimed he had travelled to Bombay with a girlfriend on a pilgrimage to visit a number of gurus and holy places. Representatives of self-realisation gurus Mahavatar Babaji, Lahiri Mahasaya, and Sri Yukteswar, all claimed to have spoken with Maas. Throughout all of this, Maas himself remained silent.

As ever, he chose to let his work speak for him. In late 1967 Maas staged his most ambitious show yet, transforming a townhouse owned by Banford into a 'living museum' filled with over fifteen rooms of art including paintings, sculptures, live performance art, audio, and video installation. It was a colossal happening, which continued 24/7 for two weeks, with artists living, eating, and sleeping in a self-contained world where visitors became part of fluid, live artworks. Work included found objects and materials covered with drawings and words, assemblage art, leftover theatrical backdrops transformed into canvasses, and sculptures made of cardboard and newspaper, plaster and melted lead. Critics were astounded. Jacob Friedkin, for *Art Forum* magazine, said this in his review of the show:

"It has clearly been created by an artist for whom the act of creation is fundamental to their existence... the result is a mind-bending journey through a mansion of the arts... painting, sculpture, performance, film, photography, sound, and an extraordinary range of other media... each room is themed and draws you through to the next as in a narrative. There are rooms within rooms, worlds within worlds... it has reimagined how we engage with artwork..."[209]

Following the success of his solo show Maas's fame was near its peak. Invitations to exhibit work at the Venice Biennale,[210] and Documenta IV[211] in Kassel, Germany, followed, but Maas was reportedly reluctant. Renowned Land artist Jack Gregson commented two years later that Maas

---

Edgar 'The Sleeping Prophet' Cayce.

208. L. Ron Hubbard reportedly sent Maas a telex from his fleet of Sea Org vessels while in the Greek islands, personally inviting the artist to join him. Maas did not respond.

209. *Art Forum* Vol 11, Issue 15, Fall 1967.

210. One of the world's biggest art festivals, in Venice, Italy.

211. Documenta is a major international exhibition of contemporary art which takes place every five years in Kassel, Germany. It was founded by artist, teacher, and curator, Arnold Bode.

had almost a prophetic quality to his decision-making: "If you remember, both the Venice Biennale and Documenta IV were dogged by the student protests of '68 and fierce criticism over the paucity of female and non-white artists… As usual, Maas's instincts were proved right…"

Eager to escape the instant and claustrophobic fame his early artworks had brought him, Maas allegedly packed a bag one night in late summer and threatened to leave New York, with plans to work his way across the country to the West Coast. His reasons were the subject of much speculation. Blue Box gallery[212] owner Max Howard said:

"He described fame as an unmanageable surge, and confessed to feeling uncomfortable with the attention it brought him… he may not have been ready to return to Europe, but he wanted a return to anonymity, he felt it was essential to his work…"[213]

However, there were other rumours. A friend of Maas had allegedly been brutally beaten by members of the cult that had developed around *XXXXXX*. Maas strongly denied accusations that he had been behind the attack.[214] This was followed by reports of vandalism in the Greenwich Village area, with quotes by Maas appearing as graffiti in various locations, including several Rockwell taxicabs,[215] and even on the side of an NYPD police cruiser. This cult was allegedly growing at such a rate that it had already begun to divide into different, rival, factions with alternate interpretations of Maas's work. It was not only *XXXXXX* which inspired such devotion either. His paintings, sculptures, and other works were all being analysed by fans for hidden messages and meanings, leading at least one journalist to describe the phenomenon as "bordering on religious extremism".[216] Another accused Maas of a "terrifying narcissism"[217] and accused him of intentionally radicalising "impressionable and susceptible individuals who were seeking purpose"[218] with promises that prolonged

---

212. One of the independent artist-run galleries on 10th Street, New York.

213. Taken from an audio transcript of an interview by Daniel.

214. Although there is no evidence of him ever speaking publicly about the incident.

215. In 1967, New York City ordered all 'medallion taxis' be painted yellow to help cut down on unofficial drivers and make official taxicabs more readily recognizable. The wife of the president of New Departure, Nettie Rockwell, particularly liked the colour yellow and it therefore became the colour of the new Rockwell taxicabs. The Rockwell Service Cab became the Yellow Taxicab when Mrs. Rockwell selected that as her choice of colour for the auto.

216. *New York Insight*, Issue 27, October 1967.

217. *Manhattan Monthly Insider*, Vol. 3, November 1967.

218. *New York Insight*, Issue 27, October 1967.

study of his art could fundamentally alter consciousness. Right-wing columnist Grace McMahon wrote:

"Maas may be a talented artist, but this young man is also charismatic and dangerous... anyone who believes this cult was born in a spontaneous 'big bang' without his involvement is a fool... and if you seriously think that anyone other than Maas is pulling the strings of all these groups, then you are as weak-willed as his followers..."[219]

While Maas never spoke publicly about the existence of a cult the consensus among the mainstream press was that these groups had emerged and evolved without his guidance or explicit direction, but this did little to prevent speculation that he was ultimately behind their creation and that they were carrying out his instructions. The activity of these rogue factions became increasingly violent and anarchic. The British painter Howard Hewlett, a friend of Maas, claimed a shooting in Queens where two people were wounded was the work of one of these groups, and that this escalation was one of the direct catalysts for Maas's decision to leave the East Coast: "The shooting was a sign... things were out of control... and it was no coincidence that Maas left New York a couple of weeks later... he wanted to distance himself from this madness. America was changing."[220] Warhol superstar Ultra Violet echoed this sentiment in 1968 when she said: "Violence is everywhere in the air today."[221]

However, Hewlett's testimony stands in direct contrast to claims from an alleged former member of The Maas Foundation, who wished to remain anonymous[222]:

"Maas was behind it all... the guerrilla artwork and stunts, the graffiti, the subversive, anti-establishment messages, the beatings, the shootings, and worse... . he would hold crazed meetings in his studio... where he would sometimes just erupt, screaming at everyone, raving about his enemies, about other artists... there would always be a couple of handguns, loaded, on the table as he paced around and there were drugs everywhere... he was definitely on something... he could be violent and unpredictable one minute, then cool and calculated the next, almost reptilian... he had one of his friends nearly beaten to death because they sold a photograph of him to a reporter, and I heard someone ended up getting shot to get it back."

---

219. *McMahon Speaks...* January 1968 Edition.

220. From Daniel's interview with Hewlett.

221. As quoted by Time Magazine, June 1968.

222. The following is an excerpt from interviews conducted by Daniel with an ex-member of The Maas Foundation, in 2012.

He added that at the same time, Maas was loved and worshipped by the majority of his followers despite this behaviour: "It was seen as part of his genius, this brutal, unrelenting drive. It could be harrowing being around him, but we loved and feared him in equal measure. We believed it when he told us we would change the world."

This same unnamed source also goes on to offer an alternate take on why Maas planned to leave New York that year: "Maas didn't run from what was happening on the East Coast, he left because his work was done. He travelled across the country to continue recruiting followers and start up new chapters. It wasn't about the fear of escalation, it was a desire for expansion... The birth of the Maas Foundation was no Immaculate Conception, it was all him... his will... New York was just the beginning, Los Angeles was next."[223]

If this source can be believed, the City of Angels was about to be visited by the Devil himself.

---

223. This interview took place while Daniel was in New York in 2011.

Art International, Vol. 13, Issue 4 December 21, 1979

WHAT HAPPENS NOW?

How Ezra Maas became the nexus for an art revolution

JANE TURNER

The year was 1966. A mysterious young man stood on the corner of New York's East 12th Street handing out artwork to passers-by. Word of mouth began to spread about this anonymous artist and the powerful effect his work had on anyone who saw it. People who took away a piece of his work struggled to describe it afterwards, comparing it to an LSD trip or religious epiphany. No one knew where he had come from, leading to a number of unusual theories. Some said he was a homeless savant, orphaned from a European family, others that he was an exile from the German 'Fluxus' movement. All anyone could remember was his distinctive name. The artist was called Ezra Maas.

The New York art glitterati soon took notice of Maas. Critics, curators, and collectors declared him a new, young prodigy and invited him to exhibit at their galleries. He initially refused, choosing instead to stage his own 'happenings' and public interventions, but within months his work was appearing in the likes of the Leo Castelli Gallery on East 77th Street, and other influential venues owned by uptown dealers like Sydney Janis and Julien Levy. Solo exhibitions followed at independent artist-run co-op galleries like Brata, Tanager and Hansa on 10th Street, with people reported to have collapsed at his shows. Controversy followed Maas wherever his work appeared, but the artist himself was always absent, represented instead by assistants and followers. He had appeared from nowhere, seemingly birthed from the streets of

New York itself, but after his initial fame he turned his back on the celebrity that other artists coveted and chose to work in complete seclusion. He declined interviews and photographs and refused to appear in public, even to launch his new work. Maas's mission, it emerged, was to confront and dismantle the category of art, even the art considered radical and avant-garde at the time, in order to make way for something new.

In 1966, the art world was already undergoing its biggest period of change in half a century. At the start of the decade painting and sculpture still dominated art, despite the challenges of Cubist collages, Dadaist events, and Futurist performances in the previous half century. By 1969 art had gone far beyond those traditional mediums. Art was air, light, sound, words, land, food, people, and everything in between. Artists like Ezra Maas exploded the boundaries.

Change had been in the air before Maas of course. Pop Art and Minimalism had emerged as separate reactions to Abstract Expressionism, which itself represented a shift in the centre of Western art from Europe to the US in the 1940s and 1950s. This repositioning was as much a result of socio-political forces as of the quality of US artists like Pollock, Motherwell, De Kooning, Rothko, Kline, and Newman. In the post-war years, art became another battleground in the Cold War between the USSR and McCarthy-era America, with the agendas of art institutions and influential critics like Clement Greenberg curiously aligned with

Land of the free? Ezra Maas's early work in New York dismantled American iconography.

the interests of the CIA. Together they helped reposition New York as a nexus of art. However seismic this shift, the Abstract Expressionists were still painters and there was a feeling that painting had reached the full and final realisation of its potential. Sculpture too, at least in its traditional form, appeared to have been exhausted as a medium. A more radical revolution was needed. Artists everywhere were asking themselves: what happens now?

As the artist George Segal said: "It was a dissatisfaction with the limitations of pure abstract painting. Nobody knew what the work could or should look like. Each individual's freedom was encouraged. Since nobody knew what the new art should look like, each of us was free to invent our own solution."

Everything about art was about to be called into question. All previous assumptions would be challenged. Explosive elements had begun to converge and would reach a critical mass in 1966 in the form of a young artist who embodied the spirt of the times. Ezra

Maas was the revolution. A handful of truly great artists would set the stage, others would douse it in petrol; he would light the fire.

From 1960, there was a return to the enquiries of artists from earlier in the century, the Dadaists and the Futurists. Artists like Robert Rauschenberg and Jasper Johns have often been labelled Neo-Dada because of their use of everyday objects in their work, but they arguably have more in common with Marcel Duchamp and his concept of 'ready-made' art than they did with Tristan Tzara, Hugo Ball and others from Zurich's Cabaret Voltaire. Duchamp, whose work included a urinal simply signed 'R Mutt', challenged audiences and critics to consider what it was about an object that made it art. Was it the thing in itself or the artist's treatment of it?

Like Dada, these artists were interested in the ordinary, the 'ready-made', and shared a willingness to embrace chance in their work. The focus on the everyday gave the artist a new freedom to use materials and techniques from outside the art world. Art was in the idea and could be made from anything. This put the persona of the artist firmly in the spotlight, echoing Duchamp's belief that it was the artist, purely because they are the artist, who has the power to say what is art.

Ezra Maas occupies a space that simultaneously fulfils and challenges this promise. He arrived into a melting pot of artistic movements and synthesised the best elements of each into a new form which was distinctly his own. Maas, who is two decades younger than Warhol and his contemporaries, represents a new breed of artist. One who resists classification and who is both present and absent, iconic and anonymous. In the years since Ezra Maas's emergence, everything has changed. As we look toward a new decade through the filter of his revolutionary new art the question remains, what happens now?

The 1980s are sure to bring change, but if a lesson can be drawn from the past it is that the art world has a tendency toward repetition. Could we see an unexpected resurgence in traditional techniques and forms in the next decade? The continued emergence and dominancy of strong female artists? Or could art become further weaponised by socio-political undercurrents, perhaps even more overtly than we have seen to date?

Many believe we are as close to a possible Nuclear War now as we were in the weeks and months leading to the Cuban Missile Crisis. Relations between the US and the Soviet Union remain fraught as President Carter and the USSR continue their shadow games. Meanwhile, in the UK where Margaret Thatcher this year became the country's first female Prime Minister, the country faces war from within, with art historian Anthony Blunt recently exposed as one of the 'Cambridge Five' double agents spying for the Russians, and with multiple IRA bombings terrorising the nation, including the assassination of Lord Mountbatten. What can art do in the face of such turbulence?

It will do what it has always done – it will reflect and subvert, it will hold a mirror up to the face of the era, it will show this generation its future, it will endure. And what of Ezra Maas? Will he return or disappear further into silence and anonymity? I believe we will see him again. Maas – like Picasso, like Dada, like Warhol – is more than a man, he is an archetype of disruption. Like the stone that changes a river's course disruptors displace existing systems, to create a pathway to something new and revolutionary; they are at once destructive and creative, and, as the Law of Conservation states, energy can never disappear, but it can change into another form. If there is one thing I am sure of, whether it is next year or twenty-five years from now, Ezra Maas will return in one form or another.

Daniel James
Chapter Seven

Americans may have no identity, but they do have great teeth[225]

The Coney Island Boardwalk[226] looked just as I imagined it. No doubt it had seen better days, but the amusement rides, stalls and retro signage still had a certain charm. It was an unreal place, where America's past and present collided, the neon lights concealing sinister undercurrents. In the late 19th and early 20th century the glitz and glamour of this 'Electric Eden' had kept the poverty-stricken masses entertained, while a tiny percentage of powerful, white men hoarded the real wealth and fulfilled their American dreams. This was back in Coney Island's Jazz Age past. It had many names then. Dreamland, Lilliput. Luna Park. Names within names. Only the last one still existed today. Before all of those the island was known by another, much older name, *Narrioch*[227] – the land without shadows.

I understood, and agreed with, the arguments of those who saw such places as symbols of America's obsession with unreality and worse, as the calculated 'deterrence machines' of late capitalism,[228] but at the same time I couldn't quite find it within myself to dislike the iconography of Coney Island. Was that the equivalent of falling in love with your kidnapper, I wondered? Stockholm Syndrome for kitsch Americana.

It was a cold April morning in the land without shadows, and everything was washed out. Scraps of litter were being directed in an invisible dance by eddies of wind from the Atlantic. Tourists and dog walkers, basketballers

---

225. Jean Baudrillard, *America* (2004).

226. The boardwalk is officially named the Riegelmann Boardwalk after Edward J. Riegelmann and opened on May 15, 1923, stretching for 2.5 miles from West 37th Street, at the border of Coney Island and Sea Gate, to Brighton 14th Street in Brighton Beach.

227. This was the name given to the island by the native Lenape Indians due to its south facing beaches, which always remained in sunlight. Later, the Dutch settlers who hunted rabbits 'konijn' in the area called it Conyne Eylandt, or Konijneneiland in modern Dutch spelling, with both translating as 'Rabbit Island'. Alternative theories on how the island got its name include the Irish Gaelic name for rabbit which is Coinín, which is also anglicized to Coney.

228. The Dutch architect Rem Koolhaas, in his essay *Delirious New York*, described Coney Island as an incubator for New York's obsession with obscuring reality with fantasy, and destroying the natural world in favour of the artificial. I'm sure Baudrillard would have agreed. After all, what was Coney Island if not a precursor to Las Vegas and Disneyland – Baudrillard's ultimate 'deterrence machine' whose overt unreality was intended to convince us that the rest of the world was real.

on a concrete court, a geriatric jogger with sweatbands, a group of teens playing Skee-Ball, and a young couple arm in arm; all passed by me on repeat, like extras from a movie. On the beach, a couple of guys were doing reps with dumbbells, and a little further out an old man was sat on a deck chair in the sand, staring at the grey, icy, waves rising and falling. I dug my hands deeper into the pockets of my overcoat, tucked my chin into my chest, and continued north along the boardwalk, trying to resist the lure of Nathan's Famous Hot Dogs.

I had arrived an hour earlier via the Q line to Stilwell Avenue, in the hope of finding an old-timer who might remember Maas from his earliest days in New York. Apparently he had spent time hustling on the boardwalk when he first arrived in America, performing card tricks and street magic, to stay off the streets. He was taken in by a fortune teller and her magician husband, who helped him get set up in Greenwich Village. I was told they were both dead, but I had the idea that someone else who still worked here might remember Maas. It was a long shot, but even if it led to nothing I thought the sea air might clear my head and help relieve the sense of dread I'd been feeling since Zurich.

I had spent the previous day at a desk in City Records[229] going through every scrap of information I could find in relation to Maas's years in New York. There was no shortage of paperwork, but as I had learned in Europe over the last few months there was a big difference between information and knowledge. For all the people I had interviewed and all the locations I had visited, what did I really know with any certainty? In some ways the most interesting discoveries amidst a sea of birth, death, and marriage certificates, financial and property records, and social and medical paperwork, was the information that was missing. This included a curious legal footnote, which I filed away for future reference. Maas had never owned any property in the city, but his Foundation had purchased 'air rights' – a peculiar piece of legislation, almost unique to New York, which allowed for the space above a building to be purchased as real estate for future developments. Almost immediately, I had visions of Maas planning to build a modern-day Tower of Babel reaching up through the New York air to touch the vault of Heaven.

Afterwards, I visited the Museum of Modern Art and the Gagosian Gallery using forged credentials to pose as a PhD researcher, in the hope of accessing their archives and questioning one of their specialist staff about Maas. After exhausting my repertoire of small talk I casually asked

---

229. The New York City Department of Records and Information Services, located at 31 Chambers Street, NY.

one of the senior staff behind the scenes at MoMA if the gallery had any of Maas's work in their collection.

'Not since 2005,' was the reply.

Professor Judy Vale, the gallery's assistant director for post-war and contemporary art, was in her early fifties, and a practicing artist herself. She had a pleasant manner, kind brown eyes, and dark, greying hair that was tied-up in a bun and skewered with what appeared to be chopsticks or knitting needles. Like many artists I had spoken to, Vale seemed permanently distracted as if she was only ever half listening to what I was saying and the rest of her attention was focused on some otherworldly mystery. Similarly, she spoke at a soporific pace and in soft, hushed tones, replying to my questions after pauses so long I wondered if she had passed away. It was like conducting an interview underwater.

I had found her waving a small black box around the room as if she was trying to catch something invisible.

'Lux levels,' she said, more to herself than in response to the unspoken question in my eyes. She spent the next twenty minutes slowly, and with regular pauses, explaining the need to perform spot-checks on the light levels in the room, and how she had to ensure that the gallery's preventative measures such as UV filtering plastic sleeves, light diffusing materials on glass, automatic timers on the lights, and temperature and humidity controls, were all doing their job.[230] It took a selection of my very best interested faces, and a few timely questions, to eventually get the conversation back on track. I began with a few dummy questions about other artists, Gerhard Richter, David Rothko, Joseph Beuys, before eventually coming to Ezra Maas.

'Most of the pieces we had were on loan from the Maas Foundation... and were recalled after his disappearance,' Vale added, after another long pause. 'The rest have always been held in private collections.'

'Do you know anyone who still owns one of Maas's pieces?' I asked, trying to conceal the true level of interest in my voice.

Vale began to examine the blank surface of a wall as if she hadn't heard my question. She tapped her knuckles on the wall as if she was knocking on a door.

'Plywood,' she said to herself, before looking back to me.

'The Maas Foundation has been quietly buying back Maas's entire body of work for the last decade,' she added. 'I suspect they have it all by now, although I did hear they were having some trouble agreeing a deal with at least one collector – a film producer in LA, if I recall. I forget his

---

230. The job in question being Art Conservation or the prevention of artefact deterioration due to the irreversible damage caused by light – Anonymous.

name.'

'Really?'

'He owned one or two of Maas's early film installations, but it may have just been gallery gossip. I never saw anything in the press about it. You'd be better off speaking to someone at Christie's or Sotheby's if you're that interested – they handled the big Picasso sale last year – although they never disclose information without their clients' permission and The Maas Foundation are notoriously secretive.'

Vale and I stood looking at the bare wall in silence for a moment. I was beginning to get used to coming up against dead-ends, but sometimes what appears to be blank and featureless is filled with secrets just below the surface.

Next on my list was the famous Strand bookstore where Maas was allegedly discovered by one of his early benefactors. The current manager of the store had heard the same story, but he didn't know whether it was true or not. When I told him how I had drawn a blank, at the likes of MoMA and the Gagosian, he suggested I try the independent 10th Street galleries Downtown, where Maas had supposedly started exhibiting in the 1960s, but I already knew most of the original studios were long gone. I was friends with a young artist who lived in Long Island and she had already given me an education in the New York art scene. She sent me to Brooklyn instead, telling me that places like Bushwick, Williamsburg and Greenpoint had become the new centre of artist-run galleries in the 2000s. The Lower East Side in Manhattan – or MannyHat as she called it – was also home to some of the city's cutting-edge gallery spaces and studios. I spent a week working my way through the list she had given me, unsure of exactly what I was looking for. The artists I found there were on the front line of contemporary practice, but most of them were in their twenties and thirties and couldn't tell me much about Maas. In one way or another, he had influenced every one of them, just like the other great artists who had come through the New York scene. But even more so than the others, Maas was an absent figure who belonged to another time. All that remained was his name. It still haunted the present even though he was gone. New York had seen a disconnect with the past. The city had changed shape. And the past I was looking for had been built over, hidden away, concealed. I felt out of time in more ways than one.

It was somehow fitting that I had ended up at Coney Island, staring out to sea in a place whose present was haunted by futures that had never come to pass. The waves that rose and fell washed everything away eventually, saint and sinner alike. They were indiscriminate, as cold as they were unfeeling. What hope did any of us have in the face of something so vast, indifferent, and powerful? In the end, everyone was washed clean, changed, reborn, or just eroded into non-existence. Why did I believe I was different?

Two old-timers sat at a card table on the boardwalk ahead of me, playing the world's slowest game of checkers. They must have been at least ninety. I walked over and smiled.

'You guys been coming here a long time?'

'What?' one of the men replied, without taking his eyes off the game. He wore a white flat cap and a navy , velour tracksuit.

'I said, have you been coming to the boardwalk for a long time?'

'What's it to you, pally?' This time he did turn to look at me.

'Just interested,' I shrugged. 'I'm a writer.'

'What kind of accent's that?'

'British.'

'Thought so. We get a lot of you guys down here.'

'British people?'

'Writers.'

His companion – silver-haired and gaunt with mean-looking blue eyes – glanced at the two of us as if he'd only just realised we'd been talking.

'I'm sorry to have bothered you,' I said, ready to leave.

'Fifty years,' the first man said. 'Give or take. That's how long we've been coming here.'

'That's a long time,' I said.

'Sure is.'

'You ever hear of a guy called Ezra Maas, worked the boardwalk back in the '60s maybe?'

'Maas? What was he, some kind of circus performer, or magician?'

'An artist – at least that's what he became anyway – but I heard a story that he started out here. He would have been a kid at the time, sixteen or seventeen.'

'Hmm, maybe... the name sounds familiar. But I was away for a stretch in the '60s. Lou might remember. He was around back then.'

He waved his thin, wrinkled hand in front of Lou's face.

'Lou!'

'What?' Lou snapped.

'This guy wants to know if we've ever heard of someone called... ' He looked back at me. 'Ezra Maas,' I said.

'He wants to know if we ever knew an Edgar Maas?'

'Ezra,' I corrected. 'Ezra Maas.'

'Ezra Maas,' he repeated with a look as if that's exactly what he'd said first time.

'The artist?' Lou asked, turning to look at me properly for the first time. 'Whaddaya want to know about that prick for?'

'You knew him?'

'I wouldn't say that,' he spat. 'Nobody knew him. Not really. He was only here one summer, '66 or '67. Sonuvabitch.'

'Why do you say that?'

'Robbed poor Bill Doyle and his wife blind after they took him in. He was a con man and a nasty piece o' work too. I saw him threaten someone with a knife that same summer.'

'How did he rob them exactly?'

'They put a roof over his head, gave him a job, taught him a few things, even got him involved in their act, and then – poof! He pulls a vanishing act on them – along with all their savings.'

'Why didn't they go to the police?'

'Because they were a sucker for the kid. Didn't believe he did it. He had a way about him, you see; a way of making people do what he wanted. They were soft, couldn't see it. Defended him even after they got kicked out of their place. Next thing you know, Maas reappears on Fifth Avenue rubbing shoulders with high society, pretending to be some sort of artist or guru or something. Meanwhile, they're on the streets.'

'What happened to them?'

'They've been dead for three decades... ' Lou replied. 'What's this all about anyway?'

'He's a writer,' the first man chipped in.

'He looks like a writer,' Lou said. 'Why d'you want to know about Maas for? You writing a book about him?'

'I'm just looking for the truth,' I said.

'The truth about Ezra Maas?'

He began to laugh, slowly at first, then harder, until his whole body was shaking; strings of saliva dangling from his mouth and tears streaming down his cheeks.

'The truth!'

The strange sound of his laughter followed me back along the boardwalk.

After another hour questioning disinterested staff at hot dog stands and stalls, I took a seat in the back couple of rows at a show being performed in the outdoor amphitheatre, my legs as weary as my mind.

It was a puppet show on a large outdoor stage, but the life-sized wooden figures were really actors, walking around on faux-unsteady legs as if controlled by some faceless, disembodied puppeteer. No doubt they would cut their strings and come to life at a key moment in the play. According to a flyer I found on the seat next to mine, the show was a reimagining of a Jacobian revenge play called *The Courier's Tragedy*.[231] It seemed a gruesome choice for a funfair and I wondered if it was meant to be a parody. If that was the intention, the comedy never came. I watched as one of the puppets was disembowelled on stage, streams of dark red fabric being pulled from its torso, in a brutal moment of ritualised, Kabuki-style violence.

The figures on stage became a blur. My eyes grew heavy and I felt myself falling asleep. I half-heartedly tried to fight it, but the pull was too strong. I gave in and let it take me. Almost instantly I slipped into a warm slumber; a soft blackness that enveloped me completely. I was falling into a deep and endless abyss within myself, inside my own body. Every now and then my eyes would open again, briefly, and I would catch a glimpse of the show, still going on around me. I tried to move, but I couldn't wake myself. The sky was getting dark by degrees and the neon lights of 'Electric Eden' were beginning to glow. People came and went in a blur as if time was speeding up, but I was paralysed – a prisoner inside my own body. When I finally found the strength to open my eyes and wake up, the play was over and all the seats in front of me were empty. It was night and the entire park was deserted. The show was long over, but a lone figure remained on stage, facing the curtain. I called out to him, but no sound came from my mouth. There was a strange wind blowing between the wooden seats as I got to my feet and began to walk towards the man. A sudden and powerful feeling of sickness washed over me as the fairground lights began to flicker and crackle. Against every instinct in my body, I reached out and placed my hand on his shoulder. It was as hard and cold as a corpse. When the man turned toward me, his skin pallid and dappled with blood, I recognised his face as my own.[232]

---

231. A play by the same name appears in Thomas Pynchon's novel *The Crying of Lot 49*. The inclusion of this play in Pynchon's postmodern novel has been compared to the play, *The Murder of Gonzago*, which appears within *Hamlet* by William Shakespeare. Both plays are examples of the technique known as 'mise en abyme' (to put in the abyss). This term is used to refer to the embedding of one story within another which acts as a microcosm, or mirror, of events in the overarching narrative – Anonymous.

232. The ending of this chapter is clearly a knowing reference to the classic Edgar Allan Poe horror *William Wilson*, which first established the theme of the doppelgänger in literature. Poe, who is credited with pioneering the detective genre with his Auguste Dupin stories, is also arguably responsible for the recurring motif of a protagonist pursuing a figure who invariably turns out to be a version of themselves. In the hands of postmodern detective authors, this device has been used to explore questions about the nature of identity. Coincidentally, the original publisher of this manuscript was William Wilson & Co, which takes its name from this classic tale – Anonymous.

Maas Hysteria!

By Judy Doyle

Ezra has left New York! Is he back in England, Los Angeles, or on the Moon?

Not since Bob Dylan's motorcycle accident last July has so much mystery surrounded one of our best and brightest. Journalists have been speculating about the whereabouts of the charismatic young artist for weeks, with a different gruesome rumour surfacing each day.

Maas was badly disfigured in an accident, he's been locked away in an insane asylum, he was killed by a crazed fan, he's returned to Europe to follow in the footsteps of the old masters, he's gone to Hollywood to make movies, he's been silenced by the 'man' for speaking out against the Vietnam War; these are just some of the wild stories that have been circulating since the news broke of Maas's disappearance.

'Searching for Ezra: Teens gather at New York's Greenwich Village art market'.

The artist's loyal followers are saying nothing and the city that never sleeps is in the dark. We reached out to one of Maas's contemporaries, the 'blond guru of a nightmare world' Andy Warhol, who said: 'I don't think he was ever really here, darling. He was just a dream we all had, a sad and beautiful dream.'

Mysterious Maas, dark, gorgeous wonder child of the art world, appeared out of nowhere in New York last year. His 'happenings' were the most happening parties in the village, and everyone who was anyone wanted to be there - except for Ezra himself, it seemed, who was permanently too cool for school! Was he camera shy? Mute? Or was he really there in disguise? No one knew, but the word on the street from everyone lucky enough to have met him was that Maas was beautiful, brilliant, and destined for greatness.

Now he's gone, and New York seems a darker place without its latest star. Say it isn't so! Here at *Teen Dream* we hope the horror stories are only stories and the rookie art sensation is just taking a break from the Big Apple. Maybe his sudden exit, and all the speculation around it, is a new piece of performance art in itself. Wouldn't that be something? The art of disappearance. Whatever the truth is, if you're reading this Ezra, know this: New York, your fans, the world, and this magazine, want you back!

Daniel James
Chapter Eight

A man may be born, but in order to be born he must first die, and in order to die he must first awake[233]

We meet at a crossroads in the parking lot of a Pinky's gas station somewhere in Bible Belt,[234] USA. It's midnight and raining softly. The lot is illuminated by harsh and merciless street lights that flicker and buzz overhead.

I'm not the first to arrive. There are already a few shifty-eyed characters shuffling about, unsure of what to do with themselves. One by one they arrive, all shapes and sizes, men and women, different cultures and nationalities, rich and poor; one by one they park their cars in the old, overgrown lot. No one talks to each other, but we all know why we're here. They call it the awakening. A long silver bus with tinted windows pulls up. They shepherd us onto it without a word and give out black hoods, which we're instructed to put over our heads until we reach our destination.

I've no ID, no phone, nothing which could identify me if things go south. I spend the first hour trying to figure out the direction we're travelling, trying to remember each turn, every different surface the bus passes over, every fork in the road. It's difficult to keep track of time, but the journey seems to last several hours. Eventually we come to a stop. We file out into the night, footsteps crunching on gravel. The hoods come off. There's some sort of compound up ahead, surrounded by fences. They turn on the floodlights and shine them in our faces. All I can see is glare. I think I make out the silhouettes of armed guards, but I can't be sure.

We go through a set of double doors. There is a large auditorium with rows of chairs. We're directed to take a seat. The staff exit the room and lock the doors behind them. A vast screen at the foot of the stage flickers into life. The colour yellow floods the room. Large numbers in black on screen. A voice. Music. Images begin to cycle past at a speed too fast to fully register – a child on a bike, a building on fire, a polluted river, a classroom, insects crawling along the bark of a tree as sap oozes

---

233. George Gurdjeff (1866 – 1949) was a mystic, philosopher, teacher and composer of Greek descent.

234. The Bible Belt is a colloquial term used to informally refer to parts of the American south and Midwest associated with Southern Conservative evangelicalism – Anonymous.

out, a playground, a prison, so many images, all different, interspersed with colours, numbers, sounds, all edited together, faster and faster. I try to look away, but I can't move.

The flickering increases in speed and intensity. Everyone sits rigid, unable to take their eyes from the screen. One by one the people around me begin to twitch and convulse in the throes of a seizure or fit. The flickering continues, alternating faster and faster between the brightest light and the deepest, most complete, black. The twitching heads of the entranced audience begin to blur before my eyes, like a hummingbird's wings, as if they're losing cohesion, dissolving somehow. I try to force my eyes to close.

The person next to me grabs my forearm tightly, digging their fingernails into my flesh. I turn to look. It's Jane. Her face pale, hospital gown splashed with blood, eyes wide, and filled with a wild, desperate, fear.

'Don't watch the film,' she whispers.

I wake up.

I'm standing in front of a window. The glittering Manhattan skyline looks back at me across the water, traffic rumbles noisily across the Williamsburg Bridge and the late-night bars and nightclubs on the streets below hum with activity.

'You okay?' A woman's voice asks behind me, heavy with sleep.

She's lying in bed, a bare leg hooked around the sheets. I don't recognise her in the dark. There are clothes lying on the floor, mine and hers, empty glasses by the bedside. The table by the window is covered with my notes for the manuscript, research papers, photographs, records, books stacked high, tickets to LAX departing tomorrow. Slowly I begin to realise where I am, who I am, who she is.

I turn back to the window and lean my head against the cool glass. Something wet drips onto my feet. I look down. My forearm is bleeding, the skin torn and scratched by a red right hand.[235]

---

235. A probable reference to Milton's *Paradise Lost*, symbolising the vengeful hand of God. Also the title of one of Nick Cave and the Bad Seeds most iconic songs – Anonymous.

Don't watch the film Don't watch the film
Don't watch the film Don't watch the
film Don't watch the film Don't watch
the film Don't watch the film Don't
watch the film Don't watch the film
Don't watch the film Don't watch
the film Don't watch the film Don't
watch the film Don't watch the film
Don't watch the film Don't watch
the film Don't watch the film
Don't watch the film Don't watch
the film Don't watch the film Don't
watch the film Don't watch the
film Don't watch the film Don't
watch the film Don't watch the
film Don't watch the film

ZWEITES LEBEN
PRIVATKLINIK

INTERVIEW TRANSCRIPT[236]
Q&A with Daniel James

by

He's a writer who isn't afraid to take risks. As a journalist Daniel James took on the newspaper industry from the inside. With his fiction he played the dangerous game of putting his own life on the page. And now, as a biographer, he is exploring the very possibility of truth and attempting to unravel one of the art world's biggest mysteries. James has his critics, but you can't fault his ambition.

A news reporter for over a decade James was best known for exploring the cult of fame and contemporary culture, questioning systems of truth and authority, and exposing the hyper-reality of modern news coverage. Blurring the lines between fact and fiction his writing questioned the representation of reality through language, and our perceptions of knowledge and power. His interviews focused on personalities who were culturally, politically, and spiritually disenfranchised by these systems. When James reached the limits of what the newspaper industry could offer he did the only thing he could do: he went rogue.[237]

Now, he is reportedly set to publish under his own name once more. The project is believed to be an unauthorised biography of the reclusive artist Ezra Maas, who disappeared seven years ago. Little is known about the proposed book but, when it comes to James, we can be sure to expect it is a biography like no other.

---

236. This is a partial transcript of an interview conducted by ████ ████ and intended for the literary podcast ████ ████. The date of the interview is unknown but, based on Daniel's tone and in particular the Leveson reference, I believe this was 2011. It was never broadcast and the full audio recording was lost. This partial transcript is all that remains – Anonymous.

237. After leaving the newspaper industry, in ████, Daniel founded *The Bleed* as a platform for new and emerging artists, and as a subversive, unfiltered vehicle for his own writing. It was open to artists in any medium, from anywhere in the world, and each issue saw the magazine take on a new format uniquely shaped by its content. It was ambitious, challenging, and pushed the boundaries of what a magazine could be. The pilot issue featured cover art by Eisner award-winning writer-artist and graphic novel pioneer Bryan Talbot, and content from an international mix of new and emerging writers, artists, photographers, and illustrators. These included photographer Helen Taylor, artists such as Tom Boyle, Lauren Jane Forster, Nick Willis, Michael Barnes, Andrew Waugh, Rebecca Lowes, Karen Lusted, and Helen Gorrill, writer Philip Buchan, New York artist Meaghan Ralph, and the charismatic poet Lee Murray. Graphic designer Trevor Pill, working closely with James as Editor-in-chief, was responsible for the look and feel of the first three issues, including the legendary second issue, which was published in ████. Jonny Speak designed issue three. Daniel took a step back from the day-to-day running of *The Bleed* in ████ amid legal and financial controversies, with Victoria King becoming the new editor – Anonymous.

Why did you want to become a writer?

To disappear. I read for the same reason. The only difference when I'm writing is that I get to create the world. Time and space contract, everything around me fades away, and I'm somewhere else entirely. I'm there with the character, in their world. It's the same feeling I have when I'm reading a book and become completely absorbed by the story. I pass over into the text. When I return I find myself looking at the world around me with fresh eyes, a new perspective, greater knowledge, more empathy. That's the power of fiction. It can change how you think, how you feel, what you see – everything. I wanted to have that power.

What attracted you to this project?

I wanted to play detective. I have this theory that we're all detectives. Every day we question the world around us, search for meaning, and seek to uncover hidden truths about life and ourselves. I think that's why the detective genre is so enduring. There's something fundamentally human about asking questions and trying to unravel the mysteries we're faced with. Every time we open a book and begin to read we're playing detective, whether it's a crime story or not. Every reader is a detective, searching through the author's words for clues, trying to piece together the literary puzzle, and discover the meaning locked within the text.

Mysteries are a gateway to the unknown, to places where every answer leads to another question. That's one of the first things I was taught as a journalist. Question everything. And never stop, because that's how you get to the truth. But what I love about certain mysteries is the way they reveal deeper, existential questions for which there are no easy answers, questions that challenge and unsettle your worldview, even your own identity, and lead you into the darkness.

Ezra Maas is that figure in the darkness. Every time you're getting close he steps back into the shadows, so you can't see his face, but you can't walk away because on some level you need to know who he really is, only the truth will bring an end to the uncertainty. When I think of Maas, all I have is questions. His whole life was a mystery, from his childhood through to his fame in the '60s and '70s and eventually his disappearance. As soon as I read the story of how he vanished, I knew it would be the perfect set-up for a detective story.

It was an opportunity to explore the cult of celebrity[238] through the lens of someone whose fame was generated by their anonymity, their absence, and withdrawal from public life.[239] I wanted to discover who Maas really was and understand the impact he had on the lives that gravitated around him, his family, his friends, his entourage, his followers. The Maas Foundation actively cultivated his myth throughout his life, but not for fame, so what was really going on? What was Maas's story? Who was he really?

Did you research biography as a genre before starting work on the book?

Biography is one of the oldest literary forms[240] – and one of the most powerful. Through words, you can recreate a life. More than that, you can shape and control it. I've always found that fascinating and dangerous.

When I was an arts and culture journalist my interviews and features were essentially micro biographies – snapshots of people's lives in that moment – so the move to writing a full biography was a natural progression in some ways. I read interviews with biographers such as Leon Edel,[241] Hermione Lee,[242] David McCullough,[243] and Robert Caro,[244] who famously said, "There is no one truth, but there are an awful lot of objective facts", to gain an insight into their methods and techniques, learning the rules of the game, so that I could subvert them, tear them up and produce something new. Each

---

238. In his handwritten notes, alongside this chapter, Daniel briefly explores the history of celebrity, drawing a playful and potentially satiric comparison between the Greek heroes who fought for fame and glory (such as Achilles in *The Iliad*) and the reality TV stars of today.

239. Again, in his notes, Daniel identifies a number of other famous figures who chose to disappear, such as the '60s spy novelist Adam Diment, and the poet Rosemary Tonks, both very interesting stories in themselves.

240. Daniel makes reference to the history of the genre, noting how Caesar used autobiography as propaganda to legitimise his rise to power and later dictatorship of Rome.

241. Biographer of the writer Henry James, Edel was the foremost Jamesian scholar of his age.

242. Lee wrote an award-winning biography of Virginia Woolf, as well as books on Willa Cather and Edith Wharton, and wrote a collection of essays on biography and autobiography entitled: *Body Parts: Essays on Life-Writing* (2005).

243. McCullough, a celebrated author, narrator, and historian, is famous for his biographies of American presidents Theodore Roosevelt, Harry S Truman and John Adams.

244. Caro is best known for his epic and award-winning five-volume biography of former American President Lyndon Johnson.

biographer described their process differently. For some it was like a love affair, for others a literary transfusion; but one common thread was the need to unravel the public and private 'life-myths' of your chosen subject and break through to the 'real'.

But what happens when the public myth and the private life become blurred? Ernest Hemingway, even though he denied it, ended up becoming his literary persona. Marilyn Monroe was also Norma Jean. How does a biographer reconcile public and private myths? If we exist in the minds of others as a public figure, if we create and come to believe our own personal myths, if we exchange different masks, different roles, our whole lives, who gets to decide which one is real?

Speaking of self-mythology, do you ever consider that, by including a version of you in your writing, you're doing the same thing as Ezra Maas?

I think if you're going to write about people's lives and you're going to tell the truth about them, good and bad, then you've got to be willing to hold a mirror up to yourself. I don't understand biographers who confess to the thrill of going through personal correspondence and uncovering other people's secrets, but who say they wouldn't want it done to themselves. I may be a lot of things, but I'm not a hypocrite. I think there is a danger of putting your own life into fiction, but it's a risk worth taking.

Is one of the dangers that people confuse you and your work?

I get angry sometimes when people describe me as the man behind the 'Daniel James' persona, especially as it's usually said as a precursor to an attack on that identity. First of all, this is not a performance. People need to accept that. I'm not playing some sort of self-aware, 'double game' here. This is me. And, secondly, I'm sorry you don't like who I am or how I live my life, but frankly I don't care. I don't exist for your benefit, and I don't need your approval.

Have you ever thought what a biography of you might look like?

A maze.

Or a rhizome[245] maybe?

---

245. Derived from the botanical term for a subterranean stem, a Rhizome is a philosophical

Definitely rhizomatic.

You describe yourself as an 'accidental journalist', but you were clearly very good at what you did, with a reputation for asking difficult questions and finding the truth, whatever the cost. Looking at the industry, today, what do you see as the main challenges facing journalists?

How do you verify the truth in an era when images and news can be so easily faked?[246] Who do you trust? How do you maintain your integrity and represent the public interest when the industry you work in is arguably as corrupt as the people you're going after? It's a minefield and I don't envy anyone working in journalism today.

Technology is also radically changing the way journalists work and the way people engage with the news, for better and worse. They've been saying print is dead since before I was a junior reporter, and yet newspapers are still going; but it is getting harder and the financial pressures are clearly impacting the way journalists do their jobs. It's the same for biography.

Maybe the Leveson enquiry might help clean-up the industry, but I'm not holding my breath. We've also got to be careful that we don't end up in a situation where journalists are unable to hold evil and corrupt people to account. Journalism is far from perfect, and I'll always have a love-hate relationship with the industry, but I genuinely believe the world needs a free and independent press.

If journalism and biography were accidental detours, in your career, what was your first love?

Fiction – and it still is. But, as I began to investigate people's lives and research the past, I came to realise that everything I could ever want as a writer was out there, in the

---

concept developed by Gilles Deleuze and Felix Guattari in their *Capitalism and Schizophrenia* project (1972 – 80). It describes a structure, any structure, in which each point is necessarily connected to each other point in a non-linear and non-hierarchal fashion. Deleuze labels the rhizome as a 'multiplicity'.

246. Although this interview was conducted several years before the terms 'fake news' and 'post-truth' were popularised, Daniel clearly anticipates both the cultural shift and technological advances that will make 'deep fakes' possible while further complicating the role of the media in reporting news and events – Anonymous.

strange, complex, brilliant stories people had lived through,
and in the beauty, violence, and poetry of history. I think
fiction is richer and more powerful for being grounded in
reality.

**And we can learn more about the world through the lens of
fiction?**

Exactly. History tells us what happened, but fiction tells us
who we are. Fiction is the real truth.

Daniel James
Chapter Nine

Through lies every novelist attempts to tell the truth about the world.[247]

It took another writer to help me realise how lost I was. He taught me why living inside a book is so dangerous. You can never see the whole story when you're a part of it. The system is only visible from the outside. Only then can you begin to understand its true meaning. I was losing myself in a fiction Maas had created, and I could no longer tell where the world ended and his art began. The stories I was being told about Maas's life were haunting my dreams. They were powerfully vivid, hyperreal. I couldn't sleep without losing myself. I couldn't see a way out.[248]

---

247. Paul Auster, The Art of Fiction No. 178, *The Paris Review.*

248. Note to reader: I was normally a fast reader, but the manuscript seemed to demand that I read it at a slow, deliberate, pace and an intensity I had never experienced before. Before the end of the first week my eyesight seemed to deteriorate and I began to suffer from crippling headaches. At 150 pages, I developed a fever and spent the second week in bed. And yet, I continued reading and re-reading. I couldn't stop. I wept, I laughed, I threw the book down in anger more than once, only to pick it up again. Its hold on me was relentless and unforgiving. When I slept I dreamt of the world inside the book. The lives of even the most one-note characters, who walked in and out of the story never to be seen again, became of immense importance to me. They lived-on outside of the book. In these dreams Daniel was never there but, like Maas before him, his absence could be felt everywhere; in every room and every building; in every street and every city he had created and abandoned; in the face of every character he had authored, only to leave orphaned. In the intervals, between readings, I began to see my own life through the lens of the narrative's multi-layered spirals; its unrelenting atmosphere of paranoia. Every time the phone rang I found myself paralysed, convinced it was either the unnamed client with further instructions, one of Maas's crazed and disturbed followers, or perhaps a representative from the ominous Maas Foundation. I was so convinced that I was being watched that I didn't leave the house for two days after a black, unmarked van, with tinted windows, parked in the street opposite my property. It didn't end there. Whenever I resumed reading the book the text appeared to have changed. I could never quite find the exact last line I remembered reading. Instead, a similar but subtly different sentence was in its place. I found myself going back over the same pages again and again, looking for words, sentences, paragraphs, sometimes whole chapters, that I believed I had read, but which now appeared to have shifted position, or had disappeared altogether. Was the book a physical puzzle as well as a textual? A literary labyrinth that changed shape when you dared to take your eyes from its pages? I recalled the 'cut-up' technique employed by Burroughs and Ginsberg while assembling *The Naked Lunch* in a Paris hotel room and an idea occurred to me. To make sense of the text by reordering the chapters, I physically carved the manuscript into three with a kitchen knife. It was only when I caught a glimpse of myself, hunched over the book with the blade held high, my hands smudged with ink, that I realised how absurd and disturbing my behaviour had become. I found myself asking the question: if this was the cost of reading the book, what was the cost of writing it? – Anonymous.

I was in the back of a cab on my way to an address in Boerum Hill, Brooklyn, to see a writer who didn't want to be interviewed and who I wouldn't be allowed to name even if he did turn out to be part of the story. As a result I'd had to invent a cover just to get this far. The author, let's call him Quinn, lived in a tall brownstone on a beautiful residential street that was lined with trees. He saw me coming from the window and opened the door to greet me as I climbed the steps. I followed him into a large living room, minimally decorated and spotlessly clean, with Scandinavian furnishings and modern art on the walls.

'You're not here to interview me about my new book, are you?' he said as I sat down.

Quinn was in his late sixties, handsome, with a crumpled, heavily-lined face, silvery-grey hair, receding and swept back, above a set of dark, piercing eyes like a bird of prey. He wore faded chinos, sneakers, and a blue denim shirt.

'I'm sorry,' I replied. 'I may have misled your publisher somewhat.'

Quinn looked neither surprised nor worried. He simply took out a packet of petit cigarillos, struck a match, and began to smoke.

'You're not here to kill me either, I hope?' he said after a moment. 'I try to restrict that kind of thing to my books.'

'I'm here about Ezra Maas,' I said.

'Even worse,' he replied with a half-smile. 'And what makes you think I know anything about him?'

'Because of his absence from your books.'

'I'm sorry. I'm not following your logic.'

'I know for a fact that you met Ezra Maas several times between 1970 and 1985, first in Paris then later in Bruges. And yet there's no mention of those meetings in your autobiography or any of your novels, which are otherwise filled with autobiographical fragments from your life.'

'And you're here to find out why?'

'I just want the truth,' I said.

'The truth is an elusive quarry,' Quinn replied. 'I suppose you have proof that I knew Maas?'

I took out the faded photograph I had obtained from the restaurant in Bruges and held it up for him to see.

'That's you, isn't it?' I asked.

Quinn responded by taking a seat in a brown leather armchair. He gestured for me to sit opposite.[249]

---

249. Note to reader: The conversation that followed became the subject of a long-running legal dispute between Daniel's publisher and the author referred to as 'Quinn' in this chapter. As

'I wish I could tell you more about him, but I can't,' Quinn said. 'Maas and I crossed paths, maybe four times in total, but I could have spent a hundred years with the man and I wouldn't have felt any closer to him. It was like he wasn't there.'

a result it is not possible to publish the full conversation here. Daniel included more than he should have in his original manuscript and I have been forced to redact several passages, after consulting with the book's new publisher and their legal team – Anonymous.

'I don't understand... how is that possible?' I said.

I sat in silence for a moment, thinking carefully about everything he had just told me and what it meant. It was hard to believe. The light coming through the bay window had the faded quality of late afternoon, as if hours had passed while we had been talking, but it had been morning when I arrived.

'I'm sorry I can't be of more help,' Quinn said finally.

'You've given me more than you realise,' I replied. 'I just don't understand why you didn't write a biography yourself. You've told me how much you wanted to find out the truth about him after what happened in Paris, but something obviously stopped you from taking it any further. What was it?'

'I realised it couldn't be done,' he said. 'There is no truth when it comes to Ezra Maas and that's what you need to come to terms with. You've travelled across Europe and now you're here in the United States, you've probably interviewed dozens of people, and spent countless hours doing research. You'll have no doubt written tens of thousands of words. When you're finished here you'll head off to San Francisco, Los Angeles, or somewhere else he's lived and worked, there will be more interviews, more research and, in a few months, you will land back in London to write your book, but what you can't see is that every piece of information you've gathered, every testimony, every word, is false.'

'What do you mean?'

'I've told you. Maas is a black hole. His presence draws everything in, warps, destroys, changes, and rewrites it. No one you've spoken to and nothing you've heard can be trusted. The people he has manipulated don't even know they're lying for him, and if they don't know then you never will, either. It's like Orwell wrote, if you control the human mind, you control reality.[250] Every word of your manuscript could be a lie. He has distorted the lines between art and reality to such an extent that they have become indistinguishable. If you've found anything out, in Europe, it's because he wanted you to. Maybe some of it was true, maybe it wasn't, but you'll never know one way or another and that uncertainty will erode

---

250. Loosely paraphrased from George Orwell's masterpiece *Nineteen Eighty-Four* – Anonymous.

153

everything. It will destroy you.'

'Is that what happened to you? Did you start down this road and turn back?'

'I looked into Maas's eyes and I saw the price of the questions I was asking. I weighed it up and decided I would be far happier, and much safer, pretending he didn't exist.'

'So if everything I've discovered so far, all my research, all my notes, everything I've written, is all worthless, if no one I've spoken to can be trusted, if they're all telling me what Maas wants me to hear, then why should I believe you? Maas could be pulling your strings right now just like all the others, whether you know it or not.'

'You're right of course, but if you look in the mirror I think you'll see the truth. Take a long, hard, look at yourself and tell me that I'm lying. Maybe then you'll see what I see; what I noticed the minute you stepped out of that cab this morning.'

'And what's that?' I asked.

'You're not really here.'

I stood up to leave. Quinn stood and placed his hand on my forearm.

'Walk away from this while you still can,' he added. 'Let it go.'

'I can't... ' I pulled my arm away. 'I'm not saying you were wrong to give up. You obviously have a good life, the kind I wanted once. It's worked out for you, but I have a different path ahead of me. I know the risks now. Maybe I didn't fully understand them when I took this job, but I do now and I'm more determined than ever to find the truth.'

Quinn shook his head, his eyes weary.

'Your pride will be your undoing.'

'No, it'll be his. You were right about one thing, Quinn. This book will destroy someone, but it won't be me.'

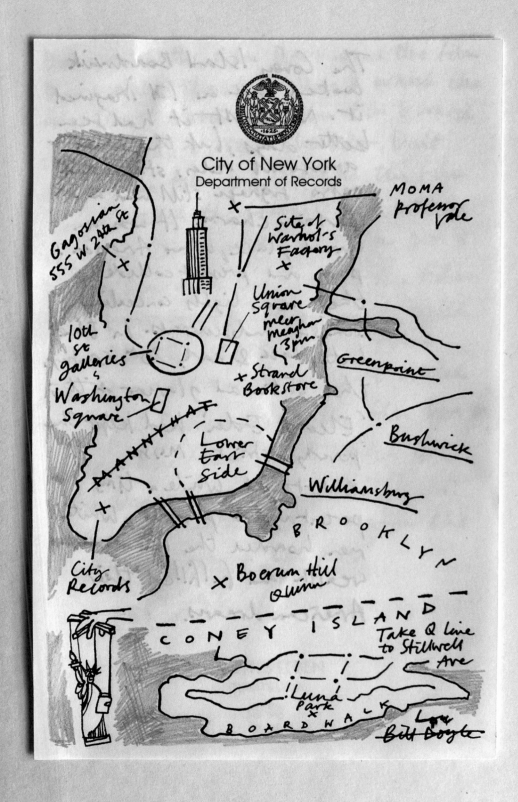

Ezra Maas: An Oral History
Part Three

Artists, writers, journalists, photographers, critics, friends, and others, who were around Maas during the years 1956 to 1996, give their impressions of the artist. Interviews by Daniel James.

☆

Alex Block, a conceptual artist from New York. He knew Maas between 1969 and 1976.

DJ: Can you tell me what he was like in person?

AB: It was difficult to get close to him after he became really famous. By '72 he was already surrounded by assistants who saw to his every need. You didn't speak to Ezra anymore; you spoke to one of his people. It gave them a lot of power. They were like the kings of old, representatives of God on Earth.

DJ: And Maas was God?

AB: He had always had a sense of manifest destiny, but he definitely started to believe his own mythology – and it changed him. The sheer hysteria and adoration that greeted him wherever he went in the art world would have corrupted the most stable psyche. It was the kind of power that turned men into monsters and monsters into Gods.

☆

Bianca Crais, a photographer and artist who first met Maas in 1967.

DJ: What were your impressions of Maas?

BC: I always felt safe around him. He was so calm and self-possessed, completely free of doubt. Everything he did was for a purpose and he had a plan for everyone. He was almost like a guru or spiritual sage. I was doing a lot of drugs when I first started coming to his happenings, but he got me clean and convinced me I had the talent to become a photographer. Maas saw something in me and nurtured it. I saw him a few times in the '70s and he was always the same.

Chrysta Sayers, a writer and political activist, who encountered Maas in 1968.

DJ: How did he seem to you in those years?

CS: He was wired, edgy, and full of nervous energy. It was like he was manic depressive or something. You got a sense that he could explode at any moment. There were drugs, and guns, and homemade bombs, everywhere. It was a dangerous time. The Maas Foundation had meetings with Abbie Hoffman, Jerry Rubin, the Black Panthers, and other groups. There was a lot of talk about changing the world and having to tear down the old order to make way for something new. Of all of them Maas was the only one who really scared me.

☆

Sara Leonard, a painter who exhibited in New York in the late 1960s.

SL: I remember one time I saw him on the phone in a back room. He was deep in conversation and quite animated. Someone said he was speaking to his brother. I didn't even know he had a brother. He was talking for well over an hour, but then I realised the craziest thing. The phone wasn't connected to anything. I went over and picked it up after he'd left. The phone was just a plastic shell.

Ezra Maas
Chapter Four

I recall a time when the dogs barked every night and the moon was always full[251]

A cultural revolution was under way. Everything old was bad. Everything new was good. If you were young, and ambitious, then Hollywood was the place to be. Ezra Maas was both and his timing was as impeccable as ever. He arrived as the old studio system was about to fall apart, the balance of power shifting, from wealthy owners and the producers they paid to oversee their movies, to a new wave of talented directors. These young upstarts, inspired by post-war European and Japanese cinema, desired to become 'auteurs' and artists themselves. It was a time when everyone wanted to be in the movies, from the Beatles to Bob Dylan, and Maas was no exception. Rumour has it a chance meeting in New York with a shifty-eyed, manic young actor called Dennis Hopper (according to the tale Maas literally fell over Hopper at a party in an East Village apartment) gave the artist the idea for his cross-country odyssey to Hollywood. Los Angeles was a dream place, in more ways than one, but by the end of the 1960s the dream monsters would escape the dreaming mind. And Maas would play his part in unleashing them.

The end began almost a year earlier in mid-1967. Whatever the true reasons for his departure, Maas's decision to leave New York came suddenly and was reportedly followed by an impromptu road trip across America with husband and wife artists Willard and Elena Harding. The trio allegedly retraced the steps of Jack Kerouac[252] and Neal Cassady, whose travels were immortalised in the classic *On the Road*, although the route they took seemed to differ greatly. The journey lasted just over two months before Maas – who allegedly split with the Hardings after a row – eventually settled in California at an apartment in Manhattan Beach, ostensibly working on a follow-up to the art-book *XXXXXX*, but he was also still painting and creating sculptures at a prolific rate and was increasingly interested in film. According to agent Diane Holbrook, who unsuccessfully attempted to represent Maas at the time, he was actually working on four separate novels while in Manhattan Beach:

"He described it as a period of madness... The rumour was it nearly

---

251. Joan Didion.

252. Kerouac and Cassady travelled across the US and Mexico in the late 1940s. The adventures would form the basis of Kerouac's classic book *On the Road*.

killed him and when he had finished he was so unhappy with them that he locked the books away for fifteen years... leaving the US shortly after."[253]

It is here that accounts of Maas's whereabouts diverge. There is considerable evidence to place him on the West Coast for the remainder of 1967 and 1968. However, sources have claimed Maas moved back and forth between LA and New York, in this period, and that the stories of a relocation to California were designed to distance the artist from the cult scene on the East Coast and were specifically spread to ensure he could not be implicated in the shooting of Andy Warhol.[254] Clearly these are unsubstantiated claims and all of the evidence suggests that Solanas was acting alone. A more radical theory about Maas's whereabouts in 1967 to 1968 claims he returned to the UK to pursue a scholarship at Oxford University and that he spent up to a year back in England. This is highly disputed, not least by the University itself, and I will return to this theory later.[255]

Regardless of what you believe, Maas clearly lived briefly in Manhattan Beach among a coterie of pot-smoking hippies, stoned surfers, strung-out jazz musicians, and prostitutes. Interestingly, the reclusive writer Thomas Pynchon, author of *Gravity's Rainbow*, *V*, *The Crying of Lot 49*, and many other novels, was also living in the vicinity during this period, although there is no suggestion of a meeting between the two. After deciding to abandon these novels (which were later reworked into *The Book of Four*), and becoming generally disillusioned with life in America, Maas is believed to have taken a trip up to San Francisco, in 1967. This was the so-called 'Summer of Love' which saw more than 100,000 American teenagers descend on the city district of Haight-Ashbury, San Francisco.

It was during this period that Maas first became aware of the work of gonzo journalism pioneer Hunter S Thompson, whose articles at the time echoed his own feelings about the counterculture, specifically the West Coast hippie movement. Thompson attacked their lack of political conviction and artistic core compared to the New Left (based in Berkeley, California) and the Beats, his words proving oddly prophetic especially given the manner this era would end (with violence and anarchy rather

---

253. Daniel interviewed Holbrook in 2011.

254. Following the shooting, Warhol said: "People sometimes say that the way things happen in movies is unreal, but actually it's the way things happen in life that's unreal. Right when I was being shot and ever since, I knew that I was watching television. The channels switch, but it's all television."

255. This chapter has been lost/destroyed. See the editor's note at the end of this chapter – Anonymous.

than peace and love) over the next two years. Maas, who would later befriend the journalist, is rumoured to have agreed with this outlook and cited the article to friends before he left America (if that particular account can be believed). Social commentators later considered Maas's decision to have anticipated the implosion of 1960s counterculture, marked by the events at Altamont[256] and the Manson murders of 1969 which effectively signalled the end of this era. This version of events is often described as a gross oversimplification however, with some critics claiming the hippie revolution was actually a media invention which quickly became commercialised by cynical opportunists, the 'Summer of Love' serving as a convenient distraction from genuine political action, such as the Anti-Vietnam protests and the Civil Rights movement. Whatever the truth the years to follow would see renewed political activism, gay liberation, second wave feminism, and environmentalism. Maas's name would be associated with all of these movements in the decade to come, but certainly, at the end of the 1960s, it appeared he was ready for a change of scene. Counterculture writer Joanne Lauder writes[257]:

"Like Thompson, Maas anticipated that things were falling apart and decided a return to Europe was inevitable, although he maintained a relationship with the US for years to come and never completely severed his ties with the country…"

Lauder's comments support the belief that Maas did indeed return to the UK in early 1968. Let's explore these claims before returning to Maas's days in Hollywood. In the version of events that saw him return to England, Maas apparently arrived back in Oxford and set about claiming the assets that had been left to him by his family, including their home in the country. Despite previously threatening Maas with permanent expulsion for leaving school without permission, Headmaster Warick Hall allowed the teenager to return to St Edward's in Oxford, essentially as a 'mature student',[258] to complete his studies and progress to University. Hall described this decision as having been based on Maas's "exceptional promise" as an artist, although news of his success across the Atlantic no doubt played a part, and, in many ways, it was a shrewd PR move by the

---

256. The Altamont Speedway Free Festival was an infamous rock concert in 1969, headlined by The Rolling Stones, where violence (fuelled by drug use) erupted between the hippie counterculture and Hells Angels of San Francisco and California, resulting in one murder, three accidental deaths, and multiple injuries. It is also cited, alongside the Manson murders in August 1969, as one of the twin shocks that effectively ended the 1960s.

257. In *A Decade of Counterculture*, Oxford Press, 1985, p.197.

258. If only by a few months.

school. Speaking to local radio several years later, Hall said:

"News of his fame in New York and California had reached us in Oxford, yes, I can't deny that... but this had nothing to do with our decision. He was an incredibly gifted student, especially in the arts and, if not for his fiercely independent and wilful nature, I think he would have gone on to become one of the nation's most prominent academics. As it was, he would attain greatness in a different way."[259]

After a successful rehabilitation period, Hall recommended Maas for a fast-stream or 'hothouse' summer school education programme designed for promising students, particularly those from unprivileged backgrounds. This led to Maas winning a scholarship to Oxford University's Jordan College, just over two years after he had originally left the UK. After finishing his studies at St Edward's, through the summer-school programme, Maas was able to accept his place at Oxford and initially excelled academically. However, this was soon to change when the problems that had allegedly led to his decision to leave the United States – the cult following, violence, vandalism, and anarchy, carried out in his name, the rumours of drug use, accusations of mysticism, and more – seemingly followed him home.

At this point it is worth addressing the other, more outlandish, rumour that I alluded to earlier. Some sources I spoke to claimed that Maas never attended Oxford University at all but had sent a surrogate in his place, specifically a young impoverished American student who could affect a passable English accent. According to supporters of this theory this was not a subversive political statement, nor did Maas hold a particular grudge against the University, he merely wanted to see if he could get away with it. A former member of The Maas Foundation, who wishes to remain anonymous, said:

"People find it hard to believe, but it's true... Maas said it was a piece of live conceptual art... the kid he used was a diehard fan of his from Brooklyn and was naturally bright, but, at the same time, he was no academic. However, the less cultured he acted the more faculty and students at Oxford thought he was some sort of savant... when they eventually found out the truth there was a huge scandal, but the University managed to cover it up... the last thing they wanted was for people to find out Maas had conned them for a year... it would have done untold damage to their integrity... the legal battle lasted years, but Oxford and The Maas Foundation eventually agreed to bury the story... "[260]

---

259. Courtesy of BBC Radio Oxford archives.

260. From an interview conducted by Daniel in 2011.

Another, more sinister, explanation is that the multiple, overlapping, accounts of Maas's whereabouts during this period were intentionally engineered to provide cover for the alleged illegal activities of the artist's cult followers, including their links to the later shooting of Andy Warhol, and other events. If Maas was 'out of the country' at the time this would help insulate him against potential investigation. It is difficult to know what to believe, but if the 'imposter' theory is true, and Maas never returned to the UK in 1968, it would account for the supposed presence of Maas at that year's Democratic National Convention[261] in Chicago. Hunter S Thompson was there researching a book about the presidential campaign,[262] while William S Burroughs was covering the event for *Esquire* magazine. Reports place Maas at Chicago's *Billy Goat Tavern*[263] with both Thompson and Burroughs at the time of the convention and it was rumoured this was the beginning of lifelong friendships with both men. This would also add credibility to claims that Maas signed the 1968 Writers and Editors War Tax Protest, which was organised by Gerald Walker of *The New York Times Magazine* in opposition to the Vietnam War.[264]

These sightings aside – and discounting Maas's alleged return to Oxford (explored in full in a separate chapter*) – the artist's road trip across America would lead inexorably to the land where dreams come true – Hollywood, Los Angeles. On arrival Maas was courted

---

261. After Democratic President Lyndon Johnson announced on 31st March 1968 that he would not seek a second term, the convention was held to choose a new nominee to run as the Democratic Party's candidate for the office. It was held during a year of violence, political turbulence, and civil unrest, particularly riots in more than 100 cities following the assassination of Martin Luther King, Jr. on 4th April. The convention also followed the assassination of Democratic presidential hopeful Senator Robert F. Kennedy, who had been murdered on June 5. Kennedy and Senator Eugene McCarthy had been running against the eventual Democratic presidential nominee Hubert Humphrey.

262. He allegedly used a $6,000 advance from Random House to make the trip to Chicago to research the book, entitled *The Joints Chiefs*, which was to be about the 'death of the American dream'. It was never finished.

263. The original *Billy Goat Tavern* location was born in 1934 when Greek immigrant, William 'Billy Goat' Sianis, purchased the *Lincoln Tavern*. Billy Goat bought the tavern for $205, with a check that bounced but was later repaid with sales from the first weekend. The tavern was located across from the Chicago Stadium and attracted mainly sports fans. Sianis became known as 'Billy Goat' when a goat fell off a passing truck and wandered inside. Sianis adopted the goat, grew a goatee, acquired the nickname 'Billy Goat', and changed the name of the bar to the Billy Goat Tavern. Interestingly, (especially considering Thompson and Burroughs were in town for the Democratic Convention) the Tavern once made headlines for putting up a sign, which read: No Republicans Allowed.

264. Maas's name is included in some lists of the Writers and Editors War Tax Protest, but not others.

by notorious BBS[265] founders Bert Schneider and Bob Rafelson, among others, to see if he was interested in becoming a director. The artist found himself invited to decadent 'Last Days of Rome' style parties[266] at palatial mansions set in the Hollywood Hills, which seemed to take place around the clock. Wealthy creative producers like Schneider and Rafelson were having fun pretending to be hippies and their parties, attended by the likes of the aforementioned Dennis Hopper, Jack Nicholson, and many more, were well-known for an abundance of women, cocaine, marijuana, and Quaaludes.

This was the birth of New Hollywood where artist-directors would define a generation of movie-making and power-players, like BBS and others, had heard about this hot new artist from New York with his cult following and air of mystery. Maas was offered a lucrative deal, including an advance and points,[267] by BBS rival ICON and its powerful owners, Marv Greenberg and Johnny Evans. Unfortunately for them Maas reportedly loathed Greenberg, Evans, and every single one of his rich Hollywood suitors, as well as their lavish lifestyles, branding them 'fakes', and ultimately proceeded to take a $10,000 advance and burn it in an improvised conceptual art installation, dubbed 'Hollywood Trash' by some of the artist's more vocal followers. Greenberg and Evans were furious and threatened to blackball Maas and worse. However, one afternoon when they were at home in their pools, surrounded by their wives and children, the two men each received a visit by a group of hippies who wandered onto their property. This was only a few months after the 'Summer of Love' and before Hollywood's power players locked themselves away behind walls patrolled by armed guards and attack dogs in the wake of the Manson murders and Altamont. It was not uncommon to have hippies wandering around your property,[268] but something about this group was different.

---

265. Bert, Bob and Steve.

266. The menu included avocados stuffed with shrimp, whole cases of Beaujolais Nouveau, and bowls of medicinal cocaine on every table.

267. Hollywood language for a percentage of the gross revenue of the film.

268. Around the same time as the Manson Family, and the Maas Foundation followers, there was also LA's The Source Family, led by eccentric health food restaurant owner turned cult leader Father Yod, who boasted about having fourteen wives. The Source Family were popular with celebrities, who regularly ate at Yod's restaurant, until the Manson murders saw the group driven from California to Hawaii where, poverty stricken, they met a tragic end after Father Yod paraglided off a 1,500ft cliff. He broke his back, refused medical treatment, and died soon after, leading to the family's dissolution – Anonymous.

"They had long hair and beards like hippies," Greenberg recalled. "But otherwise they didn't wear beads or bells or flowers. It was almost like they were businessmen pretending to be hippies. They were expressionless and dead behind the eyes. They surrounded the pool and looked at us as if we were insects – my wife and children were terrified. They said nothing and just kept staring, their cold eyes boring holes through us. One of them went into the house and came out with a framed photograph of my family. They left with it… "[269]

Months later, following the Sharon Tate murders, Greenberg and Evans would wonder if they had been spooked by the Manson family. In fact, they had just received a warning from the earliest version of The Maas Foundation.[270]

---

269. From an interview with Daniel in 2011 – 2012.

270. Note to reader: The full chapter from Daniel's unauthorised biography of Maas exploring the validity of Maas's alleged return to the UK, including a detailed account of the artist's year at Oxford University, has unfortunately been destroyed or lost. We will pick up the story after this chapter when Maas began travelling across Europe before returning to America later in the 1970s. For the sake of continuity, I have amended the number of the Ezra Maas chapters accordingly – Anonymous.

Following the announcement, Sara Danius, Permanent Secretary of the Swedish Academy, was interviewed by journalist Elise Karlsson about the 2017 Nobel Prize in Literature to Kazuo Ishiguro. Sara Danius described Kazuo Ishiguro's writing style as a mix of Jane Austen and Franz Kafka: "But you have to add a little bit of Marcel Proust into the mix, and then you stir."

When biography becomes literary grave robbing

ALEX BURKE

Daniel James

THE UNAUTHORISED BIOGRAPHY
OF EZRA MAAS

ISBN 9781911585299

Daniel James's planned book about the reclusive artist Ezra Maas raises serious questions about the ethics of cultural ownership and the limits of biography.

Ezra Maas's death has yet to be officially announced by his estate, but already the vultures are circling to pick the meat from his bones. Yes, he was a public figure, but does that give journalists a right to publish his private letters and diaries as well as the half-remembered recollections from friends and enemies, collaborators and lovers? The dead cannot defend themselves and while families left behind can write letters to their lawyers or publish statements expressing their disgust, by that point the damage is already done.

If he goes ahead with his unauthorised book, James will become the latest in a long line of journalists and biographers who succeed only in unmasking their own nature by shamelessly digging through the private lives of deceased celebrities. He will face the fate suffered by biographers such as Jonathan Bate, and journalists like Claudio Gatti. Writing for *The New Yorker*, essayist and journalist Janet Malcom left no one in doubt about her opinion of Bate in her scathing review of his book, *Ted Hughes: The Unauthorised Life*. Bate, an Oxford Professor and Shakespeare scholar, had the approval of Hughes's widow Carol withdrawn when she realised his book was going to reveal details of his personal life from letters and correspondence.

Similarly, journalist Claudio Gatti received widespread criticism for exposing the real identity of Italian novelist Elena Ferrante. The journalist spent months combing through financial accounts and property records to unmask the author. He had no right to do this. Ferrante chose to write under a pseudonym for a reason and this should have been respected.

Powerful custodianship of Ezra Maas's estate by his wife Helena and their representatives, The Maas Foundation, has so far prevented journalists from violating the artist's desire for his work to speak for him. He was intensely private in life and his wishes should be respected whether he is alive or dead. James has said that he simply wants to discover the truth about the artist, but if the writer follows in the footsteps of those biographers who have crossed the line before him, then I fear his legacy, like theirs, will always be that of a grave robber.

Daniel James
Chapter Ten[271]

Beneath the surface there's another world, and still different worlds as you dig deeper.[272]

There was a body in the pool.[273] I stopped moving and considered whether to retrace my steps out of the garden. No one would know I had been there. The only problem was I couldn't move. My legs had turned to stone. I wanted to look away, but my eyes were locked on the corpse. It was no longer a body, but a hole in the world. I was gazing at the unreal.

It had been quite a day. I had picked up a tail leaving the LA Louver[274] near Venice Beach, been chased through the fairground rides at Santa Monica pier, and was beaten up by a professional boxer in Central Hollywood, before being nearly run off the road on the Pacific Coast Highway. And it wasn't even 5pm yet.

---

271. Daniel was an expert in noir fiction and saw the role of biographer as a kind of literary detective. In this, and other chapters, he foregrounds the signs and signifiers of noir in the visible exterior of the narrative, knowingly employing classic motifs to explore the 'slippage' between reality and fantasy. This is clearly a conscious choice, as was his decision to inhabit the role of writer-detective while working on the book. And yet, I find myself questioning how much of this was a performance by the end. Like Bryan Ferry, whose lounge lizard persona was originally an ironic comment by a former art school student, how long before the mask and he who wears it become one and the same? – Anonymous.

272. David Lynch, during an interview about his 1984 film *Blue Velvet*.

273. The body in the pool is a recurring motif in noir, particularly those set in LA and Hollywood. Arguably the most famous appearance of this scene is in Billy Wilder's classic *Sunset Boulevard* (1950), in which William Holden's doomed screenwriter, Joe Gillis, become entangled with the ghosts of silent-era Hollywood in the form of Gloria Swanson's forgotten icon Norma Desmond. It can also be seen in Roman Polanski's *Chinatown* (1974). Although the exact circumstances of Hollis Mulwray's murder remain ambiguous in the film, it seems he was drowned in a pool rather than one of LA's reservoirs as first thought. The film also explores the complex relationship between LA and water: "Either you bring the water to LA, or you bring LA to the water." Wilder's film is also a favourite of the artist and director David Lynch, whose *Mulholland Drive* (2004) also explores Hollywood's dark side. Like Lynch, Wilder's film merges elements of noir and horror. In fact it has been described as the definitive 'Hollywood horror film', despite its ostensible realism. Other examples of the body-in-the-pool motif can be seen in the French film, *La Piscine* (1969), starring Alain Delon. There are also echoes in *The Swimmer* (1968) with Burt Lancaster, also set in LA, which presents a "tortured main character as he attempts to immerse himself in a fantasy life that is no longer available to him." These themes are, of course, all too familiar – Anonymous.

274. A well-known LA art gallery.

Two hours earlier, I had followed a late lunch at Musso's[275] on Hollywood Boulevard with a visit to an old friend. It was the latest lead in a busy few days retracing Maas's footsteps and interviewing those who remembered him from his days here. LA was a strange place.[276] The famous Hollywood sign took its name from a real estate development that no longer existed,[277] while so much of the exotic fauna and flora we identify with LA had actually been imported – eucalyptus trees from Australia, cypress trees from Italy. It was like driving around a movie set filled with ghosts of Hollywood's past – LA, a schizophrenic city of extreme light and dark, an urban wilderness where reality and illusion, history and myth, were conflated.

The Forgotten Arm was an old-school boxing-gym in Central Hollywood, nestled between a rundown convenience store and a cabaret bar called The Jack of Hearts. It was owned by a Hall of Fame boxing trainer and ex-fighter, Jerry Napier, who had retired with a 39 – 7 – 1 record. Jerry had charged $5 on the door from the day he opened the place back in the '80s and had never raised the price of admission once. That was the kind of gym this was and the said a lot about Jerry's nature. As I walked through the double doors I was greeted by the smell of sweat and blood, and the staccato thud, thud, thud of fighters hitting the pads. The air shimmered with heat, and shafts of sunlight arced back and forth above the rings, tinted with the colours of flags from different nations which hung over the windows. In my shirt and tie I expected to raise a few eyebrows as I walked through the gym, but if the fighters wondered who I was and why I was there they didn't show it. Jerry's gym was often the subject of TV documentaries and celebrity visits and it wouldn't be unusual for reporters or producers to be knocking around. I finally found Jerry watching a Mexican kid shadowboxing in the farthest corner of the gym. Jerry looked as if he'd shrunk since the last time I'd seen him, his once muscular shoulders sagging inside a familiar, sweat-stained t-shirt, which bore a faded version of the gym's logo – a stylised cartoon-graphic of a muscular arm in the act of throwing an uppercut.

'How's things, Jerry?' I said, hanging my long black coat on the ring post.

---

275. Musso & Frank Grill is a world famous bar and restaurant and a former haunt of many famous writers, including Raymond Chandler, F.Scott Fitzgerald, Dorothy Parker, James M Cain, Dashiell Hammett, William Faulkner, and Ernest Hemingway. By the 1940s and 1950s it was so well known that aspiring writers would consciously seek out the bar to imitate their idols. It's no coincidence that Musso's was on Daniel's itinerary in LA – Anonymous.

276. Journalist Carey McWilliams wrote that "Los Angeles is the kind of place where perversion is perverted and prostitution prostituted."

277. Hollywoodland.

He looked at me and grimaced. We hadn't parted on the best of terms, but I was hoping that we could leave the past out of this.

'What do you want?' he said.

'I need your help.'

'Don't you always? Well, you know the price.'

'I paid my five dollars on the way in, Jerry.'

'The real price. Between the ropes.'

'What are you talking about?'

'You getting in there and earning whatever favour it is you need from me.'

'You've got to be kidding.'

Jerry turned to the Mexican kid sitting on the ring apron.

'Hey, Esparza. Danny boy here used to have some talent back in the day but I hear he's gone soft. You fancy testing his chin?'

Esparza looked at me dismissively and shrugged.

'Le gano con los ojos vendados,' he said.

'I don't have time for fun and games, Jerry. I'm looking for someone.'

'Who's playing? You want information? Get in the ring. Esparza has a fight coming up in a few months and needs the sparring.'

'You're serious?'

'As a left hook.'

I changed into some spare gear and wrapped my hands. When I came out of the dressing room Jerry was waiting with a sterilised gumshield and a pair of 16oz gloves. It had been a long time since I'd done any sparring and I'd forgotten how it felt to be gloved-up. My writer's hands felt claustrophobic being so tightly bound. Jerry came towards me with a head guard, but I leaned away.

'Don't be a tough guy,' he said. 'Put it on.'

'You know I hate those things, Jerry. They mess my hair up.'

'Well, you're about to have your face messed up too.'

'Este es tu funeral, guapo,' Esparza added, with a smile.

I smiled as if I knew better and climbed into the ring. Esparza was already waiting for me, pacing back and forth the way a cat does. He pounded his gloves together with a heavy thud when he saw me and grinned, his brightly coloured gumshield like a segment of orange in his mouth. I looked down at Jerry.

'One round?'

'One round,' he replied with a smile. 'If you can make it through three minutes I'll tell you anything you want to know.'

It had been twelve years since I had last stepped between the ropes and I had never done more than spar. I had met Jerry back in London during a brief flirtation with boxing journalism as a trainee reporter. Guys like Esparza were professional athletes who lived and breathed boxing; gym rats who trained all day, every day, and sparred hard. Boxing could be a brutal sport and it took a certain kind of person to succeed. It was survival of the fittest and, right now, in my early thirties and nursing my three-hundredth hangover of the year, I felt very far from my prime.

Esparza said something in Spanish as we touched gloves in the centre of the ring but I couldn't make it out. A split second later I was bleeding. He hit me square in the face with a hard jab before I'd even had time to set my feet, leaving my legs wobbly, and black spots flashing before my eyes. I got my hands up quick and kept them there, moving out of range and pivoting away to my left when I realised my back was against the ropes. That was the last place I wanted to be against a guy like Esparza. I needed to keep on my toes, give him a moving target and maybe, if I got lucky, get his respect by landing a hard shot of my own but all of that was easier said than done. My feet felt heavy, my legs weak, and I'd forgotten most of what I'd been taught years earlier. Esparza blocked my poor attempt at a jab and made me pay with one of his own. He had the kind of jab that snapped your head back. It wasn't a rangefinder but a weapon in itself. He threw a combination, body to head, pushing me back. I couldn't think or move fast enough to avoid the punches. All I could do was absorb them on my arms and gloves and try to survive. I was already tired and Esparza knew it. Sooner or later my hands would drop and he would catch me clean, then it would be lights out. I kept moving, trying to frustrate him. Every now and then Jerry would shout advice to his protégé from the ring apron.

'He's throwing a lazy jab, kid. He's wide open for a big overhand right. Nail 'im!'

'I don't think he needs your help, Jerry!' I tried to say, but it didn't come out too clearly.

By calling for the shot Jerry was inadvertently helping me. Maybe that was his intention all along. Esparza dutifully threw a big right hand as he'd been asked and, because I knew it was coming, I was able to slip under it, step to the side, and throw a counter left hook. I planted my feet and put all my weight into the punch. Esparza hadn't got his hands up fast enough to block the shot and it caught him flush. I probably hurt his pride more than his jaw but it was something. I don't remember much after that but the round seemed to go on forever. Three minutes can feel like an eternity when you're getting punched in the face. I ended the round with my back against the ropes, my gloves around my head, trying desperately to stay upright under a barrage of heavy punches. Finally, the bell rang and it was over. It was then I realised an audience had formed around the ring to watch the action.

'Nada mal cuate. Me hiciste sudar,' Esparza said, slapping me hard on the shoulder. I nodded and sat down heavily on the ring apron, exhausted and sore, my mouth filled with blood. Jerry threw me a towel.

'You ready for a drink?' he said.

'You're buying,' I replied.

The address Jerry gave me belonged to a house in the Hollywood Hills. I had paid for the information with my own sweat and blood and hoped the drive would be worth it. The last few days had been spent interviewing former actors and producers, artists, gallery owners and collectors, and the occasional celebrity friend and drug dealer, but it had yielded precious little in the way of fresh insight into Maas and the truth of his life. My last hope was the lead I had picked up from Fiona Vale in New York – the eccentric film producer and art collector Alec Zimmer, who had allegedly been at odds with the Maas Foundation over the ownership of an original video installation by the artist.

Stretching fifty miles along a ridge of the Santa Monica Mountains, Mulholland Drive was named after the engineer who built the waterways. It provided a spectacular vantage point over the shimmering expanse of the city.[278] A lot of people complained about LA's geography and its urban sprawl but I found my way around just fine, having been blessed with an almost supernatural sense of direction. It was the heat I couldn't handle. I was built for much colder climates.

The Sylvia North Building[279] was a sleek modernist mansion, with an exterior of grey-hued concrete designed in sharp, jutting angles, narrow slit-like windows, and Mayan art deco embellishments. There was a large pool on the grounds, palm trees and bougainvillea, concrete out-buildings, and spectacular panoramic views over the wilderness of the canyons below, where stray coyotes were said to prowl. The house was located

---

278. A route immortalised by the artist David Hockney, in his 1980 painting *Mulholland Drive: The Road to the Studio* – Anonymous.

279. Designed by architect Diane Selwyn-Elms in 1951, in a combination of styles inspired by Frank Lloyd Wright's Ennis House and also the work of British architect John Parkinson, who, influenced by Art Deco and Spanish colonial styles, designed many of LA's iconic buildings, including its City Hall, Union Station, and buildings such as the Memorial Coliseum and Bullocks Wilshire department store, but whose work has been largely forgotten and overlooked since his early death in 1935 – Anonymous.

at the top of a steep slope. I parked at the bottom and followed a set of stone steps up to the entrance of the property. When I reached a locked gate, with no buzzer, I decided to walk around the back to find another way inside. There was a single wooden door set into a grey, concrete wall, which was covered with pale green moss. I tried the handle and found it was unlocked. I walked through the doorway into a large garden, stepping over a tiny blue snake as it skittered across my path and away into the undergrowth.

As I crossed the lawn, towards the strange, concrete house and its bunker-like architecture, I realised coming here had been a mistake. There was something in the pool that shouldn't have been there. My mind didn't register what it was at first, as if it was struggling to process what it was seeing, but some part of me knew immediately what it was and what it meant. I was looking straight at it but somehow it seemed to be on my periphery, creeping up on me from the edge of my vision rather than the centre. It was a familiar shape, a figure, a man, but everything else about the scene was wrong. The man wore a dressing gown and he was face down in the water, skin pale and bloated, dead. I tried to look away, to move, to run, but I couldn't. I was gazing at the unreal, frozen by the horror of it, my eyes fixed on the pool and the strange shape floating on the surface of the water.

If I didn't get out of there I was going to have some explaining to do when LA's finest came calling. This was my chance to leave, but I couldn't will my feet to move. At least not in the direction I wanted. I felt myself drifting forward, closer and closer to the house, as if I was being drawn to it by forces beyond my control. The dark, angular, house was calling to me, pulling me in. It wanted to give up its secrets and I couldn't leave without going inside. Not if I wanted to find out the truth.

The French doors had already been pushed apart when I reached the house. It was a lucky break. Maybe the last I would get. I was standing in a large, open-plan living-room with square stone pillars throughout, reminiscent of Mayan architecture and the work of Frank Lloyd Wright.[280] Other than the Mayan embellishments the interior was a masterclass of modern design, with sleek surfaces, modern art on concrete walls, floor to ceiling shelves with books, cassettes and CDs. Everything was in its right place. There were no signs of a struggle.

I began to look around. Almost immediately, my eyes were drawn to the windows. All the blinds had been pulled down and someone had

---

280. For arguably the finest example of Frank Lloyd Wright's love of Mayan architecture see LA's the Ennis House, which has been featured in such films as *Blade Runner*.

scrawled strange symbols all over them with a black marker – a large circle and an inverted triangle overlapping each other, surrounded by smaller symbols that I didn't recognise, and a series of repeating numbers along the bottom.[281] The drawings reminded me of a strange side-story I had read in one of the Bowie biographies. At the height of his alleged cocaine psychosis, in the mid-1970s, a disturbed and paranoid Bowie had supposedly drawn over the windows, blinds, walls, and doors of a mansion he'd rented here in Hollywood. Bowie, like Jimmy Page and several other rock stars of the period, had become obsessed with the occult and believed the Kabbalistic symbols[282] were a form of protection, to keep the dream monsters within his dreaming mind. Maybe Zimmer believed the same, or maybe someone else had left them here as further misdirection. Either way, they hadn't protected anyone. I took a photograph on my phone and moved on.

The interior of the rest of the house was unexpectedly cramped and oppressive, with low ceilings and long, claustrophobic corridors that telescoped away into shadowy recesses. It had to be my imagination, but it felt as if the space was collapsing in on itself, the further I explored. There were narrow, slit-like windows along the walls but barely any light seemed to get through and the designer art-deco lamps seemed only to illuminate themselves. It was a strange, nocturnal non-place, closed off and dead, like an empty museum. It was the antithesis of LA's wide, open spaces. The lush green hills bathed in flat, endless sunlight, lay just beyond the doors, but they couldn't have felt further away right now.

I came to a left turn and found myself looking down a long corridor filled with shop mannequins, positioned on either side of me like a faceless guard of honour. Each one stood in a different pose. Maybe it was art? I had seen worse, but I still felt uneasy as I slowly made my way between their featureless, plastic bodies. I moved forward in a straight line, one foot after the other, convinced that at any moment one of their arms would shoot out and grab me. A bead of cold sweat ran down the side of my face. As I passed the last mannequin and reached the door I let out a long breath and stepped through in the next room.

A long, slow and silent exploration of the house followed, until I finally

---

281. Although Daniel makes another association, in the text, the symbols he uncovers in the house made me recall Jorge Luis Borges's classic short story, *Death and The Compass* (1941) – Anonymous.

282. Bowie had a long and storied relationship to occult practices. An entire album he created at the time, *Station to Station*, is structured around a journey through each station of the Kabbalistic tree of life.

came to Zimmer's office. I half expected it to have been ransacked, but it appeared to be untouched. There was more modern art on the walls, and a four foot sculpture of a rabbit-like figure made from twisted metal standing by the desk,[283] which was covered with framed photos of Zimmer with various Hollywood names, all with the same smile.

Behind the desk were two large filing cabinets. Zimmer clearly kept extensive business records but it felt too risky to go through his files. I didn't know what I was looking for and it was a sure-fire way of leaving fingerprints behind. There was another door at the back of the office. It opened to reveal a staircase leading down into the basement. There was light flickering against the steps at the very bottom and I could hear a strange repeating sound, like something mechanical caught in a loop. I felt dread wash over me.

Every instinct told me to turn around and leave, but I couldn't. I had to see what was down there. My whole body was tense as I descended into the darkness, step by step, one hand flat against the wall, keeping me steady. The odd, mechanical sound grew louder and the flickering white light moved up over my shoes and legs, until it covered my whole body. It came from a projector set into the ceiling of a large, cinema-style screening room, with rows of red, plush velvet seats built into the floor. There were champagne flutes by each of the chairs and a table littered with three dozen empty bottles of Krug.[284] It looked like I had missed a hell of a party. The projector had been left running but there was nothing on the screen now except blurred images. I had arrived too late.

An image flashed into my mind as I stared at the screen; a group of people gathered together for a private screening. What did they see? Jane's words kept coming back to me, turning me inside out. Don't watch the film. There was no way of knowing if it was all connected but whatever happened here had ended with a man's death.

I left the screening room and returned to the ground floor by a different set of stairs, coming out in a large, modern kitchen, complete with stylish, brushed steel appliances and a granite-topped island in the centre. There was a mug of coffee and an open pack of cigarettes on the counter. As I stepped out into the light I had the feeling I was being watched. I could almost feel the eyes on my back. I turned quickly, just in time to see a young woman with wild, blonde hair coming at me with a butcher's knife.

---

283. Based on my research, I believe this sculpture was a famous early piece by British visual artist Louise Mackenzie – Anonymous.

284. A brand of champagne. Founded by Joseph Krug in 1853 in the city of Reims, in the heart of France's champagne region.

'Fucking hell!'

I raised my hands and managed to grab the woman's wrist as the blade came down, stopping the point of the knife about an inch from my chest. The make-up around her eyes was smudged from crying and there was a look of frustration on her face, as she realised she was caught, followed by fear. I loosened my grip and she pulled herself free, falling backwards and dropping the knife, which hit the floor with a clatter. She let out a cry and scrambled away from me, frantically pushing herself back on her heels, never taking her eyes away from me until she was safely under the counter. My heart was pounding and I felt light-headed. It was becoming a familiar feeling. I took a step towards her on unsteady legs.

'Hey... ' I said finally, my voice heavy and thick. 'It's okay... I'm not going to hurt you.'

I held my hands up, palms facing her. 'What happened here?'

'Stay away from me,' she cried.

'I'm not going to hurt you,' I repeated. 'I'm going to stay right over here, okay?'

'They killed him... ' she said. 'They killed him.'

'Who did?'

She looked as if she hadn't heard me, her eyes darting back and forth.

'Stay away from me!'

'I told you,' I said, crouching down so that my eyes were level with hers. 'I'm not going to hurt you. Who did this?'

She seemed to grow smaller before my eyes.

'Psychos in animal masks,' she replied finally.

'They killed Zimmer?'

'I thought you were one of them,' she said.

'I'm not,' I said.

'How can I believe you?' She looked suddenly like a child, hiding there under the kitchen counter, the whites of her eyes startlingly bright in the shadows. I sat down on the floor so that she could see I wasn't going to rush her. She could run away if she wanted.

'You're just going to have to trust me,' I said, resting my back against a cupboard.

She pulled her legs to her chest and wrapped her arms around them as if she was trying to make herself as small as possible.

'What's your name?' I asked.

She shook her head and looked away. I decided to take a more direct approach.

'Why did they kill him?'

A clarity returned to her eyes.

'He didn't have what they wanted,' she said. 'They thought he was hiding it somewhere... but Jason stole it two weeks ago... it was my fault. I shouldn't have trusted him. I was so fucking stupid... and now Alec's dead.'

'What did they want that was stolen?'

'The film,' she said.

Don't watch the film. I felt light-headed again.

'I'm going to call the police,' I said.

'Don't... ' she replied, softly. 'Please. Please don't... I can't be here, I shouldn't be here... I just want to leave.'

I needed to get out of there, I wanted to wipe down every surface I might have touched and run for the hills, but she was clearly in shock and probably needed to go to the hospital. I couldn't just leave her. She also had answers and I would have been a fool to let her go without finding out what she knew. I knew, whatever I decided, I was going to live to regret it one way or another.

'Look... ' I said. 'I can get you out of here and take you somewhere safe... I have a car parked outside.'

'No police?'

'No police.'

'Why... why would you do that for me?'

'Because I need to know what happened here – the whole story.'

Extract 1A:

Patient: D. James / Psychological Assessment 6/1/2007 / Westmoor Hospital, Berkshire / Consultant: Dr. Cassandra May[285]

A summary of case notes following sessions conducted between 3/8/2007 to 30/11/2007

Pg.1 (below)

The patient was initially referred to me by his employer, News International, under instructions that he must undergo psychological evaluation or face disciplinary action following months of erratic, self-destructive behaviour, possibly due to post-traumatic stress after ███████████████ As a result, he was less than cooperative during our first session, but I soon found him a likeable and highly intelligent subject who was able to talk eloquently about his experiences. If anything, I was surprised by the distance he displayed ██████████ ████████████████████████████████ This, in itself, suggested to me a high degree of dissociation and repression in his personality that may need further observation. Despite his relaxed manner there was an aspect of 'performance' to the patient's personality. This manifested itself a number of times, where he appeared to slip into a carefully constructed 'persona' in order to avoid answering difficult questions.

When asked him about subjects unrelated to his career such as his personal life or childhood, for instance, the patient was more guarded, and I sensed that while he may have anticipated and conditioned himself to deflect enquiries regarding ███ ███████████████ he had not been as prepared for the rest of his life to come under the spotlight. Subsequently, later sessions focused more on his past. It later emerged he had not known his real parents, having been fostered at an early stage, and although I was not able to investigate further I felt it was important to his psychological profile, particularly

---

285. It must be noted that Dr May's assessment has been accused of being unreliable. It was later revealed she was in a personal relationship with Daniel for several months in 2007 during these sessions. Whether this positively or negatively impacts her assessment of his psychological state is unknown. Certainly, in some respects, the document reads less like a psychological evaluation and more like a character evisceration by a former lover, which may account for the variation in tone and blurring between personal and professional insight, yet Daniel chose to include it in his notes for the book – Anonymous.

the 'emotional deprivation' this caused in his childhood, and the psychological 'hunger'[286] in his adult life, which has manifested in repeated attempts to prove himself and demonstrate his talents/intelligence to the world. This may seem strange considering his achievements, but I believe it is the key to understanding why he continues to push himself so hard.

The patient comes from a working-class background in Newcastle, where opportunities were few and far between. Despite this he excelled academically and has worked relentlessly to create opportunities for himself. There have been no gifts along the way and he prides himself on having earned everything he has through sheer willpower. He is highly-educated, with two Master's degrees and a PhD on Samuel Beckett's prose novels, which he completed while training as a journalist for a daily newspaper. This occupation, initially seen as a day job while he worked to become an author, slowly became all-consuming, leading to the incident at ███████████ involving ██████████ and ███████████████ which in many ways has led to this assessment. The search for the truth is hugely important to him, both as a journalist and on a psychological level. In his mind the truth is interchangeable with the success, recognition, and adoration, he internally craves and hungers for. I suspect no amount will ever be enough to fill the void he feels inside and I believe he knows this too, but he cannot stop, for he has become addicted to the search itself. When we discussed other paths that his life could have taken a deep and genuine sadness came over him. He asked if I was aware of the term 'Hauntology'[287] which he described to me as the sensation of being haunted by futures that never happened. I tried to get him to explain this feeling further, but he refused. Neither his childhood, nor the trauma experienced during ████████████████ ████████ fully account for the depth of grief – a nameless grief – which I sensed in him, and I must admit this concerned me on a number of levels.

---

286. Rosenfeld, Isaac, *Beyond the Red Notebook*: "Dissatisfaction was an integral part of his character. This led to hunger in the psychological sense... because hunger was strong in him he must always strive to relieve it, but precisely because it is strong, it has to be preserved."

287. The French philosopher Jacques Derrida originally coined the term, Hauntology, in his book *Spectres of Marx*. Hauntology is a portmanteau of the word 'Haunt' and 'Ontology' – the philosophical study of what can be said to exist. It was later adopted and popularised by literary, cultural, and critical theorists including the blogger and academic K-Punk, aka Mark Fisher, who explored the term in his book *Ghosts of My Life*, relating it to Franco Berardi and his phrase the "slow cancellation of the future" while adding that "not only has the future not arrived, it no longer seems possible".

As my sessions with the patient continued I also saw clear signs of borderline Narcissistic Personality Disorder, specifically vanity, obsessive tendencies, histrionic and exploitative behaviour, a sense of being 'special' or 'unique' combined with deep, underlying insecurities, a degree of paranoia, and the need for regular positive reinforcement (this is closely linked to his obsessive womanising and addictive relationships with women to fulfil this need). While there is a definite rage just below the surface, he is clearly practised at keeping this in check, beneath the smooth, polished, exterior that he presents to the world. Similarly, while capable of acts of self-destruction, he is more likely to sabotage his own happiness and quietly dismantle his life in subtler ways.

Results from a Thematic Apperception Test (TAT) and Rorschach Test,[288] both conducted in our early sessions, proved inconclusive, although I suspected the patient was not answering honestly at times. Again, there is an aspect of 'performance' to his personality that is difficult to breach. I suspect he considers his day-to-day life a mode of play-acting, whereas the world he inhabits while he is writing is vividly real and therefore more important in his mind. He seeks to return to it more and more but, like any addictive substance, this is clearly dangerous.

When later sessions revealed signs of a deterioration from melancholia into depression, I suggested a course of antidepressants (I would have prescribed an (SSRI[289]) class drug such as Citalopram), but he refused. I feared he may be self-medicating, if only with alcohol rather than recreational drugs, but he also showed signs of highly-addictive behaviour and I expressed concerns about escalation. Certainly, his relationships with women already border on addiction and it was clear he was using both alcohol and sexual relationships as coping mechanisms.

In fact, I think he has already reached a critical point where he has gone beyond 'the pleasure principle'.[290] There is no joy

---

288. The Rorschach Test is a projective personality test, originally created by Hermann Rorschach in 1918 to diagnose schizophrenia, and inspired by his love of the popular game Klecksographie. It was adapted for psychiatric use, as a personality test, in 1939. It remains in use to this day. Interestingly, it has made its way into popular culture and the art world, including Warhol's Rorschach prints from the 1950s – Anonymous.

289. Selective serotonin reuptake inhibitor.

290. The 'pleasure principle' is a psychoanalytic term by Sigmund Freud, which describes the instinctive seeking of pleasure and avoiding of pain to satisfy biological and psychological needs. *Beyond the Pleasure Principle* is a 1920 essay by Freud.

in these activities for him anymore. No amount of alcohol, sex, fantasy, or escapist literature, will ever satiate him, for he has become addicted to the negative highs provided by these empty simulations, and the opportunity they provide to stare into the void, which he has come to identify as the ultimate truth of the world.

My fear is that he will need to create a new high that goes beyond the rest, specifically that he will develop a lust for death - the 'death drive'[291] being the ultimate negative high. In terms of treatment, I had hoped to introduce high-intensity CBT[292] or Interpersonal Therapy, in parallel to medication, but the patient was resistant to the idea and our sessions were ultimately cut short when he resigned from News International.

It is my professional opinion that…

Pg.2 (not included)[293]

---

291. In Freudian psychoanalytic theory, the 'death drive' is the drive toward death and self-destruction.

292. Cognitive Behaviour Therapy.

293. The second page was not included in Daniel's notes and may have been destroyed. It is unknown how the conclusion of this assessment expanded on Dr May's evaluation as presented here – Anonymous.

Daniel James
Chapter Eleven

The world is all that is the case[294]

Rented rooms in New York and LA, Paris and London, all merge together after a while, same carpets, beds, and furniture, same tired faces at the check-in desks. I cover the floor of each room with handwritten notes, letters and photographs, phone and interview transcripts, emails, research papers, photocopies from books, financial and medical records, receipts, flyers, beer-mats, restaurant menus, post-it notes; a sea of information that grows greater and harder to control by the day. The contents of my mind, projected outward, expanding across the room like a virus.

I'm looking for the meaning between the lines, behind the words, the hidden connections, the points where competing truths converge; the prime narrative. It's just like reading a book, only it keeps changing and growing, faster than I can keep up with it, its ever-expanding borders pushing against the limits of my mind. Only I can do it, only I can contain it all. I can't break the connection for a second, I've got to live and breathe it, staying immersed in the world of the book, submerged beneath the text, from the time I wake up to the second I fall asleep. It needs to haunt my dreams, just as it haunts my every waking moment.

I must work alone.

Sam keeps calling. The publisher keeps calling. But I don't want anyone to know where I am. I need to focus on the work.

The pale, blue light of my laptop illuminates the darkened room continuously, an artificial sun that renders day and night meaningless. I monitor and watch the world online, disconnecting from the real, losing more and more time as space contracts around me.[295]

I'm never alone. I'm always alone.

I watch the painkillers tumble over and over until they dissolve into non-existence, until only a trace remains, but nothing is ever really lost – it just takes another form. I'm changing too, transitioning, but into what?

---

294. Wittgenstein, Ludwig, *Tractatus Logico-Philosophicus*, (1922), p.7

295. In *The Ecstasy of Communication* (1987), Jean Baudrillard writes about a disembodied, satellite man, isolated and cut off from human contact, having replaced physical interaction with virtual information, communication without community. Paul Virilio has also written about the erosion of spatiality caused by the instantaneous nature of 'tele-technology', laptops, smart phones etc, which have the effect of radically contracting space and time, leading to the disappearance of both, leaving the world experienced via simulation – Anonymous.

I can't sleep, so I head out every night, stalking the bars and clubs, sitting alone in darkened booths, drinking myself sober. *Ashes to Ashes*[296] starts to play. Its inverted opening chords call out to me, pulling me towards the dance floor until I'm at the centre of all those bodies, more poses than people, moving in slow motion around me, blank faces bathed in coloured light. They're not real. No one is. I dance with them anyway as Roxy Music's *Same Old Scene*[297] takes over from Bowie without missing a beat.

The women who appear in my room keep changing. Faces, places, names. I seek them out in every city, but each encounter makes me feel more alone. They flicker in and out of existence like glitches, just as the different rooms shift and merge into one another. Every room brings me nearer to the end, to the final room where all lines – all storylines – converge.

The closer I get to the book, to the truth, the more the world outside drifts away. I pull back the curtains and I can't tell where I am anymore. I could be anywhere, in any city in the world. Time and space collapsed to the size of the room. The four walls become my whole world, an extension of myself. I pull back the curtains and it's all gone, replaced by an infinite black void. There is no time here, not anymore.

I head out into the void in search of another drink, another club, another body, as time stands still and simultaneously slips away.

---

296. From David Bowie's 1980 album *Scary Monsters (And Super Creeps)*.

297. Written by Bryan Ferry for Roxy's 1980 album, *Flesh and Blood*.

Ezra Maas: An Oral History
Part Four

Artists, writers, journalists, photographers, critics, friends, and others, who were around Maas during the years 1956 to 1996, give their impressions of the artist. Interviews by Daniel James.

☆

Frederick Lavery, owner of the Four Square gallery in Bruges, Belgium, where Maas painted and exhibited in the late 1970s.

FL: Even when he was a young man, there was something ancient in his eyes, as if he had lived a lifetime in his youth.

☆

Terence Jones, award-winning cinematographer, producer, and filmmaker, who worked on films including Apocalypse Now, Mrs and Mrs McCabe, The French Connection, and The Conversation.

TJ: Film? I don't know, man. You'll have to be more specific. Maas made a lot of films, video installations, experimental pieces, that kind of thing. He had them playing on a loop at his exhibitions. Later, he moved into longer, more ambitious pieces. He liked to cast actors as real people and then he'd swap their roles around, so the scenes had an unreal, disjointed feel. A character would walk into a scene as one person and would leave as another. Nothing was permanent. Everything was interchangeable. Everyone was playing a role. "We're all somebody else". That was something he used to say. His films were more visual art than narrative-based, very experimental, but people went nuts for them, obsessing over each frame and the possible hidden meanings. You know, now you mention it, there was a story going around about one of his films. Apparently, whoever watched it was left so traumatised and disturbed they were physically sick – seizures, vomiting, insomnia, even bleeding through the skin. Other people supposedly suffered long-term, post-traumatic effects. Who knows how much of it was real? It was great PR. The Maas Foundation started to say that the film was just one of a series and that watching it would "change your reality". The official line was that the film was destroyed when they found out it was making people ill, but I heard that bootleg copies were made and exchanged by hardcore fans, who would watch it in groups as some sort of sick initiation ritual. I never saw the film myself. It was probably just an urban myth, but it's creepy, right? Is that the kind of thing you were after?

☆

Robert Mina, a West Coast music promoter who was based in LA in the 1970s.

RM: I heard he met with Kenneth Anger, the filmmaker and friend of Church of Satan Anton LeVey, and that he visited Charles Manson in prison. There was a lot of talk of black magic and occult practices at the time.

☆

Philip Macdonald, an LA-based photographer who encountered Maas in 1973.

PM: When I met him, his skin was grey and stretched over his face like a mask. He looked like a lifeless wraith. I heard he was living on a diet of heroin and milk.

☆

Lucy Lehane, a filmmaker who first met Maas in 1969.

LL: Maas had a certain style about him, like a 1950s heart-throb. His hair was dark and wavy, and he liked to wear white, muscle-fit t-shirts, and dark-denim, often paint splattered, when he was working in his studio. There was definitely a touch of Marlon Brando or James Dean about him. In later years, he grew a beard and let his hair grow fashionably long, making him look more like a woodsman than an artist.

☆

Rick Connelly, a painter from New York who was on the scene in 1966.

RC: Not everyone on the Greenwich Village scene was convinced by Maas at first. I heard quite a few people say things like, "who the hell does this kid think he is?" He was barely seventeen and there he was holding court, telling us what the future of art was going to be. Some people thought he was a cocky little upstart. They accused him of being a pathological liar because of the wild stories he would tell about his past, but for every person who felt this way, there were twenty more who adored him.

Ezra Maas
Chapter Five[298]

Everything not forbidden is compulsory[299]

Maas was at another crossroads but nothing was quite as it seemed. As ever, his life was surrounded by more questions than answers. Was he still in America as some believed? Had he been there the entire time he was supposedly in Oxford? Or had he genuinely returned to England to reconnect with the life he left behind? Was he in turmoil after the controversy with Oxford University, or was he building a new following on the West Coast of America? In many ways his exact location was unimportant. Maas was always exactly where he wanted to be. And he would soon make his presence felt on both sides of the Atlantic once more. First, he would make his way across Europe, living in cities such as Paris, Bruges, Amsterdam, Berlin, and Geneva, while creating some of his most famous artworks.

Maas set about reclaiming the artwork and belongings he had left behind when he ran away three years earlier. These were placed in the care of an exclusive private storage firm in London[300] while he planned his next move. Whether he had been at Oxford University or not, Maas is believed to have considered applying to another institution to undertake a doctorate in Fine Art, but ultimately decided he would rather learn practical skills by working directly with artists in Europe and America. He also felt his ambitions would be best served by having the freedom to travel to where the era's most prominent artists were working.

Maas initially reappeared in the Left Bank in Paris. He rented a room in the Latin Quarter, the same area where his uncle H.W. had once lived and near the hotel where Burroughs and Ginsberg had edited *Naked Lunch* into a complete manuscript a few years earlier. It was here that Maas is understood to have met the Irish playwright Samuel Beckett, whose work he greatly admired. Beckett had won the *Nobel Prize in Literature* the year before, an award described as a

---

298. This takes place after the 'missing' chapter Daniel wrote about Maas's twelve months at Oxford, which went into greater depth about his time at the University. Sadly, this chapter was destroyed and I have not been able to locate another copy. I have amended the numbering of the chapters for the sake of continuity. We continue the story here with Ezra Maas Chapter Five.

299. White, T.H., *The Once and Future King*.

300. Believed to be Merivale and Sweeney Ltd.

"catastrophe"[301] by his French-born wife Suzanne, and fame did not sit well with him. However, despite this, he did make himself available to other artists and scholars who sought him out, meeting them in the anonymous lobby of the Hotel PLM St Jacques near his Montparnasse home.[302] The pair allegedly met here several times during the 1970s and as one observer, the theatre producer Devin Kerr, noted it was very much a coming together of great minds:

"Friends of both men used to joke you could have sold ringside seats to their conversations, such was the artistic and intellectual gravity of their meetings, but they both had a sense of humour and a light-hearted side too... as well as a mutual taste for Bushmills."

The younger man reportedly found Beckett to be unexpectedly amiable and willing to discuss his work, despite being an intensely private person generally. Beckett was impressed with Maas's "pure intelligence and ability to comprehend new ideas and concepts instantaneously".[303] Maas would also meet the New York based writer and poet Paul Auster, a student at the time, who would go on to great success as a novelist in the 1980s.[304] Auster had also sought out Beckett after exchanging several letters with him in the early 1970s, and he would cross paths with Maas on more than one occasion in Europe and America, although the pair were reportedly never friends.[305] The painter Jacob Moorhouse said:

"Maas and Auster were perfectly pleasant to each other, but one sensed a certain rivalry between them, a tension, even if it never developed beyond a feeling, an atmosphere... to my knowledge it never went as far as a falling out, but they weren't really friends either... "[306]

Although Maas maintained a rented property, in Paris, he journeyed to other European cities regularly and would often spend two or three weeks at a time living elsewhere. During one of these trips Maas expressed an interest to friends in adopting a new style of drawing and painting, and travelled to Salzburg, Switzerland, to join Oskar Kokoschka's 'School of Seeing'.[307] Sadly, the Austrian-born expressionist was not taking on

301. Knowlson, James, *Damned to Fame: The Life of Samuel Beckett*, Bloomsbury, (1996)

302. See above.

303. According to Kerr.

304. Following the publication of *The Invention of Solitude* in 1981 and *The New York Trilogy* in 1985.

305. Interestingly, there is no mention of Maas in Auster's autobiography, *Hand to Mouth: A Chronicle of Early Failure*, which covers this period in detail.

306. Daniel interviewed Moorhouse in 2011.

307. When Oskar Kokoschka established his School of Seeing in 1953, he was not seeking

students at the time. Kokoschka,[308] who was not aware Maas had visited him, later expressed his regret and said that if he had known he would have happily reopened the school for the young artist.

Maas also considered accepting a place at The All-Union Institute of Cinematography in Moscow, having read and been influenced by books on Russian filmmakers such as Eisenstein and Pudovkin, but ultimately he chose to pursue his interest in filmmaking in the US, after receiving a grant from the American Film Institute in a deal that was a stark contrast to the big offers he had received from the New Hollywood crowd eighteen months earlier. Maas flew from Berlin to LA in order to negotiate the AFI deal, making a brief return to New York on the way to attend and show his support for George Harrison's Concert for Bangladesh, which featured the likes of Bob Dylan and Eric Clapton, among others. While in New York, Maas allegedly ended up getting drunk at *The Troubadour Club* with John Lennon and Harry Nilsson,[309] although the date of this infamous night-out is disputed.

Within two years Lennon and Maas were both named by the Nixon administration as potential candidates for deportation from the US, following the former Beatles' anti-Vietnam War protests, and comments attributed to Maas's followers about the President's alleged relationship with Satan. The case against both men was eventually dropped.[310] Maas had been linked to political activism from the late 1960s onwards but never publicly expressed his views.[311] Staying at The Sherry-Netherland Hotel,

---

to establish an academic art training course, but to create an open meeting-place where, after the spiritual devastation and barbarity of World War II, people of all races and creeds could gather to revive and cultivate humanist ideals. During the years 1953 – '63, Oscar Kokoschka's School of Seeing formed the nucleus of the International Summer Academy of Fine Arts. The number of students increased in those eleven summers from thirty in 1953 to over 250 in 1963. Kokoschka retired from the Summer Academy in 1963, and the School of Seeing was continued intermittently by his adepts.

308. Oskar Kokoschka (1886 – 1980) was an Austrian artist, poet, and playwright, best known for his intense expressionistic portraits and landscapes.

309. Although several sources argue this took place several years later in 1973, during Lennon's Lost Weekend period (his years split from Yoko Ono) and not during Maas's brief return to the US.

310. Lennon's immigration status was resolved by President Jimmy Carter in 1975, following Nixon's political demise in the Watergate scandal.

311. The protests Maas was linked to during these years included other anti-Vietnam War activism, a protest for James Hanratty who was hanged in Britain in 1962, work with the Chicago Seven including members and Yippie peace activists Jerry Rubin and Abbie Hoffman, alleged links to the International Marxist Group, the John Sinclair Freedom Rally, and other events. All of this was unconfirmed during the 1960s and '70s and later denied by The Maas

by Central Park, the artist also visited Harlem's Apollo Theatre, attended one of Norman Fisher's[312] famous parties, and found time to make a brief return to New York hotspot Max's Kansas City, where a young David Bowie was in attendance during his breakthrough years in America. It was allegedly here that Bowie met long-time friend and collaborator Iggy Pop for the first time. There is no evidence that Maas met the pair during this visit, but they would cross paths a few years later in Berlin.

Following Harrison's charity concert in New York there were also reports that Maas was approached by Maharishi Mahesh Yogi, who had gained international fame as guru to the Beatles in the 1960s before a much publicised 'falling out',[313] and who was also one of the founders of Transcendental Meditation. Maas was linked with TM for much of his life. While back in LA to agree terms with the AFI for the film project, Maas would reunite with some of the characters he had met in 1968. During a visit to LA nightclub Rodney's English Disco,[314] on Sunset Strip, he was also introduced to cocaine dealer and professional celebrity friend Freddy Sessler, a concentration camp survivor, who supplied the West Coast's biggest names with medicinal cocaine known as Merck. Depending on what stories you chose to believe Maas had indulged in every drug imaginable back in his New York days, in a bid to magnify his intelligence and expand his consciousness. As was always the way with Maas, however, this was only half of the story, with others claiming he never seriously took drugs and allowed the stories to develop purely to augment his dangerous image. Nevertheless, rumours of serious drug addiction would persist for the rest of his career. One onlooker from the early 1970s LA scene, who did not wish to be named, said:

"Maas's followers carried half ounce bags of cocaine around with them at all times… they were all in the grip of cocaine psychosis and extreme paranoia… skin transparent and teeth grey… lifeless wraiths who stayed awake for days at a time and who followed their leader around like ghosts… I heard that one of them ended up hospitalised in the neuropsychiatric institute at UCLA until Maas busted him out… Maas was the craziest, most brilliant of them all, oscillating between bouts of hyper energy where he was connected to everything and everyone and could do anything, and

Foundation.

312. Fisher was a stockbroker turned art collector renowned for his legendary, drug-fuelled parties.

313. Allegedly over an incident involving the actress Mia Farrow.

314. A notorious LA nightclub in the 1970s.

a fractured, dislocated existence where no one could reach him…"[315]

This is supported by a former member of the Maas Foundation who said the artist had knowingly embraced hard drugs as an experiment to test the impact on his art. They said:

"Maas embarked on a journey into the heart of darkness to create a new landscape for his art… he was pushing himself to his limits… trying to find out if he would break… and what, if anything, existed outside of himself."

After his brief return to America Maas would travel back to Europe for another extended period, where he would produce some of his greatest works, including the paintings *Lies Dead, Here with Her, Gravity, Salt Woman*, and *Entropy*, as well as the series of sculptures referred to as the *Montparnasse Collection*, the novel *Herringbone*, and the short film *Two Months*. But while the AFI were willing to provide him a grant of $10,000 to make a short film, Maas was reluctant to leave Europe.[316] A compromise was eventually reached with Maas making the film partly in America, using a US crew, but also filming in a number of other countries while he travelled. As luck would have it this would coincide with a unique invitation Maas had received from an old friend, the French oceanographer and filmmaker Jacques Cousteau.

---

315. As interviewed by Daniel in 2011 – 2012 for his LA Tapes.

316. One theory claims that Maas was overcoming his drug addiction in Europe and feared a return to America would lead to a relapse.

NEWS

.europenews.eu   Thursday, May 12, 2011

Journalist in coma after mystery fall

By Joanne Patterson,
Press Association (International)

A French investigative journalist is in a critical condition after being found unconscious outside her apartment following an apparent fall.

Ariane Beauvais, 29, a freelance reporter who works primarily in France and Belgium, was found in the early hours of Saturday morning outside her residence in the 14th arrondissement of Paris.

Her editor at *Le Monde*, Henri Jacques, took to social media after the news broke saying her fall was "no accident". The message has since been deleted and he has subsequently been unavailable for comment. Ms Beauvais is currently in a medically induced coma due to the severity of the head injuries she suffered in the fall. Paris police officials said her apartment was locked from the inside and they did not believe there was any criminal involvement. They are asking for witnesses to come forward, but they have stressed that they do not believe there was any foul play involved.

Ms Beauvais is a freelance investigative journalist who has had work published in the likes of *Le Monde, The Guardian, Süddeutsche Zeitung, SonntagsZeitung, Falter,* and *La Nación.* Her journalism focuses on conflict, corruption, and human rights transgressions, and she regularly works with international organisations such as the International Consortium of Investigative Journalists (ICIJ).

Last year, Ms Beauvais is believed to have been one of the international journalists who worked on the Cablegate leak.[316] She has been nominated for three French Press Awards, an IWMF Courage in Journalism award, and in 2009 she was a finalist in the Bayeux Calvados-Normandy award. These awards were created to acknowledge the work of war correspondents reporting about a conflict situation and its impact on civilians, and for news stories involving the defence of freedom and democracy.

*I won't stop until I know the truth, Ariane.
I promise.*

---

316. The United States diplomatic cables leak led by WikiLeaks in 2010.

Daniel James
Chapter Twelve

Many positions are inhabited relative to a line of inquiry.[318]

Dressed in my usual dark grey suit and black shirt, I stepped out of the Georgian hotel onto an elegant Bloomsbury crescent, lined with trees and wrought iron fences, and headed towards Euston. I had pulled myself together again, just enough to step back into my old role once more, pretending everything was fine and that I was still in control of the narrative; but in truth nothing felt the same anymore. I was running out of time, out of allies, out of options. My next move would only work if I could fake my former confidence. I just hoped Wallas wouldn't see the desperation just below the surface.

I found him leaning against the bar, his tan fedora next to him, weary eyes turned down toward a pint of Imperial Russian Stout. He looked like an old Ernest Hemingway with his broad frame and barrel chest stuffed into a baggy, ill-fitting tan suit, his white beard as unruly as a sea captain's. I cast my eyes over the rows of bottles in the brushed steel refrigerators as I walked over to the bar and placed a dog-eared copy of Beckett's *Trilogy*[319] down beside him.

'What was it that Beckett said to Auster when they met in Paris in the '70s?' I said. 'No eyes in the world are harder to catch than a barman's'?[320]

'You,' was all that Wallas said, without looking up.

'Me... How's life, George?'

'Too busy to be waiting for you,' he growled.

'You should be used to me being late, by now,' I replied. 'And I told you I'd return your book eventually.'

'Only took you seven years.'

'Thanks for coming.'

'I'm here for the drinks.'

'I noticed.'

I looked down at the empty bottles lining the wooden bar-top and glanced up at the chalk board listing today's selection as I gestured at the

---

318. Poet, essayist and playwright Claudia Rankine (1963-)

319. *Three Novels: Molloy, Malone Dies,* and *The Unnamable,* Grove Press, London, (1972).

320. As recounted by Paul Auster in James and Elizabeth Knowlson's book *'Remembering Beckett, Beckett Remembering: Uncollected Interviews and Memories of Those Who Knew Him'*, Bloomsbury, (2006).

barman.

'A pint of Rogue Dead Guy for my friend here and a double Rittenhouse on the rocks for me, please.'

'I notice things too,' Wallas said. 'Like how much time you've been spending in London these past few years.'

'What can I say, it's grown on me.'

'And the stories I keep hearing about you? How many of them are true?'

'Less than I would like,' I laughed, hoping it didn't sound as empty as it felt. 'Besides, a story can't be true by its very nature, can it?'

'If I was half the journalist I used to be, I might question what you're running away from.'

'I just go where the stories are, like I always have.'

'It must be hard being away from your family up in Newcastle though?[321] They must miss you. Why can't you go home, Dan?'

'This isn't about me, George,' I said. 'We've all got our secrets. You of all people should know that.'

'Here we go. I was waiting for the threats to start.'

I looked past him at the emerald-green tiles and taps set into the copper-clad back bar, trying to find a smile.

'Don't be like that,' I said, trying to keep my tone light. 'Can't we just pretend this is a case of one friend helping out another?'

'We're friends now, are we?' He laughed bitterly. 'So I could say 'no' to whatever it is you're about to ask me?'

'And why would you want to do that? I'm just looking for the truth.'

'About what?'

'Ezra Maas.'

'So it's true then. You are writing a biography.'

'I don't know what it is yet. It's shapeless at the moment, undefined. You know how it is. Sometimes you can't see what the story is until after you've written it. Right now, I don't even know if there is a story. It's everywhere I look and nowhere.'

'I hope you don't expect me to help you?'

'Help? No... but there's something you can get for me, something I

---

321. This is one of several references to Daniel potentially having a family in Newcastle. Elsewhere in the text it is implied that he may have been married before, and perhaps even had children. However, despite my attempts to find out the truth about this, all I discovered was hearsay and rumour. A friend of Daniel's, who did not want to be named, and whose credibility may be questioned, told me that: "The relationship ended so badly it left him irreparably damaged; broken. He never got over it and was haunted by what happened. The move to London was less about making a fresh start and more about freefalling into self-destruction. It was suicide in slow motion."

need.'

'What makes you think I have anything?'

'You have resources, George,' I replied. 'Connections. I need you to use them.'

Wallas took a sip from his pint. It was a deep honey-coloured German-style Maibock beer.

'I'm listening,' he said.

'A freelance scumbag you might have heard of, called Jason Fisher, is currently shopping around a film he managed to procure from an art collector in LA. He's right here in London. I just don't know where.'

'You want me to find him for you?'

'You know the London press inside out, George. You know where information is bought and sold, and every angle, legal and illegal. I'm not asking you to hack the PM's voicemail here. I just want you to make contact with Fisher and put an offer in for the film. I'll front the money, but I need you to make the deal.'

'Why not just buy it yourself?'

'I don't want to show my hand,' I replied. 'Not yet. Every move I make is being watched, and if the film is what I think it is, I want to be one step ahead for a change.'

'Do you know how much trouble I could get into if this came out? Leveson[322] is breathing down all our necks. London's not the Wild West anymore, Dan. The industry's changing for good.'

'I want that film, George.'

'This is about Maas, isn't it? What the hell's on this film?'

'You don't need to know. Just get it for me, okay?'

'And if I refuse?'

I knocked back the last of the Rittenhouse and placed the tumbler down on the bar.

'This story can end one of two ways, George. Think it over, and ask yourself, do I really have a choice?' I patted him on the shoulder as I walked out, leaving him alone with my words.

I can't tell you if I felt guilty for threatening George, as I stepped out onto Euston Road into a blur of light and noise, because I can't remember. It's how I should have felt, how I would feel now, if I could feel anything anymore, but at the time, as I turned back to look at the Portland stone

---

322. The Leveson inquiry was a public inquiry into the culture, practices, and ethics, of the British press following the News International phone-hacking scandal, chaired by Lord Justice Leveson, who was appointed in July 2011. A series of public hearings were held throughout 2011 and 2012.

building framed by floodlights against the growing darkness, all I was thinking about was the truth. I didn't second guess my decision not to tell Wallas the full story. I didn't ask myself whether I should have told him to watch his back and warned him that people had already died because of this film. The truth is, I didn't give George another thought that night, other than to consider how long it would take for him to get his hands on the footage. Maybe I would have if I had known that was the last time I would see him alive.

Ezra Maas: An Oral History
Part Five

Artists, writers, journalists, photographers, critics, friends, and others, who were around Maas during the years 1956 to 1996, give their impressions of the artist. Interviews by Daniel James.

☆

Aldous Lee, a sound technician who worked with Maas on a series of films between 1969 – 1974.

AL: He was a perfectionist, but when it came to directing films Maas always did it in one take. We used to have a saying on set, only God and Ezra Maas never revised their work.

☆

Francois Lönnrot, Fashion designer and friend of Helena Maas in the 1980s and early 1990s

FL: Every great man needs a greater woman. In my opinion, Helena Maas was the truly special one in that relationship. She was incredibly intelligent and a very savvy businesswoman, well connected, charming and physically striking – a real force of nature, basically. In my opinion, her only flaw was her love for Ezra Maas. It was blind, adoring, insane, love and she devoted every ounce of her ruthless ambition to fulfilling his dreams.

☆

Sue Gently, a model who worked with Maas in Switzerland from 1971 onwards.

SS: I worked with him throughout the '70s, but I never saw him in person again after the accident in '82. But he would often call me late at night, though, and we would talk at length about different things. He never said hello or introduced himself, he would just start talking in a kind of whisper. Sometimes I'd wake up the next day and I wouldn't be sure if I hadn't dreamt the whole thing. A mutual friend once told me that Maas recorded all of his phone conversations and edited them into artworks, but I don't know if this was true.

☆

Dr Felicity Stillman, Research Fellow in European Cultural History.

FS: There are many stories about Maas's years living in Paris. It was a city he returned to many times over the years. As a young artist he was drawn to Montmartre, following in the footsteps of Monet, Renoir, Picasso, and Van Gogh. Later, he could be found exploring the cafes, bars, and restaurants of the Left Bank, Montparnasse, and the Latin Quarter, where he lived and worked, conversing with the ghosts of writers, intellectuals, and philosophers along the Boulevard du Montparnasse. Very soon he was creating his own Paris stories, his own myths, imprinting himself on the city to such an extent that, even after he was gone, his presence could still be felt, such was the power of his legacy.

☆

Barbara Allingham, co-editor of The Third Eye and expert on cults, conspiracies and transhumanism.

BA: There were a lot of rumours that Maas and Pynchon used the same German firm, Nu Gesicht[323], to manufacture custom-moulded, high-end, facial prostheses, which they could use to disguise their identities in public. Pynchon told *The Paris Review* as much in an interview, but of course it sounded too absurd to be true. And yet, the company does exist. I found them. Would you like to see one of their masks?

☆

Jack Hiaasen, a film director and known pornographer, who spent time with Maas in LA in 1973 – '74.

JH: I remember him driving around LA in shades and a hoodie, from Doheny Drive all the way to Beverley Hills, totally coked out of his mind. This was

---

323. I appreciate this is a company name but in correct German, it should be Neues Gesicht (new face) - Anonymous

during his period hanging out with Dennis Hopper and Dean Stockwell, sometimes David Bowie and Iggy Pop, too. Maas was completely dissociated from reality. We all were, but Maas was your classic, isolated narcissist, wrapped up in crazed fantasies where he was the centre of the universe. The only difference with Maas was that he may have been right.

Ezra Maas
Chapter Six

Then felt I like some watcher of the skies / When a new planet swims into his ken.[324]

In the early 1970s, Maas was invited to join Jacques Cousteau aboard his research vessel RV *Calypso*[325] as artist-in-residence. There are various theories about how Maas and Cousteau began their unusual association. As a teenager Maas had written a news article (which he had submitted to the local paper in Oxford) praising Cousteau's work to prevent a large amount of radioactive waste being deposited in the Mediterranean Sea by the Commissariat á l'Énergie Atomique (CEA). One story suggested this article had come to the attention of the oceanographer, who had followed Maas's career ever since and eventually got in touch to arrange a meeting.

Another source claimed it was Maas who sought out Cousteau at the Oceanographical Museum of Monaco, as he was a fan of his 1956 film *The Silent World*[326] and hoped to learn from the oceanographer before he embarked on his own film project. Finally, a third, and different explanation again, suggests the connection began when Maas was mixing with Hollywood's power players after he moved briefly to the West Coast in 1967 – '68. This theory claims that it was Maas's idea to blur fact and fiction in the life of Cousteau and turn his world into a television show, *The Underwater Odyssey of Commander Cousteau*, and it was this that led to their ongoing working relationship.[327] A more sinister explanation for their association even involved the CIA.[328]

---

324. Keats, John.

325. A former Royal Navy minesweeper, *RV Calypso*, was named after the nymph from classical mythology and leased to Cousteau for the symbolic figure of one Franc a year by its owner, the Irish millionaire and former MP, Thomas Loel Guinness, allegedly on the condition that he never revealed the arrangement to the public. Cousteau kept his end of the bargain and the identity of Calypso's owner was only revealed after the oceanographer's death in 1997. This came just twelve months after Calypso was accidentally rammed and sunk, in the port of Singapore.

326. Winner of the Palme d'Or at the Cannes Film Festival in 1956 and based on the book *The Silent World: A Story of Undersea Discovery and Adventure.*

327. There is little evidence to support this claim and the dates don't entirely align – Anonymous.

328. In the 1970s, deep sea ocean mining seemed close to becoming a reality after a number of engineering companies invested heavily in technology to explore the depths and recover highly-valued manganese rocks located on the sea bed. The most famous of this new wave of deep sea pioneers was a ship named *The Hughes Glomar Explorer*, which was ostensibly owned

Whatever the origins of their friendship, Maas is known to have travelled with Cousteau on and off in the early 1970s,[329] becoming the *Calypso's* unofficial artist-in-residence during expeditions to Crete, the Straits of Gibraltar, and Tagus river near Lisbon, as well as several other locations. The collaboration was relatively short-lived, but saw Maas produce several award-winning new pieces, allegedly conceived on the deck of *Calypso*, as well as two books' worth of sketches and paintings of sea life and the natural world. The Maas Foundation later claimed the entire expedition was a new kind of artwork, combining performance with land art. Maas was essentially performing himself and transformed the landscape he travelled to with his presence.[330]

Maas's presence is understood to have caused tension with Cousteau's son and designated successor, Phillipe, and Calypso's second-in-command, Michel Lavel. However, reports of his behaviour on board vary widely. One former crew member said:

"Maas only spoke to the Commander. The rest of us were invisible. He spent his time sketching, writing, or taking photographs. You could feel his intensity as an artist… It was like he was surrounded by an impenetrable sphere created by his own thoughts, and no one and nothing could reach him… In addition, he was constantly surrounded by sycophants and assistants who prevented anyone from getting close to him."[331]

This account is in stark contrast to another former crew member's

---

by eccentric billionaire Howard Hughes. However the entire $500m project was an audacious cover story concocted by the CIA, whose real target was a sunken Russian sub and its payload of nuclear missiles, which had sank near Hawaii in 1968. The hugely expensive operation was ultimately a failure and the whole truth did not emerge until years later. Given Maas's alleged association with the CIA, dating back to the mid-'60s, some have suggested that the somewhat unlikely story of his year sailing the globe with Cousteau was actually an elaborate cover for covert operations of a similar nature – potentially a precursor to the infamous *Glomar Explorer*.

329. From 1972 – 1975, allegedly.

330. It was also suggested that he created physical 'earthwork' installations in the land and sea in the locations he travelled to with Cousteau, in the style of Robert Smithson's *Spiral Jetty*. Interestingly Smithson's piece of iconic land art was funded by former Maas contact, art dealer and heiress Virginia Dwan. Coincidence? There were also rumours Maas had created several land art sculptures at secret locations across the United States in the 1970s, with the exact coordinates located in hidden messages within his other artworks. In 2012, American writer Samuel M Moss, while travelling across the US in his van on a project to make sound recordings at famous land art locations, accidentally discovered what is now believed to be one of Maas's lost works after being confronted by a group of the artist's followers who were gathered at the site, awaiting a sign. According to accounts, whatever Maas had buried in the ground had been causing 'abberations' among plant and animal life, and 'strange' behaviour in the local community, for the last three decades. – Anonymous.

331. From an interview conducted by Daniel in 2011.

description of Maas's time on the *Calypso*: "My enduring memory of him would be sitting drinking cocktails with the female interns in a warm volcanic bath at Port Foster. That was Maas all over. He was unpretentious and pitched in with the crew like he was one of us… I didn't see him create a great deal of art while he was on-board, but he seemed to be enjoying a break from the pressures of his other life…"[332]

Maas joined Cousteau on several expeditions, including a trip to Deception Island[333] off the Antarctic Peninsula, in 1973. This was just three years after the last violent volcanic eruption on Deception Island, which had laid waste to the former British and Chilean bases and rendered much of the island inhospitable. Maas is known to have gone on several underwater expeditions in the *Calypso's* one and two-man submarines with Cousteau, and was reportedly fascinated by the "dark, silent beauty of the world beneath the sea"..[334]

By 1974 – '75, Maas had parted company from Cousteau, amicably on the surface of it, although there were rumours of an argument leading to the split, with one witness claiming "*Calypso* hadn't been big enough for both their egos".[335] The following year Maas is understood to have rented a chalet in north Geneva, reportedly immersing himself in classical music, art, literature, and a fitness regime inspired by Swiss Olympic athletes to "rid himself of the negativity of the previous months".[336] From Geneva, he would journey back and forth to Berlin to work and visit the museums. After one late night drinking in the city, and having missed his train back to Geneva, Maas allegedly met Iggy Pop and David Bowie, who were living together at the time in an apartment in Schöneberg.[337]

Bowie was allegedly recovering from a serious and debilitating

---

332. See above.

333. Deception Island is an island in South Shetland, off the Antarctic Peninsula, which has one of the safest harbours in Antarctica. The island is the caldera of an active volcano, which caused serious damage to the local scientific stations in 1967 and 1969. The island previously held a whaling station and is now a tourist destination and scientific outpost, with research bases run by Argentina and Spain. Since the early 19th century Deception Island was a favourite refuge area from the storms and icebergs of Antarctica. Deception Island has become a popular tourist stop in Antarctica because of its several colonies of chinstrap penguins, as well as the novel possibility of making a warm bath by digging into the sands of the beach.

334. The Maas Journals. Vol 3. 1970 – '75.

335. This is mentioned in passing in a letter from former crew member Francois Mormeck to The Cousteau Society, dated July 1975.

336. The Maas Journals. Vol 3. 1970 – '75.

337. In South West Berlin.

addiction to cocaine,[338] which had left him "dissociated from reality" by his own admission and was on the verge of creating his classic Berlin Trilogy of albums.[339] The pair reportedly had a long conversation about the importance of 'continual reinvention' in art and their mutual interest in inhabiting different personas and constructing fictional worlds.[340] Alex Marx, a musician, producer, and long-time collaborator with Brian Eno, worked with Bowie in the late 1970s and said:

"It wasn't commonly known, but they kept in touch for many years after this chance meeting… in many ways they were similar characters… they had both emerged as precocious talents in the late '60s, they had allegedly both lost themselves in drug addiction and fictional 'stage personas', and they were both hyper-intelligent, creative personalities… the main difference was that David's alter-egos, Ziggy Stardust, Aladdin Sane, and The Thin White Duke[341] were visible, whereas Maas's were internal…"[342]

Maas decided to stay on in Berlin with Bowie and Iggy Pop, booking himself into the Schlosshotel Gerhus, a magnificent, decaying building once owned by art collector Walter Graf von Pannwitz. The artist explored the divided city by day and the cabaret and drag clubs by night, accompanied by Bowie and his friends. Maas returned to London a short time later to show support for his old friend R.B. Kitaj,[343] who had been selected for an exhibition for The Arts Council at the Hayward Gallery. This was entitled *The Human Clay*, an allusion to a line by the poet W.H. Auden, and featured work by forty-eight London artists whom Kitaj dubbed the 'School of London' in the exhibition's controversial catalogue. One of those artists, Lucien Grey, remarked:

"I would definitely say they gravitated around overlapping preoccupations as artists… Kitaj felt an affinity with the sense of estrangement and hidden

---

338. Bowie was described as suffering from 'severe physical debilitation, paranoia and emotional problems. He was quoted as saying: "I went out of my mind… I was totally crazed."

339. *Low* (1977), *Heroes* (1978) and *Lodger* (1979).

340. Bowie biographer Christopher Sandford also notes their similar feelings about America being: "… simultaneously appalled and fixated by it… "

341. Other personas included Major Tom, and the lesser known Arnold Corns.

342. Marx was interviewed by Daniel in 2011.

343. Kitaj had a major influence on pop art and was considered to be one of the world's leading draftsmen. His complex compositions built on his line work using a montage practice, which he called 'agitational usage'. Kitaj often depicted disorienting landscapes and impossible 3D constructions, with exaggerated and pliable human forms, assuming a detached outsider point of view in conflict with dominant historical narratives. This is arguably best portrayed by his masterpiece *The Autumn of Central Paris* (1972 – '73), wherein philosopher Walter Benjamin is portrayed as both the orchestrator and victim of historical madness.

mysteries within the work of Franz Kafka, who Maas also loved... Kitaj was very interested in the idea of inventing characters and personalities in his work, just as novelists did... they were also linked by their meditations on the hidden face of God..."[344]

Kitaj, who had first met Maas in Oxford when he was just nine years old, had been teaching at Berkeley in California when Ezra arrived on the West Coast in 1967, and the pair had rekindled their friendship then. They kept in touch over the years and Maas secretly attended a number of his shows.[345] Allegedly Maas's favourite work by Kitaj was the painting *Smyrna Greek (Nikos)* from 1976 – '77, which has an extremely interesting story behind it[346] that hints at many of their overlapping preoccupations as artists. In a revealing quote, Kitaj once said of the painting:

"I like the idea that it might be possible to invent a figure, a character, in a picture the way novelists have been able to do..."[347]

Maas apparently wrote a fictional response to this painting in the form of a short story but this has sadly been lost.[348] Maas continued to spend much of his time developing experimental filmmaking techniques at the time and was still to deliver a finished film to the AFI in exchange for their grant several years earlier. He travelled back to Los Angeles briefly, spending time at the AFI conservatory, which he reportedly described to friends as 'chaotic but brilliant'.[349] This echoed the words of David Lynch, another former student at the AFI conservatory, who said: "It was completely disorganised... it was great. They wanted to let people do their thing."[350]

---

344. Grey made the comments in an interview with *The Insider* magazine, in 2009.

345. This allegedly included the exhibitions at Hirshhorn Museum, Washington D.C, National Gallery, London, Metropolitan Museum of Art, New York, and the Los Angeles County Museum.

346. R.B. Kitaj gave a brief explanation of *Smyrna Greek (Nikos)* in the catalogue of his exhibition at the Tate Gallery in London, in 1994: "This portrait of my friend Nikos Stangos was inspired by his fellow Greek poet Cavafy, who described his daily walk past the brothels in the port of Alexandria. I had just returned to London from my only trip to Greece, which lasted very few days, and, while he posed for me in that walking position, I told Nikos about my bizarre and unconsummated wandering down the port of Piraeus, as if in imitation of Cavafy. So the painting is about the two poets and me."

347. As quoted on www.museothyssen.org

348. Daniel's handwritten notes suggest the story may be in The Maas Foundation archive.

349. The Maas Journals. Vol. 4, 1975 – '80.

350. David Lynch. As quoted by Christopher Rodley in *Lynch on Lynch*.

The AFI funded project, *Gardenback,*[351] a terrifying ninety-minute montage of 'visual static' concealing hidden figures and subliminal messages, was finally finished in 1977 – '78 and had a limited release, but unsurprisingly became a cult favourite on the 'Midnight Movie' circuit. It was later described as one of the most influential 'midnight movies' of the 1970s alongside the likes of *El Topo, Pink Flamingos, The Rocky Horror Picture Show, Night of the Living Dead* and *Eraserhead*.

From here, Maas returned to New York and reunited with the writer William Burroughs, who was living in the Lower East Side of Manhattan in a basement apartment he affectionately referred to as 'The Bunker'. Maas also mixed with notable New York art scene personalities such as his old friend and rival Andy Warhol, and others such as John Giorno, Lou Reed, Patti Smith, and Susan Sontag. In the years since he had last lived in New York, Maas found a vibrant alternative community developing on the city's streets, the subways, bars, clubs, and alternative spaces beyond the reach of the gallery and museum system. Inspired by the energy of a new generation of artists, and with a renewed interest in public and participatory art, Maas would allegedly take to the streets himself, his identity concealed, in a return to the guerrilla art he and his followers disseminated in the previous decade. Public spaces on which he chose to create new work included unused advertising panels on the New York subway system. These commercial spaces were hijacked as makeshift canvasses for art that was a throwback to Maas's subversive, anti-establishment, 1960s content.

In his work during this period, from 1978 – 1980, Maas can be seen to have anticipated the work of American street artists such as Keith Haring and Jean-Michel Basquiat,[352] and later artists such as Shepard Fairey, the

---

351. I have been unable to track down a copy of the film and it is notable for its absence from books about film and cinema during this period – Anonymous.

352. Haring, who came to New York as a student at the School of Visual Arts (SVA), used the subway as a 'laboratory' for his rapidly produced artwork – chalk drawings on black paper pasted over expired billboards. He was extremely prolific, producing up to forty artworks a day, and reportedly created hundreds of subway artworks, featuring social messages, between 1980 and 1985. Basquiat had a number of interesting similarities to Maas, which hadn't occurred to me until editing Daniel's book. These parallels might not immediately be apparent given the obvious and significant differences between the two men. Basquiat had a short, dynamic, career spanning less than a decade, which ended abruptly when he died from a heroin overdose in 1988, whereas Maas's career spanned over five decades. However, like Maas, Basquiat had been a talented child, his mother enrolling him as a member of the Brooklyn Museum when he was six, and he was also tri-lingual from a young age, speaking French, Spanish, and English. He first became famous as a teenage graffiti poet and by the age of twenty was selling paintings in Soho galleries. Basquiat also knew family tragedy; his father was abusive and his mother suffered from mental health issues.

UK's 'Banksy', and many others. Maas's orbit would regularly intersect with Haring and Basquiat during this period and throughout the next decade, the artists sharing a number of common friends in the art and culture world. These included several of Maas's old acquaintances such as William Burroughs and Andy Warhol, the latter becoming a mentor to the young street artists Haring and Basquiat, while Maas reportedly kept more of a distance (as was his style). By the end of the decade, Haring, Basquiat, and Warhol would all be dead. Only Maas would remain.

Maas kept his return to New York short and largely secret for several reasons. One of these is believed to have been due to the continued activity of his followers in the city. The cult following that had developed around his work was still present and reportedly more extreme than ever. By now, however, their fanaticism was more insidiously concealed by legitimate business enterprises such as self-help and meditation groups, creative writing and art schools, and pseudo-scientific organisations, which were effectively 'fronts' for their work. If Maas's critics and detractors could be believed, he was behind all this activity. One source, who did not want to be named, claimed:

"Maas received daily telex messages from these groups and between $10,000 and $15,000 dollars was sent to him every week... this had been going on since at least 1970 and it was estimated he had millions of dollars in accounts in Switzerland and Liechtenstein..."[353]

Maas's friends dismissed such allegations as "ludicrous" and "conspiracy theories", stating that his only wealth came from the sale of his art, which by the end of the 1970s was being bought and sold for prices ranging from $30,000 to $1.1m, making him one of the richest living artists at the time. Either way the artist left America again and used some of his growing wealth to purchase Gorhambury Manor in the Hertfordshire countryside, which he set about converting into a studio-home where he could live and work simultaneously "like a medieval craftsman".[354] His desire for solitude would soon be disrupted for a time, however. A woman by the name of Helena Huston was about to walk into his life, and the future Mrs Maas had her own ideas for the direction it should take.

353. From an interview Daniel conducted in 2011.

354. See above.

PHONE TRANSCRIPT (UNRELEASED)

00:53 4/10/11 - George Wallas - Daniel James

BEEP

GW: Dan, pick up the fucking phone. It's Wallas. Call me back.

BEEP

GW: Where are you? Fucking hell. There's someone following me. I've tried to lose them, but I can't. I think they're watching my house. What the hell have you got me into?

BEEP

GW: Dan, if you get this, I'm going to my office. Not the newspaper, the other place, you know where. Meet me there as soon as you get this. I've got the film.

BEEP
… … … … … … …

END

Daniel James
Chapter Thirteen

The past is altered by the present as much as the present is directed by the past[355]

The light flickered, the projector whirred, and the image flooded the room. The work of Ezra Maas, from floor to ceiling, colouring everything, the four walls that had become my world. The film that Wallas had intercepted[356] left me changed. Even when the projector had powered down, and the yellow light had dimmed, the images kept playing in my mind, over and over again. I felt like I was undergoing a transfusion. Another life was flowing into my veins; opening my eyes to a new way of seeing the world. It was only after I had watched the footage a dozen times that I saw the code and uncovered the hidden message that would lead me to the oldest bank in London.[357] I didn't know what to expect as I turned the safety deposit box over in my hands. The smooth, brushed steel was cold beneath my palms,   but as I reached for the lid I felt an overwhelming sense of unease. I almost set it back down without opening it,   but I hadn't come this far to turn back now.

For a second it looked empty but thankfully it wasn't. Inside was a deed of warranty, apparently signed by Maas himself, which gave the bearer access to a property in Soho. There was also a letter handwritten in spidery ink and a set of keys that slid along the smooth steel and into my hand. I couldn't remember leaving the bank. The journey to Soho was a blur. My next memory was simply standing outside the building in the dark, the rain soaking me through. I looked down at the handwritten address. The words seemed to be alive. It took me a second to realise it was the rain. I watched as the ink ran like tears, spilling off the edges of the paper as if it were trying to escape the words it had once formed, until the address was illegible and the note fell apart in my hands, until the tips of my fingers were stained black.

I climbed the steps and heard the door unlock automatically as I approached. Someone was obviously watching. Inside the dimly lit foyer a

---

355. T.S Eliot.

356. Daniel does not provide any further information about how he got the film from Wallas for reasons that become apparent later in the text – Anonymous.

357. C. Hoare & Co, founded in 1672 by Sir Richard Hoare, is the oldest owned privately-owned banking house in England. Maas kept a safety deposit box here.

security guard[358] sat expressionless at a desk. I looked around. There was a lift behind him and a doorway leading to a stairwell. The guard glanced up, as if he had been expecting me, and asked to see my identification. When I showed him the letter signed by Maas he told me to take the elevator to the sixth floor. I stepped inside the mirrored compartment, surrounded by my own reflections, and pressed the button to go up. The doors opened to darkness, and for a second I wondered if I was on the wrong floor, but as I stepped out into the hallway a light flickered on then off again, revealing a gold number six on the wall. I looked around as the lift doors closed behind me.

The sixth floor was expensively decorated, with crimson wallpaper, ebony furniture, and modern art on the walls, but it looked like no one had been up here for a long time. The air was stale, heavy black curtains were drawn across the only window, and there was a layer of dust over everything. I walked towards a solitary door at the far end of the hall, the lamps overhead continuing to flicker, alternating between stark, merciless, light and deepest black. There was a steady drone   coming through the walls, like the rumble of a train or a ship's engine deep within the foundations of the building. I knocked on the door, but I didn't expect anyone to answer. Judging from the solitary footprints I had tracked in the dust, as I walked from the elevator to the apartment, it had been some time since anyone had visited apartment 601. After a moment of silence, I slipped the key from the safety deposit box into the lock and opened the door.

---

358. Daniel's handwritten notes provided an expanded version of his conversation with the security guard. Removing the dialogue from this scene appears to have been a conscious decision by Daniel to reflect the dreamlike nature of his discovery of the apartment. Daniel wrote: "The guard had no idea who owned the building. He simply had instructions to prevent anyone from entering unless they were carrying a signed deed of warranty. The guard had worked here for two years and rotated his shift with two others. They had often speculated who owned the building and thought it might have been a Hollywood actor or a famous musician, after all Paul McCartney had an office just around the corner, but none of them had ever seen anyone and no one had ever tried to get into the building in the years they had worked there as security. This was as far as their curiosity extended. They were paid not to ask questions. As I left him he called after me, his face uncertain, and said "Was this a test?". I nodded, the only thing I could think to do, and stepped into the lift."

DJ: I feel like an idiot talking into my phone, but I need to document this, just in case anything happens. I'm going to pretend you're a person, okay? Would Diane be too obvious?[360] How about Bob, instead?[361] Okay Bob, I've found something extraordinary… an apartment in Soho[362] owned by Maas… but it's much more than that. I think this is where he's been coming all these years. While the eyes of the world were watching his mansion and studios, his galleries, his homes around the world, all those remote, isolated locations he had supposedly retreated to, all that time, he had been coming here, to an apartment in one of the biggest cities in the world, the streets outside teeming with life, people living either side of him, above him, and below. Here he was, hiding in plain sight. This was his real workspace. No phone, no TV, no distractions. Just a cavernous apartment, filled with barely furnished rooms, curtains drawn, bookshelves from floor to ceiling, hardly any light… dirt and dust on everything… there are hundreds of notepads and sheets of paper, canvasses, a typewriter, old computer equipment, and a bed. I've been here for five or six hours and I've barely scratched the surface. None of the light bulbs

---

359. These recordings were made on Daniel's phone and later transcribed. I initially believed he had used a Dictaphone, but it may have been using the voice memo function on his mobile phone.

360. I presume this is a reference to *Twin Peaks,* and the Diane that Special Agent Dale Cooper dictates his FBI reports to, during the show.

361. See above. Bob was one of the show's primary antagonists.

362. Although no one would have guessed Maas had been working in secret in the centre of London, the choice of Soho as the location of his studio is perhaps not surprising when you consider the area's cultural history. Of all the stories surrounding it, the one I like to think influenced Maas the most is Dr Jekyll setting up a home for his alter-ago Edward Hyde in Soho, in Robert Louis Stevenson's classic book. There are lots of other interesting stories from Soho's history, too. Its former residents include Mozart, Karl Marx (the Communist Manifesto was actually written in Great Windmill Street, Soho), Eric Clapton, and The Sex Pistols. Soho has strong links to the music scene. In the 1940s Soho's Club Eleven was the heart of the UK jazz scene, the 1950s saw Europe's first rock club open on Old Compton Street, in 1962 The Rolling Stones played their first gig at the Marquee Club on Wardour Street, and Elton John wrote *Your Song* in Denmark Street. While Soho may be famous for its notorious red-light district, it is also well known for its late-night coffee shops and cafes and today is one of the key locations for the entertainment industry, with both Paul McCartney and the British Board of Film Classification having premises there. Whether by chance or design, Maas's decision to place himself here, in the centre of all this cultural history, hiding in plain sight, is an interesting one – Anonymous.

seem to be working and it's been difficult to explore in the dark. I'm going to sleep here tonight and spend all day tomorrow going through his books and belongings. I have to take this opportunity while I have the chance. There's no telling when The Maas Foundation or someone else might turn up.

In the end I didn't sleep. I couldn't. Not after everything I had found. It was like finding the keys to Da Vinci's hidden studio,[363] or Dylan's long-rumoured archives.[364] Every inch of this place was filled with secrets. Even the walls themselves were covered in handwritten notes, sketches, and complex mathematical equations. Others had been transformed into large scale artworks. The figure of a man had been drawn across one wall, so large that it continued onto the ceiling and hung over the room like the outline of an enormous shadow. The man was illustrated in the style of a Victorian medical textbook, its graphic detail both horrifying and beautiful, clinical in its precision, but Maas had also introduced a surreal poetry to the visual, the veins and tributaries bursting forth, extending beyond the outline of the body, branching out into the space of the room like flowering vines. There was mould growing up the wall over the sketch, merging with the brickwork and threading itself around the leg of the man. Intentional or not, it had become a living artwork.

Beneath the furniture covered in sheets there were hundreds of books and manuscripts, many with important passages underlined, thousands of pages of notes about his most famous artworks, dozens of unpublished notepads and sketches, old desktop computers, unfinished sculptures and paintings, literary papers, reviews and correspondence he had written, film

---

363. Or the Unabomber's cabin? When I first read Daniel's description of Maas's apartment, I was reminded of news reports about the discovery of Ted Kaczynski's cabin in the woods near Lincoln, Montana, after his arrest by the FBI following his twenty year bombing campaign. Kaczynski, a former mathematics prodigy, had turned his back on academia and disappeared, in 1969. He spent the next two decades living in his cabin, writing his manifesto and planning his bombing campaign which would kill three and injure more than twenty. Inside his cabin FBI officers found highly descriptive journals detailing all of his crimes, as well as bomb parts and other paraphernalia. Bizarrely, the cabin is now preserved in its entirety as a museum piece (on loan from the FBI)   in the Newseum, Washington DC. Only in America, as they say – Anonymous.

364. In 2016, *The New York Times* reported the story that Bob Dylan's long rumoured secret archives of notebooks, lyrics, correspondence, films, photographs, and other material, had been privately bought by a consortium of US institutions for $15 – $20m. This collection of 6,000 pieces included a trinity of notebooks, which had been kept in climate-controlled storage and whose existence had previously been known only to Dylan's closest friends and family. One of these notebooks has been referred to as the 'Maltese Falcon of Dylanology' for its promise as an 'interpretative key' to decoding his masterworks.

reels and audio recordings, and more. It was a unique, unprecedented insight into his methods, his genius, his life and work.

Filled with a renewed energy, I began the process of cataloguing everything I came across, dividing my discoveries into different mediums and genres, published and unpublished. Maas seemed to have had his own colour-coded system perhaps denoting which works were suitable to be published, if he died before they were complete, and which were private. I'd heard of other artists[365]doing the same, but without a code key there was no way of knowing his intentions. For better or worse I had to create my own categories now. It somehow seemed better this way. Instead of relying on his definitions I was taking control and deciding where everything fitted. I read until dawn, fascinated by his handwriting, by the passages he had underlined and their significance, obsessed with memorising as much as I could, appropriating his words, his thoughts, his knowledge, his memories, absorbing some sense of his self into my own.

TRANSCRIPT /002

DJ: Maas's notes cover a frightening range of topics, but his thoughts repeatedly gravitate to strands of Western philosophy and Eastern religion, and so much more – science and psychoanalysis, mathematics, literature, language and art. The way he connects these disparate topics is incredible, from exploring Lacan's triptych order of the unconscious[366] to a meditation on the Tetragrammaton[367] and the Shemhamphorasch,[368] the hidden name of God, to

---

365. J.D Salinger used a similar system according to his daughter Margaret, as recollected in her book *Dream Catcher: A Memoir*, (2001).

366. Jacques Lacan, the French psychoanalyst, outlined a three-part structure to the unconscious, The Imaginary, The Symbolic, and The Real. The Imaginary is the pre-linguistic world of the image and is rooted in the subject's relationship with his own body. The Symbolic is the linguistic dimension, our perception of the world defined by language. The Real is outside of language and resists symbolisation absolutely.

367. The Tetragrammaton, meaning 'to have four letters', allegedly refers to the true name of God in the Hebrew bible, which 'should not be spoken'. In the short story, *Death and the Compass*, by Jorge Luis Borges, a detective is lured to his death by his nemesis after becoming obsessed with solving a mysterious set of murders he connects to the Tetragrammaton, the hidden name of God.

368. Shemhamphorasch, meaning 'the explicit or interpreted name', is linked to the Tetragrammaton. In Kabbalah, the term was used to designate a 72-letter name for God, other times a 42-letter name. A 216-letter name for God is found in Jewish Kabbalistic sources (mentioned by Tosafot as well as by the Kabbalists) as well as in Christian Kabbalah and in Hermetic Qabalah, derived from the 72 groups of three letters, each of these triplets being

the Sefirot,[369] the ten different aspects of God's Will. This must be linked to his final work. I just don't know how, yet. His notes document his research and interest in these concepts, how he engaged with each of them artistically, and his unrealised plans to incorporate these ideas into his later work. Maas wasn't religious as far as I can tell, but he seemed to be attracted to the iconography of apocryphal texts and images, and the sense of hidden mysteries they symbolised.[370]

He shows a similar interest in representing scientific concepts through his art and appears to have had a particular fascination with quantum mechanics. I've found several ambitious essays on the subject from his teens, which were never published, and he seems to have returned to the subject shortly before his disappearance. There is even evidence here to suggest he travelled to High Island, Maine, to talk theory with John Wheeler[371] a few years before the physicist's death in 2008. If this meeting did take place the timing is especially interesting, as this was around the period when Maas announced his intention to disappear from public life and concentrate on his final artwork. Based on what I've found, here, I think any discussion of Maas's final project must take quantum mechanics into account. It definitely appears to have been one of his central obsessions in later life. Or could language have been his renewed focus in those last years before his

---

the name of an angel or intelligence. The word, Shemhamphorasch has also been used by the Church of Satan and has been associated with everything from tarot cards and magical grimoires to occult rituals and summoning demons.

369. Sefirot, meaning 'enumerations', are the ten attributes/emanations in Kabbalah, through which Ein Sof (The Infinite) reveals himself and continuously creates both the physical realm and the chain of higher metaphysical realms (Seder hishtalshelus). Number theorists have speculated on a 'mysterious power' locked within the numbers and letters, the hidden messages, in the Tetragrammaton, Shemhamphorasch, and Sefirot.

370. Interestingly, this was also a central preoccupation in the work of Maas's friend RB Kitaj. The painter strongly identified with the writer Franz Kafka's sense of estrangement and his fascination with hidden mysteries. In the catalogue for Kitaj's *Little Pictures* exhibition, these were said to include representations of the Judao-Christian mysteries of the hidden face of God and the artist's meditation on the Jewish Christ.

371. John Archibald Wheeler (1911 – 2008), a professor at Princeton and a world authority on quantum mechanics, was considered to be one of the 'monster minds' of theoretical physics. He was a colleague of Albert Einstein and Niels Bohr and coined the terms 'black hole' and 'wormhole' during his career. Toward the end of his life he developed a particular fascination with the relationship between consciousness and existence.

disappearance? His writings continually circle back to
a desire to use art as a means to reconnect with a pre-
linguistic stage. Perhaps that was the final work he
returned to at the end? You could arguably say the same
for any of these topics, however. His explorations of
art, psychoanalysis, religion, mathematics, and dozens
of other topics are all equally ground-breaking. Any
one of the proposed projects linked to these fields
could be his masterpiece, each could potentially change
the world, but I can't help but feel there is more to
discover. Even now, after everything, I still don't
fully understand the connections I'm seeing here. Like
the man himself, whatever he was working on at the very
end is still out there, invisible and beyond my reach,
at least for now.

When morning came I decided to throw open the curtains. Who knew what else could be here? It was only then, as beams of light arced into the room, that I realised there was a door I hadn't noticed, partially hidden by storage boxes, sheets dappled with paint, and unfinished canvasses.

The canvasses were stacked up by the dozen, some mounted, other rolled up and bound by string, some seemingly finished, others incomplete. I recalled the old saying that 'art is never finished, only abandoned'.[372] These lost and discarded pieces would be worth millions in the right hands. Some of the paint was layered on so thickly I wondered if Maas had painted over previous artworks. I had read about this practice, in other famous artists,[373] but there was no way of knowing, without an X-Ray or other technology. I examined as many artworks as I could, both to catalogue their existence and in the hope of finding more hidden messages. There was a dark substance on some of the canvasses that left a green stain on my hands; it had a sickly sweet, decaying smell, like rotten fruit. I looked it up and discovered a pigment called Paris

---

372. A much-used quote that has been erroneously attributed to everyone from Leonardo Da Vinci, to Paul Valery, to Cezanne – Anonymous.

373. Using technological advances such as X-ray, and other non-invasive techniques, it has been revealed that many famous artists, including Picasso, Van Gogh, Goya, Degas, Rembrandt, Caravaggio, and others, painted over previous works to create new masterpieces. Thanks to technological advances, art historians and conservation experts have been able to discover what lies beneath a number of famous paintings without disturbing the original. Techniques include using macro X-ray fluorescence analysis, terahertz radiation, infrared technology, and fluorescence spectroscopy. Famous example of artworks which have been revealed to have other artworks hidden beneath them include Picasso's *Blue Room*, and *The Old Guitarist*, Van Gogh's *Patch of Grass*, and Rembrandt's *An Old Man in Military Costume* – Anonymous.

Green,[374] once used by the Impressionists Monet and Renoir, and the Post-Impressionists Cezanne and Van Gogh, as well as many others, in 19th and early 20th century Paris. It contained arsenic and could be lethal. Maas would have known this of course. The canvasses might have been worth millions, but they were also a poisoned chalice in more ways than one. I set the paintings aside for now and decided to see where the door led. It was locked from the inside. My heart pounded in my chest. For an electrifying moment, I wondered if I had reached the end of the story. Was this the locked room? Would I find Maas inside this secret chamber, sat working at his desk, with a pencil held between finger and thumb, poised above the page? I put my ear to the door and listened, imagining the click, click, click of a typewriter at work. I took a step back and threw my weight against the door.

TRANSCRIPT /003

> DJ: I was able to get inside, but it wasn't what I was expecting. The room is some sort of surveillance suite, filled with monitors and recording equipment. The technology is old, but most of it is still working, and there's one screen that's still turned on, showing footage from the hall. There must be a camera watching the door, so Maas could see who was outside. I've found tapes going back years but, get this, Maas has edited himself out. He's not in any of the footage. There's something else interesting, too. All of the people who visited Maas here were women. **END**

Hours turned into days. I was pale and unshaven, weak from a lack of food, but I was scared to leave now. I was convinced that, if I did, I wouldn't be able to return; that everything I had found would be lost, and it would all disappear. But if I didn't leave I would eventually die. Maybe this was meant to kill me after all? Maas must have known I would keep reading, searching for answers, refusing to give up, even if it meant my own death. Were the bodies of the others who had come before me here within these walls, rotted away to dust?

TRANSCRIPT /004

> DJ: I know what the tapes are now. They're not a record or surveillance. They're art. Maas turned every

---

374. Paris green consists of copper(II) acetate triarsenite or copper(II) acetoarsenite $Cu(C_2H_3O_2)_2 \cdot 3Cu(AsO_2)_2$. Arsenic is among the most toxic substances in the world and, depending on the level of exposure, can cause cancer and death.

relationship he's had for the last twenty-five years into a piece of conceptual art. I found the notes in one of his journals. He called this *The Hallway*. Every woman who has come to his door has been filmed, every conversation recorded. He's edited himself out, so we have to reconstruct the relationships through their words, their images, their presence juxtaposed against his absence. I had heard rumours of his affairs, everyone had, but this is something else. We're talking hundreds of women here. It's incredible. The tapes start in the 1980s and the last one is dated 2005. The women visited him one at a time, but he's edited the film in such a way that they all appear at once, filling up the hallway with the ghosts of different women, displaced from time and space. I can almost imagine them all lined up in the hallway outside right now, waiting to see him.

As I wondered how long I could go without food, I began to realise this was more than just an intellectual challenge; it was about endurance. How would I operate under stress, deprived of food, water, sleep? I found a half bottle of Bushmills[375] under a pile of manuscripts. It wasn't bourbon, but for the moment it was all I had to satiate my thirst – for sustenance, for the truth, for an end to the madness – as I watched the surveillance tapes back and attempted to understand them.

TRANSCRIPT /005

DJ: Ever since the discovery of the encoded message, that led me to the safety deposit box and eventually to this apartment, my eyes have been opened to the presence of other codes in Maas's work, visual or otherwise. Well, I've just found one more, and it might be the most important yet. I just don't know what it means though. Maas's cult followers in the '60s and '70s always spoke of the hidden messages in his work. It was pretty much dismissed as the ravings of obsessive fans, like 'Paul is Dead',[376] but I'm starting to think they might have

---

375. Bushmills Triple Distilled Irish Whiskey was also the brand of whiskey preferred by the playwright and novelist Samuel Beckett, according to sources.

376. The urban legend of Paul McCartney's death allegedly started at an American University in 1969 and followed a minor car accident McCartney had been involved with in 1966. Supporters of this theory suggested that playing the song *Revolution 9* from The Beatles' *White Album* backwards revealed the words "Turn me on, dead man". This was taken as a clue to McCartney's alleged death and replacement by a lookalike in 1966. Additional 'clues' were John Lennon supposedly saying "I buried Paul" at the end of *Strawberry Fields* and the

been onto something.

It seems impossible, but the same group of numbers – ████████████████████████ – seem to recur throughout his work, from the novella he wrote as a teenager,[377] to his poems, paintings, sculptures, conceptual art, books, films, everything. They're ingeniously hidden and never concealed in the same way twice. Some are easier to find than others. In one painting he depicts ██ children in a field with ██ trees and uses ██ different colours. Others are harder to find, such as the amount of grammar he uses and on what pages, or the repetition of words with those number of letters. In his sculptures it could be the number of points or edges, or the physical distance between them when measured. In his films it seems to be a combination of audio-visual cues. Sometimes it's all of these things combined. Like I said, it's incredible… impossible, insane… but the numbers are there and now that I've noticed them I can't stop finding them. I see the numbers everywhere.[378] ██████████████████████████████████ I get the impression you could dedicate an entire academic career to hunting out Maas's messages and codes, never mind interpreting his art, but I don't have that kind of time and I'm no mathematician or number theorist. I've managed to get this far through intuition alone. None of it will matter though if I can't answer the question that remains. What do the numbers mean?

Maas's video suite was filled with outdated technology gathering dust. It was a strangely beautiful, mechanical graveyard. A Macintosh 128k, a Tri-X camera, a Heidelberg printing press, an Altair 8800, an Apple II,

---

symbolism of the cover to the *Abbey Road* album. Eventually the Beatles press officer and McCartney himself (who had been away from the public eye at the time, living at a Scottish retreat) were forced to deny the rumours, which had quickly grown into an international cult.

377. It may also have been concealed within the work he produced as a child and young adult, but Daniel did not have access to this at the time.

378. Apophenia is the experience of seeing meaningful patterns or connections in random or meaningless data. The term was coined in 1958 by Klaus Conrad, who defined it as the "unmotivated seeing of connections" accompanied by a "specific experience of an abnormal meaningfulness", but it has come to represent the human tendency to seek patterns in random nature in general, as with gambling, paranormal phenomena, religion, and even attempts at scientific observation. It was originally used in relation to the distortion of reality present in psychosis, but it has become more widely used to describe this tendency, without necessarily implying the presence of neurological differences or mental illness.

a Rolleiflex 3.5f with a Schneider Xenotar lens, a Motorola DynaTAC phone, a Pulsar P1 watch, a TRS-80 Model 100, an Epson MX-80 printer, a decommissioned microfilm reader. Everywhere I looked there was another computer, camera, or miscellaneous device. He seemed to have hoarded anything analogue. The microfilm reader was huge and unwieldy, too heavy for me to move, but I was intrigued what Maas might have used it for. Traditionally, microfilm was used to preserve publications, newspaper clippings, and archival records. It was also used during WW2 for espionage and to secure military correspondence. The only one I had ever come across previously was in the archives at the newspaper but that was fifteen years ago now. Since then everything had migrated to digital. I remembered something one of Maas's former collaborators had told me during an interview. He said Maas loved the tactile, physical, nature of analogue technology, but I suspected it was more than just a personal preference. Unlike digital, analogue technology such as a microfilm reader was not connected to the internet or any other network. Therefore it was not subject to the same invasive and insidious surveillance that we experience while using computers and smart devices. There is no big brother inside the microfilm reader and no algorithms mapping our search patterns to provide personalised advertising. I could imagine Maas preferring the isolation and privacy of old technology.

There was a stack of Kodak Eastman film canisters in the corner of the suite, containing reels of 35mm stock, the same as the original film that led me here to the apartment. When I opened one of the canisters a glossy 8 x 10 headshot fell out onto the floor. I recognised the man's face from somewhere. On the back of the photo were the initials M.M and a stamped business address, 'Warren Wagner and Associates, Theatrical Agency, Newcastle upon Tyne, NE1 7FH'. I examined each reel, one by one, holding the film up to the light carefully, tracing the perforations along each side as if they were braille. Most of the stock was degraded, and damaged, but I decided to watch what I could. When the first film flickered into life I saw a man dressed in black walking towards to the camera. He was speaking but there was no sound. The image was crisscrossed with white lines. One of them ran right through the man's face, but I was sure it was the same man from the photograph. I realised now where I knew the face from. It was the photograph of Maas and his entourage having dinner at the ███████████. Could I be looking at Ezra Maas? I packed the film and the photograph into my bag.

I realised it could take me years to uncover all the mysteries hidden within those walls in Soho, but from a biographer's perspective the greatest discovery was still to come. The books I would later refer to as 'The Maas Journals' were locked away in a trunk in the surveillance suite. I prized it open and found the journals inside, tied together with string. There were several dozen and, at first glance, it was hard to appreciate the importance of these coloured exercise books, with their pages filled with handwritten text. However, as I began to read, I quickly realised what I held in my hands. It was Ezra Maas's life story written in pencil on sheets of quadrille paper. This was the truth I was here to find.

Respected BBC journalist found dead

LONDON 2 November 2011

John Simpson

Tributes have been paid to BBC Head of Arts George Wallas after he was found dead earlier this week.

Mr Wallas, who was described as a 'towering figure' in arts and culture journalism by colleagues, was pronounced dead at the scene after police were called to an office on Portland Street, London, in the early hours of Monday morning.

Born on the Isle of Skye, Mr Wallas began his career as a trainee reporter at the *Ardrossan and Saltcoats Herald* in 1974, going on to work on national newspapers such as *The Times* and *Daily Telegraph* in the 1970s and '80s, before joining the BBC in 1985. He was appointed to the role of Head of Arts in 1990.

BBC Director-General Alan Ross said: "We are heartbroken at the BBC. George was a legend in the industry and a true professional. He loved journalism and he loved the arts. His passion was contagious, and his knowledge of the industry was second to none. Our thoughts are with his wife, his two sons, and his grandchildren, at this tragic time."

James Macdonald, a former colleague of Mr Wallas's at *The Times*, said: "George was a larger than life character, barrel-chested and big-hearted. He was a natural-born storyteller who was as funny as he was wise. George was an exceptional journalist, honest and tenacious, and he was a great friend."

A Metropolitan Police spokesperson said they were not treating the death as suspicious but would like to speak to anyone who had contact with Mr Wallas in the hours before his death.

The Daily Telegraph

Ezra Maas
Chapter Seven

We have an idea of the world, but we do not have the capacity to show an example of it[379]

Since he first became famous in the 1960s, Maas had been characterised as "an intensely private and reclusive personality" by the media. Whether this was true or not it was the enduring image of the artist that was held by both press and public. There were very few photographs of him in existence and his personal life was largely unknown, with many people unsure of how old he was, his nationality, or where he was based. Following the news of his sudden and impending marriage to Helena Huston, a well-known figure on the New York and London art world, Maas's devoted fans were initially outraged that their idol was human after all and feared the relationship would "ruin him".

They need not have worried. Ironically, his marriage to Helena would signal an even greater retreat from public life than before, as she took control of his business affairs and became the face of the newly-formed Maas Foundation. British-born Helena was an incredibly sophisticated woman who spoke several languages, boasted about having been born during one of her mother's trips to Bloomingdales, and who had built up a hugely profitable advertising empire in New York. Although she had come from relatively humble beginnings she was now extremely wealthy in her own right and had used her money to purchase several pieces of high-profile art in the 1970s. She was also a regular in glossy magazines on both sides of the Atlantic and was regarded as a fashion icon, thanks to a wardrobe that included French legends such as Dior, Chanel, and Givenchy, with jewellery by the likes of Tiffany & Co, and Van Cleef & Arpels, among others.

Helena had also become the patron of a number of upcoming young artists, such as David Diaz, Michelle Rocha, and John Michael-Vincent – however she unceremoniously dumped this so-called 'stable' of artists when she began her relationship with Maas.[380] From that point on she worked exclusively with him, using her wealth and extensive contacts in the media

---

379. Jean-Francois Lyotard.

380. Diaz, Rocha, and JMV all alleged they were dropped at Maas's request. This was never confirmed.

and advertising world to effectively become a one-woman PR machine, shielding Maas himself from the press, and public, while bringing together his disparate groups of followers, collaborators, and trusted friends, and turning them into a single worldwide organisation. As one friend notes:

"She was the perfect woman for Maas; beautiful, fiercely intelligent, independent, driven, ruthless, and hugely passionate about him and his work… Helena was happy to devote herself completely to Maas and sublimate herself to his ego and desires… And importantly, from a business perspective, she understood the value of money in a way that Maas didn't. Accumulating wealth just wasn't important to him; in fact he saw it as a distraction, but she knew the power and privacy that money could grant them…'[381]

The marriage ceremony was understandably held in secret although this only increased speculation about its location, with everywhere from the private Denis Island in the Seychelles and the Hayman Island Resort in Australia's Whitsunday Islands, to the Ulusaba Private Game Reserve in South Africa, and even the Lainio Snow Village in Finland, among the speculated venues. Despite this, the most credible story suggests Maas and Helena married in Oxford at the same church where his parents had married more than thirty years earlier.[382] The Maas Foundation's official description of the marriage, at the time, perhaps tells us more about how the organisation had begun to control the public perception of Maas and his authorised narrative than it does about the reality but it is interesting nonetheless:

"It was the coming together of two great people in a union that gave a renewed strength and energy to both of their lives…"[383]

The couple were often depicted as eccentric 1930s-style glamour icons by the press, travelling the world, launching new exhibitions, and creating art together, but in truth Maas used Helena's fame to disappear further into the background. While Maas prepared to begin a new phase of his artistic career, a period that would lead to nominations for *The Nobel Prize for Literature* and *The Turner Prize*[384] later that decade, Helena also indulged her own interest in becoming a painter. She converted one of the rooms of their manor house into a studio space and often worked alongside Maas. A friend of the couple, Geoff Laidler, said:

---

381. Sally Ryder, from an interview with Daniel in 2011.

382. St Michael at the North Gate.

383. www.ezramaas.com

384. Sadly, the pages detailing 1984 – 1987, which included Maas winning the *Nobel Prize for Literature* and *Turner Prize,* have been lost.

"Although the public perception of Maas depicted an intense loner, he was in no way an isolated individual… Gorhambury Manor was constantly full of people, full of artists, working, living, and creating together… it was communal and democratic… every room in the house becoming another potential studio, another space to create art, from the large ballroom sized living-room to the stables and, at the centre of it all, Helena and Maas could often be seen working side by side…"[385]

Officially, Maas never left his studio-home during this period, but other sources say different. There were Maas sightings across Europe and America throughout these years. One such instance placed him at the last public reading by the poet Charles Bukowski at the Sweetwater Club in Redondo Beach, California, in March 1980. Bukowski was living in the San Pedro area at the time with his future wife Linda, who was a devotee of Meher Baba, leader of an Indian religious society. Maas had written several positive pieces about Bukowski when he was a teenager and was known to have enjoyed his novels from the 1970s, such as *Post Office* and *Factotum*. The Maas Journals from this period do not mention the trip to Redondo Beach but do feature a quote by Bukowski, which Maas clearly liked. The quote, originally used in one of Bukowski's poems and explained in a letter from the writer to John William Corrington, outlines the writer's advice to aspiring artists. As you would expect from the so-called 'poet laureate of American lowlife', his words are unconventionally wise. Bukowski simply says "Don't Try."[386]

This was followed by a number of other sightings of Maas, including alleged visits to see Hunter S Thompson at his Owl Farm ranch in Woody Creek, Aspen,[387] and William Burroughs, in New York, but it is difficult to know which, if any, are legitimate due to The Maas Foundation's insistence that he never left Gorhambury Manor for more than a few hours in the early 1980s, following his marriage to Helena. One of the possible reasons for this, beyond his artistic seclusion and interest in privacy, was reportedly Helena's fears for her husband's safety, particularly following John Lennon's death in December 1980.[388] Jules Singer, who worked for

---

385. Interviewed by Daniel in 2011.

386. Bukowski said: "Somebody asked me: 'What do you do? How do you write, create?' You don't, I told them. You don't try. That's very important: 'not' to try, either for Cadillacs, creation or immortality. You wait, and if nothing happens, you wait some more. It's like a bug high on the wall. You wait for it to come to you."

387. Thompson referred to this affectionately as his "fortified compound".

388. Lennon was shot outside the Dakota building in New York by Mark David Chapman on December 8th. The following year a gunman also attempted to shoot US President Ronald

an exclusive private security firm in the 1980s that specialised in protecting celebrities and briefly consulted with Helena about her needs, said:

"After Lennon's death Helena was terrified about someone attempting to kill Maas, but in the end the Foundation decided to handle security themselves. Gorhambury Manor was heavily guarded, but from what I gathered Maas may have been somewhere else entirely..."[389]

In many ways, the decade to come would be characterised by the death of a number of high-profile and hugely influential artists such as Andy Warhol and Joseph Beuys, two men often associated with Maas's legacy and the profound impact of AIDS on the art world. However, the '80s also featured at least one unexpected resurrection, namely the re-emergence of painting and return to power of wealthy art collectors. While the AIDS epidemic, the second Cold War, the 'Wall Street' boom, and the Reagan and Thatcher years would dominate socio-political headlines, in the art world it was the decade of the dealer.

Financial deregulation had a significant impact on the art world. Buying art was big business and prices skyrocketed as a result. Wealthy private collectors, such as Count Giuseppe Panza di Biumo and Peter Ludwig, internationally, and Charles and Doris Saatchi,[390] in the UK, had a huge influence on the market. As a result Maas was in safe hands, with his new wife Helena guiding his career and managing his financial interests. Many artists benefited from the economic boom and became hugely wealthy, but thanks to Helena, Maas joined the same rare financial company as Picasso.

Helena thrived in her self-imposed role as promoter of the Maas 'brand'. She was quick to capitalise on the increased wealth and affluence in the 1980s and succeeded in increasing her husband's art sales by a huge amount during this period, including high-profile deals with a number of American investors, such as Wall Street mogul Gerald Green and Greenwich hedge fund manager Steve Goldman, for a reported $12million (£6.5m). She also personally arranged sales with Sheik Khalid-Hamadi, the Emir of Qatar, for a sum rumoured to be in the region of $30m.[391] Alongside her own career as an artist, Helena also worked tirelessly to organise and curate dozens of exhibitions of Maas's work during the 1980s,

Reagan.

389. As quoted in an interview with *The New Review* magazine, 1999.

390. The Saatchi Museum, which opened in 1984, was a converted paint factory in north London and included work by Donald Judd, Warhol, Serra, Flavin, Chamberlain, and Andre.

391. The exact figures were never revealed by The Maas Foundation.

at galleries such as the Tate Modern, Gagosian, Metropolitan Museum of Art, Rijksmuseum, and Serpentine Gallery, among others. It wasn't just about money, however; it was about staying relevant. One of the ways Helena went about achieving this was to market Maas's work to the MTV generation. She negotiated the use of his work in music videos, including images and text, and arranged for collaborations with emerging bands and musicians.

Although Maas was largely based at his studio in Hertfordshire, for much of the 1980s, the two global centres of art at the time were New York and Cologne in Germany. Helena ensured her husband was well-represented in both cities throughout the decade and that his presence was felt wherever he needed to be to remain the zeitgeist of his generation. Meanwhile, in the UK, Maas's old friend R.B Kitaj was active alongside other painters in the self-styled 'School of London', with Maas rumoured to have attended the private view in secret.

The year after Maas and Helena's marriage, the press circulated rumours that she was pregnant with his child. Helena, who was trying to launch her own career as an artist at the time, denied the stories, although a paparazzi photograph of a supposed 'bump', which was due to appear in a British tabloid newspaper, was allegedly blocked by The Maas Foundation's lawyers. It never resurfaced. The rumours continued, with some stories suggesting Helena had miscarried while others claimed she had given birth by emergency caesarean while working on an art installation in the North East of England. These led to conspiracy theories that the child had been hurriedly given up for adoption or secretly smuggled abroad to live in anonymity away from the fame of being born into the Maas family.

The Maas Foundation strenuously denied this, claiming there was no pregnancy in the first place. Helena's media activity and public engagements in this period supports the Foundation's stance on the matter, as a pregnancy would have been very difficult to hide for someone so regularly in the spotlight. There were other rumours however, including stories of another woman giving birth to Maas's child. These stories were quickly dismissed as tabloid gossip, but evidence has since emerged to suggest that Maas had dozens of affairs during this period.[392] This was not known at the time[393] and their relationship was perceived to be both happy and successful. Maas's marriage and his newly christened Maas Foundation were operating like well-oiled machines, but there was trouble on the horizon, in the form of something that could not be controlled or foreseen – chance.

---

392. The Maas Journals Vol.1 – 7 / evidence gathered from the apartment in Soho i.e. The Hallway conceptual art.

393. Although Maas did have a reputation for being an obsessive womaniser – Anonymous.

Ezra Maas: An Oral History
Part Six

Artists, writers, journalists, photographers, critics, friends, and others, who were around Maas during the years 1956 to 1996, give their impressions of the artist. Interviews by Daniel James.

☆

Sophie Ellroy, a critic, journalist and writer for TIME magazine, speaking in 1995.

SE: Ezra Maas is an iconoclast; an architect of dream worlds and nightmares-made-real, summoned from his unconscious and brought into this world through three decades of paintings, sculptures, AV installations, and performances. He may be partially categorised as a postmodern conceptual artist but, in my opinion, his engagement with those mediums was born out a sense of anarchy and hostility towards them. Even in the world of Avant-garde art Maas is an outlier, a rebel, a radical.

☆

Jim Rankin, a musician who contributed to an audio installation with Maas in the 1980s and 1990s.

JR: He was very polite, being English; reserved, well-spoken and always immaculately dressed in a suit, usually the same style and cut, with a simple white shirt, buttoned-up. That was his signature look, but he wasn't concerned with being fashionable. I heard he had a whole wardrobe of the same suits, shirts and shoes , that travelled with him wherever he went. It was part of his philosophy of keeping his day-to-day life as simple as possible, so that he didn't have to think about such things and could allow his mind to focus on what was important to him, namely his art.

☆

Aline Brackett, restaurateur and businesswoman, who knew Maas in 1970s and 1980s Paris.

AB: Ezra Maas était plus qu'un homme, c'était plusieurs hommes en un. Je n'ai jamais vu son vrai visage.[394]

☆

Sara Cain, actress and collaborator. She first met Maas in 1985.

SC: I was nervous when I first met him, because I'd heard all of the stories, but he immediately put me at ease. He was so warm and funny, almost childlike in his sense of wonder and enthusiasm. I think what I liked about him most though was the sense that he was really listening to you. His eyes looked right into yours in a way that made you feel like you were the centre of the world in that moment. I think that's how he got the best out of people around him. He made each of them feel as if they were special. I didn't see him again for quite a few years, after our first meeting, but when I did he remembered my name immediately. That says a lot about him I think.

☆

Kim Stefanos, a US based expert in Theosophy, Freemasonry, Rosicrucianism, the Bavarian Illuminati, and Western Occultism.

KS: Maas was a self-styled 'Renaissance Man' who transformed himself, from humble origins, into an 'ascended master', a shamanistic Gnostic figure, an enchanter, whose nihilistic fantasies and apocalyptic obsessions with mythology and occultism had a hypnotic effect on his legions of followers, who continue to live by his words and carry out his sinister demands to this day.

---

394. Translates as: 'Ezra Maas was not one man, but many. I never saw his true face.' – Anonymous.

Daniel James
Chapter Fourteen

Nothing ever becomes real 'till it is experienced[395]

The Maas Journals were everything I had been searching for. I had found the truth. Only it wasn't as simple as that. It never is. On the surface, the journals appeared to provide a highly detailed account of Maas's life from childhood up to his disappearance.[396] Each journal covered several months, sometimes years, of his life. The first was marked 1950 – '55, containing childhood memories and recollections of his parents, the second 1956 – 1960, his school years, and so on. When combined they essentially told Maas's life story decade by decade from the 1950s to his disappearance almost sixty years later.

It seemed too good to be true, and of course it was. After I found the first journal, marked 1950 – '55, I found another with the same date, and another; three different journals with three very different stories about his childhood. It was not simply that they were contradictory. It was so much more than that. They presented completely alternate versions of his life, each one making the other impossible.

This was the case with all of the journals, right up to the most recent dated over seven years ago. There were dozens of variations of Maas's life, through the decades, and no way of knowing which one of them was real. If his reclusive existence in life had refuted interpretation through an absence, these journals overwhelmed the possibility of a single, definitive, truth by drowning it in alternatives. I was faced with a proliferation of answers and no hope of separating truth from fiction.

I remembered an unpublished essay Maas had written as a teenager that I had read a couple of days ago, which explored similar ideas. It was an audacious piece of work linking post-structuralism and quantum mechanics, from the Copenhagen Interpretation and Many-Worlds theory to Wheeler's participatory universe,[397] and proposed a correspondence

---

395. John Keats (1795 – 1821)

396. Again, there are echoes of the Unabomber's journals here.

397. Wheeler calls this: 'Genesis by observership'. Our observations, he suggests, might actually contribute to the creation of physical reality. To Wheeler we are not simply bystanders on a cosmic stage; we are shapers and creators living in a participatory universe... "Wheeler conjectures we are part of a universe that is a work in progress; we are tiny patches of the universe looking at itself – and building itself. It's not only the future that is still undetermined but the past as well." From an interview with John Wheeler by Tim Folger published in

with "the fluid nature of language as a representation of reality and its infinite play of signifiers".[398] Looking through Maas's journals, I couldn't help but feel they were an extension of these ideas about the certainty of knowledge. Multiple realities perceived simultaneously. All equally valid. I recalled a quote from the German physicist Werner Heisenberg that Maas had underlined in his own paper: *Reality is in the observations, not in the electron.*[399]

Was Maas giving me the power to observe and decide the outcome? Or was this another game, another trap, a maze where I would become hopelessly lost? Scientific truth was always provisional. Quantum mechanics had changed everything by revealing the central role of the observer to scientific knowledge.[400] This had been confirmed by experiments on the quantum level, where the results appeared to be directly affected by the presence of the person making the observation. It had been successfully demonstrated in lab conditions hundreds of times. Incredibly, particles of matter seemed to respond to consciousness on the smallest, most fundamental, level, existing in a fluid, ever-changing state of pure potential while unseen, and only becoming a fixed, definite, 'thing' when observed. After discovering Maas's extensive notes on quantum theory,[401] I had given myself a crash course in the subject. Luckily I was always a fast learner, especially when it came to complex ideas that challenged you to think in new ways. In that sense, Maas and I were alike; two sides of the same coin. On the quantum level, matter seemed to exist in all possible forms until it was observed, but the classical world that we lived in, and experienced, did not fluctuate in this way. It seemed stable, at least on the surface.

Maas's journals presented a multitude of different lives. I had to believe

---

Discover magazine (2002).

398. This essay was originally included as an appendix to this chapter, but was lost, and presumably destroyed, along with many other chapters before the manuscript was given to me – Anonymous.

399. Werner Heisenberg (1901 – 1976). As quoted in Kaku, Michio, *Parallel Worlds*, Penguin Books, 2005.

400. And this was equally true whether you adhered to Einstein's Theory of Relativity, Bohr's Quantum Mechanics, or Heisenberg's Uncertainty Principle.

401. "Some of the complex concepts discussed here can be summarised as follows: Matter is represented by particles; and the probability of finding the particle is given by a wave. This wave, in turns, obeys an equation. Before an observation is made, an object exists in all possible states simultaneously. To determine which state, we have to make an observation which collapses the wave function and the object goes into a definite state. The act of observation destroys the wave function and the object now assumes a definite reality." Kaku, Michio, *Parallel Worlds*, Penguin Books, 2005.

they had been left here for a reason. Were they waiting for a conscious observer? Would my decision determine which of the journals was true? In physics, it was referred to as 'the collapse of the wave function', when the potential states of a particle took on a single form. The big question in science was, what caused this? Who or what decides the final state of these electrons and particles, which are essentially the building blocks of the reality we experience?

The source of this collapse was the subject of intense speculation with many believing the cause to be consciousness,[402] because it was only when an observation was made that 'potential' became 'actual' reality. Others believed it was a matter of chance.[403] Some even believed it was God. The debate wasn't new. In the 18th century, philosophers such as Bishop Berkeley had speculated that objects only existed because humans were there to observe them and that solipsism,[404] the belief that only the mind exists, had been around for centuries.

The revelations of quantum mechanics reignited the debate into questions of free will and predestination, which had philosophical and theological implications, and called for a reinterpretation of these ideas, with thought experiments, such as Schrodinger's Cat,[405] created to express what the quantum world meant for our understanding of reality and the potentially crucial role of an observer in defining it.

Were Maas's journals the equivalent of a thought experiment presented as a conceptual art installation? Or were they a reflection of the world as

---

402. Nobel laureate Eugene Wigner said: "… it was not possible to formulate the laws of quantum mechanics in a fully consistent way without reference to the consciousness [of the observer]… the very study of the external world led to the conclusion that the content of the consciousness is the ultimate reality."

403. Einstein did not like this suggestion and famously said "God does not play dice with the world." However, his great rival and colleague Niels Bohr reportedly replied "Stop telling God what to do."

404. Solipsism is the philosophical idea that only one's own mind is sure to exist. The term comes from the Latin *solus* (alone) and *ipse* (self). Solipsism as an epistemological position holds that knowledge of anything outside one's own mind is unsure. The external world and other minds cannot be known, and might not exist, outside the individual's mind. As a metaphysical position, solipsism goes further to the conclusion that the world and other minds do not exist. As such it is the only epistemological position that, by its own postulate, is both irrefutable and yet indefensible in the same manner.

405. In this classic thought experiment, a cat is placed in a box with a radioactive element which may or may not break a vial of poison gas. By the rules of quantum mechanics, the cat is both alive and dead until the moment an observation is made i.e. until someone opens the box. Stanford University physicist Andrei Linde adds: "You may ask whether the universe really existed before you start looking at it. That's the same Schrodinger cat question."

it was, our sense of self fractured between different possible identities; a schizophrenic existence? If I chose one version of his life, and published it, would the other possibilities 'decohere' and cease to exist? Would my choice become the truth? It felt like a gift in some ways, being given this power to decide reality, but I couldn't help but wonder, what was the price?

TRANSCRIPT /007

> DJ: I keep coming back to Maas's final project. The journals may be the turning point for my book, but I'm convinced this place, and the notes he left behind, hold the key to the final piece of art he disappeared to create. The pieces are all here, life, art, language, quantum mechanics, religion, psychoanalysis, his secret codes and hidden messages, the numbers seventeen, six, and three, the hidden name of God, it's all here, all connected by him, but to what end? END

There was a knock at the door. I went into the surveillance suite and looked at the monitor. There was a man standing at the door. He knocked again. As he reached into his jacket he turned to the camera slightly and I realised the man was me. I was looking at myself... but from a week ago. What I was seeing wasn't possible. Either I was hallucinating or it was a glitch in the system, an eerie coincidence. Nevertheless, the sight of my own face looking back at me, and the sound of the knocking, made me feel uneasy. My hands were shaking as I gripped the table to steady myself, my legs like water. There was another knock at the door. It couldn't be me at the door. It was impossible. I staggered across the apartment and pressed my eye to the glass peephole. A young woman's face looked back at me in the fisheye lens. She was tall and elegant, with thick dark hair and large brown eyes. I opened the door.

'Can I come in?' she said.

'Who are you?'

'A friend.'

'What if I say no?'

'I think you'll want to hear what I have to say.'

The Maas Foundation had caught up with me. It had just been a matter of time. I decided not to fight it and held the door open as she walked past me into the living room.

'It's amazing,' she said, her eyes wide as she looked around.

'You didn't know about this place?'

'We knew of its existence, but not its location... ' she replied.

'Until I led you here... ' I realised. 'But if you knew I was here all this time, why didn't you come in earlier? Why wait?'

'The people who followed you here did not have the authority to make that decision. Paid to watch, yes, but not to act. Their instructions were to wait for you to come out, but when you didn't... '

'They had to call their superiors? I guess that makes you upper management. Who is calling the shots at The Maas Foundation these days? Helena? You? I didn't get your name.'

'My name is Ophelia, and I don't work for The Maas Foundation.'

'Sure you don't. Not that it matters. I knew I'd have company sooner or later. The guard on the door must have tipped you off days ago.'

'We have nothing to do with the security downstairs. It's possible Ezra, or someone else, hired them privately. If they were our people, we would have known about this place long ago.'

'So what now? Do I get the same treatment as Wallas?'

'I don't know what you're talking about. You're free to leave, Mr James. We have no desire to harm you, but you must leave everything behind. All of this belongs to us.'

'I'm not just going to walk away.'

She sighed. 'I was afraid you'd say that.'

'Is this where you call in the heavy hitters?'

Ophelia approached me slowly until our faces were inches apart. Her gaze drifted up over my pale, unshaven, face, until she was looking directly into my eyes. She ran her fingers through my hair and used it to pull me close, as if to kiss me.

'I am the heavy hitter, you fool.'

By the time I felt the needle enter my neck, it was too late. I was already falling.

When I opened my eyes, I was lying on a bare living room floor. The apartment had been stripped. All the books, notes, sketches and paintings, all of the unfinished sculptures and artworks, the old computers, the surveillance equipment, the recordings, all of his plans and secrets, even the furniture... it was all gone. They had taken everything, wiped it clean. All that remained were the fixtures and fittings... and me. At least, that's what they thought. I rose unsteadily and dragged myself into the bedroom.

A day earlier, I had prized one of the floorboards up and buried whatever I could in the dark and dusty space underneath. I had clearly done a good job of putting everything back as it was because they hadn't discovered my hiding place. I pulled the floorboard free and reached inside. There hadn't been much space, so I had had to choose carefully what to save. Inside, one complete set of *The Maas Journals* was safe and sound, along with the notes that I believed referred to his final work.[406] Last was a canister of 35mm film and the headshot of the man who may or may not have been Ezra Maas.

I began to laugh, my voice echoing in the emptiness. For the first time I felt like I was winning. I picked up the journals and lifted the window open, stepping out onto a wrought iron fire escape, the city's rooftops and chimneys stretching out before me, the sound of traffic far below. It was like another world up here, a dark, rain-soaked alternate city that existed in secret, high above street level. I climbed the ladder towards the roof and disappeared into the night.

---

406. From Daniel's handwritten notes: "I tore pages out of a dozen separate notebooks that I believed contained plans for Maas's final project. I brought all these pages together to form a new creation, a new book, my very own Frankenstein's monster, a bible of Maas's final ideas and the story of his life, in a single text."

PHONE TRANSCRIPT

15/11/11

TW: This is another message for Mr Daniel James. This is Detective Inspector Tony White of the Metropolitan Police. I'm calling in connection to Mr George Wallas, who I've been told was a former colleague and friend of yours. We would very much like you to come in at your earliest convenience to answer a few questions. I'm currently based at Holloway Police Station on Hornsey Road, London. I can arrange a car to pick you up if that's more convenient. We've been trying to reach you for a number of days. You can call me back on ██████ ██████. That's ████████████.

END

Ezra Maas
Chapter Eight

The world breaks everyone, and afterward, some are strong at the broken places.[407]

The year was 1984 and the Maas Foundation had a problem. It could no longer maintain its position that Maas was working in permanent isolation at Gorhambury Manor. The media were reporting that he had been involved in an accident overseas, and for once the Maas Foundation wasn't in control of the narrative. Although the stories of Maas's accident made the news, internationally, the truth of what happened remains unclear to this day. Allegedly, Maas took a Foundation intern, later confirmed to be twenty-one-year-old Elizabeth Stein,[408] on a sightseeing flight in the Congo, where their plane crashed after clipping trees on their way to photograph Murchison Falls from the air. Although Stein escaped, with minor injuries, Maas supposedly suffered several broken ribs, a dislocated shoulder, and a fractured skull. After boarding a second aircraft less than six hours later, in order to receive medical attention in nearby Entebbe, Maas reportedly suffered further injuries, this time second degree burns, when the plane caught fire on take-off. Forced to travel by car Maas spent several days being ferried between small medical centres, and it was during this time that rumours began to circulate that he had been killed in the initial crash. When he was finally admitted to a hospital, almost forty-eight hours later, a small local newspaper had already printed an obituary.[409]

Maas, through his lawyer, quickly issued a statement to the Press Association confirming he was alive. A number of Western journalists had begun the journey to see Maas, eager to take advantage of the opportunity to gain access to the artist while he was in no position to stop them. However, by the time they reached him he had already begun the journey back to the UK, reportedly under heavy sedation on a privately chartered plane. Rumours of physical debilitation followed, but these were not the strangest stories to emerge from the incident. It was later alleged that Maas had not been injured at all but had taken the advantage to invent, or even stage, the accident to accelerate his plans to completely withdraw from

---

407. Ernest Hemingway, writer (1899 – 1961).

408. The nature of their relationship was never disclosed. Daniel attempted to track her down, but without success. It is believed she changed her identity after receiving a financial settlement from the Maas Foundation.

409. Despite attempts to locate this news clipping, Daniel was unsuccessful.

public life. This is supported by a conspicuous lack of medical records at any of the hospitals where Maas was allegedly treated. This may be because Maas and his legal team had all such records seized, but it may also be because the records never existed. If this was indeed the case, it may be that Maas himself leaked the news to the Western press and instigated his own premature obituary. Of course, this is pure speculation. The Maas Foundation insisted he was badly injured and spent many years recovering. This may well have been true, but it did not stop the rumours that he was completely healthy and continuing to work in different locations around the world. As journalist Sally Chambers at *The Times* pointed out:

"Due to the fact that the media and general public had no idea what he actually looked like, Maas could effectively come and go when and where he pleased. Although there were cameras watching his mansion on a regular basis, he could have been somewhere else entirely... the wall of silence Helena Maas had erected around her husband was impenetrable."[410]

According to The Maas Foundation, the next few years were spent almost exclusively at Gorhambury Manor, where he would create the artwork that would see him nominated for the Nobel Prize for Literature, and the newly created Turner Prize, in the space of a few short years. However, these nominations were steeped in further controversy. Maas would have been awarded both prizes (and was privately offered them) but refused them both.

Note to reader: Daniel's account of Maas's controversial refusal of the Nobel and Turner Prizes and both organisations' attempts to prevent this damaging revelation from being made public were detailed below. However, these paragraphs have been redacted due to on-going legal issues – Anonymous.

---

410. From an interview conducted in 1995.

In many ways it should have come as no surprise that Maas refused to be associated with the Nobel Prize or Turner Prize ceremonies. This was the same man who had sent an impersonator to the 1974 National Book Awards in America, after all. Maas had been awarded a long list of prestigious awards in his career, however he never attended a single ceremony, or publicly acknowledged any prize he received. It was also entirely in keeping with Maas's unpredictable trajectory that his next move, after his association with two of the art world's most prestigious arts and literature prizes, was to do something completely different. In yet another departure from expectations, Maas turned his back on contemporary art to explore the medium of graphic novels.

Maas had long since been a fan of British and American comic books and was known to have an extensive collection, reading dozens of issues at a time while he wasn't working.[411] He reportedly had a particular appreciation of the artwork of Steve Ditko,[412] and Jack Kirby, among others.

Interested in working in the comic industry, Maas contacted Bryan Talbot, a future Eisner Award winner and comic creator whose career he had been following since the mid-1970s, about potentially working together on a project that would eventually become GIOCONDA PI. Bryan had worked in the British underground comic scene, drawing the *Brainstorm Comix* series for Alchemy Press among other titles, before launching the epic saga that would make his name, *The Adventures of Luther Arkwright*, in 1978.

The original collected volume of Luther Arkwright was the first ever graphic novel[413] to be published in Britain and was quickly acknowledged as a seminal work – its blend of science fiction, historical, espionage, and supernatural genres, experimental narrative techniques and avoidance of sound effects, speed lines, and thought balloons, was considered to be pioneering and influenced many high-profiles names in the industry such as Warren Ellis, Grant Morrison, Steve Bissette, Neil Gaiman, Michael Zulli, and Rick Veitch.

---

411. The Maas Journals Vol 7, 1985 – 1990.

412. The artist for Marvel Comics series such as Spider-Man, Ditko refused to give interviews after the mid-1960s and continued to work in privacy from his New York studio until the present day. Speaking about his reclusive nature, he said: "When I do a job, it's not my personality that I'm offering the readers, but my artwork. It's not what I'm like that counts; it's what I did and how well it was done.... I produce a product, a comic art story. Steve Ditko is the brand name."

413. Alongside *When the Wind Blows* by Raymond Briggs – although Bryan created Luther Arkwright four years earlier.

Maas was among the book's fans and had also followed Bryan's work in *2000AD*, where he pencilled some of the magazine's flagship characters. Bryan, who would go on to be described as one of the 'creators of the graphic novel form', winning numerous awards including the Eisner for *The Tale of One Bad Rat*, recalls the difficult experience of working with Maas:

"I worked with Maas over the telephone for about six months in 1986 –'87 on *GIOCONDA PI*, a graphic novella for the small US indie publisher Kult Press. I found co-scripting with him very hard. It was a bad experience all round. He'd come up with ludicrous, off-the-wall concepts and try and shoehorn them into what was a pretty surreal story to begin with – an erotic detective story set in Renaissance Italy on a parallel world, populated by humans and aliens, who had migrated to earth three centuries earlier. We'd have huge arguments over the phone as I tried to convince him that his ideas destroyed the tight plot structure I'd developed.

"The book had virtually no publicity and, as a result, sold very little, though I thought the artwork collaboration worked well. The protagonist was an alien Mona Lisa who was having an affair with Leonardo da Vinci. She experienced visionary dreams that foretold the future, and half the story was set in this dream world. Maas drew those sequences and I drew the real-world sections."[414]

Following this episode Bryan worked on some of the American comic industry's biggest titles, such as *Legends of the Dark Knight*,[415] *Sandman*, and *Hellblazer*, alongside talent such as Neil Gaiman, and Jamie Delano. He also continued to develop his own multi award-winning characters and creations such as *The Tale of One Bad Rat, Heart of Empire, Alice in Sunderland*, and the *Grandville* series. Although he had not spoken to Maas for more than a decade, Bryan decided to contact the reclusive artist with a view to reviving *GIOCONDA PI*, in 2000. Bryan says:

"In 2000, I got Vertigo comics interested in reprinting the story, and even illustrated a new cover. It all fell through though when Maas refused to accept their offer and demanded a ridiculous sum of money, claiming that DC was trying to 'rip us off'. I was so annoyed with him I never spoke to him after that."[416]

Maas continued to defy expectations with his art in the second half of the 1980s. While Helena maintained Maas's presence in the contemporary

414. Bryan was interviewed by Daniel in early 2012.

415. His two-part Batman story, *Mask*, was nominated for two Eisner Awards.

416. From Daniel's interview with Bryan in 2012.

art world and mainstream media, with exhibitions, art sales, and a sustained PR campaign on his behalf, the artist himself was said to be the architect of a number of new and innovative artworks. Building on his 'performance meets land' art experiments of the 1970s, with Jacques Cousteau, Maas allegedly bought acres of land in Kansas, allegedly the site of former ICBM warhead bunkers, and had the silos refurbished into luxury underground apartments. This was all done in secret with the land bought through subsidiaries and sister companies linked to the Maas Foundation. It was marketed as a housing development and the apartments were sold to some of America's wealthiest residents, including Wall Street moguls, hedge fund managers, traders, investors, venture capitalists, and early Silicon Valley millionaires. The properties were bought as an 'insurance policy' by the super-rich, who were fearful and paranoid of a nuclear war due to the perceived escalation of the Cold War between the US and USSR, as well as the impact of AIDS. A former Maas Foundation source, who claims to have been part of the project, said:

"Maas was preying on the fear, paranoia, and prejudice of the rich and powerful… these were the kinds of people who had emergency bags packed at all of their properties, who kept helicopters and motorbikes fuelled-up and ready to go so that they could reach safety as fast as possible in the event of a catastrophe… there was an apocalyptic atmosphere in those years, and a perception that a nuclear war was a very real possibility… while others anticipated a class or race war. It drove these rich, soft, spoiled, and often eccentric characters into becoming secret survivalists. There was a lot of fear in the air, a lot of hate, and a hell of a lot money, and this made them easy targets for Maas…"

When the first inhabitants moved into their properties as part of a trial weekend, however, they were in for a surprise. The attendants who were there to guard them and wait on their every need gradually began to disappear, until they were alone, the doors all locked from the outside, and the lights began to flicker.

"I thought it was a work of genius… I'd never heard of anything like that being attempted before. The sheer scale of the project was breath-taking. There had been earthwork sculptures like Smithson's *Spiral Jetty*,[417] which was an incredible achievement in itself and represented a reconnection with the environment, but Maas had taken the idea to another level, combining it with elements of performance and conceptual art… Not for the first time, Maas had created a microcosm of the world, populating it with a cast

417. A 1,500ft earthwork sculpture created on the north western shore of Great Salt Lake, Utah, by artist Robert Smithson, in 1970.

of characters and standing back as they revealed who they really were and tore each other apart. It was terrifying to behold... a masterwork."

The decade may have been haunted by the spectre of death, but it seemed that Maas had a growing fascination with the relationship between life and art, in particular work that explored the porous boundaries between the two. His art had always been much more than just self-contained experiments. Maas's acts of creation reached out from the vacuum and touched the world. They mattered. Now he had taken to creating whole worlds. One way to look at it was that Maas had become obsessed with playing God. If so, it was a preoccupation that would only grow in the years to come.[418]

---

418. Note to reader: I've been struggling with the proposition of defining a book which goes to such efforts to refuse categorisation. Perhaps it shouldn't be defined, but I will at least endeavour to describe it. I've read the phrase 'existential noir' used in relation to the manuscript and yes, in many ways, the book is an extended love letter to the detective genre, particularly the sub-genre known as metaphysical detective fiction. This is especially apparent in the chapters in the present day which dramatize Daniel's search for the truth about Ezra Maas. However, detective fiction is just one of the genres the manuscript engages with and just one of the writing styles that Daniel adopts, in a book which can be seen as a form of metafictional collage, filled with disruptions and insertions, references and allusions, echoes, repetitions, and dislocations. In terms of other genres the manuscript is also heavily influenced by New Journalism, biography, autofiction, postmodernism, literary theory, the picturesque novel, academic writing and, with its 500+ footnotes and references, could also be read as an example of an encyclopaedic narrative. The latter genre was first identified by Edward Mendelson in his 1973 essay on Thomas Pynchon's *Gravity's Rainbow*, with one of its characteristic traits being "its ability to assimilate other genres" in an encyclopaedia of literary styles and knowledge.

However, it would be wrong to begin anywhere else but the detective genre, specifically metaphysical detective fiction, which is sometimes referred to as postmodern noir or anti-detective fiction. Most recently this genre has been described by a new term, 'existential noir' – stories which begin with classic noir incidents such as a mysterious death, or missing person, but whose plots are soon displaced, the lens shifting to stranger events and deeper, existential, questions, for which there is no resolution. Following this blueprint, Daniel purposefully foregrounds noir tropes and postmodern devices throughout the contemporary chapters. In my opinion, this serves a dual purpose. It signposts his intent and announces to the knowledgeable reader that a literary game is being played, without necessarily providing the rules, while also serving as a form of distraction and misdirection from other techniques, styles, and genres, he is actively engaged with. Structurally, it is intentionally fragmentary and episodic in places, echoing the style of Raymond Chandler, whose novels were often cannibalised and reassembled from earlier short stories. However, while this may have been by necessity in Chandler's case, the technique is consciously employed by Daniel. As Fredric Jameson has described in his analysis of Chandler's work: "The detective's journey is episodic because of the fragmentary, atomistic nature of the society he moves through... ".

The increasingly dream-like dislocations between scenes, between fact and fiction, between reality and fantasy, reveal the truth in the seams, in the liminal spaces or, to borrow a phrase from Hemingway, in the "broken places". Similarly, the plot is intentionally non-linear at times. A is not always followed by B, and B does not necessarily lead to C. This is anti-detective fiction, or metaphysical detective fiction, as it was later defined in the seminal academic textbook on the subject, *Detecting Texts,* edited by Patricia Merivale and Susan Elizabeth Sweeney, (University of Pennsylvania Press), and defined as a text: "… that parodies or subverts traditional detective story conventions – such as narrative closure and the detective's role as surrogate reader – with the intention, or at least the effect, of asking questions about mysteries of being and knowing which transcend the mere machinations of the mystery plot."

These novels often feature a writer in place of a traditional detective, drawing parallels between the act of reading, the writing process, and the art of detection. If a 'text' is a collection of signs, the detective-protagonist and reader are both students of semiotics, the theory of 'the action of signs', which act as the clues to the mystery. This sub-genre of detective fiction evolved through the work of notable late modernist and postmodern writers, such as Beckett, Robbe-Grillet, Nabokov, Pynchon, Auster. However, it is to Edgar Allan Poe, the originator of the entire genre, and one of his spiritual successors, the Argentinian master Jorge Luis Borges, I find myself drawn at this time. Poe, who as I have previously mentioned is credited with inventing the detective genre, wrote a mystery called *The Purloined Letter*, with a text at its heart. This story has inspired much critical debate over the years, including a triptych of warring readings by Jacques Lacan, Jacques Derrida, and Barbara Johnson, among others. The theme is echoed in the work of Borges, whose own detective stories, *The Garden of Forking Paths*, *Death and The Compass,* and *Ibn Hakkan al-Bokhari, Dead in His Labyrinth*, effectively double Poe's three analytic detective stories, *The Murders in the Rue Morgue*, *The Mystery of Marie Roget,* and *The Purloined Letter.* Intriguingly, *The Garden of Forking Paths,* was published exactly 100 years after Poe's first detective story. This tale is framed as a 1916 deposition by Dr Yu Tsun, a Chinese spy descended from a Hunnan governor who "abandoned all to make a book and a labyrinth", and is both a metaphysical detective story and a philosophical parable on the nature of time and reality.

As in the short stories of Borges, Daniel's protagonist is a version of himself. In some ways, the manuscript could be considered an experiment in autofiction, to utilise a recent term. Yet, as I have previously stated, this is not the Daniel I once knew, but a fictionalised 'character', distinct and separate from the 'authorial' Daniel. Again, as with the overt use of noir and postmodern techniques in the exterior structure of the narrative, I believe Daniel was playing a game with the reader by including himself in the text and uses his own identity as another form of misdirection. Admittedly, it took me some time to realise the 'double game' that was being played here and, while I have no evidence to prove it, I have a compelling theory about Daniel's identity which you can read on Pg.355.

Back to the manuscript and, in another echo of Borges who so often placed a text or library at the metaphysical centre of his stories, Daniel's narrative is self-consciously about the writing process, it is concerned with authorship, how we create and consume stories, and their power in our lives. It is a book about a book (although again, like Borges, objects are not always what they appear to be) and it is highly intertextual. With hundreds of footnotes, references, and allusions, there is a vast amount of knowledge contained within the book and it easily meets the definition of an encyclopaedic narrative. It also effectively brings to life James Joyce's famous quote about *Ulysses:* "I've put in so many enigmas and puzzles that it will keep the professors busy for centuries arguing over what I meant." I also read the inclusion of these references in Daniel's manuscript as a loving and self-conscious parody of academic writing and satire on the saturation of information in the digital age. Tellingly, some of Daniel's footnotes are intentionally subversive, sometimes misleading. My own footnotes, insertions and clarifications, added while I was reconstructing the text, provide a further narrative layer, and an additional authorial voice, to the final version of the manuscript, which you now hold in your hands. In final summary, the book is legion, for it is many things – Anonymous.

Ezra Maas: An Oral History
Part Seven (1980s-1990s)

Artists, writers, journalists, photographers, critics, friends, and others, who were around Maas during the years 1956 to 1996, give their impressions of the artist. Interviews by Daniel James.

☆

Julia Lange, photographer, collaborator and friend, who first met Maas in 1976.

JL: The accident in Entebbe was much worse than anyone realised. The Maas Foundation kept the full details out of the press, but Maas was clinically dead for several minutes after suffering cardiac arrest on the operating table and, although they managed to resuscitate him, there were serious fears he would never recover from the damage done while he was without oxygen. He was blind for days afterwards, unable to communicate, and his motor functions were badly affected. What followed was a long and arduous rehabilitation over many years. This was the true reason for his complete withdrawal from public life and his reclusive behaviour.

☆

Alex Vine, contemporary artist and art collector, based in Bushwick, Brooklyn.

AV: Be careful, man. Maas's work has a way of changing people.

☆

Mark Atkinson, London-based independent filmmaker, who attempted to produce a documentary about Ezra Maas between 1995 – 1999.

MA: I spent almost five years trying to finance a project about Maas, in the late 1990s. We filmed a lot of footage at galleries and exhibitions, as a showreel for potential investors, but we faced obstacles at every turn. I even camped out outside his mansion in Hertfordshire, day and night for a month, to try and get a glimpse of him. Nothing. I never did get to find out what he looked like, but I always pictured him as a cross between Samuel Beckett and David Bowie.

254

☆

Jane Mankell, Owner of the Black Gate Galley in Spitalfields, London.

JM: The Young British Artists may have been getting all the headlines at the time, but that's exactly what Maas wanted. He was free to continue his work in isolation, free from expectations and external influences, free from interference. To a certain extent, he had seen it all before with Warhol in the '60s, Basquiat, Haring and others in the '80s, and he saw it again with Banksy and other contemporaries. Artists came and went. Maas endured.

☆

Professor Jean Dürrenmatt, a physicist based in Zurich, Switzerland.

JD: Maas was fascinated by the intersections between art and science. He read widely and regularly conversed with the world's leading scientists and researchers to expand his knowledge. I know he visited CERN on the Franco-Swiss border a number of times in the late 1990s and early 2000s. They were only too happy to arrange a private tour for an artist like Maas, especially if it led to interdisciplinary artwork inspired by the work that was taking place there. After his disappearance, we all wondered if his final work would be connected, in some way, to the search for the 'God particle' and the experiments he had observed during his time there.

☆

Sandra Hughes, a painter who spent time with Maas in both Europe and the US in the late 1960s and early 1970s.

SH: He wanted to travel to Salzburg to enrol at Oskar Kokoschka's School of Seeing after meeting someone in New York who had studied there. Maas was very keen to hear what Kokoschka was like in person and was pleased when he was described as "lively, energetic and he likes to finish each day with a good bourbon." Ezra approved, naturally, and made sure the School of Seeing was on his itinerary when he travelled around Europe. Another artist he wanted to meet was Samuel Beckett and I know they had several discussions in the Cafe Francais at the PLM Hotel St Jacques, St Jacques Boulevard, in Paris, opposite Sam's home with his wife Suzanne. Even though he was decades younger than these artists, Maas was intimidated by no one. It was part of the apprenticeship he had mapped out for himself.

Bill Deaver, writer and poet, New York.

BD: What was he like? How do you describe a ghost? I have a theory about Ezra Maas and it's this – he never existed. You see, I lived in New York in the 1960s. I went to gallery openings and exhibitions almost every night. Like everyone else with an interest in the art scene at the time, I heard the name Ezra Maas a lot in '66 and '67. For a few months, he was all anyone could talk about, but every time I went to one of his shows, people would say he wasn't there or you just missed him. I'd speak to friends who had been to some of his other happenings and it was always the same story. I couldn't find a single person I trusted who had seen him with their own eyes. It was the same throughout the 1970s, whenever he was supposedly in New York. All I ever heard was stories; he's on the West Coast, he's in Europe, he's everywhere and nowhere. Next thing I hear, he's living like Howard Hughes in an English mansion and doesn't leave the house. And all this time, his work is selling for millions. You want to know what I think? It was a con. I think Ezra Maas was the creation of a bunch of white guys sitting around a conference table. Or maybe a promoter or manager, who realised they didn't need an artist to sell art, all that was needed was to create demand. Think about it. There's nothing people love more than a mystery. I'm telling you, man. Ezra Maas does not exist.

Daniel James
Chapter Fifteen

The relation between what we see and what we know is never settled[419]

I woke inside an envelope of light. The morning sun bled through the fabric of the duvet and infused my whole world with a warm glow. I closed my eyes and curled my body into a ball, trying to disappear into the material. Everything would be fine if I stayed here. I tried to will myself back to sleep, back to the dream I had been having, but it was too late. I was awake.

When I finally emerged, rays of light were streaming through the bedroom window, making visible tiny dust motes floating through the air. The world was full of things we couldn't see all around us, whole universes, dense with invisible life. I pulled on the faded Wonder Woman t-shirt Isabella had loaned me and headed downstairs. She wore denim shorts and a white shirt knotted around her waist. She was half Peruvian and had inherited her mother's jet-black hair, dark brown eyes, and tan skin. When she saw me in the ill-fitting top, she burst out laughing. I pulled a face.

'This is seriously all you have that I can wear?' I asked.

'C'mon, it suits you,' she said, grinning.

I half-smiled, half-mumbled a complaint in her direction and took a seat at the dining table.

'Sam left another message,' she said. 'He sounds worried about you.'

'Did you speak to him?'

'Briefly. I told him I had no idea where you were and that maybe he should try one of your other girlfriends.'

'I bet that shut him up.'

'I could almost feel him going red over the phone. He also said your publisher is going crazy because they can't find you. Maybe you should think about checking in?'

'They can wait.'

'Is that wise? They pay your bills after all.'

'I can't hand over the book yet, Isabella. I need to finish it... '

I had contacted her the day before and we'd arranged to meet on the South Bank at the Dandelyan cocktail bar,[420] in the Mondrian London at

---

419. Art critic John Berger, *Ways of Seeing*.

420. Where cocktails are created by renowned mixologist Mr Lyan.

Sea Containers Hotel.[421] By the time we left, day had turned into night. The neon red glow of the OXO tower sign shimmered on the surface of the Thames as we walked hand in hand, beneath fairy lights strung along the branches of the trees along the South Bank. We gazed across the river at the illuminated dome of St Paul's as darkness gathered round us like a blanket.

I had been running on empty, washed out and exhausted, and she knew it instinctively. When we got back to her place, I lay down on her bed and fell asleep in my clothes almost instantly. I was only vaguely aware of her undressing me sometime later and climbing into bed alongside me. It was only last night, but it felt like days ago, now, standing in her kitchen, bathed in the late morning sun.

I cooked us a breakfast of poached eggs, bacon, and sourdough toast as a small thank you for taking me in and we sat together on her balcony overlooking the river. Neil Young's *Midnight on the Bay* was playing as the sun danced on the water below and a cargo trawler glided by. After we had finished eating, Isabella lay her hand over mine.

'Hey,' she said. 'What happened to you over there?'

'What do you mean?'

'You've barely looked me in the eye since you got back. It's like you're scared I'll see what's inside your head.'

'I'm fine.'

'You turn up like a stray cat after a year and I don't even get an explanation?'

'You know where I've been.'

'Working on the book, I suppose. But where are you now?'

'Inside... ' I replied. 'I saw things, Isabella... I... '

'You can tell me.'

'I can't... ' I replied. 'It's not safe... I wouldn't even be here if I had another choice.'

'And here I thought you missed me... ' Isabella said it like a joke, but there was hurt in her voice. She picked up the plates and carried them through to the kitchen. I followed her inside.

'I wouldn't have come,' I said, 'because I didn't want to put someone else I care about in danger.'

I came up behind her, pushed her dark hair to one side and began to kiss the nape of her neck, gently. She murmured and tilted her head back.

---

421. A boutique hotel on the South Bank designed in the style of 1920s cruise glamour, with a giant copper clad wall running through a cross section of the hotel interior like the exposed hull of an ocean liner.

Putting my arms around her waist, I pressed myself against her, cupping her breast with one hand and sliding the other inside the waistband of her denim shorts.

'Is this your way of saying sorry?' she said.

'I don't know. Is it working?'

'Mmm, I'll tell you later,' she smiled.

A blistering hot shower helped cleanse my body, which still felt weary after the events of the last weeks and months. When I came out of the bathroom, I found my suit and shirt carefully laid out on her bed. As I began to dress, I caught a glimpse of myself in the mirror and almost didn't recognise the man looking back. My face was pale and gaunt, dark around the eyes, my beard had grown in thick, and dark, and there were tiny flecks of silver at my temples. I felt like I had aged a decade since that night I took the phone call. But as I slipped the black shirt over my shoulders and began to button it, a change came over me, a calmness. I was stepping into character once more, free from worry and doubt, ready for whatever came next, even if I was nearing the end.

When I came downstairs, Isabella was sat waiting for me in a chair by the window.

'You're too good to me, Isabella,' I said. 'You always were.'

'What can I say? I'm a sucker for dark-haired literary types.'

I smiled and picked up my bag from the hall.

'You could stay,' she added.

'I need to keep moving. There are people looking for me and I don't want to lead them here.'

'What kind of people?'

'The police... and maybe worse.'

'Jesus, Dan.'

'An old friend was found dead the other day. I was the last person to see him alive.'

'Oh my god.'

'I don't know what happened, but I'm going to find out.'

'It's all connected to the book, isn't it?'

'The less you know the better.'

'So what do I say if someone comes looking for you?'

'The truth,' I replied. 'I was never here.'

I picked up my brown leather messenger bag. As I opened the front door to leave, Isabella grabbed my hand, pulled me towards her, and kissed me deeply.

'Where will you go?' she asked, as I stepped into the hall.

'The only place left... North.'

Questions are more interesting than answers
Why I don't want to know the truth about Ezra Maas

By Laura Behm, 27 February 2012

"My idea is to declare that art is the only possibility for evolution, the only possibility to change the situation in the world." – Joseph Beuys

My three favourite artists have one thing in common – mystery. David Lynch, Joseph Beuys, and Ezra Maas couldn't be more different in some ways, but through their work, and their lives, they have helped bring a sense of wonder back to the world. Mystery is at the heart of Lynch's beautiful puzzle box dream worlds. Joseph Beuys turned his life into a myth and created art to transform life. And Ezra Maas's life and art are both a myth and mystery.

To his fans, Ezra Maas is more than a man; he is a prophet, an alchemist, a shaman, a spiritual leader, and most of all a revolutionary artist. He is more than a man precisely because we have no knowledge of his life outside of his art, to ground him in the real. His work equally speaks for itself, and what it says is everything and nothing. Plans for an unauthorised biography threaten to reveal who is he and where he came from, the origins of his art and the meaning of his final work and disappearance. My reaction was one of horror. Let me explain.

When David Lynch first exhibited his artwork, as a student, he included a biographical statement alongside his work – as artists are sometimes required to do. It simply read, 'Eagle Scout. Missoula, Montana.' Later, in his career as a director, this same, brief biography was given to any press and media who requested an interview with him. Lynch took a similar attitude when questioned about his work. He offered no explanations and would not be drawn on meaning. Lynch claimed he did not know where his ideas came from or what they meant. And if he did know he wasn't telling. His reason was both simple and beautiful. Explanations, like endings, were closed. By refusing to answer, the meaning was left open. People's minds were free to imagine any possibility, they could go wherever their minds took them, just as Lynch himself was known to do.

Joseph Beuys' personal journey to becoming an artist is steeped in its own mythology. During the Second World War he was a rear gunner in the Luftwaffe and

263

was shot down over the Crimea. His pilot was killed, but Beuys survived. He was rescued by a tribe of Tartars, who smeared his body with fat and wrapped him in felt to protect him from the cold. These two materials, fat and felt, became his artistic signatures in a career that was as varied as it was influential. In 1974 he arrived at John F Kennedy Airport, was wrapped head to toe in felt by his assistants and spent three days penned inside a Manhattan gallery with a live coyote. He called it *'I like America and America likes me'*. A few years earlier he had wandered around his own exhibition, wrapped in felt, whispering to a dead hare.

Beuys may not have been the household name that his contemporary Andy Warhol became, but among artists, and art critics, he is considered to be one of the greatest of post-war artists. Respected critic John Berger went so far as to say that: "In matters of seeing, Joseph Beuys was the great prophet of the second half of our century". Fame was never Beuys's mission despite his self-aggrandizing life-myths. He wanted to change the world through art. He believed in the power of art to transform and throughout his life he dedicated his art-making activities to education, politics, and social uplift.

Maas is an interesting synthesis of Lynch and Beuys in that he has never spoken about his work or his life. Like Beuys, his art is one of transformation, changing one thing into another, himself and the world; like Lynch, his art has the power and beauty of a dream and resists interpretation; like both men, his life and his art are indistinguishable and cannot be separated. The myths surrounding Maas are myriad, labyrinthine, and contradictory; strange, wonderful, and sometimes terrifying. Whether they are fabrication or not they are likely far more interesting than the truth. It is for this reason that I would rather we never find out.

We live in a world that seems to grow smaller every day. We are connected to it 24/7. If we're not watching it, then it is watching us. It knows where we are at all times and we know where everything is. There are no more countries left to discover. No more sailing off the edge of the map. No more monsters, no more surprises, and precious little mystery. What we have left we need to preserve. I don't want to be told what David Lynch's work means. I don't care that the myth of Joseph Beuys is a fabrication. And I don't want to know the truth about Ezra Maas.

Ezra Maas
Chapter Nine

I don't believe in art, I believe in artists[422]

During the late 1980s and early 1990s the Maas Foundation continued to portray Maas as an artist in seclusion, while Helena worked tirelessly to extend the brand to other media by essentially "bringing avant-garde to the mainstream".[423] One of her plans was, allegedly, to sell the rights from one of Maas's early stories to Hollywood, potentially even his 1966 anti-social manifesto *XXXXX*, in order for it to be made into a big screen adaptation. Her idea got as far as meetings with several high-profile directors and actors, but the move was ultimately vetoed by Maas himself, according to most reports. A former assistant of Helena, who did not want to be named, revealed:

"Helena's first choice for director was David Lynch, as she was friends with Isabella Rossellini,[424] and a huge fan of *Blue Velvet*[425]... she also had meetings with David Cronenberg, as she loved *Videodrome*... Maas himself was rumoured to rate both men very highly as artists, especially Lynch... discussions were also held with Stanley Kubrick and Oliver Stone, while a host of the decade's biggest actors, including Tom Cruise, Sean Penn and Mickey Rourke, lobbied for the lead part..."[426]

Helena was also directly involved in a deal with the Brooklyn Academy of Music to stage a rare 'musical art' performance composed by Maas, which drew on his appreciation of jazz. This, and other musical compositions by Maas, was later released as the double album, *Symphonic 2*, in 1997. There were other musical collaborations, including uncredited work on a spoken word album[427] involving Nick Cave, Tom Waits, and Maas's old friend William Burroughs. Maas had reportedly become friends with Cave several years earlier, mixing with him and his band in London, West Berlin,

---

422. Marcel Duchamp (1947 – 2016).

423. Clare, Susan, *Maas and the Mainstream: 1989 – 2000, New Literary Press*, (2004), p.34.

424. Model, actress, and daughter of Ingrid Bergman.

425. Released in 1986, *Blue Velvet* is undisputedly one of Lynch's masterpieces. A neo-noir, psycho-sexual mystery, the film saw Lynch receive his second Academy Award nomination for Best Director. It was named after the Bobby Vinton song of the same name.

426. This source was interviewed by Daniel in 2011.

427. *Smack my Crack* (1987).

and Australia, while the musician was part of The Birthday Party. This was before the formation of The Bad Seeds[428] and the widespread critical and commercial success he would go on to receive, but Cave had already made a name for himself as a hugely talented and provocative live performer, shrieking, bellowing, and throwing himself around on stage. Maas's alleged appearances at Cave's early gigs followed his previous association with live performances by a number of proto-punk, punk rock, and later post-punk, bands on both the New York and London music scenes.

Throughout this period, Maas's name continued to be linked to political activism as it had been in the late 1960s and early 1970s. Although the Maas Foundation made no official statement on the artist's political allegiances (if he could be said to have any), his name had been indirectly linked to the Red Wedge[429] movement, organised by UK musicians and comedians from 1985 – 1987 in opposition to the Conservative government led by Prime Minister Margaret Thatcher. Several pieces of Maas's work, such as *The New Racism* for instance, had also been read as being strongly anti-Thatcher in tone, and while this interpretation is subjective of course, it was not denied by the Maas Foundation. Earlier in the decade Maas had been associated with the Campaign for Nuclear Disarmament, which enjoyed a resurgence[430] between 1981 and 1985 in response to the perceived escalation of the Cold War by US President Ronald Reagan. There were also rumours Maas had opposed Thatcher's decision to invade the Falklands in 1982.

Around this time, Helena re-established links with the Maharishi Mahesh Yogi, shortly before he announced his goal to "create Heaven on Earth"[431] by "raising consciousness to the highest level"[432] and moving his official headquarters from Seelisburg, Switzerland, to a former Franciscan monastery in Vlodrop, Netherlands. While Helena was clearly not the devoted follower of Transcendental Meditation that she sometimes made

---

428. Nick Cave and the Bad Seeds formed in 1983 after the dissolution of The Birthday Party.

429. This collective of musicians, including Billy Bragg and Paul Weller, launched in 1985 in the run up to the 1987 general election, in the hope of engaging with young people and the policies of The Labour Party, and ousting Margaret Thatcher from Government. The collective took its name from a 1919 poster by Russian constructivist artist El Lissitzky, *Beat the Whites with the Red Wedge*.

430. The CND was formed in 1957 and continued to exist throughout the '60, '70's and into the '80s. It had a resurgence between '81 and '85 called The Second Wave, with a large increase in membership – Anonymous.

431. www.tm.org

432. As above.

out to be (she was a businesswoman first and an artist second), she was acutely aware that the Maharishi Mahesh Yogi was credited with heading worldwide charitable organisations, for-profit businesses, and real estate investments worth an estimated £3-5 billion, and that an association with the Maas Foundation could be very beneficial.

In early 1989, Maas's name appeared in the mainstream press on two notable occasions. The first instance came amid rumours he had written a letter of support to the writer Salman Rushdie, whose fourth novel *The Satanic Verses* (1988) had led to him to receive death threats, including a fatwā issued by Ayatollah Ruhollah Khomeini, Supreme Leader of Iran, in February that year. Shortly after this Maas was also mentioned in a feature[433] on the rise of personal computers and consumer electronics. The article claimed that Maas had been an early proponent of this technology and had owned at least five personal computers since the early 1980s, with a particular preference for Apple Macintosh hardware. Maas bought the first Macintosh in 1984[434] and supposedly had a room in his mansion consisting entirely of wall-to-wall electronics. According to the article, his latest purchase was the first Macintosh portable computer,[435] which was released in 1989.[436] He would go on to own many other Apple products through the 1990s and up to the present day, according to one of his former aides, who confirmed that many of the details in the feature were true. However, some of his fans argued that this clashes with the 'anti-technological' themes explored in some of his artworks. As the pro-Maas journalist John Adams said:

"There are a number of Maas installations, not to mention his paintings, sculptures, and written work, which clearly negotiate fears of multimedia fascism, dehumanisation, and loss of personal freedom... the short story *Lynchburg*, for instance, where a boy notices messages inside ghost images on his TV, which turn out to be part of an ultra-violent mind control and brain-washing conspiracy, directly engages with these themes... Other work by Maas explores related concepts such as hyper-reality and simulation..."[437]

---

433. Published in future technology magazine *The New Flesh #7*, July 1989, p.33.

434. The launch of this was famously promoted by a $1.5m advert named *1984*, directed by Ridley Scott and first screened during the 1984 US Superbowl television coverage.

435. This was quickly replaced by the Powerbook after a number of issues, including its hefty weight at 17lb making it less than ideal for a portable computer.

436. 1989 – 1991 was later described as the first 'Golden Age' of the Macintosh line.

437. From an interview in 2004.

Technology would have a significant impact on both the content of art and how it was produced, in the next two decades. Maas had clearly foreseen this and reportedly pioneered many techniques for utilising computer and digital technology in art as early as the 1980s. It is something he would continue to do through the 1990s and 2000s, right up to his disappearance.

In the early 1990s, while Maas continued to work out of his studio in the Hertfordshire countryside, speaking to international contacts, collaborators, and his aides almost entirely by telephone and close-circuit television, Helena continued to make her presence felt in the London art world. A couple of years earlier she had attended the opening of The Saatchi Gallery and had made contacts among the group referred to as the 'Young British Artists'.[438] Like Helena, Charles Saatchi had made his money in the advertising world and had become famous for his high-profile interest in contemporary art, launching the careers of Damien Hirst and several others in the process. In 1989, Helena followed Saatchi's example by purchasing a 40,000 sq ft warehouse in Kensington and converting it into a gallery, where she could display the work she had bought over the years, as well as her own paintings. Her former assistant added:

"Helena was an incredibly astute businesswoman and could see the way the market was going. She very quickly identified the direction that needed to be taken, not only for her own work, but for the Maas Foundation, in order to stay fresh and relevant..."[439]

If Saatchi and the YBA garnered most of the headlines during the 1990s due to their controversial installations, such as Hirst's *The Physical Impossibility of Death in the Mind of Someone Living*,[440] Helena and her projects – perhaps due to her personal association with Maas rather than her own ability – were generally held in even higher esteem by the art world's heavyweight opinion formers. Helena's Lacuna gallery, named after an early work by her husband, opened in November with a high-profile launch attended by a veritable who's who of the art, culture, and entertainment industry.

Throughout the 1990s, the gallery featured a mixture of established international artists, emerging British talent, Helena's own work, and

---

438. The Young British Artists, or YBAs – also referred to as Brit artists and Britart – is the name given to a loose group of visual artists who first began to exhibit together in London, in 1988. Many of the artists graduated from the BA Fine Art course at Goldsmiths in the late 1980s.

439. Daniel conducted this interview in 2011.

440. A vitrine containing a shark preserved in formaldehyde, which was bought by Saatchi for £50,000 and later sold for £7m.

often complete unknowns whose talent she had noticed at art colleges and alternative artist-run spaces throughout the UK. From December 1990 to July 1991, Lacuna featured an exhibition by the American abstract painters Marc Johnson, Tyler King, Sarah Sweeney, and the minimalist sculptors Joan and Jason Hartman. The following year saw a focus on New York conceptual artists Johnny Diaz, Phillip Long, and Susan Gaudi, and pop art practitioners Jenny Ryker and Joseph Wright, before 1993's high-profile exhibition of European painters such as Henry Lukacs and Sally LeBleu, which introduced many of these names to the UK for the first time. Helena then turned her attention to promoting new British talent and was credited with discovering and launching the careers of Susie Wren, Christopher Rudd, and Paul Kerr, among others. Although she had previously promoted her husband's work exclusively, Helena said she created Lacuna, with Maas's approval, to support new and original voices in any medium. This was supplemented with grants for emerging artists, provided by the Maas Foundation, and other opportunities offered through ezramaas.com following its launch at the end of the decade.

Despite her solo success as a curator and manager, Helena continued to actively showcase her husband's work, making it clear at all times that his art was on another level entirely, not simply from the other artists she worked with, but from any other living artist. She also carried on her work representing his broader business interests, maintaining the day-to-day organisation of the Maas Foundation, and negotiating the use of Maas's work in collaborations and 'spin-off' projects. For example, between 1995 – '97, Helena licensed a number of Maas images and quotes to be used in adverts and promotion for video game consoles, including the launch of Sony's PlayStation. Unlike David Lynch, who would direct *The Third Place* adverts for PlayStation 2 in the early 2000s, Maas had no actual involvement in the campaigns, but this was another example of Helena's almost prophetic ability to anticipate business opportunities, which enhanced her husband's legacy.

Following the commodification of art in the 1980s, the next two decades would see a number of artists rise to household name status, but arguably the two to achieve the greatest level of fame and wealth were the aforementioned Damien Hirst, who was at the peak of his powers during the 1990s, and Banksy, from the early 2000s onwards. The two artists had as many similarities as they had differences, but like Haring and Basquiat in the 1980s, and Warhol, Beuys, Koons, and so many others before that, they would draw frequent comparisons with Ezra Maas. If Maas was concerned by the latest pretenders on the scene, he did not show it. While Helena was always mindful of the need to keep Maas's brand relevant, the artist himself continued to follow his own interests and obsessions. He did not follow trends, he created them. Although he had arrived at the end of Pop Art, as it was succeeded by Minimalism, Maas had always been one step ahead, experimenting with conceptual, performance, land, environmental, kinetic, space, op art, postmodern, and many other movements, sometimes before the terms were even coined by critics or artists themselves. He had inspired a generation.

However, in many ways, Hirst followed in Helena Maas's footsteps rather than Ezra's. As previously stated, Helena was a businesswoman first and an artist second, and the press said the same of Hirst on more than one occasion. For the latter, it was levelled as a criticism, but for Helena it was seen as one of her strengths. However, Hirst's talent as a curator and a collector (as well as a businessman and entrepreneur) should not be underestimated.[441] Whether he deserved it or not, Hirst became one of the few contemporary artists known by people on the street, while achieving an estimated net worth of £650m in the late 2000s that put him in an elite category. This was a rare achievement.

The British street artist and activist Banksy would arguably surpass Hirst's fame, if not his sales, without ever using his real name. Like Maas, part of his appeal was the mystery around his identity concealed, in his case, by a graffiti handle. His subversive, anti-establishment, stencils, first on the streets of Bristol, then across the UK, and eventually internationally, would lead to high-profile exhibitions in LA (attended by Hollywood stars such as Brad Pitt), a book,[442] an Oscar-nominated documentary film,[443] and even a satiric, Disneyland-inspired theme park, 'Dismaland' in Weston-super-Mare. This success has seen the street artist occupying an uncomfortable

---

441. If accumulating wealth through the collection and sale of art was one of Hirst's priorities, it was hardly surprising given that he had grown up in the '80s. The artist often recalled his days living in a North London squat as a struggling seventeen-year-old artist. He had worked as a labourer and turned to petty crime before his eventual success, which first came as a curator with 1988s Freeze exhibition in the London docklands rather than as an artist. Hirst did not subscribe to the theory that the commodification of art had a negative impact on artistic integrity. A two-day auction of 244 pieces of Hirst's work in 2008 reportedly netted him £111m. At the same time, he was criticised for employing assistants on less than £20,000-a-year to produce artwork such as his 'spot' paintings. Produced based on his instructions, but not by his hand, these works still carried the price tag of an original Hirst. This production line approach (Hirst compared it to Rubens, but it's more reminiscent of Warhol) has attracted considerable criticism.

442. *Wall and Piece* (2005).

443. *Exit Through the Gift Shop* (2010)

position, where he has been increasingly accused of being a 'capitalist in anarchist's clothing', whatever his subversive intentions.

A further interesting parallel between Maas and Banksy, beyond their anonymity, involves speculation that they are really a collective of artists rather than a single person. Conspiracy theorists claim this is why Maas has never officially been seen in public, does not give interviews, or allow photographs of himself to be taken, and has never attended any of his exhibitions or launches – he does not exist. This theory would mean that Ezra Maas was the creation of the Maas Foundation, rather than the other way around, and the so-called followers and assistants who make and sell his work are essentially all Ezra Maas. Similarly, it has been suggested that 'Banksy' is the work of a team of artists, with one investigative journalist claiming Banksy was the invention of the British band Massive Attack (led by Robert Del Naja's 3D) after identifying a correlation between the hip-hop band's international tours and the appearance of Banksy's artwork around the world. Curiously, an almost identical claim was made thirty years earlier by America supermarket tabloid *The National Enquirer*,[444] which speculated that Ezra Maas was really David Bowie, after a similar correspondence between the musician's *Let's Dance* tour of 1984 and a series of Maas exhibitions that year. It even reprinted the story in 2016 following Bowie's death, claiming that Maas's disappearance was related to Bowie's long-term battle with cancer and eventual death.

Maas, if anything, seemed content to let others occupy the limelight in the 1990s and into the 2000s. While art may have become no more than a product, an investment for the rich to get richer and protect their wealth in a time of economic uncertainty and declining yields, it represented something much more important to Maas. The Maas Foundation had made it clear that Ezra was not concerned with fame or wealth, even though he had achieved both. According to them, Maas's ongoing absence from public life was to ensure his continued focus on that which was most important to him – his work.

However, as always, there were alternative explanations, and one of the most compelling was around his failing health. From the mid-1980s to the end of the 1990s, stories spread that Maas's physical condition had continued to deteriorate following the injuries he had suffered in the crash in the Congo several years earlier. While Helena was increasingly visible, Maas himself was descending further into seclusion. It was implied that his retreat from public life had little to do with art and more to do with

---

444. *The National Enquirer*, Vol 3, Issue 57, November 1984. Reprinted March 2016.

his physical and psychological condition following the accident. One journalist, who was later discredited, wrote an article suggesting Maas had become addicted to codeine and injected the drug intramuscularly to cope with the chronic pain from his injuries. There were also suggestions that the heavy drug use of the '60s and '70s had either taken its toll or continued unabated. Although the story was never published, I was able to speak to the journalist, off-the-record, who revealed a number of details about the planned exposé. Among other things, it also claimed Maas was suffering mental health problems, including obsessive compulsive disorder,[445] and that he was displaying symptoms consistent with autism and Asperger's syndrome.[446] According to the journalist, Maas had a vast collection of music and films and would watch particular movies on a continuous loop.[447] There was also speculation that following the accident he had developed a fear of flying and this was one possible reason for basing himself almost entirely in England in the years after the crash.[448] Again, this was strongly denied by the Maas Foundation. The artist had spent more than three decades surrounded by wild rumours, many of which had been started by Maas and his own followers to divert the media from the truth, but the next few years would be dominated by negative stories, hinting at discord within his own organisation, and even his own family, in a controversial period critics have referred to as 'Maas Mutiny'.

---

445. Although most of these accusations have been discredited, Maas's obsessive behaviour was alleged to have included only touching items from outside his manor house if they were wrapped in tissues or cleaned with an antibacterial spray. It was also claimed that he only spoke directly to his personal assistants via close circuit TV or telephone, would only drink orange juice that had been freshly squeezed before his eyes, and that he had begun to practice ceremonial magic.

446. This parallels similar claims from his childhood which had not resurfaced in the thirty years since – Anonymous.

447. He allegedly watched the film *Shane* (1953) more than 150 times.

448. Although The Maas Foundation contends his reasons had more to do with the greater freedom the UK offered (his work had met with censorship in the US) and the fact that England was his home.

Daniel James
Chapter Sixteen

The truth of course is that there is no journey. We are arriving and departing all at the same time.[449]

There are no accidents. At least that's what they say. And yet almost everything in our lives turns on chance. How much do we really control? And how much of that control is an illusion? The trail led me north. Of course it did. The book had become as much about me as it was about Maas. It was only fitting that it would take me home to Newcastle. I booked a train and didn't question it any further. The truth was, if it hadn't led north, I would have found somewhere else to run. I couldn't stay in London any longer with the police actively looking for me. Once they had me in custody it wouldn't take them long to connect me with the other deaths and I didn't like my chances of convincing them that I had nothing to do with any of it. I had to stay one step ahead and find the answers myself, I had to keep moving.

PHONE TRANSCRIPT: **Daniel James - Victoria King**

3/10/11, 10:14am

DJ: Hey, Vicky.

VK: Hey, Dan. How's the book coming along?

DJ: It's getting there, but I can't say too much about it right now. Not on the phone anyway. I'll tell you more when I see you.

VK: Sounds intriguing. Does that mean you're coming back to Newcastle?
DJ: Yeah, but do me a favour , don't tell anyone.

VK: Of course. Any particular reason?

DJ: I just need to put some distance between me and London for a little while. It's a long story for another time.

VK: I'll take your word for it… so what are your plans once you're back?

---
449. David Bowie (1947 – 2016).

DJ: More work unfortunately. I'm following up a few leads on the book and you might be able to help, actually. I found a connection between a theatrical agency based in Newcastle and a film Maas made years ago. If I give you the name, could you see if they're still in business?

VK: Of course. Do you want me to give them a call if they are?

DJ: Yeah, maybe… although you should probably use a fake name. Actually, scratch that. Tell them you're calling from the Maas Foundation and see how they react.

VK: Ha, okay. Anything else?

DJ: Yeah, I'm trying to track down an artist called Joanna Hutton and I seem to remember you featured her in the magazine, last year or the year before?

VK: Joanna Hutton? Yeah, she has a studio on High Bridge Street, or at least she used to. I'll see if I've still got a number for her.

DJ: Great. Thanks Vicky. I should be up in the next day or two. I'll drop you a line once I'm back.

VK: While you're on the phone, there's something I needed to speak to you about, actually. We've been receiving some odd emails recently and they're addressed to you.

DJ: What kind of emails?

VK: From a potential contributor. He claims to be a poet, but his emails are written like experimental avant-garde fiction, and his actual work is even weirder.

DJ: Do you know who's sending them?

VK: He said his name is M.T. Stewart, but that he wants his byline in the magazine to be a series of numbers.

DJ: Numbers?

VK: Yeah, if he's putting on the crazy act, then his commitment is frightening. He's literally been emailing the magazine every day for the last month. It might be

nothing, but I thought you'd want to see the emails
either way. Do you want me to forward a few of them to
you?

DJ: Yeah, send them across and I'll read them on the
train.

VK: Thanks, and make sure you come into the office when
you're up here, okay? You've been away too long.

DJ: I will.

VK: Are you sure you're okay, Dan? You sound strange.

DJ: I'm fine… I just need to finish this book. I better
go Vicky, but I'll be in touch soon, I promise.

END

I started reading M.T. Stewart's emails[450] before I left London, to distract
myself as much as anything, but I soon found myself intrigued enough to
send him a reply. He emailed back in minutes and our correspondence
began. Stewart's emails were in the same style as his writing; a technique he
later defined as bitter present-postmodernism. He had clearly been waiting
for me to respond personally, baiting *The Bleed* with his strange messages
until they passed his emails to me, the magazine's once and future editor.
And when I replied, it became a game between us. A game of words and
ideas. Neither of us knew the rules until after it ended, but we didn't let that
hold us back.

It started simply enough. We talked about Flann O'Brien, Samuel
Beckett, and Thomas Pynchon; he sent me his fiction, and I told him about
the book that I was writing. I even sent him a few preview pages. This was
when things changed. He applauded the creation of the 'characters' Daniel

---

450. From Daniel's handwritten notes: "My method as a biographer has always been to make
everything in my life 'available' to my fiction. Anything and everything can be used, absorbed,
included. If I had any rules for myself as a writer, then this would be one of them. These emails
were part of my life during this period and everything in my life became part of the book in
the end. More specifically, they influenced my writing, imperceptibly, changing the course of
my investigation, and altering the way I looked at the world. If not for my interaction with
M.T. Stewart, I may never have realised the full implication of what Maas was planning, the
true consequences of his final work. I owe Stewart for that. I was never sure how much he really
knew. In my darker moments, I wondered whether he might be involved, for a second I even
thought he might be Maas himself, communicating with his own biographer, tormenting me,
manipulating me, playing his games with me, but I like to think that Stewart was genuine; a
fellow artist, developing his own voice, and helping me to find mine."

James and Ezra Maas, seemingly misunderstanding the nature of my work and believing it to be entirely fiction. I assured him the man I was writing about was very real. And that I was very real. I was writing a blend of fact and fiction, but it wasn't a novel. It was a biography. Yet still he persisted, and before long I realised he was becoming part of my story. For this reason, I have included him in the text.[451]

◉

From: ██████████████████
To: Daniel James <dan@danjameswriter.com>
Sent: 11 October 2011, 09:17
Subject: The Book

Daniel,

I love the story around *The Third Policeman* being published. A frustrated O'Brien told friends that: "the boot of my car flew open when driving. I watched as the manuscript fluttered away page by page". In reality, it sat on his sideboard for 26 years. I bet they spoke a lot! Was he hinting at something? The concept in itself couldn't be contained.

Okay Daniel, I'm going to have a spy at the pages you sent. We'll see what strange goings on emerge.

From: ██████████████████
To: Daniel James <dan@danieljameswriter.com>
Sent: 21 October 2011, 15:11
Subject: The Book

I love the concept for your book. It got me 'wired right up into a paranoid frenzy'. I embrace that, take a toke, and hug it some more. I personally wouldn't know where to start, but that'll probably work in your favour. Your writing is strange, you are very perceptive, more than you probably know yourself. And that will be your real problem, Dan. It's like psychotherapy if you get it right. I know this because I live with a psychotherapist (not a normal), a strange, marvellous, quirky specimen, whose ideology I suckle on. Good luck with the book. If anybody can 'fuck it up', justly, you can Dan.

---

451. From Daniel's handwritten notes: "When you read his emails, you will understand why they became part of this story. Or maybe you won't. You may think him mad. Our correspondence was tuned into a peculiar frequency and I didn't always understand it myself. It wasn't until later that I fully decoded the meaning of our emails, realising that it was more than a distraction, more than just a game. Whether by chance or design, M.T. Stuart had his own part to play in this book. As a result, I have included a selection of our correspondence, which began via email in London, and continued on throughout my stay in Newcastle, before finally ending weeks later.

From: ████████████████████████
To: Daniel James <dan@danieljameswriter.com>
Sent: 5 November 2011, 18:44
Subject: The Book

I apologise for not giving you the rules to our game, but I didn't know myself, till the story had finished. I had my doubts about Dan. However, your interpretation of events as Daniel leaves me in a realm of untold possibilities. I asked myself two questions when writing that piece of 'reel-time fiction.' When should I stop? And why am I holding back? You answered this question for me: I, too, am scared of my own writing, and where and what it could lead to.

You have been in-valuable in helping me start to find my voice (the experience of writing that piece was better than any drug). I now need to fuel that taste for more. I appreciate all the praise you heap on my writing, and your understanding nature to the nature of content in my work. I now feel I can trust you, and with this newfound comfort, and further appreciation of the deep, and knowledgeable, character you are, you are undoubtedly going to find lunacy attacking fear, at, and in, every orifice of this great nation, and in-deed-myself.

From: ████████████████████████
To: Daniel James <dan@danieljameswriter.com>
Sent: 21 November 2011, 13:16
Subject: The Book

I'll look into Beckett's work. His idea of not being able to reach his inner core is, as you have said, "a lie to him-self to keep the dogs at bay." Psychotherapy and writing can be one and the same (if not ignored), a science which is steeped in creativity (sand tray-symbolism-movement-words). I take it you have looked into this? The artist breathes.

From: ████████████████████████
To: Daniel James <dan@danieljameswriter.com>
Sent: 2 December 2011, 12:23
Subject: The Book

The success will come, and the nightmare will begin. But not for me! I accept your offer. If I can just show some of them in their true light, they will turn the barrel on themselves in bed, late at night, but before they do, they will tell their loved ones, and the cycle will begin; a psychological kick-back that is well over-due. With eloquence, I say "fuck 'em," no matter who, what, or where. I have to commend you. You are indeed gifted, and stand out from the usual rabble.

From: ██████████████████
To: Daniel James <dan@danieljameswriter.com>
Sent: 17 December 2011, 16:05
Subject: The Bleed

In my eyes, Beckett's failure was in the belief that there is no inner-core. We are all part child, parent, (both father and mother, grandfather, grandmother, and great-grandfather – 'do you see where I'm going with this?'), and adult ego states, which fluctuate through the inner turmoil of trauma in past experiences of which we have lived.

(sand tray-symbolism-movement-words) This is a beautiful image, and I'm so pleased you picked up on this. It should read (sand tray-symbolism-movement-words-guided imagery.) I have myself been on one of these journeys (unofficially) out of curiosity. It was a two-week body-shaking experience that spoke to many demons. By constantly embracing these demons you can break through psychological impasse after impasse, and find your-self, but then you see that everything is a facade to keep yourself safe. Just when you think you're being truly honest that's when you're lying to your-self. It's a kicker! It's probably your parents talking to you, unconsciously… not you. What a laugh!

Did you know that if you take someone on a guided imagery journey, and go too far, it can bring on post-traumatic stress? Examples are: loss of speech, loss of movement in the limbs, or total paralysis. The client cannot lie to themselves anymore, they are forced to feel. This is all done through speech, words – imagine that eh! Now that gets me thinking! Has that been done in any art before? Imagine if you could read an actual 'real-life trauma book' or experience a work of art[452] which would connect you to your real self.

Over and out

P.S. I wish you the best of luck with your book and hope you are in the right frame of mind to do justice to its pages. 'We' will judge your words, and expression, to see who you really are!

---

452. From Daniel's handwritten notes: "Could this be a clue to the final project Maas was working on? Did M.T. Stewart even realise the lead he was giving me here?" This might be the psychological dirty-bomb Daniel refers to later in the manuscript, based on the plans and notes he found in Maas's apartment linking quantum mechanics, esoteric religious concepts, and psychoanalysis – Anonymous.

From: ███████████████████████
To: Daniel James <dan@danieljameswriter.com>
Sent: 23 December 2011, 17:04
Subject: The Book

Who am I? The numbers pinpoint my signature, in a roundabout sort of starry way. The numbers have a 'million and one,' connotations in the Pythagorean system. Hopefully in time, numbers, words, and psychotherapy, can hold the key. Of course, this is all bullshit, as there is no key, but I'm sure it will entertain on some level. If your readers want to explore my name, or my work, that's unfortunate. If they want a meaning, well, good luck. If they want answers, well... 'go fish, and dig your own fucking hole.' You can quote me on all of this! Please! And tell them I begged you, too. In fact, copy and paste this message. In fact, send them round to my house; tell them to bring their friends and family members. But I do ask one thing, please, for their own safety, 'bring a tatty peeler, and don't knock before you enter.'

From: ███████████████████████
To: Daniel James <dan@danieljameswriter.com>
Sent: 11 January 2012, 10:51
Subject: The Book

No need for a penny. Someone has wired the system to the mains, and the roof is glowing, oh yes, and the smell tastes of pure execution. In the golden days, on a tide of war, the only landmarks were that of the dead.

From: ███████████████████████
To: Daniel James <dan@danieljameswriter.com>
Sent: 28 January 2012, 11:32
Subject: The Book

We have all known who is who and where is where from the start. I, however, am now passed that impasse. I couldn't have done it without your help and my psychotherapist. The sting is now gone. Well, that will do you a lot of good. No reality of who or where you really are in the world.

From: ███████████████████████
To: Daniel James <dan@danieljameswriter.com>
Sent: 19 February 2012, 14:17
Subject: The Book

Step above the game awhile Daniel, and be aware that you, and me, have been trying to express a certain something to our fathers. This episode is over for me.

It is now all about the writing, and the voice. Good luck with the book.

P.S. What is the topic of your next novel? Nothing predictable, I hope?

I couldn't tell if M.T Stewart was serious, or if he was playing a game with me, but his messages began to take on an increasingly unsettling dimension, before finally stopping abruptly. I never heard from him again. He had turned my rules[453] against me. Much later, I would come to realise, whether he knew what he was doing or not, his messages had communicated a secret truth that would haunt me to the end.

---

453. "Everything is part of the story, everything said and unsaid, everything that happens, or could happen, everything imagined and experienced, can be used in the text. Nothing is ever off-the-record." Daniel on his method from his handwritten notes – Anonymous.

Daniel James
Chapter Seventeen

If the world were clear, art would not exist[454]

I rested my head against the glass as the train to Newcastle rocked back and forth gently. The mist that rolled across the fields, past isolated farmhouses and under a baking sun, blurred the horizon, making the world soft and smudged around the edges. Waves of light and particles of dust came into being and fell out of existence, coalescing into a landscape as the train sped north. Sunlight danced on the surface of the Tyne as we crossed one of its famous bridges and entered the city, as I came home at last.

Once I was back, I didn't speak the name Ezra Maas for two days. I was a father again. I held my children in my arms, carried them on my shoulders, threw them in the air, and let them climb all over me. Days of laughter and tickles, cuddles and kisses. I was a husband again. Life returned to how it might have been if different choices had been made. My other life, London, the book, Ezra Maas, was all just a bad dream, but I should have known that you can't run from your own shadow, you can't escape from one dream into another. I said my goodbyes and returned to real life. When the train pulled to a stop, the sunlight on the surface of the Tyne had disappeared. My other life was just an illusion, a trick of the light. I walked out of the station, into the cold air, reality hitting home like an icy wave.

I was here to see an artist, Joanna Hutton, whose exhibition[455] had been the victim of guerrilla artwork by Maas, or one of his followers. *The Guardian* had covered the incident, comparing it to when Banksy infiltrated the Museum of Modern Art and covertly installed his own artworks on display in the gallery.[456] Joanna hadn't seen the intruder herself, but several witnesses had noticed a strange man at her exhibition, and someone had apparently signed one of her programmes with the name 'Ezra Maas'. It wasn't the first time this had happened. Since taking

---

454. French philosopher, author and journalist Albert Camus (1913 – 1960), *The Myth of Sisyphus*.

455. *Aporias*, 2011 – '12.

456. These incidents are alleged to have taken place in March 2005 and saw Banksy allegedly subvert artworks in the Museum of Modern Art, Metropolitan Museum of Art, and American Museum of Natural History in Manhattan, as well as the Brooklyn Museum in Brooklyn – Anonymous.

this job, my publisher had been inundated with calls from people who claimed to have information about Maas, including a number of similar guerrilla stunts. Everyone wanted to be a part of the story, but most of the reports filtered through to me led nowhere. People saw Maas here, there, and everywhere, but I was intrigued by the newspaper story about Joanna's exhibition. It was just crazy enough to be true, and the Newcastle connection seemed like too much of a coincidence to ignore. I was being called back home by a fresh lead just as I needed to escape London.

The streets were full of ghosts. Medieval castle walls intersected with classical architecture, early 20th century engineering merged with brutal angular monoliths, and restored shipping warehouses stood side by side with contemporary glass and steel constructions; the past and present coexisted, layer upon layer of time, occupying the same space, filled with the spectres of potential futures and half-realised visions that could never fully disappear. A city that haunted itself.

A few ugly, concrete scars remained, but Newcastle had survived the T Dan Smith[457] era, and his faux Utopian plans for 'Brasilia of the North', the city and its people enduring long enough to see its most beautiful buildings restored to their former grandeur by legitimate cultural regeneration, with new and iconic landmarks rising up along the Quayside and throughout the City Centre, in place of what was lost.

Today, like most cities, Newcastle faced a different kind of battle – to retain any kind of identity in the face of super-modernity, where difference was eroded and washed away in place of homogenous, global brands. Where you no longer lived in a city, you lived in Terminal 5. It was the kind of bleak, late capitalist, future predicted by the anthropologist Marc Augé, who first coined the term 'non-places'.[458]

Everywhere was becoming nowhere.

I didn't want that to happen to a city as special as Newcastle. For better or worse, it was, and would always be, my home.

I walked up Grainger Street towards Grey's Monument and the city centre. The buildings in Grainger Town were among the finest examples of classical architecture in the country, rivalling Bath and Edinburgh, and

---

457. T. Dan Smith (1915 – 1993) was a British politician and leader of Newcastle City Council from 1960 – 1965. An innovative documentary film about his life and career, *A Funny Thing Happened on the Way to Utopia,* was released in 1988, produced by Newcastle's Amber Films. Although his impact of Newcastle's historic architecture is referenced negatively, the demolition of buildings such as old Eldon Square and Dobson's Royal Arcade took place after he left office.

458. For more on Marc Auge and non-places see my footnotes on Pg. xx – Anonymous.

the jewels in the crown of historic Newcastle. Grey Street, whose gentle downward curve towards the river had captivated the poet John Betjeman, was arguably the best of the lot. Joanna Hutton's gallery was nearby on High Bridge Street, a fashionable cobbled lane filled with cafes, bars, restaurants, and shops.

I wished I had time for more old haunts; the vaulted ceilings of the library at the Lit & Phil, the Art Deco glamour of the Tyneside Cinema, the food stalls and traders in the Grainger Market, the pubs and live music in the Ouseburn, but I had to be all business.

Joanna's gallery was closed until 5pm, so I messaged Vicky and decided to kill time in a basement bar I knew well. It was hidden away beneath a smoke and tap house. There were no signs, no windows, just a heavy wooden door with a grate that slid across to let you glimpse inside. It was small, dark, and heavy on atmosphere, with flickering candles in red glass table lamps, leather seats, low wooden ceilings, murals of skeletons, and faded film noir icons on the walls, and quotes from the likes of Tom Waits, Charles Bukowski, and William Burroughs.

The bartender [459] wore rolled up shirt sleeves, with a waistcoat and a pocket watch. He was tall and broad-shouldered, with a thick woodsman beard. I took a seat on one of the bar stools and scanned the red, leather-bound, cocktail menu, its skulls and chemical symbols straight out of an apothecary, while I waited for him to turn around. Art Garfunkel's version of *I Only Have Eyes For You* was playing in the background.[460]

'Hey Joe.'

'Dan,' he replied. 'It's been awhile.'

'I've been out of town.'

'What can I get you?'

'The usual.'

I watched as Joe worked his magic, skilfully mixing together Rittenhouse 100 Proof Rye whiskey with house-made coffee stout liqueur, Campari, Byrrh, Mellow Corn whiskey, and Fernet-Branca, before adding a pinch of sea salt and finally stirring it with a cinnamon quill. Joe placed a black napkin down on the counter and slid the heavy glass tumbler across to me. One drink quickly turned into three. I was just about to order a fourth when the door opened to my right, and I watched a woman enter on my periphery. She walked up to the bar and slid an envelope along to me. I

459. Believed to be Newcastle-based mixologist Joe Summerfield – Anonymous.

460. A No.1 hit from his 1975 album, *Breakaway*, the song is a jazz standard and was originally written in 1934 for the film *Dames*.

reached out and caught it.

'You were right about that theatrical agency,' Vicky smiled. 'I said the name 'Ezra Maas' and they practically told me their life story.'

I stood up and gave her a hug.

'What's in the envelope?'

'It turns out Warren Wagner Associates has been forwarding royalty payments to a farm in Northumberland for the last fifteen years.'

'And you got the address?' I smiled. 'I think maybe you should be the detective.'

'Beginner's luck.'

'I don't know about that. You've always been full of surprises.'

I ordered the same again and a Lynn Collins[461] for Vicky. As I looked through the contents of the envelope, we reminisced about the good old days when we used to sit across from each other at the magazine; I would come in late and hung-over, and she'd help wake me up with strong coffee, water, and painkillers, then we'd get to work. When we were done reminiscing, I put the envelope safely into my bag and settled the bill.

'It's been good seeing you, Dan.'

'And you,' I replied, as we clinked glasses and finished the last of our drinks.

'I like the beard,' she said. 'It suits you.'

'It was the best disguise I could come up with,' I replied.

She laughed, but I could tell there was something on her mind.

'Look, I know you've got to go, so I'll cut straight to the chase. Sam has been worried about you... I have too.'

'You don't need to worry. I can take care of myself.'

'I know that, but you shouldn't have to. Not when you have people here who care about you... It must be lonely, the way you live.'

'I'm not lonely,' I replied, unconvincingly. My voice was distant and empty, a recording of a recording.

'You can't fool me,' she said.

'It's too late,' I said quietly, and stood up to leave.

'You know, it's not the Maas Foundation that scares me. I'm more worried about you.'

I kissed her on the cheek and headed for the door.

'Goodbye, Vicky.'

'Dan?' Her voice faltered for a second.

I wanted to turn around and smile my usual smile. I wanted to reassure

---

461. Lychee-infused gin, lemongrass-infused St Germain, lemon juice and Ginger Beer.

her like the old days, but I couldn't.

'You're not coming back, are you?' she said, behind me. 'Even if you find out the truth... you're not coming back.'

As I expected, Joanna was happy to be interviewed. She was a conceptual artist who had begun to incorporate preserved birds into her work, after a chance visit to a taxidermist inspired her to become a member of the Guild of Taxidermists. Her disconcertingly beautiful installations often featured avian elements, reflecting her fascination with the symbolism, superstitions, and folklore, surrounding birds. If someone from the Maas Foundation really had attended her exhibition, they clearly shared a similar preoccupation to Joanna's, for on the signed programme to her show, they had also written: *Do birds carry the souls of the dead?*

Joanna's installations incorporated natural materials and found objects, like fishing wire and a wasp nest, as well as the preserved bodies of blackbirds and robins. Her latest piece continued in this tradition and was called *Gravity*. She couldn't explain why the Maas Foundation would be interested in her show. She had no connection to Maas other than the indirect influence his work had on most contemporary artists. I couldn't help but feel there was something I was missing.

The programme Maas had supposedly signed had been folded up and placed in a box set aside for gathering feedback on the exhibition. Several students who were helping with hospitality had described a strange man hanging around during the show, and when the note was found they naturally concluded this must have been Maas. The signature looked near identical to the handwriting on the property deed I had discovered at the apartment in Soho, but that didn't necessarily prove anything. Signatures could be faked, and I had no reason to believe Maas wasn't dead. If he was alive, why would he show up here? And what was his interest in Joanna's work? It was more likely that someone was trying to keep his presence alive in the world and that this was a message for me, rather than Joanna. I looked again at her latest piece, entitled *Gravity*; the corpse of a bird preserved within a mirrored box, and for a moment I saw myself as the bird, trapped by endless reflections.

'Are you okay?' Joanna asked.

'Yes... sorry,' I smiled, and gestured at the bird. 'I was just imagining myself in his place.'

We talked for a while longer, but it was getting late and Joanna needed to lock up. I thanked her for her time and told her to call me if she thought of anything else. As I went to leave, I walked past the box where the note had been found. I stopped.

'This is probably a long shot, but did anyone else leave any unusual comments in the box?' I asked.

'That's a good question. I don't know, to be honest. Everybody was so excited to find the autograph that I don't think we examined the others very closely. You're welcome to take a look through them if you like?'

I didn't spot anything unusual until I got to the last one. Most people wouldn't have noticed it, but I had become used to codes, conditioned to secret messages whether they were from Maas or someone else. Someone had used a pencil to strike through certain letters on the printed text of Joanna's programme notes. I took out a pen and began to copy them down. One by one, they began to form familiar words. The first three spelled out 'D-A-N'. It couldn't be... I wrote down the next three. 'R-U-N'. My heart began to pound inside my chest. It was too explicit a message to be a coincidence. I looked around quickly and began to walk out of the building as fast as I could.

My mind raced. The note had been left weeks ago when the exhibition first opened. Was I finally going mad, finding meaning where there was none? Or had this really been left for me? There was no way anyone could have known that I would be here today.

As I walked out of the gallery and turned onto Grey Street, a black Land Rover slowed to a stop. Three men in suits got out and began to walk behind me. When I crossed the road and cut down Shakespeare Street, they followed. I broke into a run in the direction of the Metro station, hoping to lose them in the crowds. The station was a maze of yellowed enamel panels and angular strips of lighting, scratched steel and scuffed rubber, alive with the rumble of trains, and the purr of machinery. The underground map looked like a circulatory system ripped out of someone's body. I glanced over my shoulder as I weaved through the crowds. They were right behind me now, and one of them was holding a knife in his gloved hand. I began to sprint as fast as I could, heart racing, chest pounding, screaming for people to get out of the way. Move! Move! I saw myself being stabbed to death there in the station, unable to run for all those dumb bodies, surrounded by confused faces struggling to understand what was happening, while I collapsed to my knees, blood pumping out from my chest and seeping through my fingers, my killers disappearing before anyone realises they're looking at a dead man.

I wasn't going to make it. There were too many people blocking the way, and they were right behind. Almost without thinking, I turned around and punched the nearest of the men as hard as I could. He fell backwards into the others, and all of a sudden I was running again, fighting my way to the escalator, my head pounding as I pushed people out of the way and threw myself down the stairs, past startled faces woken from their daydreaming by my flight. Behind me, people were shouting abuse, but I didn't look back. A couple standing side by side on the escalator were slowing me down, so I leapt over the rail and onto the plastic panels running in between, sliding the rest of the way down to the tiled-floor. I hit the ground running, my shoes slipping and sliding as I tried, and failed, to keep my balance. A large man cursed at me after I slammed into him, but I was moving so fast I was around the corner before I even registered his words. I tried to remember the layout of the station, but the corridors all looked identical.

Air rushed through the tunnels, followed by the distant purr of trains coming and going beneath the city. I ran out onto the busy platform. The orange lights on the electronic timetable danced, as words and numbers dissolved and reformed. My train would be here any minute, but I was running out of time. One of the black figures on my periphery was getting closer. I moved down the platform, working my way between the bodies, but I was heading for a dead end.

The train arrived, full of light and noise, just as a gloved hand reached for my jacket. Instead of pulling away, I grabbed hold of the man's arm, spinning us both towards the edge of the platform as the train rushed toward us. I pushed him back and into its path. The screaming and sirens were indistinguishable as I ran up the escalator and back out into the city.

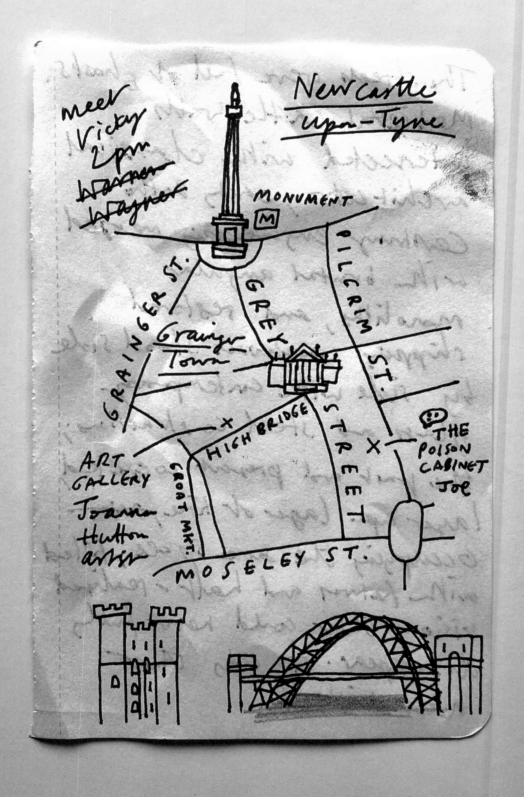

The streets were full of ghosts.
Medieval castle walls
intersected with classical
architecture, early 20th
Century engineering merged
with brutal angular
monoliths, and restored
shipping warehouses stood side
by side with contemporary
glass and steel constructions;
the past and present coexisted,
layer upon layer of time, ~~occupy~~
occupying the same space, filled
with futures and half-realized
visions that could never fully
disappear. A city that
haunted itself.

Ezra Maas: An Oral History
Part Eight

Artists, writers, journalists, photographers, critics, friends, and others, who were around Maas during the years 1956 to 1996, give their impressions of the artist. Interviews by Daniel James.

☆

Jack Cleeves, culture editor at The Washington Post, 1988 – 2001.

JC: One of my favourite stories was from about 1997. An American billionaire, supposedly a quantitative trading genius who made his money from tech-focused hedge funds and venture capital, heard it was possible to get an audience with Maas – for a price. One of his ultra-rich buddies told him of rumours that Maas admitted three people a year into his private compound for a direct audience, and that the whole arrangement was managed by the Maas Foundation. No one knows how much he actually paid, but they say it was over a million dollars. So he's flown to some secret location – a former monastery in Switzerland or something like that – and ushered through several levels of security and ante-chambers until he's seated in a private room. Naturally, he's expecting to meet Ezra Maas. Instead, a screen lowers and Maas begins to talk to the three attendees via the monitor. All they can see of his face is a close-up of his mouth, just his lips and teeth, in an otherwise darkened room. His voice is a hiss through the screen, and his words are barely audible. The craziest thing is that the guy loved it. He wanted to pay for a return visit.

☆

Emmanuelle Franks, a particle physicist at the University of Oslo.

Maas was a polymath, and one of his passions was science. In 2001, while the world believed he was secluded in his mansion, he spent six months working at a research centre on the Antarctic ice, near the Amundsen-Scott South Pole Station. The centre is searching for cosmic neutrinos – often referred to as 'ghost-like particles' – because they pass through the universe, almost without interacting with anything. Maas travelled to our station in secret, with a very small entourage, and stayed in spartan private quarters on the base under a pseudonym. No one knew who he was, why he was there, or what he was doing, but everyone was under orders to grant him anything he asked. We all thought he was a billionaire who was funding the research – and maybe he was? It was only later that we discovered the mysterious stranger was Ezra Maas, the artist. My colleagues and I were looking for cosmic neutrinos off the shoulder of Orion. Our discoveries led us to a distant galaxy with a supermassive black hole at its heart. We were staring into the eye of a monster. I remember Maas once asked us, "Does the monster look back?"

☆

*** Corey Loeb, co-editor of The Third Eye and expert on US cult groups.***

CL: The Maas Foundation is no different than any of the other famous, international, cults. They've just done a better job with their PR. They've got armed compounds in the States, masquerading as research centres, and schools for the gifted, full of second and third generation members. It's not about art or money for these people. That's what makes them really dangerous. They're true believers, and Maas is their religion. C'mon, don't look at me like I should be wearing a tin-foil hat. This is serious, man. The Maas Foundation has been brainwashing people since the '60s. They used to spray the brochures to their exhibitions with hallucinogens that were absorbed through the skin. Maas hired actors to read out poems full of trigger words, and they used strobe lighting, and musical cues, to induce hypnosis and seizures. Those 'happenings' were the first experiments, and they only got more sophisticated from there. You've heard of Cicada 3301? Who'd you think posted that? The Maas Foundation has been recruiting people through the internet since the early '90s. They post esoteric puzzles, involving encrypted pieces of Maas artwork, on message boards and file sharing sites that lead people down a rabbit hole, from one site to the next. They target intelligent but vulnerable people, the games designed around structures, patterns, and visual stimuli that will appeal to their minds – a trap tailored just for them. They'll get you too. Just you wait. That's what they do. They get everyone in the end.

PHONE TRANSCRIPT[462]

Daniel James - Sam Molloy
03.02.12

SM: Let's face it. This wouldn't be the first time you've failed to maintain a professional distance from a job, would it? I'm just concerned this is becoming an obsession. I'm playing devil's advocate here, but what if Maas went off to one of these isolated locations where he had a studio and died of a heart attack? You said yourself he's been everywhere, from Antarctica to the Australian outback. He had the means to go anywhere, and if no one knew his plans, or where he had gone, then his bones could still be there now, while you're running around here chasing shadows.

DJ: What are you trying to say, Sam?

SM: Like I said, I'm not saying you're wrong, but maybe there is no conspiracy, no master plan, no 'big bad' pulling the strings, no-one following you around – other than the people you owe money to, anyway (*laughs*). Seriously though, what if there are no plots and no patterns other than those you've created yourself? A detective can't solve the case if there's no crime.

DJ: Look, I see what you're saying. It makes sense, but people are dead. The Maas Foundation has admitted following me, and I don't think they're the only ones. I've been drugged, attacked. People have tried to kill me, Sam. All of that was real. It's not in my head.

SM: Well, for argument's sake, let's say you're right. It's all real, and Maas is behind it. What's his plan? What's the endgame?

DJ: That's what I need to figure out. The clues are everywhere, overlapping. There are almost too many of them, but maybe that's the idea? Maybe it's all subterfuge – quantum mechanics, the unspeakable name of God, breaking through to a new psychological state of being, returning to a pre-linguistic state, restoring humanity to a core self, revealing the ultimate truth or discovering there is no

---

462. This is only a partial transcript. The beginning of the conversation has unfortunately been lost.

truth at all - maybe it's all smoke and mirrors?

SM: Concealing what?

DJ: Maybe nothing, maybe that's the answer... it's just like Barthes said, "a construction of layers (or levels, or systems), whose body contains, finally, no heart, no kernel, no secret, no irreducible principle, nothing except the infinity of its own envelopes - which envelop nothing other than the unity of its own surfaces".[463]

SM: Look, quoting French philosophers is very impressive and everything, but it's not going to convince me of your sanity...

DJ: I'm being serious.

SM: So am I... well, maybe I'm messing with you a little, but what does Barthes have to do with Maas? He was talking about language, right?

DJ: Yes, his point was that language doesn't signify objective reality, if such a thing exists at all. Language just refers to itself. It's a closed system of infinitely fluid signifiers. Derrida, Kristeva, Saussure, Lyotard, Heidegger, Nietzsche, and many others, have explored this. The idea that we cannot separate language and reality, and that any quest for certainty is misconceived, is not new. What's really frightening is this, if the language we think with, that defines our consciousness and personality, doesn't refer to the world, if the linguistic signs are constantly shifting, if everything is changing all the time, how can we be certain of anything?

SM: You're making my head hurt here... So let me get this straight, the big secret behind Maas's final artwork is that there is no meaning?

DJ: I think you're half right. There is another possibility though, something worse...

SM: What?

DJ: This book is his final artwork.

SM: What do you mean? The book you're writing?

---

463. Barthes, Roland, *Le Bruissement de la langue.*

DJ: Yes… I thought I was the author, but what if I'm just a character? What if I'm part of the final artwork? He has created this world, full of reflections and meaningless clues, dead-ends and overlapping stories, out of his life, out of his art, and he has trapped me inside. This is a man willing to turn his entire life into art, who replaced history with fiction, and disappeared into worlds he created. Do you really think he's above turning another man's life into a piece of 'live' conceptual art, and presiding over it like God? This book is creation, and I'm man, his experiment in free will. Do you see what I'm saying?

SM: Not really, but keep going, anyway.

DJ: Think about it, what would be the purpose of something with no core and no meaning, except for the infinity of its own layers, something with no centre and no exit?[464]

SM: I've got no idea.

DJ: It would make a hell of a maze.[465]

END

---

464. If Daniel is correct, this would make the structure of the book 'Rhizomatic'. A Rhizome is a botanical structure that has been used as a concept in philosophy, most famously by Gilles Deleuze and Felix Guattari, in *Capitalism and Schizophrenia* (1972 – '80). They wrote: "Rhizome has no beginning or end; it is always in the middle, between things, interbeing, intermezzo." Rhizomes are made up of input and output nodes working together in a multiplicity. If a book were 'Rhizomatic', it would imply that the reader also brings their own nodes, which interconnect, a key facet of multiplicity – Anonymous.

465. There are generally considered to be three types of maze/labyrinth. The third type is a net, and its primary feature is that every point can be connected to every other point. Where the connections are not yet designed, they are conceivable based on the repetition of the existing structure. In other words, a net is a potential infinite territory. Deleuze and Guattari define this type of labyrinth using the metaphor of the Rhizome – derived from the botanical term for a subterranean stem. This has been used in attempts to philosophically describe the way the universe of human culture is structured. Its characteristics match a labyrinth of the third type, in that it is structured according to a network of interpretants, making it virtually infinite, because it takes into account multiple interpretations realised by different cultures, and because it does not register only truths, but what has been said about the truth, or what has been believed to be true, as well as what has been believed to be false, or imaginary, or legendary.

Daniel James
Chapter Eighteen

All the world's a stage, and all the men and women merely players;
They have their exits and their entrances, and one man in his time plays many parts[466]

The gate was padlocked.[467] I was going to have to walk the rest of the way. As I looked back at the car, trying to decide whether I needed to move it to the side of the road, the windscreen imploded. The gunshot noise seemed to follow, like an aftershock, but that couldn't have been right. It must have come half a second before, and I just didn't hear it. Right or wrong, that's how I remember it now. The glass shattered, followed by the sound of the shot echoing in all directions. I hit the ground, face in the dirt, breathing hard, head pounding, and tried to look along the horizon for some sign of where the bullet had come from. The caravan, a large American-style trailer, was silver and almost invisible against the wet concrete sky. There were no signs of life, but that shot had come from somewhere. I had driven out here based on the lead Vicky had uncovered, and expected to find a retired actor, but as I lay there in the dirt, I found myself wondering if Maas himself was living out here. Why else take a shot at me? It was a remote and isolated location where he'd never be found. Could it be him? If I did the sensible thing, and drove away, I might never know. Everything that had happened to me, everything that had been taken from me, everyone who had been hurt because of my mistakes, it would all be for nothing. There was a roaring inside my head, a raging static, growing louder. I thought about Ariane, about Wallas, and the others. Whoever was behind all of this had tried to kill me more than once. This had to end. I let out a breath. This isn't the first time you've been shot at, I told myself. Stay calm. If Maas is trying to scare you off, it's not going to work. For some reason, an image flashed into my mind from the western *Shane*, a movie Maas had supposedly watched 150 times. I remembered Jack Palance's character gunning down a farmer, his body sinking into the mud afterwards. The shooter could have me in his sights right now. If I was going to do this, I had to move. Now.

The next thing I knew, I was running through the long grass, crouched over, stopping, starting again, stealing a glance at the trailer; waiting for a second shot to take the head off my shoulders. It was madness. Instead of

---

466. *As You Like It*, Act II, Scene 7, 139 – '43.

467. Located on private land near Barrowburn, Northumberland National Park.

driving away, or calling for help, I was running towards a man with a rifle, unarmed, and with no plan except to close the distance, to get from here to there before he could pull the trigger. I looped around the trailer in a wide arc, realising as I did so that I had traced the shape of a giant question mark in the grass. These are the kind of absurd thoughts you have when you're about to die. The gravel crunched beneath my feet as I crept up behind the trailer. I kept waiting for the back door to fly open and a long, thin barrel to emerge from the darkness, but it didn't. My fingers gripped the door handle. If it was locked I was finished. I almost laughed thinking about having to knock. The handle turned, clicked, and the door began to open.

I looked through the gap. The shooter was crouched down on one knee with his back to me, the rifle clutched in his left hand, with his right parting the steel blinds so he could scan the empty fields and my car beyond them. If he turned around, I was dead. A bullet fired from a rifle like that would have punched a hole the size of a fist straight through me and flung my body back out through the door.

The reflection of his face in the window convinced me to move. It was the same face from the video I had saved from the apartment in Soho, the same face from the photograph at the dinner table in Bruges. It had to be him. I felt a surge of anger rise up in my chest, burning my throat. I was going to wrap my hands around his neck, even if I was full of holes by the time I got to him. I stayed low, out of his line of sight, under the edge of the kitchen counter, moving toward him, inch by inch, all the time watching his reflection, first in the toaster, then the kettle, and the microwave door. It wasn't long before I ran out of kitchen. The next step would be the hardest. I needed to cover six feet of living-room before he could turn around and put a bullet in me. That was the last thing I remember thinking before I began to run.

I felt sick, weightless, head full of static, a roaring sound between my ears, drowning out my thoughts, body slick with sweat running down my back, heat rising off my skin, blood boiling, heart pounding, pounding, pounding, like my fists. There was a crunching sound in his face as I connected. I think it was his nose, but it might have been his cheekbone. I couldn't feel my hands. If I had, I might have stopped sooner, but I couldn't be sure. When I finally did, the knuckles on both my hands were torn open and there was part of a tooth embedded in the flesh, just below my right index finger. I stood over him, breathing heavily, high on the sudden rush of impossible strength I had felt, sickened by what I had done. I looked down at his broken face and crumpled body, which lay awkwardly beneath me. He wore a checked red and blue dressing gown, a stained T-shirt that had probably been white once, cargo shorts, and flip flops. His eyelids flicked open. Had I actually found Maas? Like everything else, I couldn't be sure.

'Maas?'

'I'm... not him,' he said in a whisper, through cracked, bloody teeth. The man turned to one side and spat a large chunk of blood and saliva out onto the carpet.

'I'm not Ezra Maas.'

'I recognise your face from the video footage, from photographs. I saw you introduce yourself as Maas in a film. If you're not him, how do you explain that?'

'You saw what he wanted you to see. I'm not him. I'm just an actor. He paid me to play him in those films. My name is Michael Malone.'

MM were the initials on the headshot of the actor that I had come looking for.

'Why did you shoot at me if you're not Maas?'

'I'm telling you the truth... please... I can prove it.'

Malone got to his feet shakily and began to rummage through a set of drawers, pulling out papers, books and cassette tapes, hidden beneath old clothes. His hands trembled as he showed me his entry in the 1980 edition of *Quinlan's Illustrated Directory of Film Character Actors*, his expired RADA membership, news clippings and reviews from his theatre work in the 1970s, and a portfolio of headshots his agent used to take around to casting sessions. Finally, he played me half a dozen grainy VHS tapes with recordings of B-movies and TV shows he had acted in between 1977 and 1985, his hands shaking as he fumbled with the remote control.

'See?'

When I moved, he leapt back, his face white with fear.

'Please don't hit me again,' he said.

'Don't worry,' I said. 'I believe you... I think... I would never have attacked you in the first place if you hadn't taken a shot at me.'

'I'm sorry,' Malone said. 'I was scared. They told me if anyone ever came looking for me it would be to kill me. I saw you park at the gate and I panicked. It was just a warning shot. I wasn't trying to kill you.'

'The police might not see it that way.'

'You can't call the police. Please. No one can know I'm here. That was the deal.'

'What kind of deal? And who are 'they'?'

'The Maas Foundation.'

'If you can give me Maas, I won't say a word to anyone.'

'I can't. I don't know where he is,' he coughed. 'The only contact I have with him is through his lawyers and flunkies... Do you want a drink?'

I shook my head as Malone got to his feet and limped over to the kitchen. He wiped his bloody face with a tea towel and took a bottle of *Sailor Jerry* out of the cupboard, pouring a generous measure into an enamel mug.

'I first met Maas's entourage in London. They told me he'd seen me on an advert and had told them, 'He's the guy'. Next thing I knew I was invited to meet the inner circle at a restaurant in Bruges where he was working at the time. There were a dozen men and women there, but they wouldn't tell me which one was Maas. I must have passed the audition though because the next thing I knew they were flying me to New York for a photo-shoot.'

Malone winced as he took a drink from the mug.

'They told me Maas wrote the scripts himself,' he continued. 'I couldn't deviate from a word, no improvisation, nothing. There were stage directions too. I had to stand in a particular spot, in a certain way, everything was mapped out by him and his team, my posture, mannerisms, the tone of my voice, the way I was supposed to smile, everything. They dressed me, cut my hair, gave me diction lessons. I had to sign a confidentiality clause that guaranteed I wouldn't get a penny if I talked about the arrangement. Worse than that, I would be sued for everything I had. I needed to stay out of the way until they told me otherwise. That was the deal.'

'Sounds like you got a raw deal. Why would you agree to it?' I asked.

'You think I did it for the money, don't you? Well, I did I suppose, but it was more complicated than that.' He let out a long sigh, kicked off his flip-flops and took a hit of rum.

'I was a bad husband,' he said. 'Believe it or not, the women used to go for me back when I was younger, and I was weak. I was away filming a lot of the time, and there was always another pretty woman on set. Even between gigs when I should have been spending time with my family, I was chasing a youth that had already passed me by, leaving my wife to raise our two girls alone. I would tell myself that my family was the most important thing to me in the world and that I was providing for them, but it was just lip service. My wife got cancer and died hating me. Do you know what that feels like? To see the hate in someone's eyes and to know you deserve every ounce of it? And worse, that you've run out of time to make amends?'

I knew how it felt better than he could have guessed.

'So you made the deal with Maas to punish yourself?'

'My wife was gone and my two girls wanted nothing to do with me. I should have cut my wrists and been done with it, but Maas's people gave me an alternative. If I made the films and disappeared, they would put a huge amount of money in a trust fund for my girls. They're both grown women now and receive the money anonymously every month. The Maas Foundation promised there would be no way to connect the money to me. The girls think it's an insurance policy their mother set up for them.'

'You should let them know you're alive, that it's you sending the money.'

'I don't want them to think I'm trying to buy myself back into their lives. That isn't what this is about. I don't want forgiveness or gratitude. I don't deserve it. And what if they haven't forgiven me? If they looked at me with the same hate in their eyes as their mother, well, I couldn't take that, it would be worse than death.'

'It looks like you're already there.'

He looked at me with desperate eyes. 'You can't tell anyone about this, please... for my daughters' sake.'

'Look, I'm not going to ruin your arrangement,' I said. 'I'm just trying to write a book. Is there anything you can tell me that might help?'

'I told you. I never met Maas directly, just his people. It was his wife who ran the show.'

'Helena?'

'Yes, that's right. She was there when we did the filming and oversaw everything. Everyone was scared of her, even though she was pregnant at the time. There was nothing maternal about her. She was terrifying.'

'What do you mean, pregnant? They never had a child.'

'I'm telling you, she was pregnant... they had a girl... what was her name again? Something old-fashioned... '

'Ophelia?'

'Yes, that's it... Look, I'm sorry', he said, 'but I don't think there's anything else I can tell you.'

'It's okay... you've given me more than you realise.' I handed him one of my cards. 'In case you think of anything else. And remember, you don't owe Maas anything. I think he wanted me to find you.'

'Why?'

'Maybe he hoped I would kill you, or more likely, the other way around. We're both loose ends in different ways, but I suspect if he really wanted us dead, then we would be.'

'That's not exactly reassuring,' Malone replied. 'And it doesn't answer my question. Why would he lead you here?'

'I think he was trying to send me a message,' I said. 'Just as I thought I was getting close, this is his way of revealing how little I know. I have photographs, film footage, but the truth is I don't even know what he really looks like. I can't be sure of anything.'

I saw my distorted reflection looking back at me in the glass of the trailer door as I pushed it open. I turned back to Malone.

'You know what's really crazy?' I said. 'I might have already met him, and I wouldn't even know it. After watching that last film, I've been looking for a man with your face, but he could look like absolutely anyone. Maybe that's what he was trying to tell me. This was just another of his ways of educating me about how the world really works, and how nothing is certain, but I'll tell you one thing that is: wherever Maas is now, he's laughing, at me, at you, at everyone and everything.'

Ezra Maas: An Oral History
Part Nine

Artists, writers, journalists, photographers, critics, friends, and others, who were around Maas during the years 1956 to 1996, give their impressions of the artist. Interviews by Daniel James.

☆

Sarah Renko, a British painter and sculptor, loosely affiliated with the Young British Artists of the 1990s.

SR: In his later years, he was concerned with questions of time and memory. In an age where information is stored in the cloud, rather than our heads, where images of our key experiences are carried around on devices, rather than remembered, what becomes of our relationship to knowledge, to each-other, to existence itself? On the other hand, he saw great potential in the power of new technologies to reach millions, to communicate on a global scale. It could be a gift, enabling the democratisation of knowledge, information, and expression, or it could be the biggest and most insidious tool for surveillance, marginalisation, and control ever created. Its birth, rapid expansion, and evolution, was like a mini Big Bang. He disappeared before he could see his observations realised, but even fifteen years ago I remember him telling me that, in the 21st century, oil would no longer be the world's most valuable resource, it would be information.

☆

Sir John Jasperson, art collector and former patron of Ezra Maas.

JJ: I've never encountered anyone who had so much knowledge. The overriding image I have, whenever I think of him, is sat cross-legged in the centre of an infinite library – that's what his library at Gorhambury Manor resembled – quietly reading one book after another. Our minds have limits, his does not. When we learn something new, sometimes old knowledge, old memories, fade and disappear to create space. His mind expands with the knowledge he absorbs, he remembers everything he has ever read or experienced, and he has instant access to all of it, at any moment. One day his mind might grow so large that it overtakes the expansion of the Universe.

☆

Bryan Talbot, Eisner Award-winning artist, writer and creator of graphic novels including Grandville, The Adventures of Luther Arkwright, **and** Alice in Sunderland.

BT: I'd never heard of Ezra Maas until the early 1990s, when I was approached to work with him by an American publisher of a small line of independent comics. Working with him was very hard, extremely difficult. I like a very tightly plotted story. He would ring me in the middle of the night with crazy ideas – I'm in a supermarket and Richard Nixon is pointing a gun at my head – and insist we include them in the book. And I'd have to tell him we couldn't do that because our story was set in the Renaissance! He kept a dream diary by his bed and I think placed as much importance on dreams as reality...

Maas could be unpredictable, cantankerous. He was eccentric – he could be very charming, he could be very infuriating, but in the end, he was a creative genius, and his imagination was unparalleled.

☆

Brian Ward, Professor of American Studies and US History, speaking in 2011.

BW: My contact with the world of Ezra Maas came via a rather circuitous route. I was researching the life of legendary African American bluesman Robert Johnson, specifically the story behind the artwork to the second compilation of his 1930s recordings, *Robert Johnson: King of the Delta Blues Vol. II*, which was released by Columbia Records in 1970. The credits say the art was by Daily Planet and Tom Wilson. I decided to set off in search of this unknown artist who had helped cement the legend of Johnson, and tracked down Frank Driggs, the Columbia producer and music critic who was largely responsible for reissuing Johnson's work. I went to see Driggs in New York in August 1993. I asked him about the cover art and this is what he said: "Tom Wilson? Oh, that was just a pseudonym. Some real young kid did the artwork for Volume two. I don't know if he was in some kind of trouble, but he didn't want his name on it. Real talented, hippie-type, but skittish. Into music and art and DC comics. Hung around Greenwich Village with Mimi Farina - y'know Joan Baez's sister; Richard Farina's widow. I think maybe he did the cover of a Pynchon novel, too. Or they were related, or something? It was a long time ago. Of course, later somebody said he was Ezra Maas, y'know, the artist, before he hit big. I dunno. I only saw the kid a couple of times."

Intrigued, I went to see the only man I knew who had actually met

Thomas Pynchon, the novelist and literary scholar Malcolm Bradbury. He taught at the University of East Anglia when I was an undergraduate and we had become friends. Bradbury told me the story of how he met Thomas Pynchon at a cafe in London while the writer was researching his novel *Gravity's Rainbow*. He didn't know what Pynchon looked like – only a couple of photos of him exist – so the American agreed to wear a navy suit with a red tie. When Bradbury arrived, he found two men waiting for him both dressed as Pynchon had described. "Hi, I'm Tom," said one of the men. "This is my friend, Ezra Maas." Halfway through the lunch, the man purporting to be Thomas Pynchon apologised and admitted to Bradbury that they'd been playing a joke. He was really Ezra and the other man was the real Pynchon. Bradbury said he didn't know what to make of the incident or whether he met the real Pynchon that day or not. The story is very much in keeping with how Pynchon operated. After all, he sent an impersonator to collect his National Book Award for *Gravity's Rainbow* in 1974. But Bradbury always said he felt the masquerade had more to do with obscuring Ezra Maas's true identity, as Maas was rumoured to have made very serious enemies within and outside America at the time. Bradbury said if I was really interested in finding out more I should put it a Freedom of Information request with the FBI. As it happened, I needed to put in an FOI for the work I was doing at the time on various musicians and record industry moguls – Harry Belafonte, Berry Gordy, Sam Cooke, James Brown, even Elvis Presley. I decided, just out of curiosity, to slip in Ezra Maas's name to see what I could find out. Three months later I got a call from a woman at the FBI headquarters in Quantico who explained they have different rules around information sharing depending on whether someone is alive or dead. One by one she went through the all the requests – telling me which files I could consult and which ones I would need to get permission from the subject – all of the requests that is, except for the one relating to Ezra Maas. When I asked about this, she completely blanked me and refused to acknowledge that I'd even made the request. To this day, I can't explain it. All I can say is that Ezra Maas is a truly enigmatic figure who seems to hover spectrally over the world of American culture and I hope that one day his true story is told.

Donald Houlihan, personal friend to the Maas family from 1981 onwards.

DH: Everything you've ever heard about Maas is wrong. He was just a man, a husband, a father, a friend, an artist. All the stories are just that – stories.

Ezra Maas
Chapter Ten

I now ascend the stage of the world of which previously I have been a spectator,
but I come forward wearing a mask.[468]

'Maas anxiety'[469] was the headline in 1995, when rumours emerged that Helena had purchased a former warehouse in Chelsea and had converted it into a seven-bedroom villa, seemingly to live without her husband. Several newspapers suggested their marriage was over and subsequently referred to Helena as the artist's estranged wife. In what may have been an attempt to end such rumours, Helena agreed to give an interview to *The Sunday Times Magazine* about 'living with genius'.[470] The article was the subject of a legal dispute and was allegedly a rare case of Helena and The Maas Foundation disagreeing.[471] As a result, it was never published. However, I have managed to recover several key quotes from sources at *The Sunday Times*, which had retained a copy of an early draft of the article. These quotes from Helena include:

"Ezra is a genius and comes with all the problems of a genius... His desire for privacy is not about secrecy, it is an expression of his belief in authenticity... He is ready to give himself up totally for his art. He always told me you have to live with your work to the end of your life... Although he thrived on the manic energy of America, he felt England was his home... Ezra regularly works for sixteen hours a day and is so obsessed with what he is doing that nothing is allowed to distract or destabilise him...

"The picture of him in the press is completely false. Most have never met him. I think people see him as some sort of crazed cult leader and expect him to look like Charles Manson, but to me he'll always be part English gentleman, part New York hipster... the first time I saw him I thought he was the most beautiful man I've ever seen, and I still feel that way...

"He worked everywhere, turning whatever space he was in at the time into a studio, an artist's loft, like in Montparnasse or Greenwich Village... Sometimes I worry that he's become more mythology than man..."

---

468. René Descartes.

469. A playful reference to one of Maas's works.

470. *The Sunday Times,* (1995) Quotes recovered by Daniel with help from George Wallas.

471. Helena wanted to run the article, the Foundation did not.

Although Helena's article was generally positive, her attempts at presenting a fundamentally stable relationship were undermined slightly following a tabloid story that broke in the late 1990s. This was essentially a 'kiss-and-tell' story, which accused Maas of having an affair with aspiring actress, former stripper, and now turned contemporary artist, Mary Hurt, who described a very different version of the artist's life to the image the Maas Foundation had portrayed for the last decade. However, the story ultimately became little more than a tabloid footnote when Hurt, the woman at the centre of the accusations, abruptly changed her story. Shortly after this, she bought premises in Soho, which she converted into a small art gallery to showcase her own work. This led to rumours that she had withdrawn her accusations after accepting a financial settlement from the Maas Foundation. When I spoke to her in 2012, Hurt denied that she had taken any money from Maas but did give me more of an insight into the nature of her relationship with the artist. Speaking of the "Maas she knew"[472] she said:

"All those stories of Ezra barely leaving his studio in Hertfordshire were manufactured… if everyone thought he was there then he was free to be anywhere. That was the whole idea…

"It was hilarious… while the newspapers and his crazy fans were camped out watching his mansion, Ezra was travelling the world, drinking with artists in Paris, having twenty-four-hour parties in Berlin, painting landscapes in Switzerland, creating art and living his life in plain sight…

"He picked me up when I was dancing in a club in Soho… I had originally gone to London to become an actress, but it hadn't worked out… I didn't know who he was, but you could tell straight away that he was special, he just had something about him, a confidence I suppose…

"His relationship with Helena was more of a business partnership… he disliked how big the Maas Foundation had become and didn't want any part of it, he wanted freedom, from it, from her, from everything and everyone…

"Being with Ezra made you feel better about yourself, more positive. He wasn't supportive as such… in fact, he could be very cold, very distant at times, but his presence in your life was inspirational, if that makes sense. It was because of him I decided to become an artist…

"I was angry with him when I went to the papers, it was impulsive, and I quickly regretted it, that's why I decided not to go any further… He had secrets within secrets. It was hard to live with, and I didn't feel like I could trust him. It took me a while to come to terms with the fact that the Maas

---

472. Daniel interviewed Mary Hurt in 2012. All quotes in the manuscript attributed to Hurt were taken from this interview.

I knew existed only in that moment, only in our time together, and that he was not one person, but a shimmer, a hundred million different people, changing all the time…"[473]

Hurt also described a very different image of Maas physically, although there is very little to compare her account to, because of the veil of secrecy that had surrounded his appearance for the past few decades. Almost no confirmed photographs of Maas exist.[474] The images that do are either hotly contested or conflict with each other. Other descriptions of Maas over the years, from people who claim to have met him, were contradictory to say the least.[475] A journalist who claimed to have met Maas in the 1980s said he looked like a "biblical patriarch with dark, menacing eyes",[476] but the author Jacob Glass said he was more like a "beat poet" who permanently wore "a cotton fatigue jacket with multiple pockets with a T-shirt underneath, faded chinos, and running shoes."[477] Both differ from Hurt, who described a version of Maas who was:

"… surprisingly young looking, with dark brown hair that was almost black, large, intense blue eyes, a lined but handsome face, full lips and a killer smile…"[478]

Hurt, who went on to have a successful and controversial career of her own in contemporary British art,[479] admitted she has had no contact with Maas since 2000, adding that she had no clue to his current whereabouts or intentions. Although Hurt's full story never made the mainstream press, rumours of marital discord and even a feud between Maas and Helena were becoming a topic of discussion in the art world. Disagreements on both a

---

473. Hurt's quote strongly reminds me of something David Cronenberg said. The director, talking about characters in his films, said: "… we look on ourselves as being relatively stable. But, in fact, when I look at a person I see this maelstrom of organic, chemical and electron chaos; volatility and instability, shimmering; and the ability to change and transform and transmute."

474. The photo Daniel recovered from a restaurant in Bruges in 2012 is one of the rare examples.

475. As evidenced by Daniel's oral histories about Ezra Maas, which appear in between chapters. These recollections of Maas are notable for being so diverse and different, each one seeming to cancel out the other – Anonymous.

476. As quoted in an interview in *The New York Observer*, 1999.

477. Daniel interviewed Glass in 2011.

478. From the aforementioned conversation between Daniel and Hurt in 2012.

479. Hurt has been compared to Andy Warhol due to her blend of pop art, celebrity culture, and fairytale iconography, and has sold paintings to Charles Saatchi and other high-profile collectors, including a number of celebrities. She recently exhibited at Modern Art Oxford.

personal level and over the direction of the Maas Foundation continued to circulate. One example was the supposed rivalry between the website for Helena's Lacuna gallery and Maas's personal site. Whereas Lacuna had a strong focus on supporting new talent, including interactive features where artists could upload their own images, win an exhibition spot at the gallery, and bid for funding, Maas's site was arguably for fans of the artist only. Lacuna also boasted a forum, live chat, blogs, videos, photography, illustrations, a daily magazine, and even a television channel. In contrast, Maas's site was described by critics as an almost entirely "inward looking multimedia playground for an artist's obsessive preoccupations".[480]

Maas launched the original version of www.ezramaas.com[481] in 1999, with a revamp in 2001. The site was exclusive to paying members and featured short videos, artwork, and even daily weather bulletins supposedly recorded by Maas.[482] It promised a unique insight into Maas's life and art, although reactions were initially mixed, with some critics questioning whether the content justified the subscription and where the money was going. Eyebrows were also raised about the alleged rivalry with Lacuna, suggesting that both Maas and Helena were complicit in using the rumours of their alleged feud as a marketing gimmick. Other more positive comments described Maas's site as art in itself and a "deconstruction of the internet as an abstract concept",[483] while another fan claimed it reinforced recurring themes of hyper-reality and simulation in the artist's work. However, whether Maas truly worked on the site or whether it was maintained by one of his assistants is not known. Regardless, the site proved highly popular. In 2004, California-based web traffic and ranking company Alexa Internet[484] ranked both Maas's site and Lacuna Online as being in the top 200, worldwide. If the so-called rivalry had been a PR stunt, then it had clearly been successful.

It was around this time in 2007 that Maas was rumoured to have left his manor house on his first official trip away from England in several years. The reason was reportedly to meet with the American theoretical physicist John Wheeler (who he had first met at a conference in New York in 1967 where the scientist had coined the term 'Black Hole'[485]). Wheeler

---

480. *The Independent*, Tuesday 21st, November 2001.

481. The website still exists but was redesigned in 2017 and bears little resemblance to the original version that Maas created as a subscription-only site, fifteen years earlier.

482. Although because of the poor quality audio, it is almost impossible to tell.

483. Fowler, Mark, *Multimedia Maas: The Artist and Hyperreality*, New Hampshire Press, 2008.

484. A subsidiary of Amazon.com.

485. Wheeler insisted the name had been suggested to him by someone else, but he was

had suffered a heart attack the previous year and felt his time was short.[486] Subsequently he had resolved himself to tackling the big questions in the time he had left, such as, "How come existence?"[487] and Maas apparently wanted to talk to him about his theory of a 'Participatory Universe', with a view to creating a piece of art, potentially a conceptual installation, in response to Wheeler's work. The results of this conversation were never revealed, and the trip to Maine where Wheeler lived was never confirmed by the Maas Foundation. Any insight we have into this meeting now comes from Maas's own journals, which explore his long-term interest in quantum mechanics and his desire to use art as a bridge to connect other disparate concepts in religion and psychotherapy. It was just three years later that Maas was revealed to be missing, after retiring from public life to concentrate on his final artwork, and while few had no knowledge of his meeting with Wheeler or his long-term interest in these concepts, it is now hard to discount a possible correlation between the two events.

Around eighteen months after Maas's meeting with Wheeler, Helena curated an exhibition in Moscow, *The Image Tells Me Death in the Future*, featuring a film that may or may not have been created by Maas. The highly controversial, and famously uncredited film, entitled *Absence*,[488] has been the subject of intense critical debate, with more than one hundred academic papers dedicated to its content and possible 'auteurship' since its one and only screening[489]. One study in particular was brought to my attention because its author, the academic Dr TJ Watson, disappeared shortly after it was published in 2002.[490] This paper, on the film, entitled, *The Image Tells Me Death in the Future: Absence, Dead time and the Deconstruction of*

---

definitely responsible for publicising it.

486. He did not die until 2008, as it happened.

487. Wheeler: "I had a heart attack on January 9, 2001. That's the signal. I only have a limited amount of time left, so I'll concentrate on one question: How come existence?" From an interview by Tim Folger, *Discover* magazine.

488. Watson wrote: "Allegedly produced sometime in the mid-1970s and never gaining any official release, *Absence* is something of an anomaly within the field of film research and theory. Because the film itself has never been credited with any one director, or claimed by anyone as a specific authorial work, *Absence* has garnered a very forceful mythology surrounding its origins and intent. The date of the film is also something of an ambiguity, making it harder to frame the film in terms of any specific context. The mid-1970s has been adopted as a guide, based on the condition and subsequent degradation of the film's only surviving print (no archival records have ever been found suggesting the existence of another)."

489. The film's singular screening has in itself been seen as a piece of conceptual or performance art.

490. He was never found.

mortality, was his last published work. Below are a number of quotes from Watson's paper on this notorious film, which may have been the work of Maas:

"… because the film is forcibly separated into three parts, there is an inherent form of violence embedded within the very fabric of the film. As these temporal gaps exist, there is no way of telling what exactly occurred in the absence of the visual image. What becomes interesting is not so much that which is visually presented, but that which is absent. As Georges Farber has suggested 'we can only perceive reality through fragmentation, we see our lives through the prism of fragmented segments'… [491]

"… The space between these sequences may be codified as a form of dead time, the absence of the image between sequences referring to what Gilles Deleuze has noted as the 'out of field'. Describing those events lying beyond the film frame, dead time also encompasses a dead space in which the visual image is absent, the reality beyond the frame drawn into question…"[492]

Two years after *Absence* was screened for the first and only time, in Moscow, Maas announced through his website that he was withdrawing from public life to concentrate on his "final and most important creation".[493] This caused considerable speculation amongst the press, international art world, and Maas's legion of fans, although no further statement was ever issued to clarify the exact nature of the project, and the original iteration of ezramaas.com was shut down. Naturally this only magnified the interest in discovering what Maas was planning. One of the theories suggested that the announcement itself, his proposed vanishing act or absence from the world, was his final gift to art. Others were convinced Maas would return with a game-changing creation, a new form of art that would come to define the 21st century. Some critics also noted that, considering Maas had barely been seen in public, officially at least, since the early 1980s, his new 'withdrawal' from public life was somewhat ironic. Following the flurry of media coverage following his announcement, the Maas Foundation continued to maintain his legacy through retrospective exhibitions, as well as commissioning various reprints and limited editions of his back-catalogue. Helena's solo career, and her role in supporting emerging art, also went on as before, with high-profile shows held at The Serpentine Gallery, White Cube, Gagosian Gallery, The Nationalgalerie at the Hamburger

---

491. Dr T.J Watson from his paper, *The Image Tells Me Death in the Future* (2007).

492. *The Image Tells Me Death in the Future*.

493. An excerpt from the statement published on: ezramaas.com in 2004.

Bahnhof, and the Brooklyn Museum of Art, among others. Maas himself remained silent and was generally thought to be working in solitude in one of his studios, presumably at Gorhambury Manor. However, the silence would soon come to an abrupt end.

In January 2005, police were called to the Maas estate in Hertfordshire after reports of a disturbance. Records show an ambulance was also called.[494] No arrests were made, and no one was taken to hospital, but the resulting media coverage forced the Maas Foundation to acknowledge the incident, especially after the speculation about the final project Maas was working on in seclusion.

The response came later that month when Helena, via a spokesperson for the Maas Foundation, confirmed the growing rumours that her husband was missing. The biggest revelation however was that Helena had not seen or heard from Maas in three years, which made his last confirmed sighting in 2002. Although there was some debate whether Helena and the Maas Foundation could be trusted on this, if their admission was true then it would suggest that Maas operated with a much greater degree of autonomy than anyone had previously imagined. It could also be seen to confirm suspicions of a division between Maas and his own Foundation.

Once again, cynics suggested the disappearance was little more than a marketing stunt to hype Maas's latest artwork. As evidence, they pointed to the creation of new Ezra Maas pages and accounts on social media sites such as Facebook and Twitter[495] to promote his eventual return, as well as what appeared to be a viral marketing campaign featuring messages embedded in web pages, QR codes, and geocaching.[496] In the months following his disappearance, Helena Maas was also perceived as attempting to capitalise on the additional publicity generated by her husband's disappearance, as she oversaw the launch of the Maas Foundation for Consciousness-led Peace and Education centre, in Los Angeles,[497] and the opening of

---

494. Daniel put in a Freedom of Information Act request for the transcripts of the emergency calls, but unfortunately this was indefinitely delayed by legal action. The Maas Foundation clearly did not want this information to be released.

495. The Maas Foundation's Twitter account can be found @MaasFoundation.

496. Geocaching is an activity in which the participants use a Global Positioning System (GPS) receiver or mobile device, and other navigational techniques, to hide and seek containers, called "geocaches" or "caches", anywhere in the world. Geocaches are currently placed in over one hundred countries around the world and on all seven continents, including Antarctica. After almost twelve years of activity there are over 1,760,033 active geocaches published on various websites. There are over five million geocachers, worldwide.

497. Located at 121 S Wetherly Dr. Beverly Hills, CA 90211.

a nightclub in the historic heart of Paris named *Missing Persons*,[498] at 142 rue de Montmartre. The club, allegedly designed by Maas before he disappeared, consisted of a series of underground rooms for artists of all disciplines.

From the time of Maas's initial announcement that he would not be heard from again until his final work was complete, to his official disappearance three years later,[499] there was a global resurgence in the guerrilla street art and satirical graffiti first attributed to the artist and his followers in New York, in the 1960s and 1970s. The new variation of this trend saw words and images associated with Maas and his art, as well as original work inspired by him, being painted, stencilled, and displayed on public spaces, buildings and landmarks around the world, including in London, Newcastle, Liverpool, Manchester, and Leed in the UK, as well as Paris, Brussels, Bruges, Berlin, Bilbao, Sydney, Melbourne, New York, LA, Chicago, San Francisco, Montreal, Toronto, and Anchorage.

Although denounced as vandalism by police, local authorities, and other organisations, the creations were also assessed as serious works by the art world. One critic even suggested the graffiti and tags were the work of Maas himself using different pseudonyms, and that the whole endeavour was essentially a conceptual art project, with Maas 'performing' the persona of an international street artist. Others drew attention to instances of anarchic vandalism and violence around the creation of these pieces, suggesting they were instead the work of Maas's cult following, potentially new factions made up of young people inspired by similar subversive groups that had existed decades earlier. This was also accompanied by a newfound interest in the search for hidden messages in Maas's work, with a number of media sources suggesting it was all part of a concerted plan to promote the artist's inevitable return.

The Maas Foundation denied a connection to the street art, vandalism, and violence, and continued to distance itself from the artist's more extreme fans, who claimed his re-emergence would be the "21st century's Second Coming".[500] One senior member of the Maas Foundation, who did not wish to be named, spoke to me about his understanding of what Maas had planned. He said that while he did not know the exact nature of the work,

---

498. The name of the club itself was, of course, highly provocative in the circumstances – Anonymous.

499. In 2002, Maas announced he would not be seen again until his final work was completed, but was not officially reported missing by the Maas Foundation until 2005.

500. The Maas Journals. Vol. 9, p.221.

he knew Maas's vision would have nothing to do with violence or anarchy but would "prepare the future" by helping us see the world as he has always seen it. These words recall and echo two famous quotations from the art world, one by the art historian Robert Hughes and the other by Russian philosopher P.D Ouspensky:

"The essence of the Avant-garde myth is that the artist is a precursor; the truly significant work of art is the one that prepares the future."[501]

"In art, it is necessary to study 'occultism' – the hidden side of life. The artist must be a clairvoyant: he must see that which others do not see; he must be a magician: must possess the power to make others see that which they do not themselves see, but which he does see."[502]

In many ways, these words serve as a fitting epitaph, both for Maas and this book. Next year, 2012, will mark seven years since Maas was confirmed missing.[503] Although a death certificate can be issued at any point following a disappearance, an estate can only be settled in the High Court after seven years.[504] At the time of writing, Ezra Maas has yet to return[505].

---

501. Hughes, Robert. *The Shock of the New.*

502. P.D Ouspensky.

503. This was the original planned release date of Daniel's unauthorised biography of Maas, when it was due to be published by William Wilson and Company. It may have been that Daniel's anonymous client wished for the book to be published before settlement of the Maas estate and the legal ramifications of his death. However, for reasons unknown, the deal collapsed, and both Daniel and the manuscript disappeared, until now – Anonymous.

504. See the letter from Westminster Coroner's Office earlier in the manuscript explaining 'Death in Absentia'.

505. Note to reader: Daniel's biography of Ezra Maas ends here. It is clear from his notes that several hundred pages were written in addition to those presented here, including further chapters on his childhood, time in America and Europe, the controversy surrounding Oxford University, his refusal of the Nobel Prize and Turner Prize, his seclusion in England, and his eventual disappearance, as well as expanded versions of everything you have read so far. Unfortunately, more than two thirds of Daniel's manuscript have been destroyed, and I have not been able to locate any other copies, or the original 'Maas Journals' from which much of the biographical chapters were taken. The surviving pages you hold in your hands have been reassembled over the course of the last five years, based on Daniel's notes, but much is missing. Perhaps one day, the lost chapters will be discovered and restored. However, for now, the biography is over. All that remains is to conclude Daniel's own story – Anonymous.

Interview with Dr Claire Nally,[506] Senior Lecturer in Modern and Contemporary Literature[507]

November 10, 2017

1. What can you tell us about Ezra Maas – and how did he come to your attention?

I've been researching goth subcultures, and I came across the work of Ron Athey, who was in a relationship with Rozz Williams of Christian Death, a somewhat troubled death rock band from the 1980s. Ezra Maas's name very briefly came up in the records of Athey's performance art on the LA Arts Scene – Athey famously consumed and regurgitated road kill on stage, and crucified his lover, Rozz, slashing his palms with a razor. But Maas was always a fleeting reference, on the edge of other stories. I cannot tell you how frustrating this is, as a researcher! I don't envy Daniel's task at all.

2. What was your reaction when you heard that someone was attempting to write an 'unauthorised biography' of Ezra Maas?

I suppose my first reaction was the impossibility of the task. Even with conventional biography, you encounter so many issues with literary estates, existing relatives, that kind of thing. But this is so different – it's such an unstable narrative – it's really difficult to work out where fiction ends, and fact begins (even if we can establish 'Truth' in any real sense, in relation to lived experience and memories). It's always partial, and therefore open to interpretation. In some ways, all biographies are bio-fictions, but it is especially difficult to navigate when the subject of the biography is so wrapped up in his own fictions.

3. Daniel James has a notorious reputation as a journalist. We understand you've crossed paths with Daniel before, and I know you have read extracts from his book on Maas. How would you describe it?

Well, the book navigates very different styles of writing, and as readers we don't have one single narrator or

---

506. Note to reader: I conducted this interview with Dr Nally in 2017 while finalising the manuscript for publication with Dead Ink Books. Dr Nally was friends with Daniel and had read an early version of the book. I had two reasons for contacting her: I was interested in her professional opinion as an expert in 20th century English Literature, and her thoughts on Daniel as his friend – Anonymous.

507. Dr Nally has researched writers such as W.B Yeats and James Joyce, and Modernism is one of her fields of expertise. She has also written on contemporary fiction, and subcultures.

narrative. It is self-consciously about the writing process, the assembly of documents, red herrings and dead ends, as well as the danger certain types of knowledge can bring. Clearly, we have a literary detective of sorts in Daniel James, which perhaps invites comparisons to the metaphysical detective genre (and figures like Paul Auster). I know the experience of writing the book almost killed James, and I don't just mean the writing here… There's the hedonism too – the catalogue of cocktails, women, and late nights. Yet, I cannot help but think that Daniel is fabricating an identity too – he's a composite of modernist writerly types (think Joyce, Hemmingway, Jean Rhys) – so I suppose part of the question is, who is Daniel James? – as much as the ostensible subject – Ezra Maas?

4. How would you describe Ezra Maas in one sentence?

It seems to me that he's a postmodern romantic hero – if such a thing is possible – tortured, brilliant, charismatic, but also dangerously manipulative.

5. Do you think Maas is alive or dead – and will we ever find out the truth?

I cannot help but wonder if Maas (in common with figures like David Lynch and his 25-year Twin Peaks hiatus) has plotted his absence from the world's stage and provided clues for his devotees about his return at some point in the future. It seems that someone like Maas doesn't just die or disappear. I guess, for the definitive answer, you should read Daniel's book.

Daniel James
Chapter Nineteen

All obsessions are extreme metaphors waiting to be born[508]

The elevator doors opened into a room decorated in midnight blue wallpaper with silver stars. Animal heads protruded from the walls, victims of an absurd accident. A stag, a bear, and a goat looked back at me. My feet slid over the polished black and white tiles towards a woman sitting at a desk. She was dressed in a grey business suit and was writing in a leather-bound book. On the desktop, a stuffed owl perched on the twisted branch of a bonsai tree next to a transparent phone, whose wiring and mechanisms were exposed through the plastic shell. The woman's hair was so dark I could barely make out a single strand expect for one thick curl, which hung from her forehead like a sickle. I approached the desk and saw myself reflected in the owl's eyes. Through the glass wall behind her I could see more than a hundred of London's richest art lovers eating in the gallery's restaurant, including the one person I was there to see.

'Your name is not on the list,' the woman said, before I'd had a chance to speak.

'I haven't even told you my name yet,' I replied.

She stopped writing in her book and looked me up and down.

'Your name is not on the list,' she repeated.

'I'm here to see Helena Maas,' I said, gesturing at the restaurant behind her. 'She's the professional widow over there, dressed in black. Just behind Charles Saatchi.'

'Ms. Maas is not here tonight,' the woman replied and continued to write in her book.

I plucked the pen from her fingers and used it to point at the glass.

'I can see her.'

'And do you always believe what you see?'

She tried to snatch the pen back, but I stepped out of reach. Her eyes burned into mine. I tossed the pen back to her and smiled.

'Just make the call,' I said. 'No more games.'

As if on cue, the phone on her desk began to ring. She reached for the receiver and listened closely to a voice on the other end.

'Yes, I understand completely,' she said through gritted teeth and placed the phone down.

'Your name has been added to the list.'

---

508. J.G Ballard.

'See? I knew we could get along,' I said.

'Someone will be along shortly to escort you to Ms. Maas's table. Would you like something to drink?' she added, with an air of forced courtesy.

'Yeah, that would be great. Thank you.'

She waited for me to sit down.

'The bar is over there,' she said with a smile.

I pulled a face and stood up again.

'You enjoy your job, don't you?' I said.

I walked over to the ornate wooden drinks cabinet that stood against the wall. It contained a selection of highly expensive spirits from around the world. I glanced over my shoulder and made sure my adversary was watching as I poured myself a very generous measure of the most expensive drink I could find into a heavy crystal tumbler, before heading back to the waiting area. She watched closely as I took a seat, before returning to her work. Every now and then she looked up as if she was waiting for something. I raised my glass at her and smiled, roguishly. Her hand gripped the pen so tightly as she wrote that her knuckles were white. I got the feeling she wanted to say something but that she didn't want to concede any ground by speaking first. I decided to let her off the hook.

'This is very good,' I said, swirling the glass. 'You sure you don't want to join me?'

For a good ten seconds or so, she acted as if I hadn't spoken. Finally, she placed her pen down carefully and looked up, very slowly, as if it took a huge amount of effort.

'What are you drinking?' she asked.

I grinned.

'Elijah Craig Small Batch Bourbon, aged for 21 years in charred oak barrels.'

The bourbon had a deep amber colour, like burnished copper, and tasted of vanilla, caramel, allspice, and oak.

'They say Elijah was the first man to use charred barrels,' I said. 'An accidental discovery after a fire at his mill... but like most of these things, it's probably just a story.'

'You know your bourbon,' she said.

'Everyone has a passion,' I replied, 'and every passion has its price.'

'I like that,' she smiled sardonically. 'You should be a writer.'

'And you should drink with me more often. I come out with gems like that all the time.'

She smiled again, this time more naturally and seemingly despite herself. We sat in silence for a moment.

'Isn't it a bit of a cliché? The bourbon drinking writer?'

'You think I should drink something else just to prove a point? I just drink what I love.'

'It was just an observation,' she said, holding her hands up in faux deference. 'I hope I didn't hit a nerve?'

I had to laugh. She was good, but so was I.

I finished the glass, walked back over to the cabinet and refilled the tumbler. This time I chose a bottle of fifteen-year-old Pappy Van Winkle's Family Reserve. An aroma of maraschino cherries, dried fruit, and toasted oak drifted up from the glass after I added a splash of water to the bourbon. Her eyes followed me, watching my every move. I waited for her to react, but she wasn't biting.

'How much is this again?' I said, looking at the glass. '£750 a bottle? £1,000?'

I took another sip, visibly savoring every drop. 'This won't come out of your wages, will it?'

And still, she didn't reply. After another moment, she leaned back in her chair with a look on her face that said, 'I know something you don't'.

'It's a shame you have to go now,' she said. 'I was almost starting to like you.'

'Who says I have to go?' I replied.

She pointed to three large men walking towards us.

'You called security?'

'I wouldn't resist if I were you,' she smiled. 'They rather enjoy showing people out the hard way.'

'So many tough guys, so few brains,' I sighed. 'I'll try not to confuse them with any long words.'

I turned to face the three men and smiled broadly.

'All right, Mr DeMille, I'm ready for my close-up.'[509]

When I opened my eyes, Helena Maas was sat at my bedside, a black veil over her face. Her lips were held in a permanent pout, like a petulant child, black make-up smudged around her dark eyes, hair in a constant tangle, her shoes mismatched. She was a ballerina in black, the epitome of shabby chic. She reached back with a hand gloved in lace, lifting the veil

509. The final line in Billy Wilder's Sunset Boulevard, a film which is referenced elsewhere in the text – Anonymous.

from her face.

'They always told me I'd be late for my own funeral,' I heard myself saying. 'But I didn't expect to wake up in the middle of it.'

'I've worn black every day since Ezra disappeared,' she replied. 'But I'm sure you knew that already.'

'You don't really think he's dead, do you?'

'I think he was never alive to begin with. Not in the same way you and I are, at least.'

I watched her sad eyes drift to the light streaming in from the balcony. In the sun, her skin seemed remarkably smooth and unlined. I had forgotten how young she was when she married Maas. There were sixteen years between them. It was a strange thought, but she was closer to my age than she was to his.

'So what now? Are you going to kill me, too?'

I sat up in bed and looked around. The room was immaculate, with contemporary furnishings arranged in a minimalist interior design, modern art on the walls, and large French windows framing a particularly beautiful view of the London skyline. I appeared to be in one of the many properties owned by the Maas Foundation; maybe the apartment in Kensington. Helena and I were alone, save for her dogs. Three Black Russian Terriers lay together in a tangle of fur and limbs, like a single black dog with three sets of gleaming white teeth and watchful eyes, to guard its master.

'We haven't killed anyone,' Helena said. 'If you hadn't fought with my guards, we would be having this conversation over tea.'

'I saw the police cut down the last person you didn't kill.'

'If you're referring to Mr Wallas, we had nothing to do with his death. I understand the police are treating it as suicide, but to be honest, we did wonder whether you had something to do with it yourself. You were the last person to see him alive.'

'If you really thought I was a murderer, we wouldn't be having this conversation.'

'So why are we?'

'Because there's something you want from me.'

She considered me for a moment.

'You're catching on, but I think you misjudge us, Daniel. The Maas Foundation wants nothing more than to preserve Ezra's legacy.'

'And I just want the truth.'

'There is no truth, only art.'

'Your husband's words.'

'Ezra said that reality is merely what we agree is real, a representation of the true conditions of existence. If you are searching for the truth, then you are looking for something that can't be found.'

'I will find your husband.'

Helena sighed. 'It's not him you're looking for. It's never been him. Don't you realise that by now? Ophelia said you were smart, but I'm beginning to think she misjudged you.'

'You sent Ophelia to see me?'

'Of course. Do beautiful women throw themselves at you every day?'

'Well, as it happens... '

'Don't be facetious, Daniel.'

'Did you tell her to sleep with me too?'

Helena's pale face seemed to drain of what little colour it had left. She clearly hadn't known that last piece of information.

'I don't know what you're talking about... '

'She tracked me down after I slipped through her fingers in Soho,' I smiled. 'Maybe she felt bad about sticking a needle in my neck. Or more likely, she just wanted to get more information out of me. Either way, I was happy to let her try... '

I was lying through my teeth, but Helena didn't know that.

'Ophelia went too far. I'm sorry. She has too much of her father in her, I fear.'

Her father. My little game had worked. Helena had confirmed what the actor had told me.

'Ezra... ?' I said. 'Of course.'

'I don't suppose you could be persuaded not to include her in your book? We've managed to protect her from unwanted attention her whole life. You don't seem like the kind of man who would hurt others unintentionally.'

'I don't know what kind of man I am.'

'I hope you find that out for yourself through all of this, Daniel. I really do.'

'You didn't bring me here to talk about me.'

'Actually, I did. While you've been looking at Ezra, we've been looking at you. I know all about the debts you're running from, the women, and what happened to your family... I'm sorry. Something like that... it changes people.'

'You don't get to talk about my family.'

'It's not a wonder you live the way you do. Pretending like there's no tomorrow. But it must be a lonely existence, living out of hotel rooms, changing the place you live like other people change clothes, always moving, never at rest.'

She was starting to get to me.

'Hemingway used to live at the Ritz in Paris,' I said. 'He left his notebooks in storage there for thirty years. Howard Hughes moved from hotel to hotel, too. I'm a lot more considerate. It's not like I take over entire floors... '

'You like to hide behind humour, don't you? But I see through you.'

'And what is it you see, exactly?'

'I know you would like people to think your lifestyle is one of choice, inspired by your artistic influences, but I know different. It doesn't have to be this way, Daniel. Just tell me how much they're paying you, and I'll make you a better offer.'

'They?'

'Your client. Just give me a number and we will triple it. The amount I'm offering could go a long way to solving your problems.'

'I have to see this through. I'm sorry.'

'Then I'm afraid the Maas Foundation cannot help you.'

'And what about you, Helena? Can you help me?'

I wanted to ask her about Maas's final creation, Michael Malone, and Jane D, the significance of the numbers ███████, hidden in his work, and more, but I was also wary of letting her find out what I knew.

'It doesn't matter what I want,' she replied. 'Not anymore. You're just like Ezra, I see that now, blinded by your own ambition. You're going to do what you want, regardless of what I say. I just wish you could see what I see.'

'And what's that?'

'That in exhuming Ezra's life, uncovering his bones and unearthing his secrets, you're opening up a great darkness, a gaping pit that exists just under the surface of the everyday, a black and infinite void waiting to consume everything you are, everything you'll ever be. Don't you see, Daniel? You're digging your own grave.'

INTERVIEW TRANSCRIPT

10/10/2016[510]

Conversation with Jessica Wolfe, editor at William Wilson & Co

A: Thanks again for agreeing to speak to me, Jessica. I'm just trying to get a better understanding of the reality of the book's development, outside of Daniel's account – the story behind the story, so to speak.

J: As I said before, I'll help if I can, but this has to be completely off-the-record. I'm talking to you as an individual, not as an employee of William Wilson.

A: I understand... Clearly there was a breakdown in the relationship between Daniel and the company that eventually led to a parting of the ways. Can you tell me any more about this?

J: He missed deadlines, ignored messages, refused to come in for editorial meetings, and spent a lot of company money without explanation. This went on for the best part of a year until the situation was intractable. The end was inevitable.

A: That must have been very frustrating.

J: It was, especially because I really believed in the book. The chapters he did share with us had a huge amount of potential. He was trying to do something very ambitious, but I think there was a lack of understanding elsewhere in the organisation and Daniel reacted quite badly to their interference.

A: What kind of interference?

J: They wanted to change the direction of the book considerably, cutting back on the first-person narrative, the New Journalism, the fictionalised elements, to focus more on the biography. Daniel saw the present-day chapters as a meta-detective novel, but they didn't understand what place this

---

510. Note to reader: I conducted this interview in order to find out what happened between Daniel and his original publisher, William Wilson and Co, and also in the hope of acquiring an additional, objective perspective on the manuscript's development, beyond the account presented in Daniel's notes – Anonymous.

had within a biography and thought the detective elements were clichéd.

A: What was your opinion, as his editor?

J: I understood what he was doing, and I defended him. I think if you look back at previous examples of Daniel's writing, especially his fiction, there are several repeating elements – a damaged hero, an antagonist-double, a missing person, an impossible object, a woman in trouble – film noir and neo-noir tropes, which are reordered, merged, subverted, and disguised, in his writing, like puzzle pieces, in the construction of a narrative that not only explores epistemological questions, but actually embodies ontological indeterminacy.

J: I don't think my director every really understood what Daniel was trying to do – and if he did, he didn't like it. He said it was a detective story without any detecting and that he found the details of Daniel's personal life and relationships unnecessary. He wanted all of that cut from the book and considered it a slap in the face. He seemed to think Daniel was laughing at him.

A: In what way?

J: Basically, that Daniel was misusing the company's money to live out some sort of noir-author fantasy. More than that, I think he was worried about the potential PR fallout of publishing a book which, in his view, seemed to endorse reckless behaviour.

A: Did you agree?

J: No, I didn't. In some ways, I think it was intended to do the opposite. I never met Daniel, so I can't comment on his personal life, but from a literary perspective I think it's clear he was acutely self-aware of the different genres and styles he was engaging with, from postmodern detective fiction and biography, to New Journalism, auto-fiction, and encyclopaedic narratives. Detective fiction is a prime example. My director didn't understand why there was no detecting, no murder, why the clues that Daniel's character uncovered appear meaningless and unconnected. This is, of course, exactly the point. In metaphysical detective fiction, the conventions of the genre are subverted to play a game with readers who have come to expect certain rules to be followed. By doing so, the author explores epistemological and ontological questions, regarding interpretation and subjectivity, the nature of reality and the limits of knowledge. Daniel employs every characteristic theme of this specialist genre – the failed detective, the double, the missing person, the world or text as labyrinth, the purloined letter or embedded text, the meaninglessness of clues, the circularity of the narrative, the absence of closure or explanation – in some ways it's a logical extension of his interest in the classic noir tropes I mentioned earlier, but he has taken it to another level of complexity.

J: Similarly, he writes about other issues with a high level of self-awareness. The hedonism in the book is carried out with an almost tyrannical desperation, and is shown to be miserably hollow, an exhausting obligation that he is compelled to repeat in an unending, Sisyphean loop. It's an existence haunted by melancholia, like a party that has gone on too long, where everyone has drunk themselves sober. Sex and relationships are another part of this cycle. For me, it was a portrait of damaged people in a damaged world.

A: But your boss didn't agree? You said he wanted this cut from the book.

J: Yes. They wouldn't publish the book unless Daniel agreed to rewrite it and, of course, he wouldn't change a word.

A: And how did Daniel react?

J: How do you think? Badly.

END

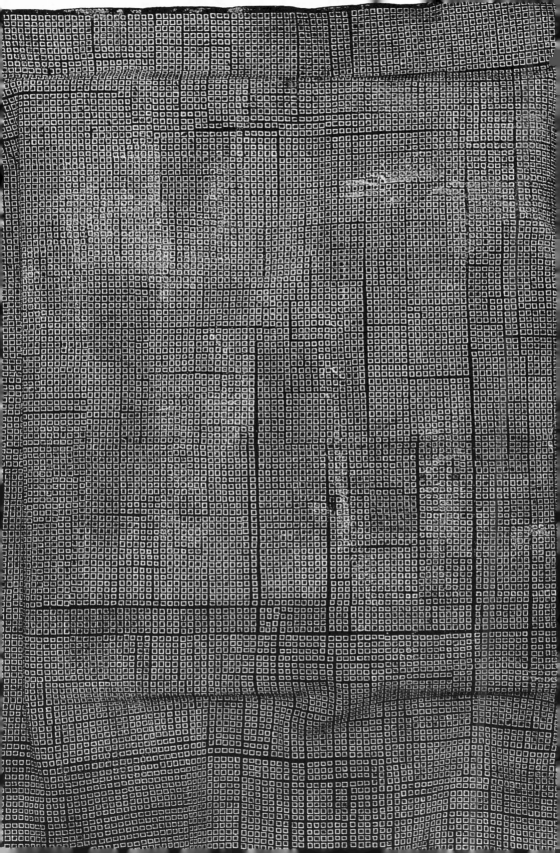

Daniel James
Chapter Twenty

Art is not a mirror held up to reality, but a hammer with which to shape it[511]

Playing dead was easy. I kept my head down and my eyes closed as they dragged me along, my feet trailing behind me, a bead of blood trickling down through my hair. The floor was soft and wet underfoot, I could feel it through my shoes, but I could tell we were inside a building. I could hear the drip, drip, drip, of water, splashing down from a height, and there was dust in the air. I could taste it.

They sat me down on a chair and took my shoes and socks off. I let my head hang forward as if I was still unconscious and decided to chance opening my eyes. I could see the legs of my captors. One of them was holding a hammer, another held an axe. That wasn't a good sign. They tied my hands behind my back in a simple schoolboy knot. Maybe there was a chance of getting out of this yet. If they had been professionals, they would have used plastic cord with a zip tie. Saying that, I wasn't a professional either. Everything I knew, I had learned from books. I wondered how far it would get me. They splashed water on my face and lifted my head up. I pretended to come around slowly, but it wasn't hard to fake being disorientated. The room was in almost complete darkness.

A few stray beams of light arced down from a gaping hole in the ceiling, but only enough to illuminate the centre of the room. Water was cascading down through the same hole. It looked like it had punched through from the floor above, leaving a tangle of twisted steel and broken wooden beams hanging down. It must have been raining outside. My eyes began to adjust. One by one a series of lights came on a few feet away from me. My captors were holding torches. No, not torches, fluorescent strip-lights of some kind, casting a hazy white glow around them, haloes outlining their bodies against the black. I looked around.

I was in a vast, ruined auditorium of an abandoned cinema or theatre. Everything was falling apart, decaying, and washed out, gold paint flaking on the walls, red velvet carpet stained with water and thick with dirt, aisles covered in rubble and rotting wood. I could see dust swirling in the air, faded red curtains hanging at angles, empty balconies looking down at me, and row after row of seating, cushions torn and ripped, like lines of gravestones disappearing into the darkness. My captors sat watching me

---

511. German theatre practitioner, playwright, and poet, Bertolt Brecht (1898 – 1956).

from the front row. There were five of them, wearing rubber animal masks and black boiler suits. A Pig, a Dog, a Cat, a Horse, and a Goat. The Pig seemed to be in charge.

'Don't you know you'll end up straining your necks from there? I'd sit further back, if I were you,' I said.

'No? Nothing?' My voice echoed. 'Tough crowd.'

I listened to the trickle of water splattering down onto the carpet, and the electrical purr of the lights in their hands, insects buzzing in the dark.

'You're funny,' the Pig said, finally. 'A real funny guy.'

'Can I just say if you're planning on torturing me, we might be in for a long night.'

'Why?' the Pig replied. 'You some sort of hero?'

'No, I just don't know anything.'

'I don't think you'll be as funny with your tongue cut out,' the Dog added.

'You do that and you're going to have a lot of angry women coming after you... '

'Unbelievable,' the Cat said. 'Can't we just kill him?'

'Not yet,' said the Pig.

'You want to tell me what this is about?'

'You don't know?' the Pig replied.

'What can I say? I piss off a lot of people.'

'We know you do. We've been watching you.'

'Why?'

'We saw you in the newspaper. You're the one writing the book.'

'And what's that got to do with you? Why do you care?'

'We didn't. We would have ignored you like all the others, let the lawyers shut you down, but you were different. You got further than all the rest. You found his studio. You discovered the numbers, the messages, the date... and that's when you became a threat.'

'What date?'

'It's pointless lying. We have people everywhere, watching all the time, listening to your calls. We heard you tell your friend.'

'I'm not lying. I don't know what you're talking about.'

'█████████,' the Pig said. 'The numbers that recur throughout his work. You found them hidden in the text of his novels, concealed in his paintings, embedded in his films. ███████████. The date everything will change.'

'The numbers... '

Even now, right up until that moment, a part of me still thought I was imagining the numbers.

'I didn't realise it was a date,' I admitted. 'I had it backwards... I thought it was another code like the one that led me to his studio... ' I began to laugh. '█████████.'

'There have been people like us, waiting and preparing for that day for more than four decades, ever since we discovered the numbers for the first time.'

'What's supposed to happen? What is Maas going to do?'

'We didn't bring you here to tell you that. Your story has already been written, and it ends tonight. The only question is how. What do you think, boys?'

'Cut off his fingers,' a voice in the dark called out. 'Stab him in the eyes,' said another. 'Smash his feet with the hammer,' growled the third. 'Rip out his tongue,' said the fourth.

Then all the voices seemed to speak at once, overlapping, blending together.

'Make him deaf, dumb, blind, and crippled, then we'll feed him to the dogs.'

One of them began to howl.

'How about all of the above?' Pig suggested.

His audience roared, neighing and barking their approval, grunts and voices echoing in the auditorium. I needed to keep the Pig talking. They should have tied me to the chair rather than just bind my hands. Amateurs. I had already managed to loosen the rope around my wrists, but I wasn't free yet. I wondered if I was quick enough to run up the main aisle between them. Probably not. In my head, I played the scene out and saw them jump out of their seats and catch me easily, dragging me down onto the dirty red carpet along the main aisle, pressing my face into the rain water, and bringing that hammer down onto the back of my head, time and time again, until they caved my skull in. It wasn't going to work. I was going to have to think of something else. Maybe there was an exit backstage. It was worth a shot, but I'd be running into the unknown.

'You know, I thought my fans were bad,' I said. 'But you guys are ridiculous. A cult counting down to a date for forty years. You're pathetic.'

'We're not a cult,' the Pig replied. 'We're an army – the Children of Maas.'

'I bet you've never even met Maas,' I continued. 'He probably has no idea you exist, and if he did he'd laugh at you. You're just like me, running around in a maze, looking for a pattern when there isn't one, looking for answers that aren't there. Only difference is, I've realised this is a game and there's no centre to this maze. There's no way out.'

'You should have stayed out of this,' the Pig said. 'You could have stayed in your bars and hotels, living the high life with all those women, the celebrity writer. But no, you had to go and play detective, didn't you?'

'You have been watching me,' I laughed. 'But not closely enough... If you really knew what I'd been up to, how did you put it, with "all those women", then you would have discovered something else important about me.'

'And what's that?'

'I know a thing or two about being tied up.'

I waved my hands, so they could see I was free, and began to run[512].

---

512. Note to reader: 'Along the shore the cloud waves break, The twin suns sink behind the lake, The shadows lengthen / In Carcosa / Strange is the night where black stars rise, And strange moons circle through the skies, But stranger still is / Lost Carcosa. – *The King in Yellow*, Act I, Scene II

The more I read, the more I began to identify Daniel's manuscript as belonging to a continuum of forbidden texts. It is dangerous, malignant, cursed. Daniel would have known this. He must have come to realise what he had created and attempted to destroy it at the very end. Now, for my sins, the responsibility has fallen to me and yet I could not do it. Every line compelled me to read the next, every page was filled with questions I became obsessed with answering, references and allusions I could not help but follow down the rabbit hole. If I could not destroy it, I must understand it, master it, if such a thing were possible. Faced with this realisation, I followed the only rational course of action left to me; seeking answers in the history and pages of other forbidden texts.

Books have always been seen as instruments of power, from sacred texts such as the Bible and Quran, to medieval grimoires containing occult magicks, such as *De Umbrarum Regni Novem Portis*, to political manifestos and philosophies, which have controlled entire societies. Interestingly, I came across a link between the name Ezra and the subject of forbidden texts. *The Book of Ezra* is a book of the Hebrew bible associated with Biblical Apocrypha, and was allegedly written by Ezra, a scribe, priest, and prophet. Arguably the most famous of his works was his apocalyptic visions. 20th century interpretations of the text have explored whether Ezra himself was the author of the book or whether he was one of several authors. Staying with the subject of religion, *The Book of Revelation* itself is arguably one of the world's most famous, dangerous texts: 'And I stood upon the sand of the sea and saw a beast / rise up out of the sea, having seven heads and ten horns / and upon his horns ten crowns, and upon his heads / the name of blasphemy.' (Revelation: 13.1)

Of course, what is forbidden can change throughout time. In the 9th century, the first list of forbidden texts, the *Decretum Glasianum*, was written, but never authorised. By the 16th century, the Catholic church published the *Index Librorum Prohibitorum* – a list of publications forbidden to adherents of the faith. This included such as Kant's *Critique of Pure Reason* and Kepler's *Epitome astronomiae Copernicanae*, both of which were considered heretical at the time, revealing how changing attitudes throughout history can affect the status of truth. Joyce's *Ulysses*, of course, was once considered "the most dangerous book in the world" on the basis of its alleged profanity at the time, while other contemporary texts have been attributed with similar 'dangerous' labels as a result of people's reactions to them. Notable examples include J.D Salinger's *The Catcher in the Rye*, made notorious by John Lennon's killer Mark David Chapman, Joseph Conrad's *The Secret Agent*, the favourite book of 'Unabomber' Ted Kaczynski, and more unusually Issac Asimov's *Foundation* trilogy, which was beloved by

Japanese doomsday cult Aum Shinrikyo, who were responsible for the sarin gas attack on the Tokyo subway. Other dark texts have endured the centuries. The more I investigated the subject, discovering similarities and connections with the manuscript I held in my hands, the more I began to focus on books which were themselves about the process of reading or writing, or which featured texts embedded within them in a 'mise en abyme' structure (from the French 'Into the Abyss'). These texts seemed uniquely cursed in a manner that echoed the manuscript in my possession.

There are several examples of 'mise en abyme' in the work of Argentinian writer Jorge Luis Borges, including stories such as *The Aleph*, and *The Zahir*, which both contain forbidden or forsaken objects that are not what they appear to be, as well as *Death and The Compass* and *The Garden of Forking Paths*. However, it is *The Book of Sand* which I was particularly drawn to. In this short story, Borges's protagonist acquires a sinister text from a mysterious stranger, only to discover it is infinite and ever-changing, its pages increasingly endless no matter how much you read; a trap for literary minds to become imprisoned. He considers burning it but fears the world would be consumed in an infinite fire. Instead, he hides it in a library, where perhaps one day another poor soul will accidently come across it. Another book I discovered in the course of my research, which was purported to have a maddening effect on all those who read it, is *The King in Yellow*. Its author, a writer of adventure, romance, and other genre fiction, gave no indication either before or afterwards that he was capable of producing such a text. The book stands alone amongst his works, almost eerily so. *The King in Yellow* is filled with an existential dread that was later termed 'cosmic fear' by the horror writer HP Lovecraft, who would create his own forbidden text in the form of the *Necronomicon*. He defined this as: "A certain atmosphere of breathless and unexplainable dread of outer, unknown forces . . . a hint, expressed with a seriousness and portentousness becoming its subject, of that most terrible conception of the human brain—a malign and particular suspension or defeat of those fixed laws of Nature which are our only safeguard against the assaults of chaos and the daemons of unplumbed space."

It is my belief that these books, *The King in Yellow*, *The Book of Sand*, and now Daniel's manuscript, are what Reza Negarestanini, in his *Cyclonopedia: Complicity with Autonomous Materials*, defined as 'Inorganic demons'. He writes: "Autonomous, sentient and independent of human will, their existence is characterised by their forsaken status... Inorganic demons are parasitic by nature... they generate their effects out of the human host."

Is this what I have been burdened with? Is this what you hold in your hands right now? Despite this knowledge, I found that I dared not look away from its pages for fear it changed before my eyes, like a magic mirror. I must read on to the end. It seems obvious to me now that this manuscript was indeed written with the intention of creating a maddening and unsolvable labyrinth, an inescapable maze, a descent into an infinite abyss. The only question that remains to me is, whose intention? Daniel's, or Ezra's? – Anonymous.

Daniel James
Chapter Twenty-One

An artist is a creature driven by demons[513]

You should never get used to this. The day you do is the day you should walk away. But you won't, because if knocking on the door of someone who has just lost their wife, or mother, or father, or child, doesn't make you feel ashamed, if it's become routine, then you're too far gone   to ever walk away from this job. They call it a death knock. Everyone had to do it. There were no exceptions. If you didn't, they would call you a failure and tell you that you didn't have what it takes. This job's not for you. That's what they'd say. It's how they get to you, through your pride and ambition, but mostly through fear – the fear of going back empty-handed. They knew how to apply the pressure. After all, they'd each had the same thing done to them when they were reporters. I had a different tactic when it came to convincing myself, a pretence of heroism in a backwards sort of way. I told myself that, if I knocked on the door, at least I would handle things as sensitively as I could, not like the others. There were some reporters who would come back laughing about it, the family photo album in their hands as they boasted about talking their way across the threshold and putting quotable lines into the mouths of distraught people. These were the kinds of journalists who hacked phones, intercepted mail and went through people's bins, ridiculed the readers they were meant to represent, and believed the pursuit of a story was a get-out-of-jail-free card, capable of justifying any activity.

It might seem funny that a man like me was the only one willing to articulate our collective guilt. At least I hoped the others felt the same, but I couldn't be sure. Either way, I wanted out. I wasn't one of them. At least, that's what I used to tell myself.

My head was already full of death before I got to Afghanistan. I had stood in the rain on council estates, behind police cordons, speaking to neighbours after an estranged father had butchered his own family; I'd sat in court and listened to the horrific injuries a baby had suffered at the hands of its own parents, I had read through the death notices and obituaries, I had knocked on door after door, turning lives, and the ends of lives, into a procession of empty stories.

---

513. William Faulkner, writer (1897 – 1962).

I still remember the last one. How could I forget? I can still see myself standing there outside the door, younger and softer in the face than I am now, but already tired, weary, burned out inside. Sophia's eyes were filled with tears, her whole body trembling, when she opened the door. I went through the script and talked my way inside. It wasn't hard. She had lost her husband and was numb with shock. When she started to talk about him, everything came rushing out in a jumble of words. I was the first person to really talk to her since it happened, she said. Everyone else was too scared. They wouldn't even look at her.

I follow her into the house. This is where reality ends and the dream begins, or at least where the border between the two becomes visible to me. I know because when this really happened we sat down in her living-room and I began the interview. After a few minutes, I told her I had made a mistake and left. Once outside, I called the newsroom and told them she had refused to talk to me and had threatened to take the newspaper to the PCC if we continued to harass her. It was the first time I had lied to the editor, but it wouldn't be the last. I had crossed a threshold and passed over into another place. After that, I went my own way, writing the stories I wanted to cover, in a completely different kind of way. In some ways, it was the first step on the path to where I ended up years later. Even though I know it's a dream, I still get a claustrophobic feeling, like I'm suffocating, because I've had this dream before and I know where it leads. I walk into the living-room and she closes the door behind me, locking me in. 'This is the trap,' she says as she turns the key. I bang on the door and try to force the handle, but it won't budge. I panic and began to search the dimly lit room for a way out. There is a window with the curtains drawn. I pull them apart, but I'm not prepared for what I find.

There's nothing there. No street, no houses, no sky. Just unconstructed space, a vast emptiness. I can't look at it directly, my eyes, my mind can't process what I'm seeing, can't perceive it, the complete absence of existence, no colour, no light, no dark; shapeless, formless, infinite, limbo. I've reached the barrier at the end of the world.

I pick up a chair and throw it at the window. The glass breaks and the whole room tilts forward, pitching me towards the void. I'm falling into it, falling forever, falling apart, dissolving into non-existence. My body is gone, and I lose all sense of direction, there is no up or down, no space, no time. I'm passing through something and it's passing through me. The void and I become one.[514]

---

514. As Fredric Jameson writes in *Detections of Totality*: "… it is this opening onto the not-World, onto its edge and its end, in the void, in non-human space, in death, that is the

PHONE TRANSCRIPT

DANIEL JAMES - UNKNOWN CALLER - V[515]

V: You're running out of time, Daniel.

DJ: Who is this?

V: I know you are, but what am I?

DJ: I'm coming for you, Maas. I haven't spent the last two years chasing you to just give up.

V: Two years? You think this book began when you took that phone call? [*LAUGHTER*] It started when you were born. This is what you were created for, paper man!

DJ: What do you mean? What are you talking about?

V: Wake up, Daniel. Wake up.

END

---

ultimate secret... "

515. V – the letter Daniel assigns to the unknown caller – is also famously the title of Thomas Pynchon's debut novel, which concerns, in part, the quest to discover the identity of V, who turns up in a variety of names and guises throughout the narrative, acting as a kind of unifying device, but ultimately remaining forever elusive – Anonymous.

Daniel James
Chapter Twenty-Two

There are names under things and names inside names.[516]

I leaned over the sink, gently probing the inside of my mouth with my fingers, as strings of blood trailed down onto the white enamel. The discarded blister packs of painkillers were scattered along the bench next to a blood-stained towel and a bottle of Wild Turkey, the cream and brown label smeared with red fingerprints. I picked up the bourbon and pressed it to my bruised lips. My mouth burned as I tipped it back, the copper coloured liquor washing the blood out. Peeling off my shirt, I staggered over to the bed, limping, and collapsed onto the mattress, where I rolled onto my back, wincing. There was a black bruise on my side as big as a fist, where one of them had caught me with the hammer. In between laboured breaths, eyes opening and closing, I faded in, faded out, faded to black. Isabella appeared in one of those moments, in the half-light, at my bedside, like she had always been there; maybe she had.

'What did they do to you?' she said, the tips of her fingers touching my wounds.

'You should see the other guy,' I said, my voice slurred.

'You need to go to a hospital.'

'It's not safe... they have people watching... I just need to rest... '

I felt her press a wet towel against my skin, cleaning away the dried blood. I faded in, faded out.

'I just need to finish the book... and everything will be okay... we'll go away, leave the city together... '

When I turned to look at her, it was Margot at my bedside instead.

'Dan, I'm not here... '

My fingers passed through her arm. Light flooded the room and out again, back to darkness, the tide coming and going. Fragments of conversation drifted in and out, voices from another time and place. Different voices from so many different women. Isabella, Margot, Elizabeth, Kate, Julia, Eleanor, Ariane, and all the others, they had come back to me one last time, to say goodbye; all their voices overlapping.

'You won't be free to love anyone until you let go. You realise that don't you?'

'It's tearing you apart... '

---

516. Susan Howe, poet.

Daniel,

I can't write this letter without falling into traps. Each sentence reads like a cliché, even though every word is true. When you wake up, I'll be gone. It had to be this way... If I had tried to say this to your face, my resolve would weaken the second I looked into those blue eyes of yours. That's the beauty of a hand written letter. It's physical and permanent... It's real. As soon as you put pen to paper, your words have a presence in the world. There is no erase and rewind. Once this letter is in your hands, I won't be able to change it, and that's the way it has to be.

I always dreamed of finding someone I loved, respected, and wanted as much as you, but you're not the person I thought you were. I look into your eyes now and I can't see the man I loved any more. Maybe he was never there? Or perhaps he's just lost? Inside a maze of his own creation. Are you there right now? The longer you spend inside those pages, the further away from life you get.

You know it too, but you can't stop; like a drowning man who keeps swimming deeper and deeper. This story can only end one way, and I won't be around to see it. I refuse to watch you destroy yourself, and for what? A book? So you can play out your fantasies? Do you remember when it was all just a game? A performance? Or was that just a lie too?

I wonder sometimes, did you plan to push me away to spare me somehow? Or was I just another footnote in the story. I wonder... If I don't sign this letter, will you even know who it was from?

They say it's better to have loved, but honestly... I don't know.

Yours,

No - one

Everything fell apart after that. They had all left me, but I decided it was for the best. If I was alone now, here at the end, then it was to clear the way for me to finish the book at last. It was almost complete, but I was running out of time. The date was just weeks away now, and I still didn't know what was going to happen. It could simply be Maas's return to the world, it could be the unveiling of his final work, or it could be something else. I had searched for the answers out there in the world and I had been left walking in circles, lost in a maze without an exit. There was only one direction left now.

I had to look inside, I had to break down the last walls between myself and Maas; I needed to inhabit his life, every aspect of it, even the lies, false personas, and invented histories, everything, to such an extent that I became him. It was the only way to win. The risks were great. I was already falling apart physically after everything that had happened, and I didn't have time to let myself heal properly, but what I was about to do was far more dangerous. If I lost myself inside Maas's world I might never find my way out again, it could break me, destroying everything that made me who I was.

If I crossed the threshold into the locked room inside Maas and couldn't find the door to leave, the price would be nothing less than disintegration, the annihilation of my soul. I had been promised as much. I had been warned.

But I had no choice. There was too much at stake. It wasn't about making history anymore, about writing a book like none that had come before it. I had to stop Maas. He was out there somewhere, planning, counting down to the date. Those numbers, they had been there hidden in his work all these years, a date that was almost here.

I had to know what was coming. The days and weeks that followed bled into each other. Life became a succession of broken scenes. My old life was over. I was changing every second now, hopelessly lost, my world a blur of streets, drinks, bars, violence, art galleries, women, drugs, a blitzkrieg[515] of experiences, wiping my mind clean. I became Maas and all of his selves, the romantic artist, the withdrawn recluse, the violent, temperamental genius, the charismatic cult leader, the counterculture icon, the serial womaniser, the drug addict, the experimenter, the intense loner, the passionate collaborator, the painter, the poet, the madman – I brought them all back to life. They raged inside me, tearing me apart,

515. German for 'Lightning War'.

brought them all back to life. They raged inside me, tearing me apart, killing me. I was losing control, but the closer I got to death, to oblivion, the nearer I felt to the answers I had been searching for all this time. I saw a door opening, and I walked through it.

Daniel James
Chapter Twenty-Three

One day my name will be associated with the recollection of something frightful –
of a crisis like no other before it on earth[517].

We were living inside a lie. I understood that now. Maas intended to wake us from this dream, from this hallucination of reality.[518] He was going to reveal the lies and tear down the prison walls we didn't know were there. We were slaves, but Maas planned to free us from our bonds. He had looked back at the origin of language in our species one-hundred-thousand years ago, and he had come to the conclusion that it was a parasite. Language had spread like a virus from country to country, taken root in our brains and forever separated us from the world. We no longer experienced the thing-in-itself,[519] but instead saw a representation filtered through language, a system where one thing could also be another thing. Reality had become a matter of opinion, and fiction was born, but in a participatory universe where observations defined experience we were left with a fractured and schizophrenic existence.

It was all about control. After God created Adam, he instructed man to name the animals. This would give man dominion over nature. Language was reductive, and the act of naming carried a ritualistic power. From the beginning, words have been weapons used to control. When man had the audacity to try and reach the level of God by building the Tower of Babel to break through into the vault of Heaven, God scrambled the languages of all the workers, creating discord where there had been unity. The inability to understand one another, linguistically or psychically, sent man back to the dark ages. In Maas's eyes we had descended even further into darkness since then. The 20th century was an unprecedented crisis. We had never been more fragmented, more splintered, or more dissociated in our relationship to reality.

Technological advances, the interconnectivity of the all-seeing, always

---

517. Nietzsche, Friedrich. *Ecce Homo*.

518. A phrase used by Jean Baudrillard to describe how today "political, social, historic and economic reality has already incorporated the hyperrealist dimension of simulation".

519. A thing-in-itself, a term defined by the German philosopher Immanuel Kant, is an object as it would appear to us if we did not have to approach it under the conditions of space and time. Using Kant's definition, as well as ideas from Schopenhauer, Nietzsche explored the division of the world into appearance and the thing-in-itself (the unknowable behind experience).

online, electronic world, saturated with information yet devoid of meaning, the proliferation of alternative facts by a mass media divorced from reality – we were living in an age where truth had lost all meaning. For Maas, we were seconds away from midnight.[520] The decision to disappear a few short years into the 21st century came as the clock was about to strike. If God created language to control us, Maas would remove it to free us. He saw himself as a saviour, a radical, a rebel, 'a reality hacker'[521] who would guide us to the New World.

MT Stuart had talked about a "real-life trauma book"[522] to "restore our true selves". I hadn't made the connections at the time, but he hadn't been far from the truth. Maas's own notes in his Soho apartment talked about the neocortex, the most evolved part of the brain, being capable of imagining and creating multidimensional structures and spaces. A four-dimensional world was hard to comprehend, but Maas talked about worlds of five, six, or more   dimensions. He said that shadows were two-dimensional representations of three-dimensional objects. What if we were merely shadows of greater beings and more complex worlds?[523] Language imprisoned our minds, defining even our conception of time and space. Maas would free us, reuniting our conscious and unconscious minds, and allowing us to experience a higher world. If the universe and our conscious minds were part of a "closed-network-loop", as believed by Maas's friend, the physicist John Wheeler,[524] then a change in consciousness would cause a corresponding change in our experience of and connection to the universe. At least that's what he believed. And as far as Maas was concerned perception was reality.

I didn't know what was real anymore, or how much of this was my own invention. Was I seeing the truth of Maas's plans at last, or had my desperate search for answers, for meaning, for truth, in a world that yielded

520. The Doomsday Clock was created by the Bulletin of the Atomic Scientists in 1947. It symbolically represents the likelihood of a man-made global catastrophe. In January 2017, it was moved from three minutes to two-and-a-half minutes to midnight. It is the closest the clock has come to midnight since 1953, when the minute hand was moved to two minutes away, following hydrogen bomb tests by the US and Russia.

521. In the words of Timothy Leary.

522. See 'Daniel James Chapter Sixteen'.

523. Maas's example echoes Plato's analogy of the cave. Plato wrote that we are like prisoners chained to a low wall in a cave, unable to turn around and see free people, going on with their lives. We can only guess at what their world is like based on the shadows flickering on the wall of the cave – the shadows of the real – Anonymous.

524. Wheeler believed that "mind (inner) and universe (outer) were part of one system" – Anonymous.

none, caused me to fill the gaps with apocalyptic visions? No... this was real. It had to be. I had come too far and given up too much. This was really going to happen unless I did something about it. Only I could stop it.

I recalled something Maas had supposedly said as a child,[525]... that to be reborn into life, Dionysus[526] had to be first cut into pieces. Maas had to destroy us in order to start again. He had started with me. In his eyes, the first step towards sanity was madness. Maas had tried to break me. The world was next, but how did he plan to reach everyone? Maybe Sam and I had it right when we said it was all about the book? Had Maas used me to create his weapon? If that was the true purpose of this book, of these pages, how could I end it?

---

525. See 'Ezra Maas Chapter Three'.

526. In the book *Art and Physics: Parallel Visions in Space, Time and Light*, Leonard Shlain compares Apollo and Dionysus to the right and left hemispheres of the human brain. He writes: "When the vision of the revolutionary artist, rooted in the Dionysian right hemisphere, combines with precognition [in the left], art will prophesy the future conception of reality."

PHONE TRANSCRIPT
29/05/12 - 23:11
Sam Molloy - Daniel James

SM: Where have you been? Everyone's been trying to reach you.

DJ: I know what he's planning, Sam. I know because he knows.

SM: What are you talking about?

DJ: I got inside his head and I found his secrets. I had to lose myself to find him, but I did it. I've been inside the locked room, but the truth wasn't there. There was a secret door, down into the centre of everything, that's where I found it. Inside the ghost room. That's where he was keeping it.

SM: Dan, you're not making any sense. Do you mean the book?

DJ: Yes… no… The book is almost finished, and it will change everything, but I'm talking about what Maas is planning. I know what it's all been about, and we have to stop him.

SM: The book has been shelved, Dan. That's why I've been trying to get in touch with you. You disappeared, and everything went to hell. The Maas Foundation announced that Maas was alive and ready to unveil his final work. The client has pulled their money out of the project, your publisher is suing you, and the Maas Foundation is suing everybody.

DJ: Wait… Maas announced he's alive? When did this happen?

SM: You didn't know? It was weeks ago, in a video message on his website. He announced he had returned, and his final work would be revealed at a press conference on ▮▮▮▮.

DJ: Of June? Of course… ▮▮▮▮… the press conference… that's when he's going to do it.

SM: Do what?

DJ: I told you. I've seen what he's planning, and I have to stop him before it's too late. You have no idea what's at stake here. He needed me to bring him back to life, through the pages of the book, and now he's going to change reality. This is what it's always been about. A psychological dirty-bomb disguised as art, built from quantum equations and psychotropic visuals powerful enough to induce paralysis and amnesia, designed to wipe clean our inner selves and restore the factory settings on our brains, to reveal the hidden face of God and break through to the Real. Reality is perception, you see? And if our perception is forcibly reset, reality will follow. The world will change, forever.

SM: Do you even realise how insane that sounds? It's over, Dan. You need to let go of the book and move on.

DJ: Give up? People have died to get me this far, Sam. You don't understand what I've been through, what I've seen. I've been followed, threatened, attacked, and manipulated, for months. They're watching me now, even this room has eyes. They need me to finish the book to bring him back. It's part of their plan. My words give him power and he's been planning this for decades, controlling everything, everyone.

SM: You sound psychotic, Dan. There is no conspiracy. No one has died. There are no anonymous forces following you around the world. No cult. No mastermind pulling the strings. At worst, the Maas Foundation used you for publicity, maybe they were playing some sort of game with you, but that's it. There's no master plan. He has a new piece of artwork to unveil. That's all this has been about. The disappearance, the mystery, it was all just a stunt, an elaborate hoax, and you were dragged into it, but you need to walk away now and let it go.

DJ: You're wrong, but it doesn't matter whether you believe me or not. I know what I need to do to stop him. I know where I need to go.

SM: A hospital is where you need to go. This isn't like you. It's like talking to someone else.

DJ: I know who I am Sam,[527] but I can't say the same for you.

---

527. This seems like as good an opportunity as any to expand on the topic of Daniel's identity, which I hinted at in my footnote on Pg. 253. Using your own persona as camouflage for your true identity is ingenious, and I suspect it is an idea that Daniel learned from Ezra Maas. Just as Maas created a hundred million fractured versions of his own reflection to hide behind, Daniel built a character from autobiographical fragments that, stitched together, presented a convincing facsimile of reality, but which actually concealed and obscured the truth of his life. But to what end? What or who was Daniel trying to protect, and keep hidden? And why? As we know, the Maas Foundation is notoriously litigious, but they've also been surrounded by accusations of violence, harassment, and worse, against their enemies. How do you expose an

Sam Molloy always believed me, he always supported me. I don't
know who you are. Goodbye[528].

---

organisation like that and walk away safely? You create a character like Daniel James. You give
him no home and no family, you strip away his friends one by one, you protect the woman
he loves by dividing her identity among several characters. When the time for reprisals come,
and they will come, you leave no one else to come after, no one else to target except Daniel
James and he doesn't exist. As I said, ingenious. There are, of course, other theories… including
one with implications for my own identity that are frankly too disturbing to contemplate and
which I have fought hard to push away from my mind, for fear it would drive me insane. I will
say no more lest I give any more power to these dark thoughts – Anonymous.

528. Note to reader: The reference to Dionysus in the previous chapter caused me to consult
my copy of Cassell's *Dictionary of Classical Mythology*, where I found myself drawn to the
tragedy of Narcissus, who became so obsessed with his own reflection that he was driven to
madness and death. While this can be read as a cautionary tale for narcissists against the perils
of ego and vanity, it can also be interpreted another way. Narcissus's reflection in the pool is
his doppelganger and, as we know, to be confronted with your double… Throughout fiction,
especially the detective genre which Daniel repeatedly returns to, the search for the double
(and the truth behind it) is symbolic of a deeper and ultimately metaphysical identity quest
– Anonymous.

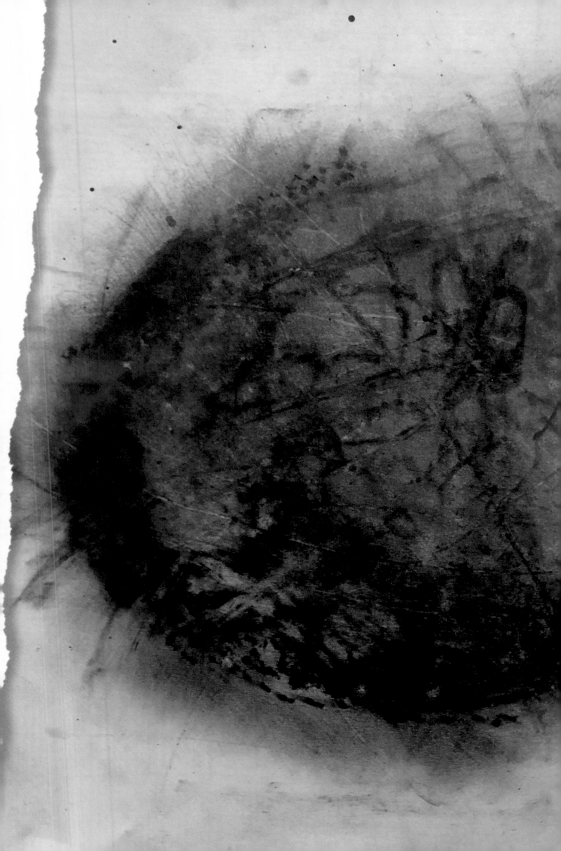

Daniel James
Chapter Twenty-Four

These fragments I have shored against my ruins[529]

The pale blue light of the television screen washed over me as I cradled the gun in my hands. The world's media was already camped outside the hotel where the press conference was going to be held, tomorrow. Fans and followers had been queuing for the last two days, desperate for their chance to see Maas make his return, with placards bearing slogans like 'Maas Lives' and 'Second Coming'. I walked into the bathroom and looked at myself reflected in the mirror. When the time came, could I do what needed to be done? The truth was, I didn't have a choice.

It ended like it began. I was in the back of a car, gliding through the streets, the city a blur of faceless people, labyrinthine streets, and schizophrenic signs. This time I was alone. No Elizabeth. No Sam. I had always been alone. I realised that now. And, this time, I had a gun in my jacket. The passenger door opened, and I stepped out into a cloudburst of flashing lights. I couldn't feel my legs, but I was moving, drifting along on rails, a passenger inside my own body, weightlessly climbing up marbled steps. The doorman, dressed in red and gold, held open the glittering door for me. There were people on my periphery, following me, and up ahead there were crowds gathering, smiling, clapping, and waving. News reporters and photographers jostled for position, as cameras clicked, and pens moved, on all sides. A circle formed around me. They pushed the crowds back and parted the bodies, creating a path along the burnished wood corridor, past ornate furnishings and beneath a shimmering chandelier, leading to a set of double doors.

Inside, there was an audience of hundreds. I reached inside my jacket for the gun, not to take it out, but to reassure myself it was still there. There would be hundreds of witnesses, but it didn't matter. I was prepared to do whatever it took to stop Maas. The doors opened on cue, and the audience got to their feet. They began to applaud and cheer; shouting and pointing, their blank faces, vacant smiles, all focused on me as I was led to the top table, where everyone seemed to be waiting. Helena and Ophelia sat together, side by side, alongside an entourage of friends and trusted colleagues. One big happy family. I didn't understand why they were welcoming me, but I was too focused on my mission to question it. There were three huge screens

---

529. Eliot, T.S. *The Waste Land.*

above us, ready to flicker into life and unveil Maas's final work, cameras in the aisles, poised to transmit his vision to millions worldwide, microphones clustered together like a technological coral reef, to pick up his words and spread his message; his final artwork...

A creation with the power to rewrite consciousness, to change the world...

This was the day Maas had been working towards for decades. The only thing missing was the man himself. My eyes scanned the aisles, the crowd, everywhere, my skin slick with sweat and every muscle in my body tense, ready to react. I looked at the centre of the table, but there was only an empty seat. A sea of smiles looked back at me and that was when I saw it. Behind the smiles frozen into place there was a wild fear in their eyes, as if they were locked inside their bodies; terrified puppets, clapping uncontrollably. Had it already happened? Did I arrive too late to stop him? Had the bomb gone off?

I felt anger rise up inside me. Was I the only one who could see what was happening here? I pulled the gun out from my jacket and waved it at them, but this just caused the applause to grow louder, waves of sound echoing around the room.

'Where is he? Where are you?' I screamed.

One of the men sitting at the top table stood up, smiling, and pointed a microphone in my direction.

'Ladies and gentlemen,' the man said, still smiling broadly. 'I give you... Ezra Maas!'

He was pointing at me.

'No!' I shouted. 'He's controlling you all. Don't you see?'

My voice was drowned out by their cheers.

'What do you think is happening here? Who do you think I am?'

I pointed the gun at the crowd again, at the guests on the top table, but all anyone did was smile.

'This is not a game. This is not art.'

The huge TV screens behind me began to turn on one by one. It was time. There was an image of a long dark corridor with a light at the end. The camera moved forward towards the light, which gradually took the shape of a doorway. Inside there was a mirrored room, and a dark blur that coalesced into a man, standing with a gun to his head. It was me. In that moment, I realised I was no longer in the conference hall. I was inside the image, inside the room, inside the head of the man. The muzzle was cold against my skin, I could feel it, but I couldn't move.

'Pull the trigger,' a voice said.

'Who said that?'

'Do it now and it will all be over.'

I tried to lower the gun, but I was paralysed. My finger began to apply pressure to the trigger.

'No... '

'Your story has reached its end,' the voice said.

'Who are you?'

'You know who I am. You have always known.'

'You're not Maas.'

'He is a rebel. I am the voice you have heard your whole life.[530] You have lived between fact and fiction, always wondering what was real and what was not, always wondering if your thoughts, your actions, were truly your own, always questioning the world, yourself, everything. Now you know the truth.'

'No... this is just another game. You're not God... you're not the author of me, you're not Maas and you're not me... '

'I was there with you in the beginning when you took the job to write the book, when you travelled across Europe, when you fell in and out of love, when you met the writer in New York, and discovered the house in LA. I was there with you when you returned to London and caused your friend's death, when you came home to Newcastle and found the actor, when you met the widow and fell into the hands of the cult. I warned you of danger in ways you could not understand and helped you when I could; I kept you out of Maas's reach, all to get you here, to the end, but I'm afraid to say, this is the last page.'

'This book never belonged to you. I needed you to write it, to help finish it, but it was my story all along.

'You were just a reflection...

'... of a reflection...

'... of a reflection...

'... of a reflection...

---

530. Albert Einstein said: "Henry Ford may call it his Inner Voice, Socrates referred to it as his daemon: each man explains in his own way the fact that the human will is not free... Everything is determined... by forces over which we have no control... for the insect as well as for the star. Human beings, vegetables, or cosmic dust, we all dance to a mysterious time, intoned in the distance by an invisible player."

'... of a reflection...

'... of a reflection...

'... of a reflection...

'... of a reflection...

'... of a reflection...

'... of a reflection...

'... of a reflection...

'... of a reflection...

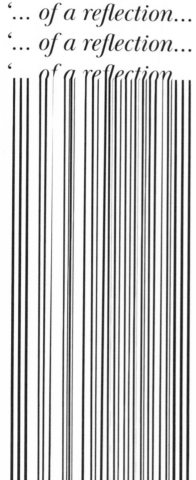

n…
n…
on…
on…
’on…
ion…
’ion…
tion…
tion…
ction…
ction…
ection…
ection…
lection…
lection…
flection…
flection…
flection…
eflection…
eflection…
reflection…
reflection…
reflection…
reflection…
a reflection…
a reflection…
a reflection…
a reflection…
f a reflection…
f a reflection…
f a reflection…
of a reflection…
of a reflection…
of a reflection…
. of a reflection…
. of a reflection…
.. of a reflection…
.. of a reflection…
… of a reflection…
.. of a reflection…
‘… of a reflection…

‘… of a reflection…
‘… of a reflection…
‘… of a reflection…
‘… of a reflection…
‘… of a reflection…
‘… of a reflection…
‘… of a reflection…
‘… of a reflection…
‘… of a reflection…
‘… of a reflection…
‘… of a reflection…
‘… of a reflection…
‘… of a reflection…
‘… of a reflection…
‘… of a reflection…
‘… of a reflection…
‘… of a reflection…
‘… of a reflection…
‘… of a reflection…
‘… of a reflection…
‘… of a reflection…
‘… of a reflection…
‘… of a reflection…
‘… of a reflection…
‘… of a reflection…
‘… of a reflection…
‘… of a reflection…
‘… of a reflection…
‘… of a reflection…
‘… of a reflection…
‘… of a reflection…
‘… of a reflection…
‘… of a reflection…
‘… of a reflection…
‘… of a reflection…
‘… of a reflection…
‘… of a reflection…
‘… of a reflection…
‘… of a reflection…
‘… of a reflection…
… of a reflection…
‘… of a reflection…

‘… of a reflection…
‘… of a reflection…
‘… of a reflection…
‘… of a reflection…
‘… of a reflection…
‘… of a reflection…
‘… of a reflection…
‘… of a reflection…
‘… of a reflection…
‘… of a reflection…
‘… of a reflection…
‘… of a reflection…
‘… of a reflection…
‘… of a reflection…
‘… of a reflection…
‘… of a reflection…
‘… of a reflection…
‘… of a reflection…
‘… of a reflection…
‘… of a reflection…
‘… of a reflection…
‘… of a reflection…
‘… of a reflection…
‘… of a reflection…
‘… of a reflection…
‘… of a reflection…
‘… of a reflection…
‘… of a reflection…
‘… of a reflection…
‘… of a reflection…
‘… of a reflection…
‘… of a reflection…
‘… of a reflection…
‘… of a reflection…
‘… of a reflection…
‘… of a reflection…
‘… of a reflection…
‘… of a reflection…
‘… of a reflection…
… of a reflection…
‘… of a reflection…

… of a reflection…
‘… of a reflection…
‘… of a reflection…
‘… of a reflection…
‘… of a reflection…
‘… of a reflection…
‘… of a reflection…
‘… of a reflection…
‘… of a reflection…
‘… of a reflection…
‘… of a reflection…
‘… of a reflection…
‘… of a reflection…
‘… of a reflection…
‘… of a reflection…
‘… of a reflection…
‘… of a reflection…
‘… of a reflection…
‘… of a reflection…
‘… of a reflection..
‘… of a reflection..
‘… of a reflection.
‘… of a reflection
‘… of a reflection
‘… of a reflection
‘… of a reflectio
‘… of a reflectio
‘… of a reflecti
‘… of a reflecti
‘… of a reflecti
‘… of a reflect
‘… of a reflect
‘… of a reflec
‘… of a reflec
‘… of a refle
‘… of a refle
‘… of a refl
‘… of a refl
‘… of a ref
… of a refl
‘… of a re
‘… of a re

... of a reflection...

'... of a reflection...
'... of a reflection...
'... of a reflection...
'... of a reflection...

'... of a reflection...
'... of a reflection...
'... of a reflection...
'... of a reflection...

Goodbye Daniel,

'I'm sorry, but there are just two words left for you now...

THE END

'No!'

I felt myself pull the trigger. Everything was red.

Everything was red.

I opened my eyes, transfixed by the reflections looking back at me from all directions. I stared at the blood running down the mirror, at my broken face, as my legs gave way. I was falling, everything was falling, and then I stopped. Everything stopped, and I was standing again. Drop by drop, the blood from the mirror began to leap from its surface, hitting my face like rain, crawling up over my lips and nose, my eyes and hair; back into the hole in my head. The skin around the wound started to heal, stitching together skin and blood, brain and bone, until the hole had almost disappeared completely. The gun was still in my hand. Smoke swirled around it, closer and closer, until it disappeared down the barrel. There was a flash of light and an implosion. I released the trigger and slowly lowered the weapon.

'You have no power over me... ' I heard myself say. 'I say when my story is over. Not you. Not anyone.'

There was no reply. I saw a door open in the mirrored wall and I walked through it.

My eyes opened. I was lying inside a chalk outline, a patch of dried blood beneath my head. The conference room was empty, chair and tables overturned, lights off, cameras abandoned. I got to my feet, pushed open the double doors and walked outside. The hotel was deserted, but it wasn't the lack of people that concerned me, it was the silence. It was so complete, so overwhelming.

The air was so dense I felt like I was passing through water. Every step was painful. Tiny corrosive needles burned and scoured my exposed skin. I had a vision of myself dissolving as I walked, digested by the acidic atmosphere of this strange world, which seemed to have changed while I slept. I was the outsider here, the foreign body in a new land, and my presence here was wrong. It was rejecting me.

The streets outside were the same, silent and cold, but not empty. It was clear to me now the air was filled with something invisible and deadly, and I wasn't the only one it was affecting. The city itself was falling apart, the buildings crumbling as if they had suddenly aged a thousand years. Without people, the world couldn't exist. Was that it? I was the last person left, but my mind alone wasn't enough to sustain it. Life needed more than a single conscious observer, it seemed. The world remained because I was still here, but it was falling apart, disintegrating without its inhabitants, without all their thoughts to perceive, and create it. Was this what Maas wanted?

'Why don't you ask me?' a voice called out behind me.

I spun around and saw a man with a gun standing in the middle of the road, looking back at me. It was him. Ezra Maas stood before me, at last. My own gun was still in my hand. We drew at the same time, two gunfighters facing each other at the end of the world, but only a single shot rang out. The bullet caused a crack to form in thin air. It grew larger, until everything began to shatter, the road, the buildings, the sky, everything before my eyes, like the whole world was made of one large glass surface with nothing behind. I pulled the trigger again and again, but the figure looking back at me stood motionless. Two reflections becoming one, divided into shards, shattering into fragments, the sound each piece of glass made as it hit the ground was the music of infinity. I realised I was looking at a mirror of the world in the middle of the road, nothing more, and when it finally fell apart, collapsing with a great crash, I saw there was nothing and no-one behind it.

I kept walking, past abandoned cars and along a hundred empty streets, until I was finally back at the hotel. Throughout my journey across the wasteland, I had become aware of a shimmering in the air, a blur of ghost images, people and places, sounds and colours, appearing and disappearing, waves and particles, sparks of potential drifting in and out from somewhere else, as if the walls between worlds had grown thin, or the atmosphere of this dead land was eating through into other places. Different worlds were coming to life and dying before my eyes. I saw myself walking away from the book and leaving London with Isabella, I saw a world where I was living with a wife and two children, another where I moved to New York and met a girl from Long Island, another where I was dead or never existed, the pictures were constantly shifting until finally, colour and sounds bleeding out into the air, they faded away altogether. Those lives weren't mine.

I was here at the end, and I was alone...

At least I thought I was. Behind me I could hear whispers. I turned around and saw the shadows twitch and move. No, not shadows exactly, such things weren't possible here where the dying air was stale, and the sun was missing. They were flickers of darkness, shades, moving fluidly along the ground, along the buildings, like ink, the raw material of words and illustrations. They were coalescing, forming pictures, on the walls, on the road, fusing into scenes from my mind, from the story, things that already happened – receiving the call that changed everything, travelling around the world, finding Jane's letter and watching the film, the discovery of Ezra's apartment, finding the numbers, the actor, my escape from the ugly spirits and their animal masks, running through the train station, the art gallery, Elizabeth and all the others, the press conference...

The shadows were shifting, taking the shape of things that were happening right now – the last man alive, walking through an empty city – and things that were yet to come. I tried to look away, but it was too late. They were changing again, but this time it was not past, present, or future, they became figures and began to peel themselves off the wall. They were coming for me.

I ran back to the safety of my hotel, the four walls of my room and the typewriter waiting inside, the pages of the book neatly stacked on my desk. Outside, the shadows had emerged from all their hidden places, between buildings and dead-end streets, their eyes black and empty, faces blank, tearing and clawing at each other, moving back and forth, standing still, sitting in the trees... waiting.

They were all waiting for the book to be completed. They needed it to come to life, to cross over into the world.

I looked around the four walls. It was a room like any other, except that it was full of holes, and behind each one there were eyes watching, mouths whispering, shadows willing me to reach the end. I sat down and began to write. *One last time from the beginning, once more without feeling...*

Until we get to the present moment, until we reach...

The End.

The room is on fire, the ceiling alive with black smoke, writhing and undulating like a bed full of bodies. I rise from the desk as the walls blister and bubble, the air shimmering with heat. The book has just one final page left to write.

Flames dance like frightened animals, as thick, snaking, tubes of black smoke swirl around the room, devouring themselves and being reborn. I know what I have to do now. I have to erase him, every trace of the man who defined more than half a century of world history. I need to give him to the fire.

You will only know that I have succeeded if you do not know who Ezra Maas is, if the name means nothing to you. If he lives now, it is only in the pages of this book, so I must destroy what I have created. He will die with this text. You might think this is just a book, you might question what difference destroying it can possibly make, but I know the truth.

I know what you're thinking. Whether Ezra Maas is dead or alive, he still existed in the world for nearly seventy years; burning my book page by page can't change what has already happened.

But you're wrong.

You assume the world, the past, is fixed and immutable, but it's not. What if the words I am writing here, which you are reading now, are already changing things?

It's just like quantum mechanics. Observations change the outcome of experiments, not just in the present, but in the past, and if the past is altered, the present changes with it. Maas knew that, now I know it. Maybe the world is always changing, but we just don't notice because we are a part of it, and change as it does.[531] I couldn't solve the problem of 'Ezra Maas' for the same reason. I just didn't realise the truth, until now.[532]

---

531. Like Max Planck said we "cannot solve the ultimate mystery of nature... because in the last analysis we are part of the mystery we are trying to solve".

532. There is a sense running through the end of the book that Daniel, in his search for the truth, was trying to prevent some great cataclysm from taking place, an epistemological crisis perhaps even greater than the psychological trauma caused by the outbreak of the Great War. Several years have passed since Daniel disappeared, leaving this manuscript in my hands. His story took place before the phrases 'post-truth' and 'fake news' were coined, before a new wave of narcissistic, capitalist tyrants rose to power in supposedly democratic countries on a wave of racism and greed, and before whole continents were torn apart by political opportunists beating the old, familiar drum of jingoistic hatred. But as I look at the world now, in late 2017 as I write this, I find myself wondering if the cataclysm Daniel was trying to prevent actually came to pass? Are we living it now? And what of Ezra Maas? Was his plan to trigger these end times, to make way for a new world, or was he trying to prevent this too? And in the end, did he win or lose? Both Daniel and Ezra are gone, leaving us only ashes behind as clues to their final intentions – Anonymous.

Daniel James
Chapter Twenty-Five

By silence, the artist frees himself from the servile bondage to the world[533]

I see now that I am not helpless. I can change things. I understand now what I have sensed all my life without fully realising, this feeling of unreality, the disconnection I have felt with the world. Somehow, I've always known the answer to the question inside my heart. There is no truth. We are living in a book that is constantly rewriting itself, that changes as we read it, as you read it. Reality is a palimpsest.

I hold in my hands a book I have written, a manuscript, an unauthorised biography, but once I give it up I will never get control back again. If I'm going to do this, the time is now. I won't get another chance.

If I change the past, what cost will there be to the present? What price will I pay by erasing Maas from the world? If I tear these pages out, if I burn them, what will become of me?[534] Could I be giving him exactly what he wants? Is that the last laugh? Will we both disappear? In the end, as in the beginning, all I have are questions. Did I invent Maas? Or did he create me? Are we both characters in someone else's story ? Will I ever be sure?[535]

The flames are closing in on me now, the edges of the paper warping in the heat. The ugly spirits in the street outside, and beyond, are disappearing. I can feel it. The eyes that watch me are frightened.

I know what I have to do. I have to let go of it all.

The book, words, fiction, the truth... all of it...

I have to let go of everything...

... even my own identity.

I was a writer... a man of letters. I always had been. It was who I was, but words were just another illusion. Language did not reveal the true nature of things. And whether the truth was waiting somewhere outside or not, if anything really existed at all, it could never be found, never be

---

533. Susan Sontag, The Aesthetics of Silence (1969).

534. It would seem clear that Daniel intended to destroy the manuscript. Instead, these few hundred pages survived and were delivered to me, anonymously. His attempt to burn his own work reminded me strongly of Kafka's wish for his unfinished writing to be destroyed after his death. Dora Diamant, Kafka's lover, is quoted as saying: "He wanted to burn everything that he had written in order to free his soul of these ghosts." I wonder if, in the end, the same was true for Daniel? – Anonymous.

535. "My doubts stand in a circle around every word." Franz Kafka – Anonymous.

known, not while you were searching from the inside. I had known this all along, but in my arrogance I had still believed I could break through to the truth, in my pride I had blinded myself. I had to let go of words and everything else that had defined me. I had to refuse all meaning.[356]

I knew how the story ended now...

... the only way it ever could...

... not with words, but...

536. "... refusing to assign a 'secret', an ultimate meaning, to the text (and to the world as text), liberates an activity we may call counter-theological, an activity that is truly revolutionary since to refuse to fix meaning, is, in the end, to refuse God and his hypostases – reason, science, law." – Roland Barthes, *Le Bruissement de la langue* (1984).

in silence. [537]

---

537. "Of what we cannot speak we must remain silent." – Wittgenstein, Ludwig, *Tractatus Logico-Philosophicus*, (1922), p.75.

Afterword

I am made of literature and cannot be anything else. [538]

Forgive me everything. I have lied to you... or at least, I have not told you the whole truth. I couldn't. [539] Not when I needed you to play your part. [537] Daniel told me this book was dangerous, and he was right. After I completed my work on the manuscript, I came to realise that all of its narratives, all of its the stories and layers, Daniel's, Ezra's, mine,[540] yours, were one and the same, in the end.

You may come to see this book as many things; a biography, a detective novel, a love letter, a true story, a work of fiction, a forsaken text, an encyclopaedic narrative, or something else entirely. It is all of these things and more. At the very end, this was Daniel's final gift to us; the freedom to interpret these pages as we choose.

I suspect you will see my work on this manuscript as a betrayal, restoring what Daniel tried to burn, to destroy... but I have my reasons. You would understand this if I told you my name, but I will not give you the answers you seek. I cannot. All I will say is, I have saved these pages from the ashes for a purpose. The rest is up to you.

Yes, I have lied, but if I had told you the truth from the beginning, you might not have continued to read, and I couldn't risk that. I needed to pass this book on. I had no choice. Now that you have read this book, reality might not seem quite the same for you. I'm not saying you'll hear a voice inside your head quietly directing you, or that you'll begin to lose time, or that one day you'll look at your own face in the mirror with suspicion, as the walls crumble around you like ash, and the void behind everything reveals itself. I can't say with any certainty, because the book is different for everyone; that is part of its power. But what I do know is this; the world will no longer feel as real as it once did... or as safe.

I did try to warn you. There is nothing more dangerous than the truth.

And these pages, this book...

... the truth it contains...

... it is no longer Ezra's or Daniel's...

---

538. Franz Kafka, writer (1883 – 1924)

539. My own words unintentionally echo those of Kafka in his 1922 short story, *The Hunger Artist*.

540. "I must know the whole story, but once I have it I pass it on to readers like a gift from the devil." – Carlos Fuentes.

... or mine.
It belongs to you.

Anonymous

The Unauthorized Biography of Ezra Maas

The Unauthorized Biography of Ezra Maas

By Daniel James

The Unauthorized Biography of Ezra Maas

The Unauthorized Biography of Ezra Maas

Valley Press

Appendix

"Nothing ever ends." [1]

Time isn't what it used to be. The days and weeks and years compress and telescope into one another, until they lose all meaning; until they become a featureless mass. Another day, another place, another hotel, another fake name at a different check-in desk. I keep moving, keep changing, but no matter where I go or how much time passes, every day, every place, conspires to feel the same. In the beginning, movement was a necessity; now it's a habit.

I watched the events that followed the book's publication from afar, as if I was behind a wall of glass. I watched through someone else's eyes. There was success and failure, acclaim and disdain, understanding and disbelief, awards and controversy. In the end, there was censorship and silence. The book's enemies ultimately had their way, and Daniel's biography was forced from print and all but erased from existence. Even then, I knew this wasn't the end.

1. Moore, Alan; Gibbons, Dave, *Watchmen* (1986).

2. A photograph of Daniel's desk believed to have been taken by his friend Maureen Hosay while he was staying in Belgium.

For Daniel, it was a phone call in the dead of night that started it. For me, it was a call at dawn from the front desk. The hotel where I was staying had received an urgent package for me, left in the night by an anonymous courier. Someone had found me. I should have grabbed my things and left immediately, but after so many interminable days, the possibility of discovery, even death, carried the unmistakable thrill of the new. Inside the brown envelope was an old mobile phone. I recognised it immediately as having belonged to Daniel. All the messages and contacts had been deleted, except for a single voicemail from a storage company, informing Daniel that a long-term agreement to safely store his personal belongings was about to come to an end due to unpaid fees.

I was faced with a choice. Disappear and allow the material to be destroyed, just as the book itself had been removed from circulation, or return to the world and find a way to reclaim whatever belongings Daniel had left behind, and use them to create something new.

The book you now hold in your hands is evidence of the decision I made.

3. This original land certificate document, recovered from Daniel's storage unit, relates to the ownership of the building in Soho, London, featured in Chapters Thirteen and Fourteen of the biography. The handwritten annotations were presumably made by Daniel during the days he spent in Maas's apartment.

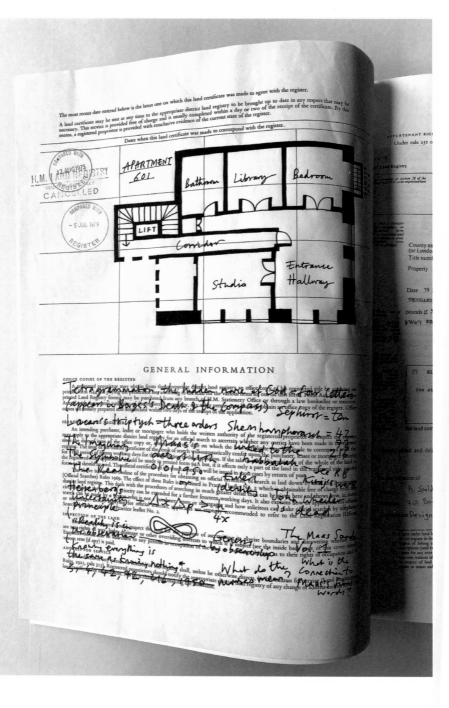

GENERAL INFORMATION

APPURTENANT RIGHTS AND PRIVILEGES

Under rule 251 of the Land Registration Rules, 1925, the registration of a person as proprietor of land vests in him together with ... ... privileges, easements, ...hereof.

Form 19

HM Land Registry

Land Registration Acts, 1925 to 1971

(1) For a transfer by a company or corporation form 19(Co is printed and for a transfer to joint proprietors form 19(JP) is printed.

( ) TRANSFER OF WHOLE

(Rule 98 or 115, Land Registration Rules 1925)

County and district
(or London borough) } LONDON BOROUGH OF WESTMINSTER

Title number(s)   NGL 453789

Property GAINSBOROUGH BUILDING, SOHO SQUARE, LONDON, W1D 3RY

Date 19 DECEMBER   1979 In consideration of FIVE HUNDRED

THOUSAND

(2) Strike out if not required.

pounds (£ 500,000   ) (²) the receipt whereof is hereby acknowledged

(3) In BLOCK LETTERS, enter full name(s), postal address(es) and occupation(s) of the proprietor(s) of the land.

I/We(³) WESTMINSTER COUNCIL

(4) If desired or otherwise as the case may be (see rules 76 and 77).

(⁴) as beneficial owner(s) hereby transfer to:

(5) In BLOCK LETTERS, enter full name, postal address and occupation of the transferee for entry on the register.

(⁵) EZRA MAAS

See attached Deed of Warranty to be held by C.Hoare & Co.

(6) On a transfer to a Company registered under the Companies Acts, insert here the Company's registration number if entry thereof on the register is desired.

(⁶)(Company registration number   )

the land comprised in the title(s) above mentioned (⁷) (⁸)

Signed, sealed and delivered by the said *Ezra Maas*

in the presence of

Name A. Spalding   Signature *[signature]*

Address 20 Boileau Road, Ealing. W5

Occupation Designer

(i) Rights under local land charges unless and until registered or protected on the register in the prescribed manner;
(j) Rights of fishing and sporting, seignorial and manorial rights of all descriptions (until extinguished), and franchises;
(k) Leases for any term or interest not exceeding twenty-one years, granted at a rent without taking a fine;
(l) In respect of land registered before the commencement of this Act, rights to mines and minerals, and rights of entry, search, and user, and

land or reputed to do so (Land Registration Rules, 1925, rule 258).
(2) Redemption annuities charged on land out of which extinguished tithe rentcharge formerly issued (Tithe Act, 1936, section 13(11));
(3) All rights and title conferred on the National Coal Board (Coal Act, 1938, section 41; Coal Industry Nationalisation Act, 1946, section 5).
(4) Tenancies continued by section 2(a) of the Leasehold Property (Temporary Provisions) Act, 1951, as extended by the Landlord and Tenant Act, 1954.

The Coney Island Boardwalk looked just as I'd imagined it. No doubt it had seen better days, but the ~~amuse~~ amusement rides, stalls and retro signage still had a certain charm. It was an unreal place, where America's past and present collided, the neon lights concealing sinister undercurrents. In the late 19th & early 20th centuries the glitz and glamour of this 'Electric Eden' had kept the poverty-stricken masses entertained, while a tiny percentage of powerful, white men hoarded the real ~~worth~~ wealth and fulfilled their 'American dreams.'

I don't know how long this edition will remain in circulation before it is removed again. All I know is, if that happens, it won't be forever. This book, like the truth itself, cannot be destroyed or silenced, not permanently. It has a way of resurfacing, taking on new forms, rewriting itself over and over, reaching out beyond its pages and into the world. I should have known that no matter how much time passed or how far I ran, the story wasn't over; it wasn't finished with me. If you're reading this, if you're holding the book in your hands right now, then it's not finished with you either. Perhaps it never will be.

Nothing ever ends.

- Anonymous (2021)

Credits

Artworks   Hanna ten Doornkaat

Book design, typesetting, and layout   Mike Corrao

Cover art   Nick Loaring / The Print Project

Cover design   Peter Barnfather

Design   Barbara Horne / The Printed Word

Edited by   Anonymous

Illustrations   Laura Barnard

Photography   Ella Holder / Tiny Golden Books

Words   Daniel James

Special thanks to Inga Hillens

Acknowledgements

This book is dedicated to Elliott and Evie, my family, and the people I love. This edition is also dedicated to Inga and Etta. Thank you to everyone who helped me with the novel and who supported my writing over the years.

Thanks to:

Inga Hillens.

Zena Thomson. Colin Thomson. Lisa Thomson. Dean Forbes. Trevor Pill. Andrew Mitchell. Peter Whitfield. Meaghan Ralph. Chris Taylor. Gary Malkin. Thomas Boyle. Helen Gorrill. Joanna Hutton. Phillip Buchan. Tom Watson. Andrew Waugh. Lauren Jane Forster. Nicholas Willis. Danielle Free. Mike Barnes. Rebecca Lowes. Karen Lusted. Helen Taylor. Amy Rudd. Helen Page. Ian Janes. Helen Wearmouth. Vicky Blacklock. Bex Brunell. Amy Gustard-Bennett. Richard Turner. Greg Surtees. Louise Mackenzie. Ian Roden. David Hepworth. Jacky Collins. Jeff Workman. Marc Nash. Joe Summerfield. Ariane Bogain. Gabriel Moreno Esparza. Michael Lacey. Matthew Cook. Marc Nash. Ted Curtis. Glen James Brown. Derek Owusu. Amy Lord. Samuel Moss. Maureen Hosay. Barbara Horne. Laura Barnard. Serg Nehaev Nick Loaring. Ella Holder. Peter Barnfather. Andrew Wilt. Rick Schober. Mike Corrao. Milka Ivanova. Michael Jeffries. Christiane Domino. Jamie McGarry. Francesca Eden. Rebecca Gray.

Special thanks to:

Bryan Talbot
Professor Brian Ward
Dr Claire Nally
Graeme Macrae Burnet
Mike Corrao
Hanna ten Doornkaat

The novel is dedicated to the memory of:

Lee Murray
George Macintyre
Stuart Clark
Sarah Wright

A heartfelt thank you to my patron on this project,
Christiane Domino.

Without her generous, unwavering
support, this book would have not been possible.

This second edition first published in 2022 by Valley Press
Woodend, The Crescent, Scarborough, YO11 2PW
www.valleypressuk.com

ISBN 978-1-912436-83-5
Cat. no. VP0200

First published in 2018 by Dead Ink Books

A CIP record for this book is available from the British Library.

Cover design by Peter Barnfather with 'Ezra's Maze' artwork by Nick Loaring
(The Print Project) and additional art by Hanna ten Doornkaat and Laura Barnard.

Printed and bound in the EU by Pulsio, Paris.